Alessandro Baricco

City

Alessandro Baricco was born in Turin in 1958. The
author of three previous novels, he has won the Prix
Médicis Étranger in France and the Selezione Camp-
iello, Viareggio, and Palazzo del Bosco prizes in Italy.
His third novel, *Silk,* became an immediate bestseller
in Italy and has been translated into twenty-seven languages. It is the basis of a forthcoming opera by André
Previn and a film to be produced by Miramax.

VINTAGE

INTERNATIONAL

Also by Alessandro Baricco

Silk
Ocean Sea

City

Alessandro Baricco

Translated from the Italian by Ann Goldstein

Vintage International

Vintage Books

A Division of Random House, Inc.

New York

FIRST VINTAGE INTERNATIONAL EDITION, JUNE 2003

Translation copyright © 2001 by Alessandro Baricco

The Library of Congress has cataloged the Knopf edition as follows:
Baricco, Alessandro.
[City. English]
City / Alessandro Baricco; translated by Ann Goldstein.—1st ed.
p. cm.
I. Goldstein, Ann, 1949– II. Title.
PQ4862.A6745 C5813 2002
853'.914—dc21 2001050727

Vintage ISBN: 0-375-72548-2

Book design by Anthea Lingeman

www.vintagebooks.com

Printed in the United States of America
10 9 8 7 6 5 4 3 2 1

City

Prologue

"So, Mr. Klauser, should Mami Jane die?"

"Screw them all."

"Is that a yes or a no?"

"What do you think?"

In October of 1987, CRB—the company that for twenty-two years had published the adventures of the mythical Ballon Mac—decided to take a poll of its readers to determine whether Mami Jane ought to die. Ballon Mac was a blind superhero who worked as a dentist by day and at night battled Evil, using the special powers of his saliva. Mami Jane was his mother. The readers were, in general, very fond of her: she collected Indian scalps and at night she performed as a bassist in a blues band whose other members were black. She was white. The idea of killing her off had come from the sales manager of CRB—a placid man who had a single passion: toy trains. He maintained that at this point Ballon Mac was on a dead-end track and needed new inspiration. The death of his mother—hit by a train as she fled a paranoid switchman—

would transform him into a lethal mixture of rage and grief, that is, the exact image of his average reader. The idea was idiotic. But then so was the average reader of Ballon Mac.

So, in October of 1987, CRB cleared out a room on the second floor and set up eight young women there to answer the telephones and tabulate readers' opinions. The question was: Should Mami Jane die?

Of the eight young women, four were employees of CRB, two had been sent by the unemployment office, and one was the granddaughter of the company president. The last, a woman of about thirty, from Pomona, was there because she'd won an internship by getting the correct answer on a radio quiz ("What is the thing that Ballon Mac hates most in the world?" "Scraping off tartar"). She had a small tape recorder that she always carried with her. Every so often she turned it on and said something into it.

Her name was Shatzy Shell.

At 10:45 on the twelfth day of the voting—when the death of Mami Jane was winning by 64 percent to 30 (the remaining 6 percent maintained that they should all go to hell, and had called to say so)—Shatzy Shell heard the phone ring for the twenty-first time that day, wrote on the form she had in front of her the number 21, and picked up the receiver. The following conversation ensued:

"CRB, good morning."

"Good morning, is Diesel there yet?"

"Who?"

"OK, he's not there yet . . ."

"This is CRB, sir."

"Yes, I know."

"You must have the wrong number."

"No, no, it's all right. Now listen to me . . ."

"Sir . . ."

"Yes?"

"This is CRB. It's the poll 'Should Mami Jane die?'"

"Thanks, I know that."

"Then would you please give me your name?"

"It doesn't matter what my name is . . ."

"You have to give it to me, it's the procedure."

"OK, OK, Gould . . . my name is Gould."

"Mr. Gould."

"Yes, Mr. Gould, now if I can . . ."

"Should Mami Jane die?"

"What?"

"You're supposed to tell me what you think . . . should Mami Jane die or not?"

"Oh, Jesus . . ."

"Do you actually know? Who Mami Jane is?"

"Of course I know, but . . ."

"You see, all you have to do is tell me if you think that . . ."

"Please, listen to me for a moment?"

"Of course."

"Then do me a favor and take a look around."

"Me?"

"Yes."

"Here?"

"Yes, there, in the room, please do me this one favor."

"OK, I'm looking."

"Good. Do you by any chance see a guy with a shaved head who's holding the hand of a big guy, and I mean big, a kind of giant, with enormous shoes and a green jacket?"

"No, I don't think so."

"You're sure?"

"Yes, I'm sure."

"Good. Then they haven't arrived yet."

"No."

"OK, then I want you to know something."

"Yes?"

"They aren't bad guys."

"No?"

"No. When they get there they'll start smashing everything up, and it's likely that they'll grab your telephone cord and twist it around your neck, or something like that, but they're not bad guys, really, it's only that . . ."

"Mr. Gould . . ."

"Yes?"

"Would you mind telling me how old you are?"

"Thirteen."

"Thirteen?"

"Twelve . . . to be exact, twelve."

"Listen, Gould, is your mother around?"

"My mother left four years ago, and now she lives with a professor who studies fish, the habits of fish, an *ethologist,* to be precise."

"I'm sorry."

"You don't have to be sorry. Life is like that, you can't do anything about it."

"Really?"

"Really. Don't you think so?"

"Yes . . . I guess . . . I don't know exactly, I imagine it's that way."

"It is that way, unfortunately."

"You're twelve, right?"

"Tomorrow I'll be thirteen, tomorrow."

"Splendid."

"Splendid."

"Happy birthday, Gould."

"Thank you."

"You'll see, it's splendid to be thirteen."

"I hope so."

"Congratulations, truly."

"Thank you."

"Your father's not around, is he?"

"No, he's at work."

"Of course."

"My father works for the Army."

"Splendid."

"Is everything always so splendid for you?"

"What?"

"Is everything always so splendid for you?"

"Yes . . . I think so."

"Splendid."

"That is . . . it often happens, yes."

"You're lucky."

"It also happens at the oddest moments."

"I think you really are lucky."

"Once I was at a cafeteria, on Route 16, just outside of town, I stopped at a cafeteria, I went in and got in line, and behind the counter there was a Vietnamese man, who could barely understand a word, so nothing was moving, you know, someone would say to him, A hamburger, and he'd say What?, maybe it was his first day of work, I don't know, so I started looking around, in the cafeteria. There were five or six tables, and people were eating, so many different faces and each face with something different in front of it, a pizza, a sandwich, a bowl of chili, they were all eating, and they were all dressed exactly how they wanted to dress, they'd gotten up in the morning and chosen something to put on, the red shirt, or the dress tight across the tits, exactly what they wanted, and now they were there, and each of them had a life behind and a life ahead, they were just *passing through* there, and tomorrow they'd do it all again from the beginning, the blue shirt, the long dress, and surely the blonde with freckles had a mother in the hospital, with all the blood tests really bad, but there she was, pushing aside the French fries with black spots, reading a newspaper propped against a gas pump–shaped salt shaker, there was a guy in a baseball shirt, who for sure had not been on a baseball field in years, he was sitting there with his son, just a kid, and he kept cuffing him on the head, on the back of the head, and every time the boy readjusted his cap, a baseball cap, and *click,* another cuff, and throughout all this never stopping eating, under a TV hanging on the wall, screen blank, the noise coming in from the highway in gusts, and sitting in a corner two men, very refined-looking, in gray suits, and you could see one of the two was crying, it was absurd, but he was crying, over steak and potatoes, he was crying silently, and the other didn't bat an eye, he had a steak in front of him, too, he was just eating, that's all, only, at one point he got up, went over to the next table, took the ketchup bottle, went back to his seat, and, very careful not to spill on his gray suit, poured a little on the other guy's plate, the one who was crying, and whispered something, I don't know what, then he put the top back on the bottle and started eating again, those two in the corner, and everything else around, a black cherry ice cream cone trampled on the floor, and on the bathroom door a sign saying "Out of Order"—I looked at all that and it was clear that the only thing you could think was *How disgusting, folks,* something so sad it would make you puke, and instead what happened was that while I was standing there in line and the Vietnamese guy kept on not getting a damn thing, I thought *Lord, how lovely,* with even a sort of desire to laugh, My goodness, how nice all this is, all of it, down to the last crumb crushed into the floor, the last greasy napkin, without knowing why, but knowing that it was true, it was all amazingly nice. Absurd, isn't it?"

"Strange."

"I'm sorry to have gone on about it."

"Why?"

"I don't know . . . people don't usually talk about things like that . . ."

"I liked it."

"Come on . . ."

"No, really, especially the part about the ketchup . . ."

"He grabbed the bottle and poured some out onto . . ."

"Yes."

"Dressed all in gray."

"Funny."

"Right."

"Right."

"Gould?"

"Yes."

"I'm glad you called."

"Hey, no, wait . . ."

"I'm still here."

"What's your name?"

"Shatzy."

"Shatzy."

"My name is Shatzy Shell."

"Shatzy Shell."

"Yes."

"And there's no one there wrapping the telephone cord around your neck, right?"

"No."

"You'll remember, when they get there, that they're not bad?"

"You'll see, they won't come."

"Don't count on it, they'll get there . . ."

"Why is that, Gould?"

"Diesel *adores* Mami Jane. And he is seven feet six inches tall."

"Splendid."

"Depends. When he's *very* angry it's not at all splendid."

"And now he's *very* angry?"

"You would be, too, if they were taking a poll on whether to kill Mami Jane, and Mami Jane was your ideal mother."

"It's only a poll, Gould."

"Diesel says it's all a trick. He says they already decided months ago that they would kill her off, and they're only doing this for show."

"Maybe he's wrong."

"Diesel is never wrong. He's a giant."

"How giant?"

"Very."

"I was once with a guy who could slam-dunk without even standing on tiptoe."

"Really?"

"But his job was taking tickets in a movie theater."

"And did you love him?"

"What sort of question is that, Gould?"

"You said you were *with* him."

"Yes, we were together. We were together for twenty-two days."

"And then?"

"I don't know . . . it was all sort of *complicated,* you know what I mean?"

"Yes . . . For Diesel, too, it's all sort of complicated."

"That's how it is."

"His father had a toilet made specially for him—it cost him a fortune."

"I told you, it's all sort of complicated."

"Yes. When Diesel tried to go to school, down in Taton, he arrived one morning . . ."

"Gould?"

"Yes?"

"Excuse me a moment, Gould."

"OK."

"Stay on the line, OK?"

"OK."

Shatzy Shell put Gould on hold. Then she turned to the man who was standing in front of her desk, looking at her. It was the head of the department of development and promotion. His name was Bellerbaumer. He was one of those people who suck on the eyepiece of their glasses.

"Mr. Bellerbaumer?"

Mr. Bellerbaumer cleared his throat.

"Miss Shell, you are talking about giants."

"Exactly."

"You have been on the telephone for twelve minutes and you are talking about giants."

"Twelve minutes?"

"Yesterday you talked happily for twenty-seven minutes with a stockbroker who at the end made you a proposal of marriage."

"He didn't know who Mami Jane was, I had to . . ."

"And the day before you were on that telephone for an hour and eleven minutes correcting the homework of a wretched little boy who then gave you as his answer 'Why not do in Ballon Mac?'"

"It's an idea. You might think about it."

"Miss Shell, that telephone is the property of CRB, and you are paid to say only one goddam sentence: Should Mami Jane die?"

"I'm trying to do my best."

"So am I. And so I am going to fire you, Miss Shell."

"Excuse me?"

"I am compelled to let you go, Miss Shell."

"You're serious?"

"I'm sorry."

" . . ."

" . . ."

" . . ."

" . . ."

"Mr. Bellerbaumer?"

"Yes."

"Would you mind if I finish my phone call?"

"What phone call?"

"The phone call. There's a boy on the line, who's on hold."

" . . ."

" . . ."

"Finish your phone call."

"Thank you."

"You're welcome."

"Gould?"

"Hello?"

"I'm afraid I have to hang up, Gould."

"OK."

"They've fired me."

"Splendid."

"I'm not so sure about that."

"At least now they won't strangle you."

"Who?"

"Diesel and Poomerang."

"The giant?"

"The giant is Diesel. Poomerang is the other, the one with no hair. He's a mute."

"Poomerang."

"Yes. He's a mute. He can't speak. He hears but he can't speak."

"They'll be stopped at the door."

"Generally they never get stopped, those two."

"Gould?"

"Yes."

"Should Mami Jane die?"

"They can all go to hell."

"'I don't know.' OK."

"Tell me something, Shatzy?"

"I have to go now."

"Just one thing."

"Go ahead."

"That place, that cafeteria . . ."

"Yes . . ."

"I was thinking . . . it must be a pretty nice place . . ."

"Yes . . ."

"I was thinking I might like to have my birthday there."

"What do you mean?"

"Tomorrow . . . it's my birthday . . . we could all go and eat there, maybe the two men in gray are still there, the ketchup ones."

"It's a funny idea, Gould."

"You, me, Diesel, and Poomerang. I'll pay."

"I don't know."

"It's a good idea, really."

"Maybe."

"855 6741."

"What's that?"

"My number. Call me, if you feel like it, OK?"

"You don't sound like a thirteen-year-old."

"I will be tomorrow, to be exact."

"I see."

"Then OK."

"Yes."

"OK."

"Gould?"

"Yes?"

"Bye."

"Bye, Shatzy."

"Bye."

Shatzy Shell pressed the blue button and hung up. She started to gather up her things and put them in her bag; it was a yellow bag with "Save the Planet Earth from Painted Toenails" written on it. She took the framed photographs of Walt Disney and Eva Braun. And the little tape recorder that she always carried with her. Every so often she turned it on and said something into it. The seven other women looked at her silently, while the telephones rang in vain, forfeiting precious opinions on the future of Mami Jane. What Shatzy Shell had to say, she said as she took off her sneakers and put on her heels.

"So, for the record, in a little while a giant and a guy with no hair, a mute, will come through that door. They will break up everything and strangle you with your telephone cords. The giant's name is Diesel, the mute's is Poomerang. Or the other way around, I can't remember. Anyway: they're not bad guys."

The photograph of Eva Braun had a red plastic frame, and a foot that folded out from the back, covered in fabric: to hold it up, if necessary. She, Eva Braun, had the face of Eva Braun.

"Get it?"

"More or less."

"He played the piano in an enormous department store, on the main floor, under the 'up' escalator. There was a piece of red carpet on the floor and a white piano, and he wore a tuxedo and played for six hours a day—Chopin, Cole Porter, stuff like that, all from memory. He had been given a printed card that said, in fancy lettering, 'Our pianist will return immediately': when he had to go to the bathroom he brought it out and set it on the piano. Then he came back and started up again. He wasn't bad like other fathers, I mean, not bad the way . . . he didn't beat anyone, he didn't drink, he didn't screw his secretary, nothing like that. Even when it came to the car . . . he didn't buy one for himself, he was always careful not to have a car that was too . . . too new, or fancy, he could have, but he didn't, he was careful, it came naturally, I don't think he had a specific plan, he just didn't do—he didn't do any of those things, and that was the problem, you see? Right there, that was the origin of the problem . . . that he didn't do those things, or a thousand others; he worked and that was all, he did it, *as if life had insulted him,* and so he had withdrawn into that job that was a defeat, without any desire to get himself out of it; it was like a black hole, an abyss of unhappiness, and the tragedy, the real tragedy, the heart of all that tragedy was that he had dragged us down, totally, me and my mother, into that hole along with him, all he did was drag us down, every moment of his life, every instant, with a miraculous constancy, devoting every gesture to the insane demonstration of a lethal theory, which was: that if he was like that it was *for* us two, *for* me and my mother, this was the theory, *for* us two, because we existed, because of us, for our protection, the two of us, for for for, and the whole damn time he was reminding us of this idiotic theory, his whole life with us was this one long, uninterrupted, exhausting action, which, on top of everything else, he purposely carried out in the cruelest and cleverest way possible; that is, without ever saying a word. No, he never said a word about it, never said anything, he could have spoken to us, clearly, but he never did, not a word, and that was terrible, that was cruel, never to say a thing, and then to be saying it the whole damn time, in the way he sat at the table, and what he watched on television, and even how he had his hair cut, and all the goddam things he didn't do, and his expression when he looked at you . . . it was cruel, it's the sort of thing that can make you turn out crazy, and I was turning out crazy. I was a child, a child can't defend itself. Children may be nasty but in certain areas they have no defenses, it's like if you beat a child, what can the child do, he can't do anything, I couldn't do anything, I was turning out crazy, so one day my mother took me aside and told me about Eva Braun. It was a good example. The daughter of Hitler. She told me to think of Eva Braun. She managed, so you can manage. It was an odd conversation, but it made sense. She told me that at the end, when he killed himself with a cyanide capsule, she killed herself, too: she was there in the bunker, and she killed herself along with him. Because even in the worst of fathers there is something good, she said to me. And you must learn to love that something. I thought about it. I tried to imagine in what way Hitler could have been good, and I made up stories about him, such as he comes home at night, all tired out, and speaks softly, and sits in front of the hearth, staring at the fire, dead tired, and I—I was Eva Braun, right?—a child with blonde braids, and pale white legs under my skirt, I watched him from the next room, without getting any closer, and he was so splendidly tired, with all that blood dripping from him everywhere, and so handsome in his uniform, all you could do was just stand there looking at him, until the blood disappeared and you saw only the tiredness, the marvelous tiredness, so I stood there adoringly, until at last he turned towards me, and saw me, and smiled at me, and got up, in all his dazzling tiredness, and came towards me, right up to me, and squatted down beside me: Hitler. Pretty crazy. He spoke to me, whispering, in German, and then with his hand, his right hand, he slowly caressed my hair, and although you might have thought it would be icy, that hand was soft, and warm, and gentle, it had a kind of wisdom in it, it was a hand that could save you; and although you might have thought it would be repulsive, it was a hand you could love, which in the end you did love, in the end you thought how lovely it was that it was the right hand of your father, gently caressing you. That was the sort of stuff I had going through my head. It was my exercises, you see? Eva Braun was my gym. In time I became very good. At night I'd stare at my father, sitting in his pajamas in front of the TV, until I saw Hitler, in his pajamas in front of the TV. I'd focus on that image for a while, drink it in, then it would go blurry and I'd go back to my father, to his real face: goodness, how sweet it seemed, all that tiredness, that unhappiness. Then I went back to Hitler, then I pulled out my father again, and so I went back and forth with my fantasy; it was a way of escaping the torture, the silences, all that shit. It worked. Except for a couple of times, it worked. All right. A few years later I read in a magazine that Eva Braun wasn't Hitler's daughter but his lover. Wife, I don't know. The point is she slept with him. It was a blow. It confused the hell out of me. I tried to readjust, somehow, but there was no way. I couldn't get out of my mind the image of Hitler going up to that child and starting to kiss her and all the rest, it was disgusting, and the girl was me, Eva Braun, and he became my father. It was a mess, just terrible. My little game was shattered, and there was no way to put it back together; it had worked, but it didn't work anymore. It stopped right there. I never loved my father again until he changed trains, as he put it. It's a funny story. He changed trains one ordinary Sunday. He was playing the piano, under the escalator, and a lady all covered with jewels, who was a little tipsy, came up to him. He was playing 'When We Were Alive,' and she started dancing, in front of everyone, with her shopping bags in her hand, and her face beaming. They went on like that for half an hour. Then she carried him off, and she carried him off forever. At home all he said was: I've changed trains. At that point, to tell you the truth, I went back to loving him somewhat, because it was like a liberation, I don't know, he even did his hair in a sort of Latin lover style, with the part as if carved into his white hair, and a new shirt—right then and there I began to love him, at least for an instant, it was like a liberation. I've changed trains. Years of domestic tragedy wiped out by a trivial sentence. Grotesque. But lots of times things are like that, in fact they almost always are: you discover in the end that the suffering, all that suffering, was pointless, that you've suffered horrendously, and it was pointless, neither just nor unjust, not good or bad, merely *pointless,* all you can say in the end is: it was pointless. Stuff to drive you crazy if you think about it, so it's better not to think about it, all you can do is not think about it any more, never, you see?"

"More or less."

"Is the hamburger good?"

"Yes."

Diesel and Poomerang never made it to the offces of CRB, anyway, because at the intersection of Seventh Street and Bourdon Boulevard they saw in the middle of the sidewalk, right before their eyes, the heel of a black shoe that had rolled there from somewhere or other but was now motionless, like a tiny rock in the full flood of people heading out on their lunch hour.

"What the hell," Diesel said.

"What is it?" Poomerang didn't say.

"Look," Diesel said.

"What the hell," Poomerang didn't say.

They stared at that black heel, a spike heel, and it took no time to see—a moment after the inevitable flash of an ankle in dark nylon—the *step* that had lost it, the exact step, imagined as rhythm and dance, compass female varnished nylon dark. They saw it first in the pendulum swing of the legs, and then in the gentle bounce of the bosom, under the blouse, which sent it on to the hair—short and black, thought Diesel, short and blond, thought Poomerang—smooth and light enough to dance to that rhythm, which by now in their eyes had become female body, and humanity and history, when it suddenly tripped on the tiny syncopation of a heel that began to totter on one step, and on the next gave way, detaching itself from the shoe and from that whole rhythm—of woman humanity and history—forcing it to falter—not really fall—and from there to find again the equilibrium of immobility—silence.

They were surrounded by noise and confusion, but it was as if nothing could dislodge them, Diesel even more bent over than usual, his eyes fixed on the ground, Poomerang rubbing his shaved head with his left hand, back and forth: the right, as always, hanging onto Diesel's pants pocket. They were staring at a black spike heel but in reality they were seeing the woman as she wavered, slowed down; they saw her turn for an instant and say

"Shit"

and not think even for a second of stopping, as a normal woman would—stop, turn back, retrieve the heel, try to stick it back on supporting herself with one hand on a street signpost, wrong way—not even think of doing such a reasonable thing, but continuing instead to walk, just out of habit saying

"Shit"

at the very moment when, refusing to let the syncopation of an involuntary limp wrinkle her beauty, she takes off the damaged shoe with a casual gesture, still not stopping, and then indeed for those two she becomes heroic by taking off the other—shoeless compass chromed nylon dark—she picks up the shoes, tosses them into a blue trash can as she looks around, searching for what she immediately finds, a yellow vehicle slowly cruising the street: she raises an arm, something gold slides down from the wrist, the yellow vehicle puts on its turn signal, stops, she gets in, gives an address as she pulls her slender leg—foot shoeless—onto the seat, lifting her skirt and, for a moment, flashing a warm prospect of lace that disappears, replaced by an inch of thigh—white—and then reappears on the edge of her panties: little more than a flash, yet it registers in the eyes of a man in a dark suit who doesn't stop walking but keeps going, follows along behind, the warm flash imprinted on his retina, burning his consciousness and breaking on the defenses of his stupor—the stupor of a wearily married man—with a loud crash of metal and lament.

What happened was that Diesel and Poomerang stayed with the dark-suited man, sucked in by the quiet wake of his distress, which moved them, so to speak, and pushed them on, until they saw the color of his bathrobe—brown—and smelled the odors of his kitchen. They ended up sitting at the table with him, and noticed that his wife laughed too hard at the jokes spinning out of the blaring television, while he, the man in the dark suit, poured some beer in a glass for her, and got himself a bottle of mineral water, warm and non-carbonated, the kind he had been drinking for years, thanks to the memory of four long-ago renal colic attacks. In the second drawer of his desk they found seventy-two pages of a novel, unfinished, which was entitled "The Last Bet," and a visiting card—Dr. Mortensen—with two purple-painted lips printed on the back. The clock radio was set on 102.4, Radio Nostalgia, and, shading the bulb in the lamp on the bedside table, there was a pamphlet from the Children of God, whose theme was the immorality of hunting and fishing: the title, a bit scorched by the bulb, was: *I will make you fishers of men.*

They were rifling through Mrs. Mortensen's intimate lingerie when, by a banal and vulgar association of ideas, in their blood rose the memory of the woman dark metallic nylon compass—a violent shake that compelled them to rush all the way back to the yellow taxi, and remain there, on the edge of the street, a little dazed by the disastrous discovery: the disastrous disappearance of the yellow taxi into the bowels of the city—a whole avenue full of cars but empty of yellow taxis with heroes making themselves comfortable on the backseat.

"Gone," Poomerang didn't say.

"Christ," Diesel said.

On the curved surface of the black spike heel they stared at an entire city, at thousands of streets, hundreds of blank yellow cars.

"Lost," Diesel said.

"Maybe," Poomerang didn't say.

"Like looking for a needle in a haystack."

"Not the car."

"There are thousands of them."

"Not the yellow car."

"Too many cars."

"Not the car, the shoes."

"Where, exactly, can a yellow car go?"

"Shoes. A shoe store."

"Where she said she wanted to go."

"A shoe store. The nearest shoe store."

"She looked at the taxi driver and said . . ."

The nearest shoe store. Shoes with black spike heels.

". . . the best shoe store, near by."

"Toxon's, Fourth Street, second floor, women's shoes."

"Toxon's, for Christ's sake."

They found her in front of a mirror, black shoes on her feet, spike heels, and a salesman who was saying

"Perfect."

They never lost her again after that. For an indeterminate number of hours they catalogued her gestures and the objects around her, as if they were testing perfumes. It was something that by now they breathed, when, after an endless dinner, they followed her to the bed of a man who smelled of eau de cologne, and who, using the remote control, played Ravel's *Bolero* over and over again. In front of the bed there was an aquarium with a purple fish in it, and a lot of stupid bubbles. He made love in religious silence; he had put his gold wedding band on the night table, next to a five-pack of a brand-name prophylactic. She pressed her nails into his back, hard enough so that he could feel it, gently enough not to leave a mark. At the seventh *Bolero* she said

"Excuse me,"

slid off the bed, got dressed, put on the spike-heeled black shoes, and left, without a word. The last thing they saw of her was a door closed, gently.

Rain. Asphalt mirrorlike around the black spike heel, a shiny eye staring at them.

"Rain," said Diesel.

They looked up, to a different light, gray, not many people, sound of tires and puddles. Soaked shoes, water down their necks. The time on their watches was no use.

"Let's go," Diesel said.

"Let's go," Poomerang didn't say.

Diesel walked clumsily, slowly, dragging his left foot, the ridiculous immense shoe suspended on a leg that changed course below the knee and bent awkwardly, twisting every step into a Cubist dance. And he breathed heavily, like a cyclist going uphill, a smudged rhythmic painful breathing. Poomerang knew that walk and that breathing by heart. He was attached to them and he danced them gracefully, with the weary look of someone emerging from a tango marathon.

The one and the other, close together, and the soaked stretches of the city on the way home, the liquid lights of traffic signals, cars in third that sounded like toilets flushing, a heel on the ground, farther and farther away, the eye wet, without, any longer, an eyelid, without a brow, finished.

The photograph of Walt Disney was a little bigger than the one of Eva Braun. It had a pale wood frame, and a foot that folded out from the back: to hold it up, if necessary. Walt Disney had white hair and was standing astride a little train, and smiling. It was a train for children, with a locomotive and a lot of cars. It didn't have rails, it had rubber tires, and was in Disneyland, in Anaheim, California.

"Get it?"

"More or less."

"So he was the biggest, had been the biggest. A terrible reactionary, if you like, but he was good at happiness, it was his talent, he got to happiness directly, without many complications, and he brought everyone along with him, really everyone. He had happiness for hire, the most ever seen, he had some for every pocket, for every taste, with his stories of ducks and dwarfs and Bambis, if you think about it, how he did it, and yet he started there and distilled from that whole big mess something that if someone asks you what is happiness, even if it kind of makes you sick, in the end you have to admit that, maybe it's not quite that, but it has the flavor, the taste, I mean, as in strawberry or raspberry, happiness has that taste, no way around it, maybe it's a fake, maybe it's not authentic happiness, original, so to speak, but those were fabulous copies, better than the original, and anyhow there's no way of . . ."

"Done."

"Done?"

"Yes."

"How was it?"

"All right."

"Shall we go?"

"Let's go."

Shall we go? Let's go.

1

"This house is disgusting," said Shatzy.

"Yes," said Gould.

"It's a disgusting house, believe me."

Technically speaking, Gould was a genius. This had been determined by a committee of five professors who had examined him at the age of six, subjecting him to three days of tests. On the Stocken scale, he turned out to belong in the delta band: at that level intelligence is an abnormally developed mechanism whose limits are difficult to conceive. Provisionally they assigned him an IQ of 180, a prodigious figure in itself. They had taken him out of elementary school, where for six days he had tried to seem normal, and had entrusted him to a team of university researchers. At the age of eleven he had graduated in theoretical physics, with work on the solution of the Hubbard model in two dimensions.

"What are the shoes doing in the refrigerator?"

"Bacteria."

"Meaning?"

"An experiment with bacteria. Inside the shoes are glass slides. Gram-positive bacteria."

"And the moldy chicken has something to do with bacteria?"

"Chicken?"

Gould's house was two stories high. It had eight rooms and features such as a garage and a cellar. In the living room there was a carpet with a pattern of imitation Tuscan terra-cotta tiles but since it was two inches thick the idea didn't work all that well. In the corner room, on the first floor, there was a table-soccer game. The bathroom was completely red, including the fixtures. The general impression was of a house belonging to rich people where the FBI had gone to look for a microfilm of the president screwing in a Las Vegas brothel.

"How do you manage to live here?"

"I don't really live here."

"It's your house, isn't it?"

"More or less. I have two rooms down at the college. And there's also a cafeteria there."

"A child shouldn't *live* in a college. A child shouldn't even study there, in a place like that."

"Then what should a child do?"

"I don't know, play with his dog, fake his parents' signatures, have a bloody nose all the time, things like that. Certainly not live in a college."

"Fake something?"

"Forget it."

"Fake?"

"At least a governess, they could at least have a governess for you, has your father ever thought of that?"

"I *have* a governess."

"Really?"

"In a certain sense."

"In what sense, Gould?"

Gould's father was convinced that Gould had a governess, and that her name was Lucy. Every Friday, at 7:15, he telephoned her to find out if everything was OK. Then Gould handed the telephone to Poomerang. Poomerang imitated Lucy's voice very well.

"But isn't Poomerang a mute?"

"Right. Lucy's a mute, too."

"You have a mute governess?"

"Not exactly. My father thinks I have a governess, and he pays her every month by money order. I've told him that she's very good but she's mute."

"And to find out how things are going *he telephones her*?"

"Yes."

"Brilliant."

"It works. Poomerang is terrific. You know, it's not the same thing listening to an ordinary person be silent and listening to a mute be silent. It's a different silence. My father wouldn't fall for it."

"Your father must be a very intelligent man."

"He works for the Army."

"I see."

The day of Gould's graduation, his father had flown in by helicopter from the military base at Arpaka, and had landed on the lawn in front of the university. There was a big crowd of people. The rector had given a very good speech. One of the most significant passages was the one about billiards. "We look at your human and scientific adventure, dear Gould, as at the masterly course that the intelligence of a divine arm, leaning over the green felt of the billiard table of life, has imparted to the billiard ball of your intelligence. You, Gould, are a billiard ball, and you run between the cushions of knowledge tracing the infallible trajectory that will let you, with our joy and sympathy, roll gently into the pocket of fame and success. It is in confidence but with enormous pride that I say to you, my son: that pocket has a name, and the name of that pocket is the Nobel Prize." Out of the whole speech what impressed itself in Gould's mind above all was the sentence "You,

Gould, are a billiard ball." Since he was, understandably, inclined to believe his professors, he had adjusted to the idea that his life would roll out with a predetermined exactitude, and for years afterward he tried to feel under the skin of his days the soft caress of the green felt: and to recognize in the intrusion of unforeseen sorrows the geometric trauma of precise, scientifically infallible cushions. The unfortunate fact was that the pool halls he needed to enter were prohibited to minors, and so for a long time he was prevented from discovering that the gilded image of a pool table could be converted into a perfect metaphor for failure, a place that demonstrated the human inability to approach exactitude. A single evening at Merry's could have furnished him with useful hints on the inevitable incursion of chance into any geometric figure. Under the smoky light hanging over the grease-stained green felt he would have seen faces on which was enacted, as if in hieroglyphics, the unmaking of an illusion, an illusion that harmoniously intertwined intention and reality, imagination and deed. It would not have been difficult, that is, to discover an imperfect world where it was extremely unlikely that among the physiognomies of the players you would come upon the solemn and reassuring face of God. But, as stated, you entered Merry's only if you could produce a driver's license, and this allowed the rector's fine metaphor to remain for years illogically intact in Gould's imagination, like a holy icon that escapes a bombardment. And so he found it untouched inside himself years later, on the day when he suddenly decided to devastate his life. He even had time to look at it again, at that moment, with affectionate and hopeless attention, before giving it the most brutal farewell he could imagine.

"Do you have a job, Shatzy?"

"No, Gould."

"Want to be my governess?"

"Yes."

2

Behind Gould's house was a soccer field. Children played there, while the grown-ups sat on the sidelines shouting, or in the little wooden bleachers, eating and shouting. There was grass everywhere, even in front of the goals and in the middle of the field. It was a beautiful soccer field. Gould, Diesel, and Poomerang sat for hours at the bedroom window watching. They watched the games, the training sessions, everything there was to watch. Gould took notes. He had a theory. He was convinced that every position corresponded to a precise physical and psychological type. He could recognize a forward even before he had changed and put on the No. 9 jersey. His bravura act was reading team pictures: he'd study them for a while and then he could tell you what position the one with the sideburns played and which was the right wing. He had a margin of error of 28 percent. He was working to get it under 10, and practiced whenever he could on the boys on the ball field behind the house. He was still struggling with the defenders, because although it was relatively easy to identify them, to figure out which one played right and which left was a problem. In general, the right back was physically more compact and psychologically cruder. He had a logical approach to things, and proceeded by deductive reasoning, usually without imaginative variations. He pulled up his socks when they slipped down and seldom spat on the ground. The left back, on the other hand, tended, over time, to take on characteristics of his direct opponent, the notoriously volatile right wing, who had strong anarchic tendencies and obvious mental weaknesses. The right wing transforms his area of the field into a land without laws where the only stable reference is the lateral line, a white chalk stripe that he looks for obsessively, desperately. The left back, who, as a defender, has a psychology founded on order and geometry, is forced to adapt to an ecosystem that is uncomfortable for him, and he is therefore, by vocation, a loser. The need to continually adjust his reactions to unpredictable patterns condemns him to a permanent spiritual and, often, physical instability. This may explain his conspicuous tendency to wear his hair long, to be thrown out for protesting, and to make the sign of the cross at the starting whistle. Given this, to distinguish him from a right back in a photograph is nearly impossible. Sometimes Gould was successful.

Diesel watched because he liked headers. He felt an extraordinary pleasure when he heard the impact of skull against ball, and every time it happened, every single time, he said, "Amazing," a big smile on his face. Amazing. Once, a boy hit the ball with his head, the ball hit the bar, ricocheted off, the boy hit it again with his head, it struck the wood, and he dived forwards and went for the header before it touched the ground, just grazing it and getting it in the net. Then Diesel said, "Really amazing." Usually, though, all he said was "Amazing."

Poomerang watched because he was looking for a move he had seen years before, on TV. In his opinion it was such a good play that it couldn't have disappeared forever; it must be roaming the soccer fields of the world, and so he was waiting for it to show up there, on that children's playing field. He had found out the number of soccer fields in the world—one million eight hundred and four—and he was perfectly aware that the chances of seeing the move take place right there were minimal. But Gould had calculated that the chances were not much less than those of being born mute. So Poomerang was waiting. The move was the following: the goalkeeper makes a long throw, the striker, a little beyond midfield, sends the ball on with his head, the opposing goalkeeper comes out of the penalty area and kicks it on the fly, the ball sails back beyond midfield, skipping over the heads of all the players, hits the ground at the edge of the penalty area, and, bouncing over the stunned goalkeeper, goes into the net just grazing the wood. From a strictly soccer point of view, it was lamentable. But Poomerang claimed that in a purely aesthetic sense he had rarely seen anything more harmonious and elegant. "It was as if everything were happening in an aquarium," he didn't say, trying to explain. "As if everything were moving through water, slowly, smoothly, the ball swimming through the air, unhurried, and the players turned into fish, scattered and wandering, looking up open-mouthed and all together rolling their heads to the right and to the left, while the ball bounced over the goalkeeper, his gills wide open, and in the end a wily fisherman caught in his net the fish-ball and the eyes of all, a miraculous catch in the absolute, deep-sea silence of an expanse of green algae with white lines made by a mathematician diver." It was the sixteenth minute of the second half. The match ended two-nothing.

Every so often Gould went out and sat down at the edge of the field, behind the goal on the right, next to Prof. Taltomar. Minutes passed, and they said nothing. Always with their eyes on the field. Prof. Taltomar was of a certain age, and behind him were thousands of hours of soccer watching. The game mattered relatively little to him. He observed the referees. He studied them. He always had an unfiltered cigarette in his mouth, unlighted, and from time to time he muttered phrases like "too far from the play," or "play the advantage, asshole." Often he shook his head. He was the only one who applauded decisions like a sending-off or a retake of a penalty kick. He had some questionable convictions that he had summarized in a single maxim, and for years it had been his comment on any discussion: "Hands in the penalty area is always intentional, offsides are never in doubt, all women are whores." He claimed that the universe was "a match played without a referee," but in his way he believed in God: "He is the linesman, and always screws up offsides." Once, half drunk, he admitted in public that he had been a referee, as a young man. Then he retreated into a mysterious silence.

Gould attributed to him, not wrongly, an infinite knowledge of the rules and sought in him what he could not find in the illustrious academics who were daily coaching him for the Nobel: the assurance that order was one of the properties of infinity. This was what happened between them:

1. Gould arrived, and, without even saying hello, sat down beside the professor and watched the field.
2. For minutes they exchanged neither a word nor a glance.
3. Eventually Gould, continuing to watch the game, said something like: "Cross from the right, striker volleys it to the right midfielder, the ball hits the bar, which breaks in two, then caroms off the referee, ends up between the feet of the right wing, who kicks it at the net. A defender blocks it with one hand and then hurls it back up the field."
4. Prof. Taltomar took his time removing the cigarette from his lips and shaking off an imaginary ash. Then he spat some bits of tobacco on the ground and murmured softly: "Game suspended while the bar is fixed, with consequent fine against the home team for carelessness in maintaining the field. When play resumes, penalty kick for the visiting team and a red card for the defender. A one-match ban, unless he escapes with a warning."
5. They continued to stare at the playing field for a while, without comment.

6. At a certain point Gould left, saying, "Thank you, Professor."
7. Prof. Taltomar murmured, without turning, "Take care, my boy."

This happened more or less once a week.

Gould enjoyed it a lot.

Children need certainties.

One last thing that was important happened at the soccer field. Every so often, while Gould was sitting there with the professor, a ball would roll past the goal, heading towards them. Sometimes it passed right beside them and stopped a few yards farther on. Then the goalie would take a few steps in their direction and shout, "Ball!" Professor Taltomar didn't move a muscle. Gould looked at the ball, looked at the goalkeeper, and didn't move.

"Ball, please!"

Gould, bewildered, stared straight ahead, into space, not moving.

3

On Friday, at 7:15, Gould's father telephoned to find out from Lucy if everything was OK. Gould said that Lucy had gone off with a traveling watch salesman she had met at Mass the Sunday before.

"Watches?"

"And other stuff, chains, crucifixes, stuff like that."

"Christ, Gould. You'd better put an ad in the newspaper. The way we did the other time."

"Yes."

"Get the ad in the paper right away and then use the questionnaire, OK?"

"Yes."

"But wasn't that girl a mute?"

"Yes."

"Did you tell the watch salesman that?"

"She told him."

"She did?"

"Yes, on the telephone."

"People are unbelievable."

"Right."

"Do you still have copies of the questionnaire?"

"Yes."

"Make some photocopies, just in case, OK?"

"Hello?"

"Gould?"

"Hello."

"Gould can you hear me?"

"Now I hear you."

"If you're running out of questionnaires, make some photo-copies."

"Hello?"

"Gould can you hear me?"

". . ."

"Gould!"

"I'm here."

"Did you hear me?"

"Hello?"

"This is a bad connection."

"Now I hear you."

"Are you still there?"

"I'm here . . ."

"Hello!"

"I'm here."

"But what the hell's happening to . . ."

"Bye, Dad."

"Are these damn telephones made of shit?"

"Bye."

"Made out of shit, these teleph"

Click.

Since he couldn't come and do the interviewing himself, Gould's father had the applicants fill out a questionnaire that he had put together and mail it to him, so that he could choose a new governess for Gould based on the responses he received. There were thirty-seven questions, but it was very rare for applicants to get to the end. Generally they stopped around the fifteenth question (15. Ketchup or mayonnaise?). Often they got up and left after reading the first (1. Can the applicant reconstruct the series of failures that led her today, at her age, and unemployed, to apply for a job that is not very well paid and has obvious risks?). Shatzy Shell set up the photographs of Eva Braun and Walt Disney on the table, put a sheet of paper in the typewriter, and tapped out the number 22.

"Read me 22, Gould."

"Really, you're supposed to start at the beginning."

"Who said so?"

"That's No. 1, people always begin at No. 1."

"Gould?"

"Yes."

"Look me in the eyes."

"Yes."

"Do you truly believe that when things have numbers, and one thing in particular has the number 1, that what we have to do, what you have to do, and I, and everyone, is to start right there, for the simple reason that that is the number-one thing?"

"No."

"Splendid."

"Which do you want?"

"22."

"22. Can the applicant recall the nicest thing she ever had to do when she was a child?"

Shatzy sat shaking her head for a moment and murmuring incredulously "had to do." Then she began to write.

When I was little the nicest thing was to go and see the Ideal Home Exhibition. It was at Olympia Hall, which was an enormous place, like a station, with a cupola-shaped roof. Enormous.

Instead of trains and tracks there was the Ideal Home Exhibition. I don't know if you remember, Colonel. They did it every year. The incredible thing is that the houses were real, and you walked around as if you were in some absurd town, with streets, and street lamps at the corners, and with the houses all different, and very clean, and new. Everything was in place, the curtains, the front walk, and gardens, too—it was a dream world. You might have thought it would all be cardboard, and yet the houses were built out of real bricks, even the flowers were real—everything was real. You could have lived there, you could go up the steps, open the door. They were real houses. It's hard to explain, but as you walked into the middle of it you felt something very strange, a sort of painful amazement. I mean, they were real houses and all, but then, in actuality, real houses are different. Mine was six stories tall, and had windows that were all alike, and a marble staircase, with a little landing on each floor, and a smell of disinfectant everywhere. It was a beautiful house. But those houses were different. They had odd-shaped roofs, and fashionable features like bay windows, or a front porch, or a spiral staircase, and a terrace or balcony, things like that. And a light over the entrance. Or a garage with a painted door. They were real, but not real: this was what bothered you. If I think back on it now, it was all in the name, the Ideal Home Exhibition, after all what did you know then about what was ideal and what wasn't. You had no concept of *ideal*. So it took you by surprise, from behind, so to speak. And it was a strange sensation. I think you would understand what I mean if I could explain to you why I burst into tears the first time I went there. Seriously. I cried. I had gone because my aunt worked there, and she had free tickets. She was tall and beautiful, with long black hair. She had been hired to play a mother working in the kitchen. You see, every so often the houses were animated, that is, there were people who pretended to live there, I don't know, a man sitting in the living room reading a newspaper and smoking his pipe, or maybe even children, in their pajamas, in bed—they were bunk beds, marvelous, we had never seen bunk beds. The idea was always to give that impression of the *ideal,* you see? Even the characters were *ideal.* My aunt played the *ideal* in the kitchen, looking elegant and beautiful, in a patterned apron: she was arranging things, opening the kitchen cabinets, and she opened and closed them continuously, but gently, all the time taking out cups and plates, things like that. Smiling. Sometimes even film stars came, or famous singers, and they did the same thing, while photographers took pictures and the next day the pictures were in the paper. I remember one woman, all in furs, a singer, I think, with diamond rings on her fingers, who gazed at the camera while she ran a Hoover vacuum cleaner up and down. We didn't even know what a vacuum cleaner was. This was another great thing about the Ideal Home Exhibition: when you left, your head was full of things you'd never seen before and would never see again. It was like that. Anyway, the first time I went with my mother, and right at the entrance there was an exact replica of a mountain village, with meadows and paths, it was something. Behind it was an enormous painted backdrop, with mountain peaks and blue sky. My head began to feel very queer. I would have stood there looking forever. My mother dragged me away, and we went to a place where there was nothing but bathrooms, one after another, bathrooms you wouldn't believe. The last was called "Now and Then," and there were a lot of people watching—it was like a play, on the right you saw a bathroom from a hundred years ago, and on the left the identical bathroom but everything was modern, very up to date. The incredible thing is that in the bathtubs were two models, no water but two women, and here's the clever part, they were twins, you see? Two women, twins, in the exact same position, one in a copper tub, the other in a white enameled one, and the really crazy thing is that they were *naked,* I swear, completely naked, and smiling at the public, and they held their arms very carefully so that you could get a peek at their tits but not really see them, and everyone was making serious remarks about the bathroom fixtures, but the fact is their eyes were continually darting away to see if by chance the twins had moved their arms just a bit, just enough so their tits were visible; the twins, by the way—you see the odd things that one ends up remembering—were called the Dolphin sisters, although now, thinking back, I suppose it was a stage name. I'm telling you this story about the bathroom because it has something to do with the fact that I burst into tears at the end. I mean, it was a whole combination of things that disconcerted you, from the start, a stratagem that wore you out and predisposed you, so to speak, to something special. Anyway, we left the naked twins and entered the central hall. There were the Ideal Homes, one after another, all in a row, each with its yard, some antique, or old, and others more modern, with a sports car parked out front. It was marvelous. We walked slowly, and at one point my mother stopped and said Look how lovely this is. It was a two-story house with a front porch, a peaked roof, and tall red-brick chimneys. There was nothing extraordinary about it—it was ideal in a very ordinary way—and maybe that was why it struck you. We stood there looking at it, in silence. There were so many people passing by, chatting, and so much noise, the way there always is at the Ideal Home Exhibition, but I began not to hear it any more, as if, little by little, it were all fading from my mind. And at some point I happened to see through the kitchen window—a big window on the ground floor, with the curtains open—I saw the light go on inside, and a woman came in, smiling, with a bunch of flowers in her hand. She walked over to the table, put down the flowers, got a vase, and went to the sink to fill it with water. She did all this as if no one were looking at her, as if she were in a remote corner of the world, where there was only her and that kitchen. She picked up the flowers and put them in the vase, and then she placed the vase in the center of the table, nudging back a rose that was escaping from one side. She was blonde, and her hair was held in place by a headband. She turned, went to the refrigerator, opened it, and reached in for a bottle of milk and something else. She closed the fridge by giving it a little shove with her elbow, because her hands were full. And although I couldn't hear it, I distinctly felt the click of the door as it closed, precise, metallic and slightly warm. I have never heard anything so exact, and definitive, and redeeming. So I looked at the house for a moment—at the whole house, the garden, the chimneys, the chair on the porch, everything. And then I burst out crying. My mother was frightened, she thought something had happened, and in fact something had happened, but what she thought was that I had wet my pants, it was something that often happened, when I was a child, I'd wet my pants and start to cry, so she thought that was what it was and started dragging me to the bathroom. Then, when she saw that I was dry, she began asking me what was wrong, and she wouldn't stop. It was torture, because obviously I didn't know what to say, I could only keep saying that everything was fine, that I was fine. Then why are you crying?

"I am not crying."

"Yes, you are crying."

"No, I'm not."

It was a kind of *piercing, painful amazement*. I don't know if you know, Colonel. It's rather like looking at toy trains, especially if there's a model landscape, in relief, with the station and the tunnels, and cows in the fields and lighted signals at the grade crossings. It happens there, too. Or in a cartoon when you see the house where the mice live, with matchboxes for beds, and a painting of the grandfather mouse on the wall, and bookshelves, and a spoon that serves as a rocking chair. You feel a kind of comfort inside, almost a *revelation*, that opens your soul, so to speak, but at the same time you feel a kind of pain, the sensation of an absolute, irremediable loss. A sweet catastrophe. I think it has to do with the fact that at those moments you are always *outside*, you are always looking in *from the outside*. You can't go in and get on the train, that's a fact; and the house for mice is something that's on television, while you are inescapably *in front*, all you can do is look. That day, you could go inside the Ideal Home if you wanted, you waited in line for a while and then you could go in to see the rooms. But it wasn't the same. There was a whole lot of interesting stuff—it was weird, you could even touch the knick-knacks—but you no longer had the same sense of wonder as when you saw it from the outside. It's a funny thing. When you happen to see the place where you would be *safe*, you are always looking at it *from the outside*. You're never in it. It's *your* place, but you are never there. My mother kept asking me why I was sad, and I would have liked to tell her that I wasn't sad; on the contrary, I would have had to explain to her that it had to do with something like happiness, the devastating experience of having suddenly glimpsed it, and in that idiotic house. But how. Even now I wouldn't be able to. There's also something a little embarrassing about it. That was a stupid Ideal Home, which had been built just to con people, it was a big stupid business of architects and builders, it was a deliberate trick, to tell you the truth. As far as I know, the architect who designed it might be a complete imbecile, one of those guys who on their lunch hour wait outside schools to rub against the girls and whisper Suck my dick and stuff like that. Besides, I don't know if you've noticed this, but generally, if something strikes you as a *revelation*, you can bet that it's bogus, I mean, that it isn't *true*. Take the example of the toy train. You can look at a *real* station for hours and nothing happens; then just glance at a toy train and, *click*, all sorts of good things start up. It doesn't make sense, but it's the damn truth, and sometimes the more idiotic the thing that grabs you is, the more it sticks, with its wonder, as if there had to be a dose of deceit, of deliberate deceit, as if everything had to be false, at least for a while, to succeed in becoming something like a *revelation*. It's the same with books, or films. Any more bogus than that and you'd die, and if you go to see who's behind there you can bet that you will find only solemn sons of bitches, but meanwhile inside you see things that, walking around on the street, you dream of but in real life you'll never find. Real life never *speaks*. It's a game of skill, you win or you lose, they make you play it to distract you, so you won't think. My mother used that ploy. When I didn't stop crying, she dragged me over to a machine that was all lights and signs. It was a lovely machine—it looked like a slot machine or something. It had been set up by a company that made margarine, and had been very carefully designed. There were six cookies on a plate, some made with butter and some with margarine. You tasted them, one by one, and every time you had to say if the cookie was made with margarine or butter. In those days margarine was rather exotic, people didn't really know what it was; they thought it was healthier than butter and basically gross. That was the problem. So the company came up with that machine, and the game was this: if you thought the cookie was made with butter you pressed the red button, and if it seemed to taste like margarine you pressed the blue one. It was fun. And I stopped crying. No doubt about it. I stopped crying. Not that something had changed in my mind: I still had stuck inside me that sensation of piercing, painful amazement, and in fact I would never again be without it, because when a child discovers there's a place that is his place, when *his* home flashes before him for a second, and the *meaning* of a Home, and, above all, the idea that such a House *exists*, then it's forever, you've been screwed to the very end, there's no going back, you will always be someone who's passing through by chance, with a piercing, painful sense of amazement, and so you're always happier than others and always sadder, with all those things to laugh and cry about, as you wander. In this particular case, anyway, I stopped crying. It worked. I ate cookies, I pushed buttons, the lights went on, and I wasn't crying anymore. My mother was happy, she thought it was over, she didn't understand, but I did, I understood it all perfectly, I knew that nothing was over, that it would never be over, but, still, I wasn't crying, and I was playing with butter and margarine. You know, there were so many times, later, when I felt that sensation inside again . . . It seems as if I'd never felt anything else since. With my mind somewhere else, I stood there pressing blue and red buttons, trying to guess. A game of skill. They make you play it to distract you. As long as it works, why not? Among other things, when the Ideal Home Exhibition was over that year, the margarine company announced that a hundred and thirty thousand people had played the game, and that only 8 percent of the contestants had guessed right about all six cookies. They announced it rather triumphantly. I think that was more or less my success rate. I mean that if I think of all the times I tried to guess, pushing the blue and red buttons of this life, I must have hit it right more or less 8 percent of the time—it seems to me a plausible percentage. I say this not at all triumphantly. But it must have gone more or less like that. As I see it.

Shatzy turned to Gould, who had not missed a line.

"How's that?"

"My father isn't a colonel."

"No?"

"General."

"OK, general. And the rest?"

"If you keep going at this rate by the time you finish I won't need a governess anymore."

"That's true. Let me see . . ."

Gould handed her the list of questions. Shatzy glanced at it, then stopped at a question on the second page.

"This is a quick one. Read it . . ."

"31. Can the applicant briefly state the dream of her life?"

"I can."

My dream is to make a Western. I began when I was six and I intend not to die before I finish it.

"*Voilà.*"

From the time she was six, Shatzy Shell had been working on a Western. It was the only thing she truly cared about, in life. She thought about it constantly. When good ideas came to her, she turned on her portable tape recorder and spoke them into it. She had recorded hundreds of tapes. She said it was a wonderful Western.

4

They killed off Mami Jane in the January issue, in a story entitled "Killer Rails." That's the way things go.

5

That business about the Western, among other things, was true. Shatzy had been working on it for years. In the beginning she had collected ideas, then she had started writing things down, filling notebooks. Now she used a tape recorder. Every so often she turned it on and spoke into it. She didn't have a definite method, but she went on, without stopping. And the Western grew. It started with a cloud of sand at sunset.

The usual cloud of sand at sunset, every evening wafted by the wind over the earth and into the sky, while Melissa Dolphin sweeps the road in front of her house; whipped by the river of circling air she sweeps, with unreasoning care, and futile. But carrying her sixty-three years calmly and gratefully. Twin sister of Julie Dolphin, who, swinging on the verandah, sheltered from the worst of the wind, watches her now: watching her, through the dust, she alone understands her.

To the right, laid out along the main street, runs the town. To the left, nothing. There is no frontier beyond their fence, only a land that has been decreed useless, and has been abolished from thought. Rocks and nothing. When someone dies in these parts, people say: the Dolphin sisters saw him pass by. No house is farther out here than their house. Nor elsewhere, they say.

So it is with astonishment that Melissa Dolphin raises her gaze to that nothingness and sees the figure of a man slowly approaching, blurry in the cloud of sand and sunset. Although she has occasionally seen something disappear in that direction—thornbushes, animals, an old man, useless glances—something *appear,* never. Someone.

Julie, she says softly, and turns towards her sister.

Julie Dolphin is standing, on the verandah, and in her right hand she's holding a Winchester model 1873, octagonal barrel, .44-.40 caliber. She looks at the man—he walks slowly, with his hat lowered over his eyes, duster down to the ground, leading something, a horse, something, a horse and something, a bandanna protects his face from the dust. Julie Dolphin raises the rifle, slides the wooden butt against her right shoulder, bends her head to align eye, sight, man.

Yes, Melissa, she says softly.

She aims at the middle of his chest, and fires.

The man stops.

He looks up.

He lowers the bandanna that hides his face.

Julie Dolphin looks at him. She reloads. Then she bends her head to align eye, sight, man.

She aims at his face, and fires.

The echo of the shot is swallowed up in the dust. Julie Dolphin knocks the cartridge out of the bolt: Morgan red, .44-.40 caliber. She remains standing, watching.

It takes the man a few minutes to get to Melissa Dolphin, motionless in the middle of the road. He takes off his hat.

Closingtown?

It depends, Melissa Dolphin answers.

Shatzy Shell's Western began exactly like that.

6

"I'm going with you."

"Why?"

"I want to see this damn school," Shatzy said.

So they went out, the two of them; there was a bus or you could walk. Let's walk part of the way, then maybe take the bus. OK, but cover up.

"What did you say?"

"I don't know, Gould, what did I say?"

"Cover up."

"No way."

"I swear."

"You dreamed it."

"You said cover up, as if you were my mother."

"Come on, let's go."

"You said it."

"Stop this."

"I swear."

"And cover up."

The street sloped slightly downhill, and the ground was littered with leaves that had fallen from the trees, so Gould shuffled his feet as he walked, as if he had moles instead of shoes, moles that were tunneling through the leaves, making a noise like a cigar being lighted, but multiplied a thousand times. A red and yellow noise.

"My father smokes cigars."

"Really?"

"He'd like you."

"He *does like me,* Gould."

"How do you know?"

"I can tell, from his voice."

"Really?"

"You can tell a lot of things, from a person's voice."

"For example?"

"For example, let's say you hear someone with a beautiful voice, really beautiful, a man with a beautiful voice, OK?"

"OK."

"Then you can bet on it, he's ugly."

"Ugly."

"Worse than ugly, really ugly, a greaseball, you know, he's too tall, or he has fat hands that are always sweaty, always sort of moist, you get the picture?"

"So."

"What do you mean, so?"

"I don't know, I don't like to shake hands. In fact I don't have much experience of hands."

"You don't like to shake hands."

"No. It's stupid."

"Oh?"

"Grown-ups' hands are always too big. It's pointless for them to shake hands with *me,* just thinking about it is stupid, and in the end it's always embarrassing."

"Once, on TV, I saw the Nobel Prizes being given out. Well, one person went up there, in a fancy outfit, and then all he did was shake hands, from start to finish."

"That's another story."

"It's a story I'm interested in. Tell it to me, Gould."

"What do you mean?"

"The Nobel Prize."

"What about it?"

"How did they decide to have you win it?"

"They didn't *decide* to have me win it."

"You mean you just won it?"

"They don't give the Nobel Prize to children."

"They could make an exception."

"Stop it."

"OK."

". . ."

". . ."

". . ."

"All right, then how did it happen, Gould?"

"Nothing, it's nonsense, you know—a way of talking, I think."

"Odd way of talking."

"So you don't like it?"

"It's not that I don't like it."

"You don't like it."

"I find it odd, that's all. How can you think of telling a child that he's going to win the Nobel Prize? He may be intelligent, and what have you, but you can't know—maybe he's not *that* intelligent, maybe he doesn't *want* to win the Nobel, and anyway, even if he does, why tell him? Isn't it better to leave him alone, let him do what he has to do, and then one morning he'll wake up and they'll say have you heard the news? You've won the Nobel Prize. The end."

"Look, no one's said anything to me . . ."

"It's the way you talk to someone when he's going to die."

"..."

"..."

"..."

"It was only an example, Gould."

"..."

"Come on, Gould, it was only an example ... Gould, look at me."

"What's the matter?"

"It was only an example."

"OK."

Gould stopped and looked back. There were the two furrows dug by his feet through the leaves, like long, even stripes, vanishing into the distance. You could imagine that someone would come along, perhaps hours later, and walk with his feet in the two lanes, slowly, having fun keeping his feet in the lanes. Gould jumped to one side and moved on, walking carefully, trying not to leave tracks. He looked back at the two stripes that had been suddenly interrupted. *The Adventures of the Invisible Man,* he thought.

"There's the bus, Gould. Shall we take it?"

"Yes."

It went to the end of the avenue and then turned, going up the hill, skirting the park, and passing the animal hospital. It was a red bus. Eventually, it arrived at the school.

"Hey, it's nice," said Shatzy.

"Yes."

"It's really nice, I'd never have imagined it."

"You can't tell from here, but it keeps on going back. There are all the playing fields, and then it goes on, for a long way."

"Lovely."

They stood there next to each other, looking. Boys were going in and out, and there was a big lawn in front of the steps, with paths and a couple of enormous, slightly twisted trees.

"You know the field behind the house, where they play soccer?" said Gould.

"Yes."

"Those are the same boys, the ones who play soccer."

"Yes."

"The odd thing is that even when there's no ball around they play. Every so often you see them kicking in the air, or pretending to dribble. Maybe they'll make a header, but there's no ball, they're just jogging a little while they wait for the coach to get there, or for the game to begin. Sometimes they're not even dressed to play—they've got their schoolbags, they have their coats on—but still they'll make a pass to the midfielder, or they'll be dribbling a chair, stuff like that."

" . . . "

" . . . "

" . . . "

"For me it's the same."

" . . . "

"School, I mean, for me it's just like that."

" . . . "

"Even if there's no book, no professor, no school, nothing, I . . . it's the same thing . . . I never stop my . . . I never stop. You see?"

"I guess."

"It's something I like. I never stop thinking about it."

"Funny."

"You see?"

"Yes."

"The Nobel Prize has nothing to do with it, you see?"

The thing is, they weren't even looking at each other; they were still standing there, eyes wandering over the school, the lawn, the trees, and everything else.

"I wasn't serious, Gould."

"Really?"

"Of course not. I was talking just to talk, you shouldn't listen to me, I'm the last person you should listen to on the subject of school. Believe me."

"OK."

"All in all, school's not my strong point."

". . ."

"Excuse me, Gould."

"It's nothing."

"OK."

"I'm glad you like it."

"What?"

"Here."

"Yes."

"It's nice here."

"But you'll come home, later, OK?"

"Of course I'm coming home."

"Do it: come home."

"Yes."

"OK."

Then they looked at each other. At first, they didn't. They sort of looked. Gould had on a wool cap, slightly askew, so that one ear was covered and the other wasn't. Looking at him, you would have had to have very sharp eyes to see that he was a genius. Shatzy pulled his hat down over the uncovered ear. Bye, she said. Gould went through the gate and started out along the central path, across the big lawn. He didn't look back. He seemed very small, in the middle of that whole school; Shatzy thought that she had never, in her whole life, seen anything smaller than that boy with his schoolbag, as he went along the path, becoming smaller and smaller with each step. She thought it was scandalous to allow a child to be so alone, and that at the very least he should have had a band of hussars behind him, or something of the sort, to escort him along the path and into his classes, a couple of dozen hussars, maybe more. But like this it was terrible.

"It's terrible," she said to two boys who were coming out, with books under their arms and comic-book shoes.

"Is something wrong?"

"Everything's wrong."

"Oh?"

The boys sneered.

"Do you know someone called Gould?"

"Gould?"

"Yes, Gould."

"The kid?"

They sneered.

"Yes, the kid."

"Of course we know him."

"What is there to sneer at?"

"Mr. Nobel, who doesn't know him?"

"What is there to sneer at?"

"Hey, cool it, sister."

"So, do you know him or not?"

"Yes, we know him."

"Are you friends of his?"

"Who, us?"

"You."

They sneered.

"He's not friends with anyone."

"What do you mean?"

"He's not friends with anyone, that's what it means."

"Doesn't he go to school with you?"

"He lives there, at school."

"So?"

"So nothing."

"He goes to class like everyone else, doesn't he?"

"What's it to you? What are you, some kind of a journalist?"

"I'm not a journalist."

"She's his mama."

They snorted.

"I am not his mama. He has a mother."

"And who is she, Marie Curie?"

"Fuck you."

"Hey sister, cool it."

"Cool it yourself."

"You're out of your mind."

"Fuck you."

"Hey."

"Leave her alone. She's nuts."

"What the fuck . . ."

"Come on, forget it . . ."

"She's nuts."

"Let's go, come on."

They weren't sneering any more.

"YOU WON'T BE SO SMART WHEN THE HUSSARS ARRIVE," Shatzy shouted after them.

"Just listen to her."

"Forget it, come on."

"THEY'LL HANG YOU, AND PEOPLE LIKE YOU, BY THE BALLS, AND THEN THEY'LL USE YOU FOR TARGET PRACTICE."

"She's nuts."

"Unbelievable."

Shatzy turned back towards the school. They'll hang you by the balls, she murmured softly. Then she blew her nose. It was very cold. She looked at the big lawn and the twisted trees. She had seen trees like that before, but she couldn't remember where. In front of some museum, perhaps. It was very cold. She took out her gloves and put them on. Damn it all, she thought. She looked at the time. There were boys coming out and boys going in. The school was white. The lawn was turning yellow. Damn it all, she thought.

Then she began to run.

She turned onto the path and ran all the way to the steps, took the steps two at a time, and went into the school. She proceeded to the end of a long corridor, took the stairs to the second floor, went into a kind of cafeteria and out the other side, went down one floor, opened all the doors she could find, ended up outside the school again, crossed a playing field and a garden, entered a three-story yellow building, climbed the stairs, looked in a library and the bathrooms, stuck her head into offices, took an elevator, followed an arrow that said "Grabenhauer Foundation," turned back, went along a green-painted corridor, opened the first door, looked inside the classroom, and saw a man standing behind a lectern and nobody at the desks but one boy, sitting in the third row, with a can of Coke in his hand.

"Shatzy."

"Hi, Gould."

"What are you doing here?"

"Nothing, I just wanted to see if everything was going OK."

"Everything's OK."

"All in order?"

"Yes."

"Good. How do you get out of here?"

"Go downstairs and follow the arrows."

"The arrows."

"Yes."

"OK."

"See you."

"See you."

Gould and the professor remained in the classroom.

"That's my new governess," said Gould. "Her name is Shatzy Shell."

"Cute," observed the professor, who, to stick to the facts, was called Martens. Then he resumed the lecture, which, to stick to the facts, was his Lecture No. 14.

And in effect this appears to be the heart of that singular experience, although obscure and for the most part impenetrable, Prof. Martens asserted in Lecture No. 14. Take the example of a passer-by who, methodically synchronizing his action to a prior plan, determined that morning, sets off with a precise goal, taking a well-defined and unambiguous route along a city street. And suppose that he suddenly happens to come upon the negligible presence, on the pavement, of a black spike heel, unforeseen and, at the same time, unforeseeable.

And suppose he stands there as if bewitched.

He alone—pay attention—and not the thousand other human beings who, in an analogous situation of mind and body, also saw the black spike heel but carefully and automatically relegated it to the useful marginal area of peculiar objects essentially not suitable for penetrating the system of attention, in accordance with the pragmatic setting of the aforementioned system. While our man, instead, having been suddenly subjected to a blinding epiphany, stops walking, spiritually and otherwise, because he has been irremediably taken out of himself by an image that resounds like an ineluctable call, a song that seemingly echoes into infinity.

It's strange, Prof. Martens asserted in Lecture No. 14.

When, in the swarm of material that perception is charged with handing over from experience to us, one detail, and only that one, slips out of the magma, and, evading all checkpoints, actually *strikes* the surface of our automatic non-attention. Generally there is no reason for such instants to occur, and yet they do, suddenly kindling in us an unusual emotion. They are like a promise. Like the gleam of a promise.

They promise worlds.

One might say—Prof. Martens asserted in Lecture No. 14—that certain epiphanies consisting of objects that have escaped the equalizing insignificance of the real are tiny peepholes through which we are allowed to intuit—perhaps reach—the fullness of worlds. Worlds. In the meaninglessness of a spike heel lost on the street light percolates, the light of woman, of a world—Prof. Martens asserted in Lecture No. 14—so that one must ask oneself, in the end, if just that / perhaps that is the single portal to the authenticity of worlds

there is in no woman all the woman that

there is in a spike heel lost on the street / right there, within reach of your hand something that resembles / something that is the kernel of the vast collective experience and history sheltered under the name of woman / we could say its iridescent truth / more precisely, that which in the real world corresponds to what on our perceptual horizon occurs as the emotion and sensation catalogued under the linguistic expression *woman*

there is in no woman all the woman that there is in a spike heel lost on the street: and if this is true, authenticity must be a subterranean metropolis, discernible in the gleam of tiny peepholes announcing it, glowing objects cut into the armored surface of the real, blazes that are annunciation and shortcut, beacon and portal, angels—Prof. Martens asserted in his Lecture No. 14. Adding: don't even mention to me Proust's madeleine. *Settled* there, in that obscenely homey, bourgeois, tearoom image / the burn of true peepholes is neutralized, they are reduced to phenomena, insignificant in themselves, of involuntary and—who knows why, since it's involuntary—revelatory memory / lying on the doctor's couch we have sold off the epiphanic flashes from the underground like depressing regurgitations from the personal and individual subconscious / we have consigned them to a soothing remedy, as if they were kidney stones, to be expelled, pissed away in a pee of memories, memories / memory / diuresis of the soul / unpardonable cowardice / as if—Prof. Martens asserted in his lecture No. 14, leaving the lectern and going over to Gould—

as if the man who stands bewitched by the spike heel, a black spike heel, were at that moment himself: and had his *own* biography, and his *own* memory. This is the lie. The eyes that see the flashes are unique terminals for the world. They are combinations of things that have happened, objective constellations of possibilities meeting in a single moment in the same place. There is nothing subjective. Every flash is an instance of objectivity. It is the authentic that disfigures the real

think of it,
what wonderful eyes, capable of being real and that's all, eyes
without history

afterwards, only afterwards, then it's history

listen
to me, afterwards, only afterwards, then it's story

the ambition to
render that flash eternal converts it to a story, as far as it can

think
of the mind that can do it

how much lightness, and strength, to
hold a flash suspended for the time necessary to see it melt into a
story

that would be to coin stories, *that* is what one should know
how to do, listening as long as necessary, waiting for the clearing
hidden in the piercing glare, greeting the step and the measures,
the breath, the pace, walking its paths, breathing its tempos, until
you have, in hand, in the voice, that instant opening up into a
place, and *softened* in the curved line of a story, to the straight line
of a story *sharpened*

can you imagine a more beautiful gesture?
Prof. Martens asserted in Lecture No. 14.

Professor Martens was Gould's instructor in quantum mechan-
ics. He had a passion for bicycles, though he fell off frequently,
because of ear lesions that hadn't healed properly. One of his
ancestors had fought in the battle of Charlottenburg, and he had
the evidence. He said.

7

Another good scene was the menu scene. In the saloon. Not the menu. The scene. It took place in the saloon.

Where a whole great confusion of things was dancing around—voices, noises, colors—but don't forget, said Shatzy, the stink. That's important. Keep in mind the stink. Sweat, alcohol, horses, rotten teeth, pee and aftershave. Got that? She wouldn't continue until you swore you had that firmly in your mind.

In the beginning it was all between Carver, the guy who worked in the saloon, and the stranger, the one who'd been at the Dolphin sisters'. Whenever Carver talked, he dried glasses. No one had ever seen him wash one.

"Are you the stranger?"

"What's that, a new brand of whiskey?"

"It's a question."

"I've heard some more original."

"We keep the good ones over here, for the customers with money."

The stranger places a gold piece on the bar and says:

"Let's see."

"Whiskey, *señor?*"

"Double."

Shatzy said that there was still some stuff left to record, but essentially it was almost perfect. The dialogue, she meant.

"Do you folks always shoot people who show up in town?"

"Dolphin sisters, eh?"

"Two ladies. Twins."

"That's them."

"Nice pair."

"Never seen anyone use a rifle like them," Carver says, and starts drying another glass.

"What do you mean?"

"You haven't heard the story of the jack of hearts yet?"

"No."

"They're famous, on account of that story. It goes like this. They stand forty paces away from you, you throw a deck of cards in the air, they shoot, you pick the cards up off the ground, and when you're done you find you've got fifty-one normal cards and one with two holes in the middle."

"The jack of hearts."

"Right."

"Jack of hearts every time?"

"They like that card. There must be something behind it."

"And when can you catch this number?"

"You can't. The last time was two years ago and a fellow got killed. End of the run."

"The two of them did him in?"

"He was a guy who came from somewhere else, a fool. He had heard the story of the jack of hearts and didn't believe it; he said those old maids couldn't hit a playing card if you rolled it up and stuck it in the gun barrel. For days he went around saying that, it made him laugh like a lunatic, that business of rolling up the card and so forth. Finally the Dolphin sisters decided they'd had enough. It wasn't so much the business about the card, it was the stuff about the old maids that made them furious, everyone here knows it's best to avoid the subject, and instead that jerk couldn't shut up, the old maids this, the old maids that. It made them crazy. Another whiskey?"

"First the story."

"Finally, he bet a thousand dollars that they couldn't do it. He seemed very sure of himself. They showed up, with their guns. The whole town turned out to watch. The fool laughed, totally cool, counted out the forty paces, took the pack of cards, and threw them up in the air. He was stretched out on the ground while the cards were still in the air, falling like dead leaves: two shots straight to the heart. Dead. The Dolphin sisters turned and, without a word, went home."

"Bingo."

"We all stood there, like stone, and didn't even know where to look. A silence like the grave. Only the sheriff moved: he went up to the corpse, rolled him onto his back, and stood looking a while. He seemed to be searching for something. Then he turned to us: he shook his head and smiled."

Carver stopped wiping the glass. He smiled, too.

"That fool had been very clever. He'd taken the jack of hearts out of the pack and hidden it. Guess where."

"Vest pocket."

"Just above his heart. I remember it still, that card. Covered with blood. And in the middle: two holes, just so, like a signature."

"Whiskey, Carver."

"*Sì, señor.*"

At the trial—said Shatzy—the judge searched through his books for something that would allow an unarmed cheat to be killed without the killers' ending up on the gallows. He couldn't find anything. So he said, Fuck you, not guilty. He took the sheriff aside and said something to him alone. Then he went and got violently drunk.

"Carver?"

"*Si, señor.*"

"Why am I alive?"

"This is a saloon, the church is farther along, on the other side of the street."

"How is it that the Dolphin sisters shot me and yet I'm here, drinking whiskey?"

"Blanks. The sisters don't know it, Truman Morgan makes them, red, .44-.40 caliber, they did a good job, exact likenesses of the real ones. But they're blanks. Sheriff's orders."

"And they don't know it?"

Carver shrugs his shoulders. The stranger empties his glass. There is a stink of sweat, alcohol, horses, rotten teeth, pee and aftershave. If you asked Shatzy what the hell it had to do with the menu, she said it does, it does. Don't worry, this is only the beginning.

8

Since the bathroom was at the top of the stairs, when Shatzy went up to bed she passed it. Gould was in there. And what she heard from outside was his voice. His voice imitating other voices.

"We're not at your fucking college, Larry, you know? Look at me and breathe . . . come on, breathe . . . AND GO SLOW WITH THAT STUFF, CHRIST!"

"Your eyebrow's a mess, Maestro."

"Go slow, just the same, for God's sake . . . listen Larry, are you listening to me?"

"Yes."

"If you don't stop playing the little rich kid that guy will send you home with somebody else's face."

"Yes."

"Would you like to have somebody else's face?"

"No."

"Breathe . . . like this, Mr. Mama's boy."

"I am not a . . ."

"YES, YOU ARE, YOU FUCKING MAMA'S BOY, breathe . . . give him some water . . . WATER . . . listen to me, are you listening to me? You won't beat him if you stand there waiting, get it?"

" . . ."

"Shorten up, Larry, you have to get inside there and stay with his punches, you have to look for those punches, understand, stop running, you're not here to look good in the photos, watch for his punches, NO MORE WATER, when you feel his fists then you're at the right distance, that's where you have to work, left to the liver and uppercut, that guy's got a defense you could drive a truck through, LARRY!"

"Yes."

"Go with his punches and then hit him. Repeat after me."

"My hand . . . my hand hurts."

"REPEAT IT, BY GOD!"

"Go with his punches . . ."

"Go with his punches, Larry."

DONG!

"Fuck you, Larry!"

" . . . fuck."

Third round here in the ring at the Toyota Master Building, Larry Gorman and León Sobilo, scheduled for eight rounds, Gorman's face already looks tired, Sobilo stays in the center of the ring . . . in his usual position, not too refined but effective . . . a great fighter, remember his match with Harder . . . twelve brutal rounds . . . left jab from Sobilo, another jab . . . Gorman backpedals, Gorman at the ropes, then he slides down, gracefully . . .

"WHAT WAS THAT, LARRY? YOU'RE NOT DANCING THE TANGO, FOR GOD'S SAKE."

Sobilo doesn't ease up, again with the jab, and again . . . right hook, DOUBLES WITH THE LEFT, GORMAN WAVERS . . . LOOKS FOR THE CORNER, BOTH STANDING . . . Sobilo on the attack, Gorman crouching in the corner . . .

"NOW, LARRY!"

UPPERCUT FROM GORMAN, RIGHT HOOK, LEFT TO THE BODY, SOBILO SEEMS TO BE HIT HARD, BACKS UP TOWARD THE CENTER OF THE RING

FINISH HIM LARRY, FUCK, NOW . . .

Gorman presses him . . . holds his arms down at his sides, a really weird sight, all you folks out there listening . . . Sobilo stops . . . Gorman's torso wobbles, he still has his arms lowered . . . jab from Sobilo, Gorman ducks, AND GETS INSIDE SOBILO'S DEFENSE

RIGHT

STRAIGHT RIGHT

LEFT

LEFT HOOK . . .

AND RIGHT

RIGHT HOOK, SOBILO TO THE CANVAS, TO THE CANVAS, SOBILO GOES DOWN, A DEADLY COMBINATION, SOBILO TO THE CANVAS, HE DOESN'T SEEM TO HAVE THE STRENGTH TO GET UP . . . RIGHT LEFT RIGHT WITH DIZZYING SPEED . . . SOBILO TRIES TO GET UP . . . GETS UP, SOBILO ON HIS FEET, THE COUNT IS OVER, SOBILO ON HIS FEET BUT IT'S OVER, IT'S OVER, THE REFEREE STOPS THE FIGHT, IT'S OVER, AT A MINUTE AND SIXTEEN SECONDS INTO THE THIRD ROUND, TECHNICAL KNOCKOUT, ALL YOU LISTENERS OUT THERE, ONE AMAZING BURST WAS ENOUGH FOR LARRY GORMAN TO CARRY OFF THE VICTORY HERE AT THE TOYOTA MASTER BUILDING . . .

"Where the fuck did you learn that tango step?"

"In college, Maestro."

"Don't bullshit me."

"I'll teach you if you want."

"Put this on, let's go."

"Whose face do I have?"

"Yours."

"OK."

Sound of running water. Then the faucet, and brushing of teeth. Then nothing. The door opened and Gould was in his pajamas. Shatzy stood there motionless, looking at him.

"And what was that?"

"What?"

"That TV."

"It's a radio."

"Ah."

"Ugly son of a bitch, that Sobilo."

"Italian?"

"Argentinean. A fighter. Ugly to look at, but a stubborn son of a bitch. Never went down before."

"Gould?"

"Yes."

"Why don't you just pee when you're in the bathroom, like other little boys?"

"I do it in bed, it's more comfortable."

"True."

"Night."

"Night."

9

Shatzy invited them all out to dinner on Saturday, so in the afternoon they went to Wizwondk's, the barber's, to get their hair cut. It was crowded; there was a line out the door. Everyone gets a haircut on Saturday.

"At my house we all have a bath on Saturday," said Diesel.

The man lying back in the chair, soaped up to his nostrils, kept clearing his throat, but in that position, of course, he couldn't spit, and so it accumulated. Horrifying to think what he might cough up, at the right moment. Fan blades turning on the ceiling whirling hair stubble old Brilliantine ads and the smell of cologne. Yellow walls, Brigitte Bardot, who has never aged in Wizwondk's heart, pasted on mirrors; someone says he was a priest, at home, then something about girls, some such story. Wizwondk the barber: on Thursday he cut hair free, "I know why, and I'll never tell you." Poomerang had his head shaved. Gould: "Cut as little as possible, please." Diesel didn't sit in chairs, so he stood, leaning on the sink, and Wizwondk climbed up on a stool, up and down, and cut, tapered in the back, center part. For now, anyway, people were lined up outside in the heat, waiting.

"Technical knockout in the third round," said Gould.

"Shit," said Diesel, taking a greasy bill out of his pocket and handing it to Poomerang. "You want to explain to me how he stayed on his feet all that time?"

"I told you, that guy was a stubborn son of a bitch."

"You can't hurry an artist, and Gorman is an artist," Poomerang didn't say, pocketing it.

"And what about Mondini?" asked Diesel.

"Mondini made a face like this, he didn't want to utter a word. He says Larry's trying to be clever, he gets up there and dances the tango."

"*Baila, baila.*"

"Next," said Wizwondk.

Mondini was Larry's trainer. The Maestro, they call him. The one who discovered Larry. His hair was stiff and curly, like steel wool. He had a story of his own.

POOMERANG: Mondini was a tinker; he didn't know much about it, but he did it. He fixed a toilet in a gym and fell in love with boxing. In his first fight he ended up on the mat six times. Back in the locker room, he got dressed, then went out and waited for the guy who had flattened him. He had a Russian name, Kozalkev. Mondini could barely stand up because of the hits he'd taken, but he followed him, without being noticed, until the Russian went into a bar. Mondini went in, too. He ordered a beer and sat down next to him. He waited awhile, then said to him: Teach me. Kozalkev had fought fifty-three times, he sold fights, and every so often he had himself set up with a few greenhorns to straighten his record. Fuck you, he said. Very calmly, Mondini emptied his beer on the fighter's pants. That started them brawling, hitting and kicking and throwing glasses, until they were forcibly separated and thrown into a jail cell, down at police headquarters. For an hour they sat in the semi-darkness, in solitary silence. Then the Russian said: First of all, you box if you're hungry—it doesn't matter for what. By morning they had gotten as far as how to punch your opponent in the kidneys without the referee's seeing you, and then how you protest when the opponent does the same. A fist in the kidneys, incidentally, hurts all the way up to the eyes.

DIESEL: Mondini said that it takes one night to learn how to box. And a whole lifetime to learn how to fight. He stopped at thirty-four. A career, like so many, with one memorable match. Twelve rounds at Atlantic City, against Barry "King" Moose. They ended up on the mat four times each. It looked as though they were going to murder each other. They spent the last round leaning on each other, head to head, exhausted, their fists swinging like pendulums winding down: and for those last three minutes they insulted each other like pigs. In the end the victory went to Moose, he'd gotten some hooks in. Mondini tried to forget. But one time, when they were all watching TV, and there was something about a murder in Atlantic City, someone heard him mutter: Great place, I spent a week there once, one Sunday night.

"Shall I touch up all this white hair?" said Wizwondk. On Monday, his day off, he visited the cemeteries; he seemed to have relatives everywhere. And at night, at home, he played the guitar. The neighbors opened their windows and listened.

POOMERANG: Mondini stopped when he was thirty-four. His last fight was against a black guy from Philadelphia. He was at the end of the line, too. Mondini called his wife, who always sat in the first row, and said to her:

"Did you take the money?"

"Yes."

"OK. All on me, on points."

"But . . ."

"Don't argue. Me, on points. And let's just hope the guy manages to stay on his feet to the end."

Mondini went to the mat in the second round and again in the seventh. He didn't fight badly, but he just didn't see that damn left hook coming. The black guy did a good job of getting it off, you couldn't see it coming. He let him have one in the tenth, and put him out cold. Mondini saw stars for a while. Then he saw his wife looking at him, leaning over the cot in the locker room. He attempted a smile.

"Don't worry. We'll start over."

"Done," his wife said. "I put it all on the other guy."

It was with that money that he opened the gym. And he became Mondini, the real thing. The Maestro. Try finding another like him.

The kid sitting right under the Berbaluz calendar (hair dyes and shampoos) began to tremble like a condemned man. His whole body was trembling, violently. He slid off the chair and lay on the floor. He was gnashing his teeth and foaming at the mouth. With every breath he let out a frightening hiss. Wizwondk stopped, scissors and comb in his hand. They were all staring, no one moved. The big fat man who was sitting in the chair next to him said

"What's with him?"

No one answered. The boy was in bad shape. He was beating his arms and legs on the floor, and his head was bobbing on its own, his eyes were crossed and the slobber was fouling his face.

"Fucking disgusting!"

The fat man got up, looked at the boy lying in front of him, and ran his hands over his jacket, as if wiping them off. He was pale, and his forehead was shiny with sweat.

"Are you going to make him stop, or not? It's indecent!"

Wizwondk couldn't move. Someone else got up but no one dared approach. An old man who had remained sitting in his chair murmured something like

"You have to let him breathe . . ."

Wizwondk said

"The telephone . . ."

The boy hit his head on the floor, he didn't complain, nothing, only that dreadful hissing . . .

DIESEL: A really fine gym. Mondini's Gym. Right above the door, so there would be no mistake, was written, in red, "Boxing: Do It If You're Hungry." Then there was a picture of Mondini as a young man, with his fists in the air, and one of Rocky Marciano, autographed. There was a blue ring, a little smaller than regulation. And equipment everywhere. Mondini opened at three in the afternoon. The first thing he did was plug in the clock, the one that timed the rounds. It only had a second hand, and every three circuits it rang and then stopped for a minute. Mondini had a kind of reflex. When the bell rang he'd spit and then smile: as if he had emerged unharmed from something. He lived in his own time, divided into three-minute rounds and one-minute pauses. When he closed the gym, late in the evening, the last thing he did, in the dark, was unplug the clock. Then he went home, like a ship whose sails have been lowered.

POOMERANG: He took a couple of kids to the national title, kids without much talent, but he worked them well. He killed them with training exercises, and then, when they were ready, he sat them down and began to talk. About everything. And among the other things, boxing. After half an hour they got up. They wouldn't have been able to repeat a thing, but when they went into the blue ring to fight, it all came back to their minds: how to defend, how to fake a hook, how to duck a left. Leaning on the ropes, Mondini watched them in silence, not missing a move. Then he sent them home without saying a word. The next day, it started again. His students trusted him. He managed to bring out the best in each of them. When the best was to get beaten soundly every time they went into the ring, Mondini would call them over, one evening like all the others, and say I'll take you home, OK? He'd load them into his old sedan, twenty years old, and, talking about other things, drive them home. When they got out of the car, they also got out of the ring. They knew it. Some said: I'm sorry, Maestro. He'd shrug. And that was the end. It went on like that for sixteen years. Then Larry Gorman showed up.

The boy started to pee on himself. His pants flattened out and the pee ran over the linoleum floor tiles. The fat man walked around the boy, he was beside himself:

"God damn it, this is disgusting . . . stop it, you fucking bastard, will you stop it?"

No one was thinking of going near him, because the boy was still writhing, and the fat man was frightening he was so angry. He went on shouting.

"Cut it out, you bastard, you hear me? Cut it out, he's peed all over himself, little bastard, shit, he's peed on himself, like an animal, God damn . . ."

He was standing in front of the kid, and suddenly he kicked him, in the ribs, and then looked at his shoe, a black loafer, to see if it was dirty, and that utterly enraged him.

"Fucking shit, can't you see how revolting it is, disgusting, make him stop!"

He began kicking him all over. Wizwondk took two steps forwards. He had the scissors in his hand. He held them like a dagger.

"Now that's enough, Mr. Abner," he said.

The fat man didn't even hear him. He was like a madman kicking the boy. He shouted and struck, the boy was still trembling, there was drool all over his face, and every so often he made that hissing sound, but weaker, as if from a distance. Everyone was terrified. Wizwondk took another two steps forwards.

DIESEL: Larry Gorman was sixteen. A good build, a light heavyweight's; a good face, not like a fighter's; a good family, from an exclusive neighborhood. He came into the gym late one night. And he asked for Mondini. The Maestro was leaning on the ropes, watching two guys who were sparring. One of them, the blond, was always leaving his right side unprotected. The other didn't have his heart in it. The Maestro was brooding. Larry went up to him and said: Hello, my name is Larry, and I want to be a boxer. Mondini turned, looked him over, pointed to the red letters over the door, and went back to the two who were fighting. Larry didn't even turn around. He had already read the words. Boxing:

Do It If You're Hungry. As a matter of fact, he said, I haven't had dinner yet. The bell rang, they stopped fighting, Mondini spat on the floor and said Very funny. Get out. Someone else would have left, but Larry was different, he never left. He sat down on a bench in a corner and didn't move. Mondini kept at it for two more hours, then the gym began to empty out, people picked up their stuff and left. Until it was just the two of them. Mondini put his coat on over his gym clothes, turned out the light, headed towards the clock and said: if anyone comes, bark. Then he unplugged the clock and left. When he came back the next day, at three in the afternoon, Larry was there. On the bench. Give me one good reason why I should train you, Mondini said to him. To see what it's like to train the next world champion.

POOMERANG: In a sense, Mondini hated him. But he spent a year remaking his body, with a killing regimen of training. He took the money off him, as he put it. Larry worked without discussion, and meanwhile he watched others, and learned. A model pupil, except he had this mania of never being quiet. He talked continuously. He commented. As soon as anyone was in the ring, he started. Maybe he was jumping rope, or even on the floor doing his eightieth kneebend. At the first punch, he began to comment. He gave his opinion. He corrected, he counseled, he got mad. Generally, he kept his voice fairly low, but still it was exhausting. One night, about a year after his arrival, there were two guys in the ring, sparring, and he wouldn't stop. It annoyed him that the shorter one couldn't hide his punches, and was too slow on his feet. What's the matter, he shit in his shoes? he said. Mondini stopped the fight. He made the shorter one get out of the ring, turned to Larry, and said Get up there. He put on the gloves, the headgear, and inserted the mouthpiece. Larry had never been in the ring and had never punched anyone in his life. The other was a light heavyweight, with six fights behind him, all of which he had won. Promising. He looked at the Maestro because he didn't really know what to do. Mondini gave him a nod that meant let him have it till I stop you. Larry put up his fists. When he met the other's gaze, he smiled and with the mouthpiece wobbling in his mouth managed to say: Scared?

Wizwondk was now standing right in front of the fat man. But the man didn't even see him. He kept on kicking the boy and shouting—he had totally lost his head.

"You little bastard son of a bitch, go home and be revolting, go and die in your own house, just leave me alone, get it, this is a civilized place, tell him this is a civilized place, he can't be allowed . . ."

The fat man looked around. He was searching for someone to say he was right, but they were all terrified, they watched in silence, immobilized, not one could take his eyes off him. Only Wizwondk, with the scissors in his hand, still seemed to be alive.

"Get away from there, Mr. Abner," he said, in a loud voice.

Mr. Abner, still shouting, thrust one foot in the boy's face, right in all that slobber, and began to crush it, as if he were putting out an enormous cigarette, and at the same time he pulled up his pant leg, so it wouldn't get dirty. Wizwondk took a step forward and stuck the scissors in his side. Once, and then again, without a word. The fat man turned, he was astonished, and to stay upright he had to take his foot off the boy's face. He was swaying back and forth, and he wasn't shouting any more, but he went up to Wizwondk and, grabbing him by the neck, squeezed with both hands, while the blood dripped down his jacket and his pants. Wizwondk raised the scissors again and plunged them into his neck, and then, when the fat man staggered, into his chest. The scissors broke. Blood gushed in rhythmic bursts from the fat man's jugular and spurted all over the room. He fell to the floor, taking the magazine table with him. The boy was still there, you could hear the sound of his head beating the floor, incessant, like a clock gone crazy, no part of his body was still. Only his breath seemed to have stopped. Wizwondk let the handle of the scissors, which he was still holding, drop to the floor. The other piece was sticking out of Mr. Abner's chest, and it was dripping with blood.

DIESEL: Three minutes passed, and the bell rang. Mondini said, That's enough. He took Larry's headguard off and began to untie the gloves. Larry was panting. Mondini said to him I'll drive you home, OK? It took a while, in the old sedan, to get to the exclusive neighborhood. They stopped in front of a house that was all lights and windows. Mondini turned off the engine and looked at Larry.

"Three minutes and you didn't throw a single punch."

"Three minutes and I didn't take a punch, either," Larry answered.

Mondini fixed his eyes on the steering wheel. It was true. For the entire round, Larry had been moving his legs with impressive agility, dancing in all directions, as if he had wheels under his feet. The other fighter had thrown all the punches he knew, and hadn't been able to hit him. He'd left the ring raging like a beast.

"That's not boxing, Larry."

"I didn't want to hurt him."

"Don't talk nonsense."

"Really, I didn't want to . . ."

"Don't talk nonsense."

Mondini glanced at the house. It looked like an advertisement for happiness.

"Why the hell do you want to be a boxer?"

"I don't know."

"What the hell kind of answer is that?"

"That's what my father says. What the hell kind of answer is that? He's a lawyer."

"I see."

"Nice house, isn't it?"

"I can see that from your face."

They sat there a while, in that silence of the wealthy. Larry toyed with the car's ashtray. He opened and closed it. Mondini didn't toy with anything, because he was thinking back to what he had seen in the ring: the biggest talent that had ever fallen into his hands. He was rich, the son of a lawyer, and hadn't the slightest reason to box.

"See you tomorrow," said Larry, opening the door.

Mondini shrugged his shoulders.

"Fuck you, Larry."

"Fuck," he answered happily, and went into the house.

It remained their way of saying goodbye. Even during a fight, when they were in the corner, and the bell rang, Larry would get up, Mondini would take away the stool and they would unfailingly say to each other:

"Fuck you, Larry."

"Fuck."

Larry went on, and he won. He won twelve in a row. Thirteen, with Sobilo.

Wizwondk fell to his knees. A few feet away, the fat man was spurting blood all over the place, his eyes staring wide and his hands, every so often, groping in the air. Around him, the others woke from their spell. Some ran off. Two men went over to Wizwondk and picked him up, speaking to him. Someone grabbed the phone and called the police. Gould found himself pushed forward, a few steps from the two bodies jerking like fish at the bottom of a pail. He tried to turn back, but couldn't. Suddenly there was a terrible smell. He turned and saw on one of the mirrors a black-and-white photograph, of a soccer team posing, all sweaty and smiling, around a big cup sitting on the ground. He pushed his way through the crowd until he was right in front of the picture. He leaned over the sink and tried to shut out everything around him. He started with the right wing: he was in T-shirt and shorts, but his socks had fallen down, he had a silly moustache, and his smile betrayed an intense sadness. The sweeper was the only one who wasn't sweaty, and he was also the tallest: easy. He recognized the stopper in the contorted face and stocky build of the player at the edge of the picture and the center forward in the actor's face of the one who was grasping a handle of the cup and staring into the camera. He began to have trouble when it came to the fullbacks. They all had the faces of fullbacks.

He tried to study the legs, when they were visible. But there was such an uproar—people shoving, someone shouting—that he couldn't concentrate. He gave up a moment before realizing that the one in the uniform, but sweaty, was the left back, who naturally had been thrown out of the game. He closed his eyes. And began to vomit.

Wizwondk spent several years in prison. When they realized that he was harmless, they allowed him to have his guitar. He played every night, light cheerful numbers. In the other cells, the other prisoners listened to him.

10

Edge of the field, behind the goal at the right. They sat there, watching. Prof. Taltomar with the cigarette butt between his lips. Gould with a wool cap on his head, hands in his pockets.

Minutes and minutes.

Then Gould, not taking his eyes off the game, said:

"Wild storm on the field. Twenty minutes into the second half. Pass from the left, the home team forward, obviously offside, stops it with his chest, the referee puts the whistle to his mouth, but the whistle, full of water, doesn't work, the center forward kicks with his instep, the ref tries the whistle again but again it misfires, the ball goes into the upper corner of the net, the referee tries to whistle with his fingers but spits in his hand, the forward heads like one possessed for the corner flag, takes off his jersey, leans on the flag, performs some stupid Brazilian dance steps, and then is incinerated by a bolt of lightning that destroys the above-mentioned flag completely."

Prof. Taltomar took his time removing the cigarette from his lips and shaking off an imaginary ash.

The situation was, objectively, complex.

Finally he spat some crumbs of tobacco on the ground and murmured softly:

"Goal disallowed because of illegal position. Center forward warned for taking off his jersey. When his ashes have been removed from the field, the bench can make the necessary substitution. Once the substitution is authorized by the referee's whistle and a new corner flag is installed, play resumes with a free kick in the exact place where the offside occurred. No penalty for the home team. We haven't yet reached the point where someone is responsible if the opposing center forward has extremely bad luck."

Silence.

Then Gould said

"Thank you, Professor."

And went off.

"Take care, my boy," murmured Prof. Taltomar without even turning to look at him.

The game was tied at nothing-nothing.

The referee didn't run much but he knew what was what.

It was bitterly cold.

Children need certainties.

11

"Give me Miss Shell."

"All right."

Gould handed the receiver to Shatzy. His father was on the line.

"Hello?"

"Miss Shell?"

"It's me."

"Any relation to the oil company?"

"No."

"Too bad."

"I agree."

"Your answer to question No. 31 was that you're making a Western."

"Right."

"That the dream of your life is to make a Western."

"Yes."

"Do you think it's a good answer?"

"I didn't have any other."

"   . . ."

"   . . ."

"But what is it?, a film?"

"I beg your pardon?"

"This Western . . . what is it, a film, a book, a comic strip, what in the world is it?"

"In what sense?"

"Can you hear me?"

"Yes."

"What is it? a film?"

"What's what?"

"THE WESTERN, what is it?"

"It's a Western."

"   . . ."

"   . . ."

"A Western?"

"A Western."

"   . . ."

"   . . ."

"Miss Shell?"

"I'm here."

"Is everything all right there?"

"Marvelous."

"Gould is special, you do understand that?"

"I think so."

"I don't want to have any sort of upset around him, am I clear?"

"More or less."

"He should think about his studies, and everything else will follow."

"Yes, General."

"He's a strong boy, he'll manage."

"Probably."

"You know the story of the hand of Joaquín Murieta?"

"Pardon?"

"Joaquín Murieta. He was a bandit."

"Fantastic."

"The terror of Texas—for years he spread terror there. He was a fierce bandit, and he was very good at it: he laid out eleven sheriffs in three years, he had a price on his head that looked like a collection of zeroes."

"Really?"

"Finally, they had to mobilize the army to capture him. It took a while, but they got him. And you know what they did then?"

"No."

"They cut off one hand, the left hand, the hand he shot with. They packed it up and sent it on a trip around Texas. It made a tour of all the cities. The sheriff would receive the package, put the hand on display in the saloon, and then pack it up and send it on to the next city. It was like a warning, you see?"

"Yes."

"So that people would understand who was stronger."

"I see."

"Well, you know the odd thing about the whole business?"

"No."

"It's that they sent around four hands belonging to Joaquín Murieta, to speed things up, the real one and three others cut off some other poor Mexicans, and one day they made a mistake in their calculations, and in a city called Martintown two hands arrived at the same time, two hands belonging to Joaquín Murieta, both left hands."

"Splendid."

"You know what people said?"

"No."

"I don't, either."

"I beg your pardon?"

"I don't, either."

"Oh."

"It's a good story, don't you think?"

"Yes, it's a good story."

"I thought it might be useful, for your Western."

"I'll think about it."

"The last time I was there, in the fridge there was a yellow plastic airplane and the telephone book."

"Now everything's fine."

"I'm counting on you."

"Of course."

"The boy needs to drink milk, get the kind with vitamins."

"Yes."

"And calcium, he has to have calcium, he's always been a bit low in calcium."

"Yes."

"Someday I'll explain."

"What?"

"Why I'm here and Gould is there. I imagine it doesn't seem much of an idea, to you."

"I don't know."

"I'm sure it doesn't seem to you much of an idea."

"I don't know."

"Someday I'll explain, you'll see."

"All right."

"That was a problem before, with that mute girl. She was a fine girl, but it wasn't very easy to explain things."

"I imagine."

"I feel more comfortable with you, Miss Shell."

"Good."

"You can speak."

"Yes."

"It's much more practical."

"I agree."

"Good."

"Good."

"Give me Gould?"

"Yes."

Gould's father telephoned every Friday, at 7:15 in the evening.

12

Beautiful was the whore of Closingtown, beautiful. Black-haired was the whore of Closingtown, black-haired. There were dozens of books in her room, on the second floor of the saloon, and she read them when she was waiting, stories with a beginning and an end, if you ask her she'll tell you the stories. Young was the whore of Closingtown, young. Holding you between her legs she whispers: *my love.*

Shatzy said that she cost the same as four beers.

A thirst for her, in all the pants in town.

Sticking to the facts: she had come there to be the schoolteacher. The school had been converted to a storehouse, since Miss McGuy had left. So eventually she had arrived. She had put everything in order, and the children had begun to buy notebooks, pencils, and the rest. According to Shatzy, she was a very good teacher. She did easy things, and had books they could understand. Finally, even the older kids got to like it: they went when they could, the teacher was beautiful, and you ended up being able to read what was written under the faces of the outlaws, the ones hanging in the sheriff's office. These were boys who were already men. She made the mistake of staying with one of them, alone, in the deserted school, one ordinary evening. She fondled him, and then she made love with all the will in the world. Afterwards, when it got to be known, the men would have let it go, but the women said that she was a whore, not a teacher.

True, she said.

She closed the school and went to work on the other side of the street, in a room above the bar. Slender were the hands of the whore of Closingtown, slender. Her name was Fanny.

They all loved her, but only one loved her truly, and that was Pat Cobhan. He stayed below, drinking beer, and waited. When she was finished, she came down.

Hello, Fanny.

Hello.

They walked up and down, from one end of the town to the other, holding each other tight, in the dark, and speaking of the wind that never stopped.

Good night, Fanny.

Good night.

Pat Cobhan was seventeen. Green were the eyes of the whore of Closingtown, green.

In order to understand their story—Shatzy said—you have to know how many shots a pistol had in those days.

Six.

She said it was a perfect number. Think about it. And sound that rhythm. Six shots, one two three four five six. Perfect. You hear the silence afterwards? Yes, that's a silence. One two three four. Five six. Silence. It's like a breath. Every six shots is a breath. You can breathe quickly or slowly, but every breath is perfect. One two three four five. Six. Now breathe silence.

How many shots were there in a pistol?

Six.

Then she told you the story.

Pat Cobhan laughs, downstairs, with foam from the beer in his beard and the smell of horses on his hands. There's a violinist playing, and he has a trained dog. People throw him money, the dog retrieves it, and then, walking on his hind legs, goes back to his master and puts the money in his pocket. The violinist is blind. Pat Cobhan laughs.

Fanny is working, upstairs, with the preacher's son between her legs. *My love*. The preacher's son is called Young. He's kept his shirt on, and his black hair is soaked with sweat. Something like terror, in his eyes. Fanny says to him Fuck me, Young, but he grows rigid and slides away from her parted thighs—white lace-trimmed stockings that come just above the knee and then nothing else. He doesn't know where to look. He takes her hand and presses it on his sex. Yes, Young, she says. She caresses it, you're handsome, Young, she says. She licks the palm of his hand, looking him in the eyes, then caresses him again, barely touching him. Come on, says Young. Come on. She clasps his sex in the palm of her hand. He closes his eyes and thinks I must not think. Of anything. She looks at her own hand, and then the sweat on Young's face, on his chest, and again at her hand sliding over his sex. I like your dick, Young, I want it, your dick. He is lying on his side, leaning on one arm. The arm trembles. Come, Young, she says. His eyes are closed. Come. He turns to lie on top of her, and pushes between her open thighs. That's it, Young, that's it, she says. He opens his eyes. Something like terror, in his eyes. He grimaces, and slides off. Wait, Young, she says, holding his head in her hands and kissing him. Wait, he says.

Pat Cobhan laughs, downstairs, and glances at the clock, behind the bar. He asks for another beer and plays with a silver coin, trying to balance it on the rim of the empty glass.

Want to marry me, Fanny?

Don't talk nonsense, Pat.

I'm serious.

Stop it.

Do you like me, Fanny?

Yes.

I like you, Fanny.

The coin falls into the glass, Pat Cobhan turns the glass upside down, the coin falls out, on the wood of the bar, what's left of the beer drips out, liquid and foam. He takes the coin and dries it on his pants. He looks at it. He would like to sniff it. He places it on the edge of the glass. He glances at the clock. He thinks: Young, you bastard, will you finish up? Sweet is the scent of the whore of Closingtown, sweet.

Fanny glides her lips over Young's sex, and he looks at her: he likes this. He puts one hand in her hair and pulls her to him. She moves the hand away, still kissing him. He looks at her. His hand is in her hair again, she stops, raises her eyes to him and says Be good, Young. Be quiet, he says, and with his hand pushes her head towards his sex. She takes it in her mouth and closes her eyes. She slides faster and faster, back and forth. Like that, whore, he says. Like that. She opens her eyes and sees the skin on Young's stomach shiny with sweat. She sees the muscles contract, suddenly, as in a kind of agony. Come on, he says. Don't stop. A kind of agony. He looks at her. He likes her. Looks at her. He places his hands on her shoulders, holds her tight, and then, suddenly, shoves her back and lies on top of her. Slowly, Young, she says. He closes his eyes and moves against her. Slowly, Young. With her hand, she feels for his sex, he moves her away. He pushes hard between her thighs. Shit, he says. Shit. His hair, wet with sweat, is pasted to his forehead. Shit. He slides away again, suddenly. She turns her head to one side, lifts her eyes to heaven for an instant, and sighs. And he sees her. Sees her.

Pat Cobhan lifts his eyes to stare at the clock, behind the bar. Then he looks at the stairs that lead to the second floor. Then he looks at the full glass of beer in front of him.

Hey, Carver.

Pat?

Keep it cold for me.

You going?

I'll be back.

Everything all right, Pat?

Everything's OK, yes, it's OK.

All right.

Keep it cold for me.

He stands up and leans on the bar. He turns and glances at the door of the saloon. He spits on the floor, then crushes the knot of saliva with his boot, and looks at the wet dust, on the floor. He raises his head again.

Make sure no one pees in it, OK? and smiles.

Why don't you go home, Pat?

Go yourself, Carver.

You ought to go home.

Don't tell me what to do.

Carver shakes his head. Pat Cobhan snickers. He picks up his glass of beer and takes a swallow. He puts the glass down, turns, looks at the stairs that lead to the second floor, looks at the black hands on the yellowed white dial, You bastard, he says softly.

Young has turned, he has stretched out one hand towards the belt hanging on the chair, he has taken the pistol out of the holster and now he holds it tight in his fist. He slides the barrel over Fanny's skin. White is the skin of the whore of Closingtown, white. She starts to get up. Stay put, he says. He sticks the barrel of the pistol under her chin, presses it there. Don't move. Don't cry out. What on earth are you doing, she says. Quiet. He slides the gun barrel over her skin, lower and lower. He spreads her legs. He rests the pistol on her sex. Please, Young, she says. Slowly he pushes the gun in. He takes it out and slowly sticks it back in. Do you like that? he says. She starts to tremble. Isn't that what you wanted? he says. He pushes the pistol deep in. She arches her back, puts a hand on Young's cheek, gently. Please, Young, she says.

Please. She looks at him. He stops. Calm down, she says. You're a good boy, Young, right? You're a good boy. She's weeping, the tears falling all over her face. Give me a kiss, I like kissing you, come here, Young, kiss me. She speaks softly, without taking her eyes off him. Stay with me, let's make love, would you like that? Yes, he says. And he starts moving the gun again, back and forth. Let's make love, he says. She closes her eyes. A grimace of pain that contorts her face. I beg you, Young. He looks at the gun barrel moving in and out of her flesh. He sees that it's covered with blood. He cocks the trigger with his thumb. I like to make love, he says.

Fuck, says Pat Cobhan. He moves away from the bar. I'll be back, he says. He passes the Castorp brothers' table, he greets them, touching two fingers to the brim of his hat. Black.

Top of the world, Pat?

Yes, sir.

Bitch of a wind today.

Yes, sir.

It'll never stop.

My father says it will get tired.

Your father.

He says no horse can gallop forever.

The wind isn't a horse.

My father says it is.

Does, does he?

Yes, sir.

Tell him to come see me, every so often.

Yes, sir.

Tell him.

Yes, sir.

Bravo.

Pat Cobhan waves and heads for the stairs. He looks up and sees nothing. He climbs a few steps. He thinks he'd like to have a gun. His father doesn't want him to have one. That way, you don't get in trouble. No one shoots at an unarmed kid. He stops. He glances at the clock, down behind the bar. He can't remember exactly how much time has passed. He tries to remember, but he can't. He looks down into the saloon and thinks he's like a bird perched on a branch. It would be nice to open your wings and fly, grazing their heads and landing on the hat of the blind musician. I would have shiny black feathers, he thinks, while his right hand feels in his pants pocket for the hard outline of his knife. It's a small knife, the blade folded into the wooden handle. He looks farther up the stairs and sees nothing. A closed door, no sounds, nothing. I'm just being stupid, he thinks. He stands there, lowers his gaze, sees his boot on the step. Dust thick on the worn leather. Taps twice, with his heel, on the wood. Then he leans over and with a finger polishes the tip. Just at that moment he hears from above the dry sound of a shot and a brief cry. And he realizes it's all over. Then he hears a second shot, and, one after the other, the third and the fourth and the fifth. He is frozen. He waits. He has a strange buzzing in his head and everything seems far away. He feels someone shove him, and people are running up the stairs, shouting. In his eyes is the shiny tip of his boot. He waits. But he hears nothing. Then he gets up, and goes slowly down the stairs. He crosses the saloon, goes out the door, gets on his horse. He rides all night and at dawn he reaches Abilene. The next day he heads north, passing through Bartleboro and Connox, following the river as far as Contertown, and then for days he rides towards the mountains. Berbery, Tucson City, Pollak, to Full Creek, where the railroad goes. He follows the tracks for miles and miles. Quartzite, Coltown, Oldbridge, and then Rider, Rio Solo, Sullivan and Preston. After twenty-two days he comes to a place called Stonewall. He looks at the tops of the trees and the way the birds fly. He gets off his horse, picks up a handful of dust, and lets it slide slowly between his fingers. There's no wind here, he thinks. He sells the horse, buys a gun belt, holster and gun. That night he goes to the saloon. He doesn't talk to anyone, he sits there, drinking and watching. He studies them all, one by one. Then he chooses a man who is playing cards, who has white uncallused hands, gleaming spurs. A narrow beard, cut with care and deliberation.

That man's cheating, he says.

Something wrong, kid?

I don't like bastards, that's all.

Get your shit tongue outside, and fast.

I don't like cowards, that's all.

Kid.

I've never liked them.

Let's do one thing.

Let's have it.

I didn't hear a word, you get up, you disappear, and for the rest of your days thank heaven it ended like this.

Let's do something else. You put down the cards, get up, and go cheat somewhere else.

The man pushes back his chair, slowly gets up, stands there, his arms by his sides and his hands on his guns. He looks at the boy.

Pat Cobhan spits. He looks at the tips of his boots, as if he were searching for something. Then he raises his eyes towards the man.

You fool, the man says.

Pat Cobhan suddenly grabs his gun. But he doesn't draw. He feels the sixth shot, now. Then nothing else, forever.

Silence.

What a silence.

Shatzy had a poem by Robert Curts stuck on the door of the fridge. She had copied it because she liked it. Not all of it, but she liked the bit near the end where it said: Lovers die in the same breath. It also had a nice closing, but the best part was that line. Lovers die in the same breath.

And another thing. Shatzy was always humming a rather stupid song, which she had learned as a child. It had a lot of stanzas. The refrain began like this: Red are the fields of our paradise, red. It wasn't much, as a song. And it was so long that you might be dead before you'd sung the whole thing. Truly.

Young died in his cell, the day before the trial. His father went to see him, and shot him in the face, point-blank.

13

Gould had twenty-seven professors. The one he liked best, how-ever, was Mondrian Kilroy. He was a man of about fifty, with an oddly Irish face (he wasn't Irish). On his feet he always wore gray cloth slippers, so they all thought that he lived at the university, and some that he had been born there. He taught statistics.

Once Gould had gone into Classroom 6 and had seen, sitting at one of the desks there, Prof. Mondrian Kilroy. The curious thing was that he was crying. Gould sat down a few desks away, and opened his books. He liked to study in empty classrooms. One didn't usually find professors crying there. Mondrian Kilroy said something, very softly, and Gould was quiet for a bit, then said he hadn't heard him. Mondrian Kilroy, turning towards him, said that he was crying. Gould saw that he didn't have a handkerchief, or anything, and that the back of his hand was wet, and the tears were dripping down inside the collar of a blue shirt. Do you want a tissue? he asked. No, thank you. Would you like me to bring you something to drink? No, thank you. He was still crying, there was no doubt about it.

Although peculiar, it couldn't be considered completely illogical, given the direction that for some years the studies of Prof. Mondrian Kilroy had been taking, that is to say given the nature of his research, which, for some years, had centered on a rather singular subject, that is to say: he studied curved objects. You have no idea how many curved objects exist; only Mondrian Kilroy, and even in his case it was only by approximation, was able to appreciate the impact on man's perceptual network and, therefore, on his ethical-sentimental disposition. In general he found it difficult to recapitulate the argument in front of his colleagues, who were often inclined to consider his research "excessively lateral" (whatever such an expression might mean). But it was his conviction that the presence of curved surfaces in the index of existence was anything but accidental, and in fact represented in some sense the flight path by means of which the real escaped the rigid framework of its destiny, that fatally blocked orthogonal structure. It was what, in general, "set the world in motion again," to use the exact words of Prof. Mondrian Kilroy.

The sense of all of that emerged clearly—and yet in an undoubtedly bizarre form—in his lectures, and in some in particular, and with unusual brilliance in one, the one known as Lecture No. 11, which was devoted to Claude Monet's *Waterlilies*. As you all know, *Waterlilies* is not properly a painting but, rather, a group of eight great wall panels that, if set next to each other, would give the impressive final result of a composition three hundred feet long and six feet high. Monet worked on the paintings for an unspecified number of years, and decided, in 1918, to give them to his country, France, in homage to its victory in the First World War. He continued to work on them to the end of his life, and he died, on December 5, 1926, before being able to see them exhibited to the public. A curious tour de force, they received contradictory critical judgments, being at times described as prophetic masterpieces and at times as, at best, decorations for dressing up the walls of a brasserie. The public, however, continues even today to regard them with unconditional and rapt admiration.

As Prof. Mondrian Kilroy himself was fond of pointing out, the *Waterlilies* presents an obviously paradoxical feature—disconcerting, he was fond of saying—and that is the despicable choice of subject: for three hundred feet of length and six of height, they immortalize solely a pond of waterlilies. Some trees, fleetingly, a bit of sky, perhaps, but essentially: water and waterlilies. It would be difficult to find a subject more insignificant, in effect kitsch, nor is it easy to grasp how a genius could have conceived of devoting years of work and hundreds of square feet of color to such nonsense. A single afternoon and the outside of a teapot would have been more than sufficient. And yet it is precisely in this absurdity that the genius of the *Waterlilies* begins. It is so evident—Prof. Mondrian Kilroy would say—what Monet intended to do. He intended to paint nothingness.

To paint nothingness must have been such an obsession for him that the last thirty years of his life seem, in hindsight, to have been possessed—utterly consumed—by it. And from the exact day when, in November of 1893, he bought an extensive piece of land adjacent to his property at Giverny, and conceived the idea of constructing a large pool for aquatic flowers—in other words, a pond filled with waterlilies. A project that could, reductively, be interpreted as an old man's taking up of an aesthetic hobby, and which, on the other hand, Prof. Mondrian Kilroy did not hesitate to define as the conscious, strategic first move of a man who knew perfectly well where he was going. In order to paint nothingness, he first had to find it. Monet did something more: he produced it. He surely understood that the solution to the problem was not to obtain nothingness by leaving out the real (ordinary abstract painting can do something like that) but, rather, to obtain nothingness by a process of progressive breakdown and dispersal of the real. He understood that the nothingness he was looking for was the whole, caught in an instant of momentaneous absence.

He imagined it as a free zone between what existed and what no longer existed. He was not unaware that this would be a rather lengthy undertaking.

"Excuse me, my prostate is calling"—Prof. Mondrian Kilroy customarily said when he reached this point in Lecture No. 11. He would go to the bathroom and return a few minutes later, visibly relieved.

The record tells us that in those thirty years Monet spent much more time working in his garden than he did painting: ingenuously, the record splits in two an action that in fact was one, and that Monet performed with obsessive determination every moment of his last thirty years: *creating* the *Waterlilies*. Cultivating them and painting them were simply different names for the same adventure. We can imagine that what he had in mind was: waiting. He had had the wit to choose, as a starting point, a corner of the world in which reality was characterized by a high degree of evanescence and monotony, a muteness nearly without meaning. A pond of waterlilies. The problem then was to induce that portion of the world to unload any residual dross of meaning—to bleed it, empty it, dissipate it to the point of near-total disappearance. Its lamentable *existence* would then become little more than the simultaneous presence of various vanished absences. To achieve that ambitious result, Monet relied on a rather banal but well-tested stratagem—a stratagem whose devastating efficacy is attested to by married life. Nothing can become so meaningless as whatever you wake up beside every morning of your life. What Monet did was to bring into his house the portion of the world that he intended to reduce to nothing. He created a lily pond in the very place where it would be impossible for him to avoid seeing it. Only an ass—argued Prof. Mondrian Kilroy in his Lecture No. 11—could believe that to impose on oneself daily intimacy with that pond was a way of knowing it and understanding it and stealing its secret. It was a way of demolishing it. One can say that every time Monet's gaze rested on that pond he came a step closer to absolute indifference, burning up residues of amazement and remnants of wonder. One can even hypothesize that that ceaseless work on the garden—attested to by the record—touching up here and there, planting flowers and pulling them up, laying out and relaying out borders and paths, was nothing other than a painstaking surgical operation on everything that refused to be worn down by habit, that persisted in rippling the surface of attention, disrupting the picture of absolute meaninglessness that was taking shape in the painter's eye. Monet was looking for the rotundity of nothingness, and where habit showed itself to be impotent he didn't hesitate to intervene with the scalpel.

Vran, Prof. Mondrian Kilroy noted, with onomatopoetic effect, accompanying the expression with an unmistakable gesture.

Vran.

One day he woke up, got out of bed, and went into the garden; he reached the edge of the pond, and what he saw was: nothing. Another man would have been content. But one of the components of genius is a boundless obstinacy which causes it to pursue its goals with an overdeveloped anxiety for perfection. Monet began to paint: but shut up in his studio. Not for a moment did he think of setting up his easel at the edge of the pond, facing the waterlilies. It was immediately clear to him that, having labored for years to create those waterlilies, he had to remain shut up in his studio to paint them, that is, confined in a place where, in order to stick to the facts, he was unable to see the waterlilies. Sticking to the facts: there, in his studio, he could *remember* them. And this choice of memory—rather than the direct approach of sight—was an extreme, brilliant modification of nothingness, since memory—as opposed to sight—assured an infinitesimal perceptual counter-movement that kept the waterlilies a step away from being too meaningless, warming them with a glimmer of recollection, just enough to stop them an instant before the abyss of non-existence. They were nothing, but they *were*.

Finally he could paint them.

Here, customarily, Prof. Mondrian Kilroy paused somewhat theatrically, returned to his desk and sat down, and allowed his audience a few minutes of silence that were filled in various ways, though for the most part politely. This was the moment when, generally, his colleagues left the room, displaying a web of facial micro-expressions that were meant to signify lively approval, along with sincere regret for the myriad tasks that, as one could understand, prevented them from staying longer. Prof. Mondrian Kilroy never gave any sign of noticing them.

Not that to Monet it was important, exactly, to paint nothingness. His idea was not a sort of weary-artist affectation, or even an empty ambition to create a virtuosic tour de force. What he had in mind was something more subtle. Prof. Mondrian Kilroy stopped for a second at this point, stared at the audience, and, lowering his voice, as if he were about to let out a secret, said: Monet needed nothingness so that his painting could be free to portray, in the absence of a subject, itself. Contrary to what a naive observer might suggest, the *Waterlilies* represents not waterlilies but the gaze that gazes at them. It is the mold of a determinate perceptual system. To be precise: of a wildly anomalous perceptual system. Other colleagues, surely more authoritative than I—Prof. Mondrian Kilroy noted with nauseating false modesty—have already pointed out that *Waterlilies* has no coordinates, that is, the waterlilies appear to be floating in a space without hierarchies, in which closeness and distance do not exist, nor up and down, nor before and after. Technically speaking, *Waterlilies* represents the gaze of an impossible eye. The point of view that looks at the waterlilies is not at the edge of the pond, not in the air, not on the surface of the water, not at a distance, not close up. It is everywhere. Perhaps an astigmatic god would be able to see this way— Prof. Mondrian Kilroy was fond of commenting, ironically. He said: The *Waterlilies* is nothingness, seen by the eye of no one.

Therefore to view the *Waterlilies* means to gaze at a gaze—he said—and furthermore a gaze that does not refer to some former experience of ours but is unique and unrepeatable, a view that could never be our own. To put it another way: to look at the *Waterlilies* is an outer limit of experience, a nearly impossible undertaking. This did not escape Monet, who for a long time was occupied, and preoccupied, in searching, with maniacal fastidiousness, for a particular arrangement of the *Waterlilies* that would reduce as much as possible its non-visibility. What he managed to find was an elementary device, in itself simple, which even today demonstrates a solid effectiveness and which, as an irrelevant corollary, was the means by which those waterlilies slipped into the radius of Prof. Mondrian Kilroy's research. Monet wanted the *Waterlilies* to be arranged, according to a precise sequence, on eight curved walls.

Curves, ladies and gentlemen—announced Prof. Mondrian Kilroy, with transparent satisfaction.

For a scholar who had devoted extensive essays to rainbows, hard-boiled eggs, the houses of Gaudì, cannonballs, highway interchanges and river bends—for a scholar who had consecrated to surface curves years of reflection and analysis—for Prof. Mondrian Kilroy, in short, it must have been a poignant epiphany to discover how that painter of old, impelled to balance on the edge of the impossible, had found salvation in the company of mercifully curved walls—walls that had escaped the condemnation of any corner. Thus it was with a thrill of satisfaction that Prof. Mondrian Kilroy felt he had the right to project slide No. 421, which was a view of the two rooms of the Orangerie, in Paris, where Monet's *Waterlilies* was installed in January of 1927, and where the public would still, today, be able to see it, if only *seeing it* were not a term utterly inadequate to the impossible action of looking at it.

(Slide No. 421)

There is not a single inch of the *Waterlilies* that is not a curved surface, ladies and gentlemen. And with this Prof. Mondrian Kilroy came to the true heart of Lecture No. 11, of all his lectures the most brilliantly lucid. He moved closer to his audience, and from here to the end it unrolled with a floodlike, yet methodical, passion.

I have seen the men and women there, with the *Waterlilies* upon them. They come through the door and immediately feel lost, as if HURLED from the habitual act of seeing, EJECTED from their dwelling place in a specific point of view and diffuuuuused in a space where they search in vain for the beginning. A beginning. In a certain sense the *Waterlilies,* although immovable, revolves around them, set in motion by the curvature that arrays the panels like shells around the empty spaces of the rooms in such a way that they seem to be the walls, fatally suggesting a sort of panorama to which the visitors yield, attempting to turn in a circle as their eyes orbit 360 degrees, in childish wonderment: not infrequently tinged by a smile. Perhaps for a moment they have the illusion that they have *seen*, adjusting to a mode of perception related to that of the cinema, but as they try, mechanically, to find the right distance and the proper sequence the disappointment is immediate, for it is precisely distance and sequence which the cinema dictates at every step, and so they have become unused to looking freely, have unlearned how to choose, cinema being a continuously forced looking—so to speak vicarious, despotic, tyrannical: whereas these waterlilies seem to suggest the vertigo of a liberated perception—an impossible task, as everyone knows. And so men—they feel lost. At this point they allow some time. They wander, they take another turn around, they stroll, stand still again, line up, back up, sometimes they sit down—on the floor or on convenient, compassionate benches—conscious of seeing something they love, yet anything but certain of seeing it, truly seeing it. Many begin to wonder how. How long it must have taken, how high it is, how many pounds of paint he used, how many feet long it is, how. They're escaping, obviously; they like to think that knowing what you have before you makes it possible, finally, to have it, in effect, before you, and not above, under, on, beside; that is, where the *Waterlilies* resides, heedless of any quantification—simply everywhere. Sooner or later, they dare, and they move in. They are going to see. But only from close up. They would touch if they could—their eyes rest there, since their fingers can't. And ultimately they stop seeing, unable to grasp anything, perceiving only thick anarchic brushstrokes, like the bottoms of dirty plates, blue mustard and mayonnaise, or chromatic commas on the walls of impressionist toilets. They laugh. And immediately they go back to regain the point at which they knew at least what they were *not* seeing: some waterlilies. As they step back they do not fail to wonder how that man could see from a distance and paint close up, a subtle trick that charms them, leaving them, at the end of their little journey backwards to the center of the room, as hopeless as before, and also bewitched: and at this exact moment the consciousness of not knowing how to see acquires a painful streak, coupled, as it now is, with the subterranean certainty that what escaped their gaze would have been a piercing pleasure, an unforgettable memory of beauty. Then they give up. And place their hand on the supreme surrogate of experience, on the seal of every failure to see. They liberate from the warmth of a gray felt case their undoing: the camera.

They photograph the *Waterlilies*.

How touching. A crutch hurled at the enemy's cannons. Fifty-millimeter lenses launched in a nosedive, kamikaze retinas against flotillas of fleeing waterlilies. No flash is permitted by the pitiless dictates of the regulations: they take pictures, searching for human shots—impossible—and making adjustments with humiliating kneebends, contortions of the upper body, oscillations past the center of gravity. They are supplicants for any glimpse, trusting perhaps in the miraculous chemical aid of the darkroom. The most poignant—of all, the most poignant—announce their defeat by interposing between lens and waterlilies the mortifying bodily presence of a relative, who is generally placed—as in a symbolic gesture of surrender—with his back to the waterlilies. For years afterwards, he will greet guests and friends, from the wall above a chest of drawers, with the tired smile of a cousin shipwrecked, years ago, in a pond of *nymphéas, hélas, hélas.* Thus the wily old painter carries them off, lost in their impossible task of gazing at a non-existent gaze, overwhelmed and vanquished, simply devastated by his skill, by him, his waterlilies, colors, damn brushes, the view that he sees, never to be seen again, water, waterliliiiii-ieeeeees. I would still hate him today, for that reason. Prophets are not forgiven for obscure prophecies, and for a long time I thought he was of that breed, the worst of all, evil masters, I was convinced that the view he imagined was worthless, being inaccessible to others and reserved for him—that he had been unable to make it visible. That was why he was despicable, for if you took away the optical acrobatics—that mad excursion beyond point of view, in search of the infinite—if you took away that pioneering adventure in sensibility, what remained was a sea of out-of-focus waterlilies, an overextended essay on impressionism, this noxious pimp's technique, in which the average bourgeois intelligence loooooooves to recognize the irruption of the modern, electrified by the idea that here was a revolution, and moved by the idea of being able to love it, even though it's a revolution, noting that it hasn't hurt anyone—*new for you,* at last a revolution conceived expressly for young ladies of good family, free sample of the emotion of modernity in every box—ugh. You couldn't help hating him, for what he had done, and I hated him every single time I went into the two rooms of the Orangerie, in Paris, emerging defeated, every single time, for twenty years. And I would hate him still today—that vain desecrater of curved surfaces—if, on the afternoon of June 14, 1983, I hadn't happened to see someone—a woman—enter Room 2, the larger room, and, right before my eyes, see the *Waterlilies*—see the *Waterlilies*—thus revealing to me that to do so was possible, not for me, perhaps, but in principle, for someone in this world: that view existed, and there was a where that was the beginning of it, the parabola, and the end. For years, in fact, I had watched women there, suspecting instinctively

that if there was a solution a woman would discover it, if for no
other reason than the objective complicity between enigmas.
Naturally I observed beautiful women—above all, beautiful
women. This woman separated herself from her group, Oriental
woman, big hat partly hiding her face, strange shoes, she left the
group and headed towards a wall in Room 2—she had been in the
middle of the room, at first, with her group of Oriental tourists,
all women—and she separated herself from them, as if she had
lost the tie that bound her to them, as if a singular force of gravity
were now drawing her towards the waterlilies, the ones displayed
on the eastern wall, where the curvature is greatest—she let herself drift towards the waterlilies, suddenly assuming the motion of
an autumn leaf—she fell pendulumlike, swaying with opposing
and harmonically contorted movements—I like to say: curves—
two wooden crutches pressed under her armpits—her feet soft
black clappers broken inside playing phocomelic steps—a shawl
over her shoulders—invalid's shawl—the arms badly shriveled—
she seemed a splendid-exhausted moth, and I watched her—as if
she had arrived after a long migration, exhausted, splendid. She
gained every inch with immense difficulty, yet did not seem to
know the hypothesis of stopping. Every movement spiraled
around the axis of her deformity, and yet she proceeded, rolling
out tremors interpretable as steps, and so she advanced, a patient
snail, inseparable from the illness that was her abode—a strip of
spittle, behind her, marking the trajectory of that grotesque
walk—the embarrassment of the others crossing over it, grinding
out shame and irritation, in search of escape routes for their eyes,
but it was hard to stop looking at her—you couldn't look anywhere else—there were a lot of people, there was me, and at a certain point there was only her. She got just close enough to graze
the waterlilies, then she began to slide along beside them, replicat-
ing the curve of the wall, enriching it with kinetic vocalizations,
the curved line crumpled into a scribble that at every jolt became
wearier, as, at every instant, the distance, no less indefinite than

the waterlilies, adjusted itself, because dispersed by that movement in a thousand directions, exploded in that body without a center. She went around the entire room like that, getting closer and moving away, jerked by the drunken pendulum that marked time within the tempo of her illness, while people moved aside, careful not to disturb even the most unexpected evolutions of her progress. And I, who for years had tried to look at those waterlilies, who had never succeeded in seeing anything but rather kitschy and, above all, deplorable waterlilies, let her pass by me and suddenly I understood, without even observing what she was doing with her eyes, with total clarity I understood that she was seeing—she was the gaze that those waterlilies were portraying— the gaze that had forever seen them—she was the exact angulation, the precise point of view, the impossible eye—her stumpy black shoes were it, her illness was it, her patience, the horror of her movements, the wooden crutches, the invalid's shawl, the rattle of arms and legs, the pain, the force, and that singular drooled trajectory in space—lost forever when she reached the end, stopped, and smiled.

From June 14, 1983, the life of Prof. Mondrian Kilroy inclined to melancholy, consistent with his theoretical principles that, based on an analysis of Monet's *Waterlilies,* had determined the objective superiority of the state of pain as the *conditio sine qua non* of a superior perception of the world. He was convinced that suffering was the only way to get beyond the surface of the real. It was the curved line that evaded the angular structure of the inauthentic. Moreover, Prof. Mondrian Kilroy had a happy life, without serious troubles, sheltered from the caprices of misfortune. Thus things were problematic for him, given the theoretical premises set out above, and made him feel inexorably inadequate: in the end his only cause for suffering was the pain of not having pain. The victim of a banal theoretical-sentimental short circuit, Prof. Mondrian Kilroy slid little by little into a nervous depression that at irregular intervals brought on memory loss, attacks of vertigo, and random mood swings. It happened that he surprised himself crying sometimes, without definite reasons or justifications. For a certain period he enjoyed that indulgence, but he wasn't such a slave to his own theories as not to feel, every time, a little ashamed. One day, while he was weeping—completely gratuitously—in Classroom 6, he saw the door open, and a boy came in. It was a student of his, named Gould. He was famous at the college because he had graduated at the age of eleven. He was a prodigy. For a while he had even lived there, at the college, right after that unfortunate business about his mother. She was a beautiful woman, a blonde, very nice. But she wasn't well. One day her husband had taken her to a clinic, a psychiatric clinic. He said that there was nothing else he could do. It was then that the boy had ended up at the college. No one really knew what he had understood, of the whole affair. No one ever dared to ask him. He was a well-behaved boy, no one wanted to frighten him. Every so often Prof. Mondrian Kilroy looked at him and thought he would like to do something for him. But he didn't know what.

The boy asked if he wanted a tissue, or something to drink. Prof. Mondrian Kilroy said no, he was fine. They stayed there awhile. The boy was studying. There was a nice light, which came from the windows. Prof. Mondrian Kilroy stood up, took his jacket, and started for the door. When he passed the boy, he touched his head with his hand, and murmured something like You're a good boy, Gould.

The boy said nothing.

14

"Hi."

"Hi," said Shatzy.

"What can I get you?"

"Two cheeseburgers and two orange juices."

"Fries?"

"No, thanks."

"It costs the same with fries."

"It doesn't matter, thanks."

"Cheeseburger, drink, and fries, that's Combination No. 3," she said, pointing to a photograph behind her.

"Nice photo, but we don't like fries."

"You could have a double cheeseburger without fries, Combination No. 5, which costs the same."

"Same as what?"

"A cheeseburger and an orange juice."

"A double cheeseburger costs the same as a single cheeseburger?"

"Yes, if you take Combination No. 5."

"Incredible."

"Combination No. 5?"

"No. We want single cheeseburgers. One each. No double cheeseburgers."

"Whatever you say. But you're throwing away money."

"That's all right, thank you."

"Two cheeseburgers and two orange juices, then."

"Perfect."

"Dessert?"

"Do you want cake, Gould?"

"Yes."

"Then add one piece of cake."

"This week, for every dessert you order you get a second one free."

"Splendid."

"What do you want?"

"Nothing, thanks."

"But you *have* to take it, they're giving it away."

"I don't like desserts, I don't want it."

"But I *have* to give it to you."

"Why?"

"It's the special of the week."

"I see."

"So I *have* to give it to you."

"What do you mean you have to give it to me, I don't want it, I don't like it, I don't want to get big and fat like Tina Turner, I don't want to wear XXL underpants, do I have to wait until next week to get a cheeseburger?"

"You can always not eat it. Take the free dessert and just don't eat it."

"Then what do I do with it?"

"You can throw it away."

"THROW IT AWAY? I don't throw away anything, you throw it away. Hey, go ahead, you throw it away, OK?"

"I can't, they'd fire me."

"Christ . . ."

"They're very strict here."

"All right, OK, forget it, give me the cake."

"Syrup?"

"No syrup."

"It's free."

"I KNOW IT'S FREE BUT I DON'T WANT IT, OK?"

"Whatever you want."

"No syrup."

"Cream?"

"Cream?"

"There's cream, if you want."

"I don't even want the *cake*, how can you even imagine that I want CREAM?"

"I don't know."

"Well, I do: no cream."

"Not even for the kid?"

"Not even for the kid."

"OK. Two cheeseburgers, two orange juices, one cake with nothing. This is for you," she added, holding out toward Shatzy two items wrapped in clear paper.

"What the hell is that?"

"Chewing gum. It's free, inside there's a sugar marble, and if the marble is red you win ten more pieces of gum, if it's blue you win a Combination No. 6, free. If the marble is white, you eat it and that's the end. Anyway, the rules are printed on the paper."

"Excuse me a moment."

"Yes?"

"Excuse me, but . . ."

"Yes?"

"Let's say just for fun I take this damn chewing gum, OK?"

"Yes."

"Let's say, even more for fun, that I chew it for a quarter of an hour and then I find a blue marble inside."

"Yes."

"Then I bring it over to you, all covered with saliva, and put it down here, and you give me a fat, fried, hot Combination No. 6?"

"Free."

"And in your opinion, when would I eat it?"

"Right away, I think."

"I want a cheeseburger and an orange juice, get it? I wouldn't know what to do with three pieces of fried chicken plus a medium fries plus a buttered corn on the cob plus a medium Coke. I DON'T KNOW WHAT THE HELL I'D DO WITH THEM."

"Usually they eat them."

"Who? Who eats them? Marlon Brando, Elvis Presley, King Kong?"

"People."

"*People?*"

"Yes, people."

"Listen, would you do me a favor?"

"Of course."

"Take back the chewing gum."

"I can't."

"Put it aside for the next obese person who comes by."

"I can't, really."

"Christ . . ."

"I'm sorry."

"You're sorry."

"Really."

"Give me the chewing gum."

"It's not bad, it's papaya flavor."

"*Papaya?*"

"The exotic fruit."

"Papaya."

"It's this year's fashion."

"OK, OK."

"That's it?"

"Yes, dear, that's it."

They paid and found a table. Hanging from the ceiling was a TV monitor tuned to the food channel. Questions appeared on the screen. If you had the right answer you wrote it in the proper space on the paper placemat and gave it to the cashier. You could win a Combination No. 2. Just then the question was: Who scored the first goal in the World Cup final in 1966?

1. Geoffrey Hurst.
2. Bobby Charlton.
3. Helmut Haller.

"Three," murmured Gould.

"Don't even try it," Shatzy hissed at him, and opened the package with the cheeseburger in it. On the inside cover appeared a flaming red patch. On it was written "CONGRATULATIONS!!! YOU HAVE WON ANOTHER HAMBURGER!" And in smaller letters: "Bring this coupon to the cashier immediately, you will receive a free hamburger and a drink at half price!" There was another sentence, written on the diagonal, but Shatzy didn't read it. She calmly closed the plastic package, leaving the cheeseburger inside.

"Let's go," she said.

"But I haven't even started," said Gould.

"We'll start another time."

They got up, leaving everything there, and headed for the door. A man in a clown suit, with a cap displaying the restaurant's logo, intercepted them.

"A complimentary balloon, miss."

"Take the balloon, Gould."

On the ball was written I EAT HAMBURGERS.

"If you tie it to the door of your house you can enter the SUNDAYBURGER contest."

"Tie it to the door, Gould."

"Every Sunday there's a drawing, and one house with the balloon is chosen and a truck delivers 500 bacon cheeseburgers to the door."

"Remember to clear the front walk, Gould."

"There is also a 75-gallon-capacity freezer on special deal. To store the bacon cheeseburgers in."

"Naturally."

"If you take the 100-gallon capacity you also get a microwave."

"Splendid."

"If you already have one you can get a professional hair dryer with four speeds."

"In case I should want to shampoo the bacon cheeseburgers?"

"Pardon?"

"Or shampoo myself with ketchup."

"Excuse me?"

"They say it makes your hair shiny."

"What, ketchup?"

"Yes, haven't you ever tried it?"

"No."

"Try it. Also béarnaise sauce isn't bad."

"Seriously?"

"Gets rid of dandruff."

"I don't have dandruff, thank goodness."

"You'll certainly get it if you go on eating béarnaise sauce."

"But I never do."

"Yes, but you wash your hair with it."

"Me?"

"Of course, you can see from the dryer."

"What dryer?"

"The one you have tied to the door."

"But I don't have one tied to the door."

"Think hard—you put it there when the four-speed microwave flew away."

"Flew away from where?"

"From the freezer."

"From the freezer?"

"Sunday, don't you remember?"

"Are you kidding?"

"Do I look like someone who's kidding?"

"No."

"Correct. You have won 100 gallons of balloons, and they will be delivered to you in cheeseburgers. See you, bye."

"I don't get it."

"It doesn't matter. See you, OK?"

"The balloon."

"Take the balloon, Gould."

"You want red or blue?"

"The child is blind."

"Oh, sorry."

"That's OK. It happens."

"Do you want to take the balloon?"

"No, he'll take it. He's blind, not stupid."

"Shall I give him red or blue?"

"Don't you have vomit color?"

"No."

"Odd."

"Only red or blue."

"Go for the red."

"Here."

"Take the red balloon, Gould."

"Here, take it."

"Say thank you, Gould."

"Thank you."

"You're welcome."

"Do we have anything else to discuss?"

"Excuse me?"

"I guess not. Goodbye."

"Good luck on Sunday!"

"Thanks."

They left the restaurant. The air was cold and clear, as if cleansed by winter.

"It's a shit planet," Shatzy said softly.

Gould stood there, still, in the middle of the sidewalk, with a red balloon in his hand. On it was written I EAT HAMBURGERS.

"I'm hungry," he said.

15

"Larry! . . . Larry! . . . Larry Gorman is approaching our position . . . he's surrounded by his people . . . the ring is mobbed . . . LARRY! . . . it's not easy for the champion to make his way through . . . there's Mondini, his coach . . . a lightning-fast win tonight, here at the Sony Sports Club, let's recap, just 2 minutes 27 seconds is all . . . LARRY, here, Larry, we're on the air, live on radio . . . Larry . . . we're on the air, so, fast work . . ."

"Is this microphone working?"

"Yes, we're on the air."

"Nice microphone, where'd you buy it?"

"I don't buy them, Larry . . . listen . . . did you think it would be over so quickly or . . ."

"My sister would like that a lot . . ."

"I mean . . ."

"No, seriously. You know, she imitates Marilyn Monroe, she sings and she's the spitting image of Marilyn, the same voice, I swear, only she doesn't have a microphone . . ."

"Listen, Larry . . ."

"Usually she manages with a banana."

"Larry, you want to say something about your opponent?"

"Yes. I want to say something."

"Go ahead."

"I want to say something about my opponent. My opponent is called Larry Gorman. Why do they keep on setting me up with those zeroes wearing gloves and no clothes? They're always under my feet. So eventually I have to knock them down."

"DAMN IT, GOULD, WILL YOU GET OUT OF THERE?"

It was Shatzy's voice. It came from outside the door. The bathroom door.

"I'm coming, I'm coming."

Music of flushing. Tap on. Tap off. Pause. Door opens.

"They've been waiting half an hour for you."

"I'm coming."

Some people from the local TV station had come to Gould's house. They wanted to do a feature for the Friday evening special. Title: *Portrait of a Child Genius*. They had set up the camera in the living room. What they had in mind was a half-hour interview. They counted on working up a sad story of a boy condemned by his intelligence to solitude and success. Its brilliance lay in their having found someone whose life was a tragedy not because he was terribly unfortunate but, on the contrary, because he was terribly fortunate. If it wasn't exactly brilliant at least it seemed like a good idea.

Gould sat on the sofa, in front of the camera. Poomerang was beside him, also sitting. Diesel didn't fit on the sofa, so he sat on the floor, although it took him a while to get there. And then it wasn't clear how he would ever get up. Anyway. They arranged the microphones and turned on the spots. The interviewer smoothed her skirt over her crossed legs.

"Everything all right, Gould?" she said.

"Yes."

"Let's just test the microphone."

"Yes."

"Would you like to say something into it, any old thing?"

"No, I don't want to say anything into this microphone, I wouldn't do it even if you paid me a gazillion . . ."

"All right, everything's set, OK, let's start. Are you ready?"

"Yes."

"Look at me, OK? Forget the camera."

"All right."

"Let's begin."

"Yes."

"Mr. Gould . . . or can I call you simply Gould?"

" . . . "

"Let's just say Gould, then. Listen, Gould, when did you realize that you weren't an ordinary kid—I mean, that you were a genius?"

POOMERANG (not saying): It depends. You, for example, when did you realize that you were an idiot? Did it happen all at once, or did you discover it little by little, first when you compared your grades with your friends' grades, then when you noticed at parties that no one wanted to be on your team for "Name That Film"?

"Gould?"

"Yes?"

"I was wondering . . . if you remember, from when you were little, an incident, something, when you suddenly felt different from others, different from the other children . . ."

DIESEL: Yes, I remember very well. See, I used to go to the park, with the others, all the neighborhood kids . . . there were swings, a slide, all those things . . . It was a nice park, and we went there in the afternoon if it was sunny. Well, I didn't know then that I was . . . different, let's say, in other words, that I was already big but . . . a child can't tell if he's different or something . . . I was the biggest, that's all, and one day I climbed the steps of the slide, for the first time, you weren't allowed on it if you were too young, but no one saw me—besides, no one even knew exactly how old I was—so I climbed the steps, and what happened is that when I got to the top I sat down on the slide and it was a disaster, I didn't fit, my bottom didn't fit in the slide, you know? I tried as hard as I could, but that bastard of a bottom wouldn't get in . . . It was silly but there was nothing to do, my bottom didn't fit in the slide. So finally I had to go back. I got down from the slide, but by the steps. Do you know what it means to go down a slide on the steps? Have you ever tried it? with everyone looking at you? have you ever felt that sensation? Maybe you've felt it, right? There are plenty of people around, who get off a slide by going down the steps. Have you noticed? There are plenty of people for whom it went wrong, that's the truth.

"Gould?"

"Yes?"

"Everything OK?"

"Yes."

"OK, OK. So, listen . . . would you tell us about your friend-ships with other boys. Do you have friends? Do you play any games, sports, anything like that?"

POOMERANG (not saying): I like to go underwater. It's different down there. There's no noise, you can't make a sound, even if you want to you can't do it, there's no noise there. You move slowly, you can't make sudden movements, I mean fast movements, you have to go slowly, everyone is compelled to go slowly. You can't hurt yourself, people can't give you stupid slaps on the back or things like that, it's a great place. And especially it's the ideal place for talking, you know? What I really like is to talk down there, it's ideal, you can talk and . . . you can talk, well, everyone can talk, anyone, if he wants to, can talk, it's fantastic how people talk down there. Only, it's too bad that there's never . . . there's almost never anyone there, that's the real drawback, that there's no one down there, apart from you, I mean, it would be a fantastic place, but there's almost never anyone there to talk to, mostly you can't find anyone. It's too bad, don't you think?

"Would you like to have a break, Gould? We can stop and start again when you want."

"No, this is fine, thank you."

"You're sure?"

"Yes."

"Is there something you'd like to talk about?"

"No, I'd rather you asked me questions, it's easier."

"Really?"

"Yes."

"OK . . . now . . ."

" . . ."

"Well . . . the fact that you're . . . special, if I can put it that way . . . special . . . I mean, you get along with other kids? It's OK?"

DIESEL: You know something? It's their problem. I've thought about this a lot, and I understand that things are like that, and it's their problem. I have no problem being with them, I can take them by the hand, talk to them, play with them, I—I'm not the one who always remembers I'm like that—I forget about it, they're the ones who never forget. Never. Sometimes you can see that maybe they'd like to play with me, too, but it's as if they were somehow afraid of hurting themselves, or something like that. They don't know how to take it the right way. Instead, they get a lot of stuff in their heads, about what I can do and can't do, who knows what they imagine, they're always thinking of ways to annoy me, to insult me, or make me mad, so everything's ruined. They don't have to be that way. No one has explained to them that people who are a little special, as you put it, really are normal, they have the same desires as other people, the same fears, it's not any different—you can be special in one thing and normal in all the rest—someone should explain it to them. It becomes too complicated, and so in the end they get tired, and then they forget about it. You can understand it, if they stay away—you're a problem for them, you see? A problem. No one goes to the movies with a problem, believe me. I mean: if you have even just an apology for a friend to go to the movies with, you wouldn't dream of going with a problem. You wouldn't dream of going with me. That's how it is.

"Would you prefer to talk about your family, Gould?"

"If you like."

"Tell me about your father."

"What do you want to know?"

"I don't know . . . do you like being with your father?"

"Yes. He works for the Army."

"Are you proud of him?"

"Proud?"

"Yes, I mean, are you . . . proud . . . proud of him?"

" . . . "

"And your mother?"

" . . . "

"Would you like to tell us about your mother?"

" . . . "

" . . . "

" . . . "

"Would you prefer to talk about school? Do you like being what you are?"

"What do you mean?"

"I mean, you're famous, people know you, your schoolmates, your professors, they all know who you are. Is it something that you enjoy?"

POOMERANG (not saying): Listen, I'll tell you a story. One day someone comes to my neighborhood, someone from somewhere else, runs into me in the street and stops me. He wanted to know if I knew Poomerang. If I knew where he could find him. I didn't say anything, so he started explaining to me, he told me he's a guy with no hair, about your height, and he never speaks, you must know him, don't you?, the one who never speaks, everyone knows him. I didn't say anything. He began to get mad: come on, he said, he's even been in the newspapers, he's the one who unloaded a truckful of shit in front of CRB, because of that business with Mami Jane. Come on, he always wears black, everyone knows him, he usually goes around with a friend of his, a kind of giant. He knew everything. He was looking for Poomerang. And I was right there. In black. Not speaking. Finally he got mad. He was yelling that if I didn't want to talk to him I could go to hell, what kind of manners are these, you can't even ask someone something, what sort of world is this. He was yelling. And I was right there. Do you understand? Do you see how stupid it is to ask me if I like it or not? Hey, I'm talking to you, do you understand me?

"Don't you feel like talking, Gould?"

"Why?"

"We can stop, if you like."

"No, no, I think it's going very well."

"Well, it's not as if you're making things easy for me."

"I'm sorry."

"It's OK. It happens."

"I'm sorry."

"I don't know, what would you like me to ask you?"

". . ."

"I don't know, do you have dreams, for example . . . is there anything you dream about, for when you're grown up, anything that . . . well, a dream."

DIESEL: I'd like to see the world. You know what the problem is? I don't get in cars and I can't fit on a bus, I'm too big, there's nowhere for me to sit, it's like the slide. Always the same thing, and there's no solution. Ridiculous, right? But meanwhile I'd like to see the world, and there's no way: I just have to stay here and look at the pictures in the newspapers, or in the atlas. It's the same with trains, a disaster—I tried, it was a disaster. There's no way. All I want is to sit and watch the world go by outside the windows of something big enough to transport me, that's all. It seems like nothing, and yet. If you really want to know, it's the only thing that I really miss, I mean, I'm happy to be the way I am, I wouldn't want to be an ordinary person, the same as everyone else, I'm glad to be the way I am. There's just that one thing. I feel I'm too big to be able to see the world, like a grown-up. Only that. Really, it's the only thing that makes me mad.

"I think maybe we've had enough, Gould."

"Yes?"

"In other words, we can stop here."

"Good."

"You're sure you don't want to say anything?"

"Like what?"

"Is there something you want to say, before we stop? Anything."

"Yes. Perhaps there is. One thing."

"Good, Gould. Then say it."

"Do you know who Prof. Taltomar is?"

"Is he one of your professors?"

"More or less. He's not at school."

"No?"

"He's always sitting on the edge of a soccer field, just behind the goal. We sit there together, the two of us. And we watch, you see?"

"Yes."

"Well, I wanted to say that every so often someone takes a shot and the ball goes out of play, past the goal. Sometimes it rolls right by us and stops a little farther on. Then the goalie, usually it's the goalie, takes a few steps off the field, sees us, and calls Ball, please, the ball, thanks. And Prof. Taltomar never moves, he goes on staring at the field, as if nothing had happened. This has happened dozens of times, and we have never gone to get the ball, you see?"

"Yes."

"So the professor and I, it's not that we talk much, we watch, that's all, but one day I decided to ask him. I asked him: Why don't we ever go and get the damn ball? He spat some tobacco on the ground and then he said: Either you watch or you play. He didn't say anything else. Either you watch or you play."

". . ."

". . ."

"And then?"

"And then that's all."

"Is that what you wanted to say, Gould?"

"Yes, that was it."

"Nothing else?"

"No."

"All right."

". . ."

"All right, then, we'll stop here."

"Is that all right?"

"Yes, that's all right."

"Good."

What are we to make of this stuff? said Vack Montorsi when he saw the tape. Vack Montorsi was the producer of the Friday night special. It wouldn't even keep a cokehead awake, he pointed out while, hand on the remote, he fast-forwarded, looking for something that wasn't depressing. They had tried to interview Gould's father, but he had said that as far as he could tell television journalists were a bunch of perverts and he wanted nothing to do with them. So they were left with just a few shots of Gould's school and a series of distinctly boring statements released by his professors. They said things like "talent must be protected" or "the intelligence of that boy is a phenomenon that leads one to reflect on the." Vack Montorsi fast-forwarded and shook his head.

"There's a point where one of them is crying," said the interviewer, playing her last decent card.

"Where is it?"

"Farther on."

Vack Montorsi fast-forwarded. A professor appeared, in slippers.

"It's him."

It was Mondrian Kilroy.

"But he's not crying."

"He cries later."

Vack Montorsi hit "play."

". . . in large part that is only nonsense. People believe that the difficulties of a prodigy originate in the pressure placed on him by those around him, in the terrible expectations they have of him. That's nonsense. The real problem is within, and others have nothing to do with it. The real problem is talent. Talent is like a cell gone mad, it grows uncontrollably and under no compulsion. It's as if someone had built a bowling alley in your house. It ruins you completely, yet it's also beautiful, and maybe in time you learn to bowl, brilliantly, and you become the greatest bowler in the world, but your house, how in the world can you put it right, how can you save it, how do you manage to hold on to something so that eventually, at the right moment, you can say This is my house, get out, you pigs, it's my house. You can't do it. Talent is destructive, it's objectively destructive, and what happens around it doesn't count. It works from the inside, and destroys. You have to be very strong, to save something. And that is a boy. Can you imagine a bowling alley in the middle of a boy's house? Just the noise it makes, every blessed day, a constant uproar, and the certainty that silence, true silence—you can forget about it. Houses without silence. What sort of houses are they? Who can restore that boy's house to him? You, with your video camera? I with my lessons? I?"

And here, in fact, Prof. Mondrian Kilroy blew his nose, took off his eyeglasses, and wiped his eyes with a large wrinkled blue handkerchief. It was, if you will, something like crying.

"That's it?" asked Vack Montorsi.

"More or less."

Vack Montorsi turned off the video recorder.

"What else do we have?"

"The twins and the story of the fake *Mona Lisa*."

"The *Mona Lisa* is revolting."

Friday night a special on a pair of English twins was aired. For three years they had taken turns going to school and no one had realized it. Not even their fiancée. Who now had a bit of a problem.

16

Gould was sitting on the floor, on the two-inch-thick wall-to-wall carpet. He was watching television. It was after ten when Shatzy got home. She liked to go shopping at night, she claimed that the groceries were tired and so made no resistance to being bought. She opened the door and Gould said hi, without taking his eyes off the television. Shatzy looked at him.

"Don't expect much, but it would be an improvement if you at least turned it on."

Gould said that it didn't work. He pushed all the buttons on the remote but nothing happened. Shatzy put the groceries down on the kitchen table. She glanced at the turned-off TV set. It was of fake wood, unless it was real wood.

"Where did you get it?"

"What?"

"Where did you get the TV set?"

Gould said that Poomerang had stolen it from a Japanese guy who sold Japanese dishes made of wax. He said they were dishes in the sense of things to eat, like chicken and celery, raw fish, things like that, and it was incredible how perfect they were, impossible to believe they were fake. Someone had even managed to make soups. He said it couldn't be easy to make a soup out of wax, you had to know how to do it, it wasn't something you could improvise, just like that, on the spot.

"What do you mean, *stole?*"

"He took it away from him."

"Did he go crazy?"

"The Japanese guy owed him money."

He said that Poomerang washed the display window every morning and the Japanese man always had an excuse for not paying him, so Poomerang had not told him that he was fed up with waiting, and had seized the fake-wood TV set and carried it off. He said that maybe it was even real wood, but if you're in a place that has stuff to eat made of wax that's exactly the same as the real thing, you kind of expect that everything in there is fake, you can't make exact distinctions anymore. Then Shatzy said it must indeed be like that, and added that it happened to her when she read the newspaper. Gould pushed a red button on the remote, but nothing happened.

"Do you know anyone who's crazy, Shatzy?"

"Crazy crazy?"

"Someone the doctors say is crazy."

"A real crazy person."

"Yes."

Shatzy said she thought she had seen one or two, yes. They hadn't made a good impression at first. They smoke all the time, and they have no sense of shame. They're likely to come up to you and meanwhile they're holding their weenie in their hand, she said. They don't do it out of malice, it's that they lack any sense of shame. Which is really fortunate, she added. After a bit you get used to it and then it can be a very pleasant thing, even though pleasant isn't the right word. Affecting. She said it could be an affecting thing.

"Do you know what happens in the head of a person who goes crazy?" Gould asked.

Shatzy said it depended on what sort of crazy it was. Ordinary crazy, said Gould. I don't know, said Shatzy. I think that something breaks inside, so there are pieces that don't respond to orders any more. The orders are given but they get lost on the way, they never get there, or they get there very late and then they can't go back, the same orders keep on going, obsessively, and there's no way to stop them. So everything goes to pieces, it's a kind of organized anarchy: you open the tap and the light goes on, the telephone rings when you turn on the radio, the blender starts up whenever it wants, you open the bathroom door and find yourself in the kitchen, you look for the door to the outside and you can't find it anymore. Likely it isn't there anymore. Disappeared. You're shut in there forever. Shatzy went over to the television. She wanted to touch the fake wood. She said if you can't go out anymore, out of a house like that, you have to find a way of living in it. And they do it. From the outside you can't understand it, but for them it's all very logical. She said that a crazy person is someone who sticks his head in the oven to wash his hair.

"It seems like a lot of fun," Gould said.

"No. I don't think it is a lot of fun."

Then she said that according to her it was real wood.

Gould was sitting on the floor, on the two-inch-thick carpet. He was still watching television. Shatzy said that at her house there had been a green plastic table, but if you went up close to it and looked hard you discovered it was wood, which is stupid, if you think about it, but at the time there was a real mania for plastic, everything had to be plastic. Then Gould said that his mother had gone crazy. It had happened one day. Now she's in a psychiatric hospital, he said. Shatzy said nothing, but she leaned over the television set where there was a dent, a kind of dent, and with her nail she chipped off a piece of something hard and dark. Then she said that TV set must have been dropped, it was no wonder it didn't work. A dropped television set is a dead television set, she said.

"They came to get her one day and I haven't seen her since. My father doesn't want me to see her like that. He says I mustn't see her like that."

"Gould . . ."

"Yes?"

"Your mother left four years ago to live with a professor who studies fish."

Gould tried pushing some buttons on the remote again, but nothing happened. Shatzy went to the kitchen and came back with an open can of grapefruit juice. She balanced it on the edge of the couch. It was a blue couch, and was more or less in front of the television set. Gould began scratching one leg with the remote, just above the calf. If there is one thing that can drive you mad it's when the elastic on your socks is too tight. He kept scratching himself with the corner of the remote. Shatzy picked up the can again, looked around, then put it down on the table, next to a vase of petunias. She looked like someone who had come to decorate the apartment. You could hear the noise of the refrigerator in the kitchen producing cold, trembling like an old drunk. Then Gould said that they had taken her away early in the morning, so he had heard some uproar but had gone on sleeping, and when he woke up his father was there walking back and forth, dressed in civilian clothes, with his tie a bit loose on the open collar of his shirt. He said that once he had gone to look for the hospital, but he hadn't been able to find it because no one knew anything about it, and he hadn't met anyone willing to help him. He said that at first he had thought of writing to her every day, but his father claimed that she had to stay very quiet and avoid emotions, so he had asked if reading a letter could be an emotion, and after thinking about it a little had concluded that it was. So he hadn't written any more. He said he had investigated and had been told that sometimes people who go to those hospitals come back later, but he had never dared to ask his father if she would come back. His father did not like to talk about it, and in fact now that some years had passed he didn't talk about it anymore at all, only sometimes he said that Gould's mother was well, but he didn't say anything else. Gould said it was strange but if he had to remember his mother he always remembered her laughing, snapshots of a sort came to mind and in them she was always laughing, and this was in spite of the fact that as far as he could remember he wouldn't say that she laughed often, but this was what happened to him, if he thought of her he thought of her laughing. He said also that all her clothes were still hanging in the bedroom closet, and that she knew how to imitate the voices of singers, she sang with the voice of Marilyn Monroe, and looked just like her.

"Marilyn Monroe?"

"Yes."

"Marilyn Monroe."

"Yes."

"Marilyn Monroe."

Shatzy began repeating softly Marilyn Monroe, Marilyn Monroe, Marilyn Monroe, without stopping, and at a certain point she picked up the can again, and poured the juice into the vase of petunias, Marilyn Monroe, Marilyn Monroe, down to the last drop, then set it on the table again, and said Marilyn Monroe over and over again as she went into the kitchen, came back, looked for the keys, locked the house door, and then headed towards the stairs. She took off her shoes. And a barrette that was holding her hair back. She put the barrette in her pocket. She left the shoes there.

"I'm going to bed, Gould."

". . ."

"Excuse me."

". . ."

"Excuse me, but I have to go to bed."

Gould sat there, looking at the television.

He thought he ought to tell Poomerang to take it back.

The Japanese man had a nice radio, an old model, he could take that. It had the names of the cities on the glass front, and if you turned the dial you could move a little orange pointer and travel all over the world.

He thought that with a television, there were some things you couldn't do.

Then he stopped thinking.

He got up, turned out the lights, climbed the stairs, went into the bathroom, moved in the darkness to the toilet, raised the lid, and sat down on the seat, without even pulling his pants down.

"I just slipped."

"My ass."

"I'm telling you, I slipped."

"Shut up, Larry. Breathe deeply."

"What the fuck is this stuff?"

"Don't make a fuss, just breathe deeply."

"I DON'T NEED THIS STUFF, fuck, I just slipped."

"All right, you slipped. Now listen to me. When you get up look carefully at what's in front of you. If you see two or three black guys wearing gloves, then wait, hold them off with a jab, but don't hit hard, or you'll get the wrong one. You have to wait, understand? just keep them off you, and when you can, go into a clinch, stay there and breathe. Don't hit hard until you see only one of them, get it?"

"I can see perfectly."

"Look at me."

"I can see perfectly."

"Until you feel well forget your fists and use your head."

"I'm supposed to take him down with a header?"

"It's no time to joke, Larry. The guy took you down."

"Fuck, do I have to prove it to you, I slipped, you're the one who can't see, you know something? you'd better watch out, you can't see any more . . ."

"CUT IT OUT, GOD DAMN IT . . ."

"You're the one who . . ."

"CUT IT OUT."

". . ."

"You're making me curse, you dirty . . ."

GONG

"I don't want to lose this, Larry."

"You're going to win, Maestro."

"Fuck you."

"Fuck."

Tensions are high here at St. Anthony Field, with Larry Gorman, favored to finish up in the third round, hit hard by a really quick hook from Randolph, now it's a question of seeing if he's recovered, it's a new situation for him, the first time in his career he's been to the mat, the quick hook from Randolph took him by surprise, START OF THE FOURTH ROUND, Randolph comes out like a fury, RANDOLPH, RANDOLPH, GORMAN IMMEDIATELY AT THE ROPES, it's not starting off well for the student of Mondini, Randolph seems to have gone wild, UPPERCUT, UPPERCUT AGAIN, Gorman tightens his defense, breaks away on the left, breathes, RANDOLPH COMES FROM BELOW, it's not a very tidy action but it seems effective, Gorman is forced to back up again, his legs are still moving well, RANDOLPH LANDS A JAB, ANOTHER JAB AND RIGHT HOOK, GORMAN STAGGERS, STRAIGHT FROM RANDOLPH MISSES, GORMAN'S BODY SWAYS, RANDOLPH GOES AFTER HIM, GORMAN AGAIN ON THE ROPES, THE CROWD IS ON ITS FEET . . .

Gould got up from the toilet. He flushed, then realized that he hadn't even peed, and this seemed to him stupid. He went to the sink and turned on the light. Toothpaste. Teeth. The toothpaste was bubble gum–flavored. It had some kind of stars in it—like something made of rubber with stars inside. It was made that way because children liked it, and would brush their teeth without making a fuss. On the tube it said: for children. Afterwards it was as if you had chewed gum for an entire physics lecture. But you had clean teeth, and you didn't have to stick anything under the desk. He swished cold water in his mouth and spat it all straight into the drain in the sink. As he dried himself he looked in the mirror. Then he turned and went back to the toilet. He unzipped his zipper.

"Christ, there were three of them, Maestro."

"Really?"

"You can't fight against three."

"Right."

"Two is no problem, but three is too many. So I thought I'd get rid of one."

"Excellent idea."

"You know the odd thing? When he went down, the other two disappeared as well. Funny, isn't it?"

"Very funny."

"Right, left, right, and poof, all three gone."

"Explain something to me: how did you choose which one to hit?"

"I chose the real one."

"Was it written on his forehead?"

"It was the one that stank the worst."

"I see."

"Scientific. You said it yourself: use your head."

"You're a lucky bastard, Larry."

"Right, left, right: have you ever seen such a fast combination?"

"Not from someone who looked like he was dead."

"Then say it, come on, stop grumbling and say it."

"I've never seen a dead man pull off such a fast combination."

"You said it, Christ, you said it, hey, where are the microphones, for once when they'd be useful where are they?, you said it, I heard it, with my own ears, you said it, you said it, right?"

"You're a lucky bastard, Larry."

Flush.

A little cheap, Gould thought.

Everything had gone slightly wrong that evening, he thought. Then he pulled up his zipper, turned out the light, and went to bed.

Time passed.

Pieces of night.

At some point he woke up. Shatzy was sitting on the floor, next to his bed. She was wearing a nightgown with a red terry-cloth bathrobe over it. She was chewing on the end of a blue pen.

"Hi, Shatzy."

"Hi."

The door was half open, and light came in from the hall. Gould closed his eyes.

"Something occurred to me," said Shatzy.

". . ."

"Are you listening to me?"

"Yes."

"Something occurred to me."

She was silent for a moment. Maybe she was searching for the words. She was biting the pen, you could hear the sound of the plastic, and a sound like a straw. Then she started talking again.

"Here's what I thought. You know what a trailer is?, you attach it to a car, a trailer, you know?"

"Yes."

"Trailers have always made me horribly sad, I don't know why, but when you pass them on the highway you feel a terrific sadness, they're always moving slowly, with the father in the car, staring straight ahead, and everyone's passing him, and he's got the trailer attached, so the back of the car's a little lower than the front, it slopes, kind of like an old lady with an enormous shopping bag, who walks bent over, and so slowly that everyone passes her. It's incredibly sad. But also it's something you can't help looking at, I mean, while you're passing it, you always give it a glance, you *have* to, even if you know it's going to be sad, no kidding, you turn and look, every time. And if you think about it, the truth is that there's something that attracts you about something like that, about the trailer, if you dig and dig, under all those layers of sadness, finally you reach an intuition that there's something that, ultimately, attracts you, something that's been hidden, as if it wanted to become more *precious*, in a way, something that you would *like*, but like seriously, only if you had to discover it. See what I mean?"

"More or less."

"I've been following this notion for years."

Gould pulled the covers up a little, it was quite cold. Shatzy wrapped her bare feet in a sweater.

"You know what? It's kind of like oysters. I would really like to eat them, it's wonderful to see them being eaten, but I've always been revolted by them, there's nothing to do about it, they remind me of catarrh, you know?"

"Yes."

"How can you eat them if they remind you of catarrh?"

"You can't."

"Exactly. You can't. It's the same thing with trailers."

"They remind you of catarrh?"

"What does that have to do with it? They don't remind me of catarrh, but they make me sad, you see? I've never been able to find a reason, not the ghost of a reason, to think God, how nice it would be to have a trailer."

"Yes."

"For years I've thought about it and I've never found a shred of a good reason."

Silence.

Silence.

"You know something, Gould?"

"No."

"Yesterday I found one."

"A good reason?"

"I found a reason. A good one."

Gould opened his eyes.

"Really?"

"Yes."

Shatzy turned toward Gould, rested her elbows on the bed and leaned over him until she looked him in the eyes, close up. Then she said:

"Diesel."

"Diesel?"

"Yes. Diesel."

"Why?"

"You know that stuff you told me? About how he would like to see the world but he can't get on a train, or a bus, there's no way for him to fit, and he won't get in a car, all that. You told me yourself."

"Yes."

"A trailer, Gould. A trailer."

Gould pulled himself up a little in the bed.

"What do you mean, Shatzy?"

"I mean that we're going to see the world, Gould."

Gould smiled.

"You're nuts."

"No. *I'm* not, Gould."

Gould went back down a little, under the covers. He stayed there thinking about it, in silence.

"You think Diesel would fit, in a trailer?"

"Guaranteed. He sits in the back, and if he wants he can lie down, and we take him on a trip. He'd have his house, and he'd go wherever he wants."

"He'd like that."

"Of course he'd like it."

"It's something he'd like."

It was quite cold. There was the light coming through the doorway, and nothing else. Every so often a car went by in the street. If you wanted to, you could hear it: ask yourself where it was going at that hour, and embroider a lot of stories around it. Shatzy looked at Gould.

"We'd have our house and we'd go where we like."

Gould closed his eyes. He thought of a trailer he'd seen in an animated cartoon, it went like a crazy person along a street hanging over nothing, it went like a lunatic, skidding in all directions, it always seemed about to fall over the edge, but it never did, and meanwhile, inside, everyone was eating, and they were in their house; the trailer was small, but it held them all like a hand that holds a little animal without crushing it, and carried them around. The fact that someone had to drive the car had been forgotten, so they were all in there eating, and they were surrounded by something like happiness, but it was something more, a splendid *ridiculous* happiness. He opened his eyes again.

"Who would drive?"

"Me."

"And who would buy the trailer?"

"Me."

"You?"

"Me, of course. I've got some money."

"A lot?"

"Some."

"A trailer costs a lot."

"You're joking. They ought to pay you, to buy a trailer."

"I don't think they think that."

"Well, they should."

"They won't."

"So then we'll pay."

"I have some money, too."

"See? There's no problem."

"There must be one that doesn't cost much, don't you think?"

"Of course there is. You think that in this whole damn country there isn't a trailer that costs exactly the amount of money we have in our pockets?"

"It would be dumb."

"It would be unbelievable."

"Really."

They both had highways in their eyes, and highways, and highways.

"Let's go see the world, Gould. Enough of this babble."

Her voice was light and happy. Then she got up. Her feet were tangled in the sweater. She untwisted it somehow and stood there, next to the bed. Gould looked at her. Then what she did was she leaned over him, slowly came closer, rested her lips on his just for an instant, and remained standing there, looking at him from very close. He pulled one hand out from under the covers, placed it in Shatzy's hair, sat up a little, kissed her in the corner of her mouth and then right on the lips, first softly and then hard, with his eyes closed.

17

In September 1988, eight months after the death of Mami Jane, CRB decided to suspend publication of the adventures of Ballon Mac, the superhero dentist. Sales had continued to fall with surprising regularity, and even the decision to introduce a female character who frequently revealed her breasts had proved to be ineffectual. In the final issue, Ballon Mac left for a distant planet promising himself and his readers that "one bright day in a better tomorrow" he would return. "Amen," Franz Forte, the business manager of CRB, had remarked, with satisfaction. Diesel and Poomerang bought a hundred and eleven copies of the last issue. For months they devoted themselves, methodically and despite the dubious quality of the paper, to the task of wiping their bottoms, whenever necessary, with a page from the magazine. They then folded the page in fourths, very carefully, and sent it to Franz Forte, Business Office, CRB. Since they used envelopes taken from hotels, government offices, sports clubs, it was impossible for Franz Forte's secretary to identify them before they arrived on the boss's desk. He resigned himself to opening the mail, every day, with a certain circumspection.

Gould had his fourteenth birthday. Shatzy took everyone out to dinner at a Chinese restaurant. There was a family at the next table: father, mother and small daughter. The daughter's name was Melania. The father took it into his head to teach her to use chopsticks. He had a somewhat nasal voice.

"Hold the chopstick in your hand . . . like this . . . first just one, sweetheart, hold it tight, see?, you have to squeeze it between your thumb and your middle finger, not like that, watch . . . Melania, watch Daddy, you have to hold it like this, there, good, now squeeze it a little, not so much, you only have to hold it . . . Melania, look at Daddy, between the thumb and the middle, see, like this, no, which is the middle, Melania?, this is the middle finger, sweetheart . . ."

"Why don't you leave her alone?" the wife said at that point. She said it without raising her eyes from her soup: abalone and soybean sprouts. She had dyed red hair and a yellow shirt with shoulder pads. Her husband went on as if no one had said a word.

"Melania, look at me, look at Daddy, sit down, and take the chopstick, come on, like this . . . there, see how easy it is, there are millions of children in China and you don't think *they* make all this fuss . . . now take the other one, MELANIA, sit up straight, look how Daddy does it, one stick and then the other, in your hand, come on . . ."

"Leave her alone."

"I'm teaching her . . ."

"Can't you see she's hungry?"

"She'll eat when she learns."

"It will be cold by the time she learns."

"FOR HEAVEN'S SAKE, I'M HER FATHER, I CAN . . ."

"Don't shout."

"I'm her father and I have the obligation to teach her something, seeing that her mother evidently has better things to do than to educate her only daughter who . . ."

"Eat with your fork, Melania."

"DON'T EVEN TALK TO HER, Melania, sweetheart, listen to Daddy, now let's show Mommy that we can eat like a good little Chinese girl . . ."

Melania began to cry.

"You've made her cry."

"I DID NOT MAKE HER CRY."

"Then what is she doing?"

"Melania, there's no need to cry, you're a big girl, you mustn't cry, take this chopstick, come on, give me your hand, GIVE ME THAT HAND, there, good, gently, you have to hold it gently, Melania, everyone's looking at you, stop crying and take the goddam chopstick . . ."

"Don't swear."

"I DID NOT SWEAR."

Melania began to cry even harder.

"MELANIA, Melania, you're about to get a spanking, you know that Daddy is patient but there's a limit to everything, MELANIA, HOLD THIS CHOPSTICK OR WE'LL GET UP AND GO HOME IMMEDI-ATELY, and you know I'm not joking, come on, first one chopstick and then the other, come on, between the thumb and the index finger, not the index finger, THE MIDDLE, now squeeze it, like that, good, see you can do it, come on, now take the other one, the other chopstick, sweetheart, WITH THE OTHER HAND, STUPID . . . take it with THE OTHER HAND and put it in THIS hand, get it?, it's not hard, now stop crying, what is there to cry about?, do you want to grow up or not?, do you want to be a silly little girl forever . . ."

Diesel got up. It was always a big job for him, but he did it. He went over to the table where the family was sitting, picked up the child's chopsticks in one hand, and, tightening his grip, pulverized them, right over the father's plateful of Peking duck.

Melania stopped crying. The restaurant had fallen into a silence that smelled of deep-frying and soy sauce. Diesel spoke softly, but they could hear him even in the kitchen. He limited himself to one question.

"Why do you have children?" he said. "Why?"

The father was motionless, staring straight ahead, not daring to turn. The wife had her spoon halfway between her mouth and her bowl. She looked at Diesel with bewildered regret: she was like a contestant on a quiz show who knows the answer but can't remember it.

Diesel leaned over the child. He looked her in the eyes.

"You splendid little Chinese girl."

He said.

"Eat with the fork or I'll kill you."

Then he turned and went back to his table.

"Will you pass me the Cantonese rice?" Poomerang didn't say.

It was a nice birthday, in its way.

In February 1989 a research group at the University of Vancouver published in the authoritative journal *Science and Progress* a ninety-two-page article setting forth a new theory of the double dynamics of pseudo particles. The authors—sixteen physicists from five different countries—maintained, in front of the TV cameras of half the world, that a new epoch was opening for science: and they claimed that, in the space of a decade, their research would make possible the production of low-cost energy with minimal environmental risk. After three months, however, a two-and-a-half-page article in the *National Scientific Bulletin* demonstrated that, upon careful study, the mathematical model on which the Vancouver researchers had based their theory had turned out to be largely inadequate, and essentially unusable. "Rather infantile," stated the two authors of the article, to be exact. The first was named Mondrian Kilroy. The second was Gould.

Not that, in general, the two worked together. It was by chance more than anything else. Everything had begun in the dining hall. They happened to be sitting across from each other, and at some point Prof. Mondrian Kilroy, spitting out his purée, had said

"What is this? Did they make this stuff in Vancouver?"

Gould had read the ninety-two pages in *Science and Progress*. He didn't think the purée was bad, but he knew that something was wrong in that article. He passed Prof. Mondrian Kilroy his serving of spinach and said that in his view the mistake was on page twelve. The professor smiled. He ignored the spinach and began to cover the paper napkin on which he had spat out the purée with calculations. It took them twelve days. On the thirteenth day, they copied everything neatly and sent it to the *Bulletin*. Mondrian Kilroy would have liked to give the article the title "Objection to the Vancouver Purée." Gould convinced him that something more innocuous would be better. When the media discovered that one of the authors was fourteen years old they went wild. Gould and the professor were forced to call a press conference and a hundred and thirty-four journalists came, from all over the world.

"Too many," said Prof. Mondrian Kilroy.

"Too many," said Gould.

They spoke to each other while they were waiting in the corridor. They turned, made their way out through the kitchens, and went fishing in Lake Abalema. The rector considered their behavior unacceptable and they were suspended.

"From what, exactly?" asked Prof. Mondrian Kilroy. What it was *exactly* no one knew. So the suspension was suspended.

More or less around the same time Shatzy remembered that, if she wanted to get a trailer, it was crucial to have a car. "True," said Gould, agreeing how odd it was that they hadn't thought of it before. Shatzy said maybe they could talk to his father about it. He must have a car, right?, somewhere. He's a male. Males always have a car, somewhere. Gould said, "True." Then he added that it was better, however, not to say anything about the trailer. You can bet on that, said Shatzy.

"Hello?"

"Miss Shell?"

"It's me."

"Everything OK there?"

"Yes. We just have one small problem."

"What problem?"

"We could use your car."

"My car?"

"Yes."

"What car are you talking about?"

"Yours."

"You're telling me I have a car?"

"It seemed plausible."

"I'm afraid you're mistaken, Miss Shell."

"That's surprising."

"Why, don't you ever make mistakes?"

"I didn't mean that."

"What did you mean?"

"You're a male and you don't have a car, that's what I meant. Isn't that surprising?"

"I'm not sure."

"It's quite surprising, believe me."

"Would a tank do? I have plenty of those."

For a moment Shatzy envisioned a trailer pulled by a tank.

"No, I'm afraid that doesn't solve the problem."

"I was joking."

"Oh."

"Miss Shell?"

"Yes."

"Will you kindly tell me what the problem *is*?"

Shatzy thought of Bird, the old gunfighter. Strange mechanism, the mind. It works the way it wants to.

"What is the problem, Miss Shell?"

Rather, it was that sort of weariness. Like a weariness on

you. The same music that Bird danced to. The old gunfighter.

"Miss Shell, I'm asking you what the problem is—would you mind answering me?"

Bird.

Roads on his face, roads walked by innumerable gunfights, said Shatzy. His eyes swallowed up in his skull, and hands of olive-wood, quick hands, like branches in winter. The comb, in the morning, dipped in water, parting the white hair, transparent by now. Tobacco lungs in the voice that says softly: What a wind today.

Nothing worse for a gunfighter than not to die.

Look around, every unfamiliar face could be that of yet another fool arriving from far away to become the one who killed Clay "Bird" Puller. If you want to know when you become a legend, then listen: it's when your enemies always come from behind. As long as they come at you from the front you're only a gunfighter. Glory is a trail of shit, behind your back. Hurry up, asshole, I said to him without even turning around. The boy wore a black hat, and in his pocket was some piece of crap that was the memory of a distant hatred, and the promise of some sort of vengeance. Too late, asshole.

With these roads on my face, cowardly old age, peeing on myself in the night, the goddam pain below the belt, like a burning rock between belly and ass, day never comes, and when it comes it's a desert of empty time to cross. How did I get here?, me.

The way Bird shot. He wore his holster backwards, with the butts of the guns facing forwards. He would draw with his arms crossed, the right gun in his left hand and vice versa. That way, when he came towards you, his fingers touching the gun butts, he seemed like a condemned man, like a prisoner on his way to the gallows, with his arms crossed in front. A second later he was a bird of prey opening its wings, a whip in the air, and the straight flight of two bullets. Bird.

What is that, creeping through the fog of my cataracts, I am forced to count the hours, I who knew instants, and that was the only time that existed for me. The swerve of a pupil, the whitened knuckles around a glass, a spur in the side of the horse, the shadow of a shadow on the blue wall. I lived an eternity where others saw seconds. They saw a flash where I saw a map, a star where I saw heavens. I looked within the folds of time that for them were already a memory. There was no other way, I had been taught, to see death before it arrives. What is that, creeping through the fog of my cataracts, I am forced to spy on the cards of others, searching for cues from my seat, always in the second row, in the evening throwing rocks at the dogs, in my pocket an old man's money that the whores don't want, a mariachi player will take it when he comes, may your song be long and sad, boy, sweet your guitar and slow your voice, I want to dance tonight, until the sunset of this night, I'll dance.

They said that Bird always carried a dictionary with him. French. He had learned all the words, one after another, in alphabetical order. He was so old that he had already been around once and now was in the Gs for the second time. No one knew why in the world he did it. But once, in Tandeltown, they say that he went up to a woman, she was beautiful, tall, green-eyed, you had to wonder how she had ended up there. He went up to her and said: *Enchanté.*

Clay "Bird" Puller. He'll have a wonderful death, said Shatzy. I've promised him: a wonderful death.

"Miss Shell?"

"Yes, hello."

"Can you hear me?"

"Yes, very well."

"The line was interrupted."

"It happens."

"It's hell, with these telephones."

"Yes."

"I think it would be easier to send a bomber there and hit my son on the head than to succeed in talking to him on the telephone."

"I hope you won't do that."

"What?"

"No, nothing, I was joking."

"Is Gould there?"

"Yes."

"May I speak to him?"

"Of course."

"Take care."

"You, too."

Gould was in his pajamas, even though it was only 7:15. He had caught a flu that the papers called Russian. It was nasty, and the worst part was that, besides the fever, it emptied out your insides. So you had to spend hours on the toilet. It gave the career of Larry Gorman a sudden and, as we will see, decisive impetus. Within a few days he had sent to the canvas Park Porter, Bill Ormesson, Frank Tarantini and Morgan "Killer" Bluman. He beat Grey La Banca on account of an injury, in the third round. Pat McGrilley did himself in on his own, slipping and hitting his head on the mat. By now Larry Gorman had a record that could not go unnoticed. Twenty-one fights, twenty-one victories before the distance. The papers were beginning to talk about a world championship.

DIESEL: Mondini found out from Drink, his assistant. Drink told him that the newspapers were talking about Larry. He had clippings, he'd gotten them from his nephew. Mondini took out his glasses and began to read. It made an odd impression on him. He had never seen the name of a student of his mentioned alongside the names of real champions. It was a little like buying *Playboy* and finding a photo of your wife inside. Some of the papers were dismissive, saying that of those twenty-one wins only a couple were against true fighters. One paper, in particular, claimed that it was all a scam and explained that Larry's father, a wealthy lawyer, had spent a pile of money to get his son there, even though it didn't say exactly *how* he had spent it. The article was clever, and made you laugh. Because of his father being a lawyer, Larry was referred to as Larry "Lawyer" Gorman. Mondini found that it made him laugh quite a lot. Apart from that, though, the papers took the idea very seriously. *Boxing* put Larry in sixth place in the world rankings. And in *Boxing Ring* there was a short piece about him entitled "Heir to the Crown." Mondini realized while he was reading it that his glasses were misting.

"Hey, Larry . . . Larry! A word or two for the radio audience . . ."

"I'm not fighting tonight, Dan."

"Just a couple of words."

"I've come to see some good fighting, and that's it, this time I'm going to enjoy myself outside the ring."

"Do you have anything to say with regard to certain articles that have appeared in . . ."

"I like that nickname."

"What do you mean?"

"*Lawyer.* I like it. I think I'll use it."

"Let's remind our listeners that a tough article on Larry appeared in one of the dailies, written by . . ."

"Larry Lawyer Gorman, sounds good, doesn't it? I think I'll use it. Do me a favor next time, Dan . . ."

"What's that, Larry?"

"On your radio show call me Lawyer. I like it."

"Whatever you want, Larry."

"Larry Lawyer."

"Larry Lawyer, all right."

'You have a spot on your collar, Dan, a grease spot."

"What?"

"You have a grease spot, on your collar . . . there, see it? . . . it must be grease."

POOMERANG: Mondini finished reading and realized that things had taken a bad turn. The way he saw it, it was a bad turn. The world of boxing was a strange one, it had everything, from the guy who liked to hit a punching bag to guys who earned a living in the ring, trying to get out alive. There were clean fighters and fighters who played dirty, but it was for the most part a true world, and he liked it. Boxing. As he had known it. He liked it. But the title, the world championship, the crown: that was another story. Too much money in it, too many people who were hard to understand, too much fame. And heavy punches, punches of a different type. The way he saw it, it was something to steer clear of.

He realized that things were escalating when a fellow with dark glasses and new teeth walked into the gym. He was from the world of the casinos, where the important fights were arranged. Mondini remembered him as a fighter—there had even been talk once of their fighting, then nothing had come of it. He didn't like him: the fellow was one of those fighters who last two rounds, then begin to wonder what the hell they're doing up there, with so many good movies to see. A programmed loser. Now he had grown fat, and had a slight limp. He had come to "say hello." They had a little chat. Larry wasn't there.

DIESEL: Larry was in training, and he never mentioned the title. Mondini worked him hard, and he didn't let up. It was as if he were in a bubble, where nothing could touch him. Mondini had seen that before: it was something champions had. A mixture of indisputable strength and utter solitude. It sheltered them from defeat, and from happiness. Thus, unbeaten, they would waste their whole life. One day Larry arrived at the gym with a girl, a small thin brunette called Jody. She wore a tight sweater and shoes with a lot of laces. She looked pretty to Mondini and, in a way, nice. She sat in a corner and watched Larry work out, without saying a word. Before the workout was over, she got up and left. Another day Larry was sparring with a kid who was younger than him, a brave kid but young, and at one point he began to go down on him a little too hard. Mondini didn't wait for the clock to sound the three minutes: leaning on the ropes he said: That's enough. But Larry wouldn't stop. He kept hitting with a peculiar brutality. And he went on till the end. Mondini didn't say anything. He let Larry come out of the ring. He saw how Drink dried off his back and took off his gloves: with respect. He saw him walk by the mirror, before going back to the dressing room, and pause for a moment, right in front of it. Then he remembered the silent girl, for some reason, and a lot of other things. He cursed in a low voice, and realized that the moment had arrived. He waited for Larry to come out, in his elegant cashmere overcoat. He unplugged the clock. Then he said

"I'll take you home, Larry, OK?"

POOMERANG: They drove across town without saying a word. Mondini's old sedan would run only with the choke pulled out as far as it would go. Stopping at traffic lights the car looked like a pressure cooker three hours into the minestrone. When they got there Mondini parked and turned off the engine. An exclusive neighborhood, with low lights on the broad lawns.

"You trust me, Larry?"

"Yes."

"Then I'm going to explain something to you."

"All right."

"You've had twenty-one fights, Larry. Sixteen of those I could have won myself. But the other five, those were real fighters. Sobilo, Parker, Morgan Bluman . . . That's a type that makes you lose the will to fight. And they couldn't even go the distance with you. You have a way of boxing that they have never dreamed of. Every so often, when you're up there, I look at your opponents, and it's crazy how . . . old they seem. They're like black-and-white movies. I don't know where you learned, but that's what it is. Boxing like that wouldn't exist except for you. You believe me?"

"Yes."

"Then listen carefully. There are two things you have to understand."

"OK."

"First: you have never taken a real punch in your life."

"What do you mean?"

"Everybody throws punches, Larry. Then there are three, four fighters in the world who are capable of something more: they can hit. Theirs are true punches. You have no idea what they're like. Those are blows that could redesign the body of a car. They've got it all: coordination, power, speed, precision, brutality. They're masterpieces. Schoolchildren should be taken to see them, like museums. And it's great to see them when you're sitting in front of the TV, with a beer in your hand. But if you're up there, Larry, it's fear, no way around it, it's pure fear. Terror. You can die from a punch like that. Or be a vegetable for the rest of your life."

Larry didn't move. He looked straight ahead, through the windshield. He said only:

"And the second thing?"

Mondini said nothing for a while. Then he turned the rear-view mirror towards Larry. What he would have liked to say was that world champions don't have a face like that. But the words wouldn't come. He wanted to say that to risk your life in the ring you have to have a black hole ahead of you instead of the future, otherwise you're just a crazy young fool, in love with yourself, and that's all. Perhaps he also wanted to say something about that silent girl. But he didn't know what, exactly.

Larry looked at himself in the mirror.

He saw a lawyer's face. World champion of boxing.

Mondini found something to say. It wasn't much, but it gave the idea.

"You know how to recognize a great fighter? He knows when the time has come for him to stop. Believe me, Larry: your time has come."

Larry turned towards the Maestro.

"I should stop?"

"Yes."

"*I* should stop?"

"Yes."

"You mean to tell me that Larry Lawyer Gorman should stop?"

"*You*, Larry, *you* have to stop."

"Me?"

DIESEL: Everybody knows that rich people don't understand a damn thing about the rest of humanity, but what no one realizes is that the rest of humanity doesn't know a damn thing about rich people, hasn't got a chance of understanding them. You have to have been there, to understand, you have to have been rich when you were six, when you were in your mother's belly, when you were a gleam in your wealthy father's eye. Then maybe you can understand. If not, all you can do is shoot off your mouth. How do you know, for instance, what's important for them? What really counts? Or what frightens them? You could say it about yourself, maybe. But them, what does it have to do with them? They're in another ecosystem. Like fish, so to speak. Who can understand what they want, or where they're going, and why. They're fish. And they can die of what for you is life. A breath of air and they're gone, a breath of ordinary air, the air that for you is life. Dead. Larry was a fish. He had his own sea around him, and gills that were almost invisible, and you can't understand the air he breathes if you're standing here on the shore and looking at the sea.

POOMERANG: Larry didn't even think about it too long. He put the rear-view mirror back in place, looked straight into the eyes of Mondini and said

"I want to get there, Maestro. I want to know what you see, from up there."

Mondini shook his head.

"Not much if you're lying on the canvas with your eyes rolled up in your head."

He didn't say it to bring bad luck, he said it just to say something, to keep things from becoming too serious. But for Larry it was serious. Larry, who joked about everything, now he was totally serious.

"I want to try, Maestro. Will you take me?"

Mondini wasn't there expecting to answer questions. He was there to make that kid get out of the ring.

"Please, will you take me?"

Mondini wasn't expecting that.

"Yes or no, Maestro?"

The winter of 1989 was extremely cold, and the soccer games, behind Gould's house, were often called off because of the state of the field. At times the teams resigned themselves to playing in impossible conditions, just so that the schedule wouldn't be completely shot. One day Gould, Poomerang and Diesel happened to see them play in the snow. The ball bounced, and so for the referee it was all regulation. One team wore red shirts, the other purple-and-white-checked stripes. Some of the players wore gloves and one of the two goalies had put a Cossack hat on, with the ear flaps lowered and tied under his chin. He looked like an Antarctic explorer rescued from the pack ice by a cruise ship from Club Med. Halfway through the second half Gould left the house and went to his usual place, behind the right-hand goal. Prof. Taltomar wasn't there. It was the first time. Gould waited a while, then went home. The reds won, with a lucky goal in the twelfth minute of the second half.

The professor no longer showed up at the field, and so Gould went to look for him. Finally he found him, in an old people's home, with pneumonia that might be cancer, no one was sure. He was in bed, and looked as if he'd got smaller. In his mouth was an unfiltered cigarette, unlighted. Gould moved the chair next to the bed and sat down. Prof. Taltomar had his eyes closed, maybe he was sleeping. For a while Gould sat in silence, then he said:

"Nothing-nothing at two minutes from the end. The center forward runs into the penalty area, the referee blows the whistle. The captain protests, starts screaming like a madman. The referee gets angry, pulls out a gun, and shoots him point-blank. The gun misfires. The captain hurls himself on the referee and they end up on the ground. The players run over and separate them. The referee gets up."

Professor Taltomar didn't move. For quite a while, he didn't move. Then he slowly removed the cigarette from his lips, tapped off a little of the imaginary ash, and murmured softly:

"Red card for the captain. Penalty enforced. Play resumes until the expiration of regulation time plus time added on for the scuffle. Expulsion of the referee according to Rule No. 28 of the handbook that goes as follows: Dickheads are not permitted to referee."

Then he coughed and put the cigarette back in his mouth.

Gould felt good, inside.

He stayed a bit longer, in silence.

When he got up he said:

"Thank you, Professor."

Prof. Taltomar didn't even open his eyes.

"Take care, my boy."

More or less around the same time, Shatzy negotiated the purchase of a secondhand trailer, a '71 Pagoda model. Inside it was all wood-paneled. Outside it was yellow.

"How did you happen to choose a yellow one?"

"May I point out that it's you who are buying it, not me."

"I know, but twenty years ago it was you who bought it. You're not going to tell me there were no other colors?"

"If you don't like yellow you can always repaint it."

"I like yellow."

"You do?"

"I do, yes. But in general a person has to be a retard to buy a yellow trailer, don't you think?"

Prof. Bandini inclined his head, reminding himself that he had to be very patient with this girl. He had to remain calm, or he would never get rid of the damn trailer. He had been trying to unload it for months. There aren't many people who have at the top of their wish list a '71 Pagoda trailer. Yellow. He had put ads everywhere, including the newspaper of the university where he taught. It was Gould's university. Gould had cut out the ad and stuck it among the others on the refrigerator. Then it was Shatzy who decided. She preferred Catholics and intellectuals: usually they were embarrassed to talk about money. Prof. Bandini was a Catholic intellectual.

So one day, while he was giving a lecture to a hundred students, in Classroom 11, he saw the door open and that girl came in.

"Are you Prof. Michael Bandini?"

"Yes, why?"

Shatzy waved the newspaper clipping.

"Are you the one selling a used trailer, '71 Pagoda, fairly good condition, price negotiable, no exchange?"

Without exactly knowing why, Prof. Bandini was embarrassed, as if someone were returning to him an umbrella left in a porn movie house.

"Yes, that's me."

"Can I see it?, the trailer, I mean, can I see it?"

"I'm in the middle of a lecture."

Only then did Shatzy seem to become aware of the students, who filled the lecture hall.

"Oh."

"Would you mind coming back later?"

"Of course, I'm sorry. Can I wait, maybe I'll just sit here, do you mind? I might learn something interesting."

"Please."

"Thank you."

Prof. Bandini thought to himself that the world was full of lunatics. Then he continued from where he had left off.

"Usually," he said, "the *porch* is situated at the front of the house. It consists of a roof, varying in width—but seldom wider than twelve feet—which is held up by a series of posts, and covers a wooden platform whose elevation with respect to the ground is generally between eight inches and five feet. A railing and the necessary access steps complete the basic framework. From a purely architectural point of view, the porch represents a rather rudimentary development of the classical idea of the façade, the expression of an affluent poverty and of a primitive luxury. From a psychological, not to say moral, point of view, on the other hand, it's a phenomenon that makes me crazy and that turns out, upon close analysis, to be poignant, yet repulsive and, finally, epiphanic. From the Greek *epiphaneia:* revelation."

Shatzy approved with a slight nod of her head. In the West, in fact, almost every house had a front porch.

"The anomaly of the porch," continued Prof. Bandini, "is, obviously, that it is inside and outside at the same time. In a sense, it represents an extended threshold, where the house no longer exists, but has not yet vanished into the threat of the outside. It's a no man's land where the idea of a protected place—which every house, by its very existence, bears witness to, in fact embodies—expands beyond its own definition and rises up again, undefended, as if to posthumously resist the claims of the open. In this sense it may seem the ultimate weak place, world in the balance, idea in exile. And it's not impossible that its identity as weakness contributes to its attraction, since man tends to love places that seem to incarnate his own precariousness, the fact that he is exposed, a creature of the borderland."

In private, Prof. Bandini summed up his argument with an expression that he considered it imprudent to use in public, but which he regarded as a happy synthesis. "Men *have* houses: but they *are* porches." He had once tried saying it to his wife, and his wife had laughed until she was sick. That had rather wounded him. She later left him for a translator, a woman twenty-two years her senior.

"However," Prof. Bandini continued, "it is curious how this condition of 'the weak place' dissolves as soon as the porch ceases to be an inanimate architectural element and is inhabited by men. On a porch, the average man sits with his back to the house, generally in a chair equipped with a special mechanism to make it rock. Sometimes—if we are to compose the picture with pinpoint precision—the man holds a loaded gun on his lap. Always, he looks straight ahead. If we now return to the image of precariousness which was the porch considered as a simple architectural element, and enrich it with the presence of the man—his back to the house, rocking in the rocking chair, a loaded gun on his lap—the image will shift noticeably toward a sense of strength, security, determination. One could even say that the porch ceases to be a frail echo of the house it is attached to and becomes the confirmation of what the house just hints at: the ultimate sanction of the protected place, the solution of the theorem that the house merely states."

Shatzy especially liked the detail about the loaded gun.

"Finally," continued Prof. Bandini, "the man and the porch together constitute an icon, secular, and yet sacred, too, which celebrates the human being's right to possess a place of his own, removed from the vague state of simply existing. Further: the icon celebrates the human being's right to defend that place, using the weapons of a methodical cowardice (the rocking of the rocking chair) or of a well-equipped courage (the loaded gun). The entire human condition is summed up in that image. Because exactly this seems to be man's predestined dislocation: facing the world, with himself in back."

This was something that Prof. Bandini believed, beyond any academic necessity—he simply believed that things were that way, he believed it even when he was in his bath. He thought, indeed, that men are on the porch of their own life (and therefore in exile from themselves), and that this is the only possible way for them to defend their life from the world, since as soon as they venture to re-enter the house (and therefore be themselves) the house is immediately reduced to a fragile refuge in the sea of nothingness, destined to be swept away by the wave of the Open, and the shelter becomes a fatal trap, for which reason people hurry out again onto the porch (and therefore out of themselves), taking up the only position from which they can block the invasion of the world, and save at least the idea of a house of their own, even if they must resign themselves to the knowledge that that house is uninhabitable. We have houses, but we are porches, he thought. He looked at men and in their poignant lies he heard the creak of the rocking chair on the dusty planks of the porch; and the outbursts of pride and painful self-assertion—in which, in others and in himself, he saw the sentence of perennial exile hiding—were, for him, ludicrous loaded guns. It was all very sad, if you thought about it, but also moving, because, in the end, Prof. Bandini knew that he felt affection for himself and for others, and compassion for all the porches he was surrounded by

there was something infinitely dignified in the endless delay on the threshold of the house, one step in front of you

nights when the fierce wind of truth rises, the morning after you are forced to repair the roof of your lies, with perfect patience, but when my love returns everything will be all right again, we will watch the sunset together drinking colored water

or when a man, in his weariness, asked you to sit before him, and he opened his mind to you, dragging out everything, truly everything, and even then you understood that you were sitting on his porch but he had not let you enter the house, he himself had not gone into the house for years now, and this, paradoxically, was the reason for his weariness, as he sat there, in front of you

those evenings when the air is cold and the world seems to have retreated, you suddenly feel silly there on the porch, standing guard against no enemy, and it's exhaustion that gnaws at you, and the humiliation of feeling so pointlessly foolish, finally you get up and go back into the house, after years of lies, of pretenses, you go back into the house knowing that you may not be able even to orient yourself inside, as if it were someone else's house, and yet it's yours, it still is, you open the door and enter, a

curious happiness you didn't remember, your house, how marvelous, this warmth a womb, peace, myself, at last, I will never go
out again, I put the gun down in the corner and learn again the
forms of the objects and the shape of the space, get used again to
the forgotten geography of the truth, I will learn to move without
breaking anything, when someone knocks at the door I will open
it, when it's summer I will throw wide the windows, I will stay in
this house until I am, BUT

BUT if you wait, and from the outside
watch this house, maybe an hour goes by, or an entire day, BUT in
the end you will see the door open, and, though you will never
know or understand, ever, what could have happened inside, you
will see the door open and, slowly, the man emerge, invisibly
pushed outside by you will never know what, BUT surely it must
have to do with some vertiginous fear, or inadequacy, or condemnation, so pitiless that it pushes the man out, onto his porch, gun
in hand, I adore

I adore that moment, said Prof. Bandini, the exact
moment when once again he takes a step, gun in hand, looks at
the world before him, feels the sharp air, turns up the collar of his
jacket, and then—marvelous—returns to his chair, sits, and, leaning back, sets it in motion, the gentle swaying that had ceased, the
reassuring roll of the lie that now rocks again the regained seren-
ity, the peace of the craven, the only one we get, people pass by
and greet us, Hey Jack, where did you go? Nothing, nothing,
I'm here now, Take it easy, Jack, one hand caressing the rifle butt,
he looks into the distance, narrowing his eyes a little, how
much light, o world how much light do you need, the tiniest flame
was enough for me, in there, when?, I don't remember when,
BUT it was a place I said farewell to, and then no more, he will
never speak of it again, as he rocks forever on his painted wooden
porch

if you think about it, think of the empty houses, by the hundred, behind people's faces, behind their porches, thousands of

houses in perfect order, and empty, think of the air inside, the colors, the objects, the changing light, all happening for no one, orphaned places, the ones that should be THE PLACES, the only true ones, but destiny's odd sense of urban planning has made them the wormholes of the world, abandoned cavities beneath the surface of consciousness: if you think about it, what a mystery, what about them, the true places, my true place, what about ME while I was here defending myself, doesn't it ever occur to you to ask yourself? Who knows how I am, ME? while you're there rocking, repairing bits of the roof, polishing your rifle, greeting passers-by—suddenly that question comes to mind, who knows how *I* am?, I want to know only this, how am *I*? Does anyone know if I'm good, or old, does anyone know if I'm ALIVE?

Shatzy went up to the lectern. The students were leaving and Prof. Bandini was arranging his papers in a briefcase.

"Not bad, your lecture."

"Thanks."

"Seriously. There was a lot of interesting stuff."

"Thank you very much."

"You know what it made me think?"

"No."

"Here's what I thought, Hey, that professor is, unfortunately, right, I mean, that's how things are, men have houses, but in reality they are porches, I don't know if I'm explaining myself, they have houses, but they are . . ."

"What did you say?"

"When?"

"Just now, about houses."

"I don't know, what did I say?"

"You said that sentence."

"What sentence?"

They walked down the street together, Shatzy and Prof. Bandini, talking, then they said goodbye and he told her that the trailer was in his yard, and if she wanted to come by that afternoon he would be there, and she said fine, so that afternoon in fact she went, and it was then that they started discussing the color and, to be exact, what Shatzy said was:

"How did you happen to choose a yellow one?"

"May I point out that it's you who are buying it, not me."

"I know, but twenty years ago it was you who bought it. You're not going to tell me there were no other colors?"

"If you don't like yellow you can always repaint it."

"I like yellow."

"You do?"

"I do, yes. But in general a person has to be a retard to buy a yellow trailer, don't you think?"

Twenty yards away, Gould, Poomerang, and Diesel stood in the shade, leaning against the side of Prof. Bandini's garage and watching the scene.

"He doesn't know it, but he's crazy about her," Poomerang didn't say.

"Where did Shatzy get that awful blouse?" Diesel asked.

"A strategic blouse," said Gould. "If she coughs the top button comes unbuttoned and you get a glimpse of her tits."

"Really?"

"Well, you have to know how to cough the right way. Shatzy practices in front of the mirror."

Poomerang began to cough. Then he looked at the buttons of his shirt. Then he looked again at the two who were going in and out of the trailer, discussing.

"What happened in the end with Mondini? Does he take him to the world championship or not?"

"Maybe."

"What do you mean?"

"It's not clear."

"What do you mean, it's not clear?"

"Now some people came from the Tropicana, the casino, and offered to put a lot of money on a match between Larry and Benson."

"Really? Benson?"

"Benson."

"Fuck."

"Right. Except that Mondini said Thanks a million, another time."

"No!"

"Yes. He says that first Larry has to have one more fight."

"Is he crazy?"

"It's not clear what he has in mind. All he says is that first Larry has to have another fight, and then they'll see."

"But Benson is a shortcut to the championship, if Larry beats him . . ."

"Nothing to do about it, Mondini's deaf in that ear."

"He's gone mad, the old man."

"No, he's got something in mind. The other night, Larry went to him directly and said Maestro, you owe me an answer. Mondini looked at him and then he said: After the next fight, Larry, and I'm going to choose it."

"Come on . . ."

"Then Larry put on a smile and said All right, OK, whatever you like, Maestro, who am I supposed to take out?"

"Right, who the hell is he supposed to take out?"

"Now comes the best part."

"Which is?"

"Mondini is a weird guy, it's hard to tell what he has in mind."

"What on earth do you mean, Gould?"

"With all the fighters to choose from, it's odd, really, incomprehensible . . ."

"So who the hell did he choose?"

"You'd never guess."

"So, come on . . ."

Gould turned for a second to look at Shatzy, over there with Prof. Bandini. Then he said softly:

"Poreda."

"Who?"

"Poreda."

"*Stanley* Poreda?"

"Yes."

"Poreda the one with the broken arms?"

"That's the one."

"What the hell's going on?"

"I said you wouldn't believe it."

"Poreda?"

"Stanley Hooker Poreda."

"That son of a bitch."

"You can say that again."

"Poreda . . . fuck."

"Poreda."

POOMERANG: Stanley Poreda had retired two years earlier. To be exact, he had had to retire. He had sold a fight, only things had gone wrong. His opponent was a guy related to a boss in Belem. His form was good, but in terms of power he was a disaster, he couldn't have beaten a drunk. Poreda was an artist in simulating the KO, but in the first four rounds he didn't take a single hit that bore the slightest resemblance to a real blow. He would have liked to go down and head home. But there was no way to get a decent punch out of that worthless wimp. So, just to do something, at the end of the fourth round he went in with a jab and doubled it with a hook. Nothing special. But the wimp went down. Saved by the bell. When Poreda returned to his corner, a very well dressed guy appeared, with a gold-filtered cigarette in his mouth. He didn't even take it out of his mouth when he leaned over and whispered: You worm, try that again and you're fucked. He only took it out when, a second later, he spat into the water bottle and said to the corner: Give the boy something to drink, he's thirsty. Poreda was, in his way, a professional. He grabbed the bottle and took a drink without turning a hair. Then the bell sounded. The wimp got up, staggering a little, but, when he got to the center of the ring, he had the strength to say to Poreda: let's get this over with, you creep. Right, Poreda thought. He opened his defense with a couple of jabs, then went in with an uppercut and ended with a right hook. The wimp flew backwards like a puppet. When he landed he looked like someone who had fallen from a tenth-floor window. Poreda took off his mouthpiece, went straight to the wimp's corner, and said: Give the boy something to drink, he's thirsty. Ten days later, two thugs with guns came to his house. They broke both his arms, crushing them, one after the other, in the door. End of the line, Poreda thought.

DIESEL: He had started out with Mondini. Two or three fights, then the Maestro had caught him going down on a ridiculous punch, and had understood. It's a profession like any other, Poreda had said to him. It's not mine, Mondini had said. And he had thrown him out of the gym. Mondini had continued to follow his progress, from a distance. He wasn't a great fighter, Poreda, but he was like an animal that has found in the ring its habitat. He knew all the tricks, he had even invented a few, and some he executed with indisputable perfection. Above all: he was strong. He was strong like almost no other active fighters. It was a skill. When he decided to, he was capable of unloading in a single punch all hundred and eighty pounds of himself, it was as if for one instant every ounce of his body went into that glove. Even his butt, Mondini said. He had a kind of admiration for him. So, when this business of Larry and the world championship started up, that was who came to mind: with all the other fighters around: him.

POOMERANG: It wasn't a stupid idea. Apart from the real champions, Poreda was the dirtiest, toughest, strongest, and most skillful opponent he could find for Larry. He was boxing after you took away the poetry. He was combat reduced to the bone. Only, he had to be persuaded to return to the ring. Mondini put on his good overcoat, went to the bank, withdrew some of his savings, and went to find Poreda in the gym where he was a trainer. Maybe it was just a coincidence, but the slaughterhouse was nearby.

"That's some money," Poreda noted, weighing the stack of bills. "Too much to buy a fighter who stopped selling fights two years ago."

Mondini didn't blink.

"You don't understand, Poreda. I'll pay you if you win."

"If I win?"

"Exactly."

"You're crazy. That kid has talent, you've got a real treasure there, and you're paying someone to beat him."

"I have my reasons, Poreda."

"No, no, I don't want to know about that stuff any more, I'm finished with betting, I don't have any other arms to break, I've had enough."

"Betting doesn't enter into it, I swear to you."

"Then what is it, now you're training people to see them lose?"

"It happens."

"You're crazy."

"Maybe. You'll do it?"

Poreda couldn't believe it. It was the first time he had ever been paid a bribe to win.

"Mondini, let's not kid around, that Gorman is quite a little talent, but you know, if I want to, I'll figure out a way to get him."

"I know. That's why I'm here."

"There's a risk you'll lose your money."

"I know."

"Mondini . . ."

"What?"

"What's behind this?"

"Nothing. I want to see if the kid can still dance once I soak him in shit. You're the shit."

Poreda smiled. He had an ex-wife who was after him for alimony, a girlfriend who was fifteen years younger than he, and a taxman who was taking a thousand dollars a month to forget his name. So he smiled. Then he spat on the ground. It had always been his way of signing a contract.

"She coughed."

"What?"

"Shatzy . . . coughed."

"We're at the good part."

"He's mad about her, he'll sell it to her, positively he'll sell it to her."

"Is the button open?"

"You can't see from here."

"It must be open."

"I don't think it will be enough."

"Ten that he does it," Poomerang didn't say, and took a greasy bill out of his pocket.

"Done. And another twenty on Poreda."

"No bets on Poreda, guys, Mondini swore to him."

"What does that have to do with it, we always bet."

"Not this time, this time it's serious."

"The other times weren't?"

"This is more serious."

"OK, but it's still boxing, isn't it?"

"Mondini swore to him."

"Mondini, not me, I never swore I wouldn't bet . . ."

"It's the same thing."

"It is not the same thing."

Right at that moment, Prof. Bandini said to Shatzy:

"Would you like to have dinner with me tonight?"

Shatzy smiled.

"Another time, Professor."

She held out her hand and Prof. Bandini shook it.

"Another time, then."

"Yes."

Shatzy turned and went back down the stone path. Just before she reached the garage, she rebuttoned the button, the one over her breasts. When she stopped in front of Gould her expression was serious.

"His wife left him. For a woman."

"Splendid."

"You could have told me."

"I didn't know."

"Isn't he your professor?"

"He doesn't lecture about his marriage."

"No?"

"No."

"Oh."

She turned. The professor was still there. He waved to her. She waved back.

"He's a nice guy."

"Yes."

"He didn't deserve a yellow trailer. Sometimes people punish themselves for reasons they don't even understand, so, just for the taste of punishment . . . they decide . . . to punish themselves."

"Shatzy . . ."

"Yes?"

"WILL YOU PLEASE TELL ME IF YOU RIPPED OFF THAT BLASTED TRAILER, YES OR NO?"

"Gould?"

"Yes."

"Don't shout."

"OK."

"You want to know if I managed to buy a '71 yellow Pagoda trailer for almost nothing?"

"Yes."

"GOD DAMN YOU CHICKEN BASTARD, OF COURSE I DID."

She shouted so loud that she popped the button over her tits. Gould, Diesel and Poomerang were dumbstruck, their eyes looked like eggs in gelatin. Not because of the button, because of the trailer. It had never crossed their minds that it would really happen. They looked at Shatzy as if at the reincarnation of Mami Jane, returned to cut off the balls of Franz Forte, the business manager of CRB. God damn you chicken bastard, she had done it.

Two days later, a tow truck brought the trailer to Gould's house. They parked it in the yard. They washed it carefully, even the tires, the windows, everything. It was very yellow. It was like a toy house, something made for children. Neighbors passing by stopped to look at it. Someone once said to Shatzy that it wouldn't be bad to have a porch on the front, a plastic porch, like the ones sold at the supermarket. They even came in yellow.

"No porch," said Shatzy.

18

Pitt Clark's body was found after a four-day search, buried under two feet of dirt, near the river. Doc examined it and said that Pitt had died of suffocation, probably he had been buried alive. He had bruises on his arms, his neck and his back. Before he was buried, he had been raped. Pitt was eleven years old.

Now listen to a strange story, Shatzy said.

The same day Pitt was found, an Indian everyone called Bear disappeared from the Clark ranch. Someone saw him leave town, on horseback, heading for the mountains. Bear was Pitt's friend. Pitt always listened to him. They often went swimming together, down at the river. And they hunted snakes. They'd keep them alive for a while, feeding them mice. Then they killed them. Bear must have been about twenty. They called him that because he was odd. With people, he was odd. Under his cot they found a tin can and in the can a bracelet that Pitt always wore on his right wrist. It was made of snakeskin.

Shatzy said that many people volunteered to go after the Indian. It was intoxicating, to hunt a man. But the sheriff said: I'm going. Alone. His name was Wister, and he was a fine man. He didn't like hangings and he believed in trials. He knew Pitt, every so often he'd taken him fishing, and he had also promised him that when he was fourteen he would teach him to shoot—to hit a bottle, at ten paces, with his eyes closed. He said: Bear is my business.

He left in the morning, while the wind raised whirlpools of dust under the grill of a burning sun.

Now pay attention, Shatzy said. A manhunt is pure geometry. Points, lines, distances. Draw it on a map: an intoxicated but implacable geometry. It can last hours or weeks. One flees, the other follows. Every minute takes them farther from the land that brought them forth and that, if questioned, would recognize them. Soon they become two points in a void where the good can no longer be distinguished from the bad. Then even if they wanted to they would be unable to change anything. They are objective trajectories, geometries calculated by destiny starting from a wrong. They will wind down only in a final result, written as a footnote to life, in blood-red ink. Music.

Shatzy did the music, with her mouth closed, something like a big orchestra, violins and trumpets, it was done well. Then she asked you: Everything clear?

More or less.

You'll see, it's not hard.

All right.

Shall we go?

Let's go.

Sheriff Wister heads for the mountains. He takes the trail for Pinter Pass. He goes up through a forest, looks for Bear's tracks and figures he must have half a day's advantage. When the trees thin out he stops to rest his horse. Then he starts off again. He goes along the mountain ridge, slowly, studying the hoofprints on the trail. It takes a while but finally he is able to recognize those of Bear's horse. He imagines that the Indian, if he wanted, could have made them vanish. The boy must be sure of himself, and relaxed. Maybe he believes he can reach the border. Maybe he doesn't think he's being followed. He spurs his horse and goes up towards Pinter Pass. By the time he arrives it's evening. He looks down, at the narrow valley that descends to the desert. Far away, he seems to see a tiny wake of dust rising in the midst of the emptiness. He goes down a few hundred yards, finds a cave, stops the horse. He is tired. He spends the night there.

On the second day, Sheriff Wister wakes at dawn. He takes his binoculars and looks down into the valley. He sees a small dark patch along the trail. Bear. He gets on his horse, carefully makes his way down the steep mountain ledges. When he gets to the valley floor he spurs his horse to a gallop. He rides for an hour, without a break. Then he stops. He can see Bear with his naked eye, a mile or so ahead. He seems to have stopped. Wister gets off his horse. He shelters under a big tree and rests. When he starts off again, the sun is at its zenith. His horse goes at an easy pace, and not for a second does he take his eyes off Bear's silhouette, small and dark ahead of him. He still appears not to be moving. Why doesn't he flee? thinks Sheriff Wister. He rides for half an hour, then stops. Bear is no more than five hundred yards away. He is motionless, sitting in the saddle of a dappled horse. He could be a statue. Sheriff Wister loads his rifle and checks his pistols. He looks at the sun. It's about to go behind him. You're finished, kid. He takes off at a gallop. A hundred yards, then another hundred, he rides without a pause, finally he sees Bear move, leave the trail and head to the right. Where are you going, kid, that way is the desert, he plants his spurs in the side of his horse, leaves the trail and follows him. Bear turns to the east, then west again, and again east. Where are you going, kid? thinks Sheriff Wister. He slows down, Bear stays five hundred yards ahead, after a while he stops, Wister sees this and urges his horse to a gallop, Bear takes off, turns to the east again, the colors fade, and suddenly night falls. Wister stops. OK, kid. I'm not in a hurry. He dismounts, makes camp, lights a fire. Before he goes to sleep, he sees in the darkness the light of Bear's campfire, five hundred yards ahead. Good night, kid.

On the third day, Sheriff Wister wakes before dawn. He stirs up the fire, heats the coffee. He sees no lights in the darkness. He waits. At daybreak, he sees Bear in the distance, standing motionless beside his dappled bay. He takes the binoculars. The boy doesn't have a rifle. Maybe a pistol. Sheriff Wister sits down on the ground. The first move is yours, kid. They stay like that for hours. Sun burning the emptiness all around. Every half hour Sheriff Wister takes a swallow of water and one of whiskey. The light is blinding. Suddenly he sees Pitt again, laughing, running. Then he sees him shout, shout, shout. He looks at his hands and they are trembling. Die, you son of a bitch, die you Indian bastard. He gets up. He feels his head spinning. He takes the reins in his hand and begins to walk, leading the horse. He walks slowly, but he realizes that Bear is getting closer. The boy isn't moving. He doesn't get on his horse, doesn't run away. Three hundred yards. Two hundred. Sheriff Wister stops. He shouts: End it, Bear. He says softly: Get yourself killed, like a good boy. And again shouting: Bear, don't be a fool. The boy remains motionless. Wister checks rifle and pistols. Then he climbs into the saddle. He takes off at a gallop. He sees Bear mount his horse and go. They ride for half an hour, like that. No more than two hundred yards separates them. A pueblo appears on the horizon, forgotten in the emptiness. Bear heads for it, Wister follows. Ten minutes later Bear enters the pueblo at a gallop and disappears. Sheriff Wister slows down and gets off his horse. He draws his gun before reaching the first houses. Not a living soul. He walks slowly, keeping close to the walls, alert to the slightest sound. He looks in every window, reads every shadow. He feels his heart pounding in his ears. Stay calm, he thinks. Probably he's not even armed. All you have to do is find him and get rid of him. He's just a kid. He sees an old woman standing in the doorway of a *posada*. He approaches. He asks her in Spanish if she's seen an Indian, on a dappled horse. She nods yes, with her head, and points towards the other end of the village, where the trail goes on into the emptiness. Wister aims the rifle at her head. Don't lie, he says in Spanish. She makes the sign of the cross, and again points to the far end of the village. Do you have anything to drink? The woman goes into the *posada* and comes out with some whiskey. Sheriff Wister drinks. Did he take water, the Indian? The woman nods yes. You know who he is? Then the woman says: yes. *Es un chico que va detras de un asesino.* Sheriff Wister stares at her. Did he tell you that? Yes. Sheriff Wister takes another swallow of whiskey. You're dead, kid, he thinks. He gets on his horse, tosses a coin to the old woman, puts the whiskey in his pack, and proceeds, slowly, to the edge of the village. When he passes the last house he looks ahead. Nothing. He turns right. He sees Bear motionless in the saddle, no more than two hundred yards away. *Es un chico que va detras de un asesino.* Sheriff Wister quickly grabs the gun from the saddle, aims, and shoots. Twice. Bear doesn't move. The echo of the shots disappears slowly in the air. Sheriff Wister throws away the cartridge. Stay calm, he thinks. Don't you see he's too far away? Stay calm. He watches Bear. He wants to shout something at him, but doesn't know what. He turns his horse, goes back to the first house, and dismounts. He spends the night there. But he can't sleep. A gun, always, in his hand.

On the fourth day, Sheriff Wister leaves the pueblo and sees Bear in the distance, on the trail that leads to the desert. He gets on his horse and follows him, slowly. He lets the horse carry him. Every so often he falls asleep: from the heat, the exhaustion. After three hours he stops at a spring. The Indian might have poisoned it, he thinks. He refills his canteens and sets off. I mustn't let him reach the desert, he thinks. We'll both die there. He has a swallow of whiskey. He waits until the sun is lower on the horizon. Then he takes off at a gallop. Bear doesn't seem to be aware of him. He keeps going, slowly, without turning. Perhaps he's sleeping. He's mine, thinks Sheriff Wister. Three hundred yards. Two hundred yards. A hundred yards. Sheriff Wister draws his gun. Fifty yards. Bear turns, he has a rifle in his hand, aims and shoots. One shot.

Wister's horse swerves to the right, then collapses on its front legs. The animal is lying on its side. It lifts its head, tries to stand up. Wister manages to slide out from under it. He feels a burning pain in his shoulder. Then he hears a second shot enter the animal's flesh. He raises his head, and, leaning against the horse's body, fires three shots, one after the other. Bear's horse rears up on its hind legs and rolls over on its back, legs in the air, kicking. Sheriff Wister grabs his rifle from the saddle. Bear regains control of his horse and gallops off, trying to escape. Wister aims and fires two shots. It seems to him that he sees Bear fold over the animal's neck. Then he sees the horse break its stride, stagger, move another twenty yards, and collapse. He sees Bear's body flung in the dust. Adios, kid, he thinks. He loads the gun, takes aim. Bear is trying to get up. Wister fires. He sees a swirl of dust, twenty yards in front of Bear's body. Shit, he says. He fires again. The second bullet hits beside the first. Bear has gotten up. He retrieves his gun. With the other hand he unhooks the saddlebags from the saddle. He stands there, staring at Wister. Eighty yards between them. A gunshot. Something more. Sheriff Wister looks at the sun. Still a couple of hours before dark, he thinks. His shoulder hurts, he can't move the arm without feeling a sharp pain. *Muy bien,* kid. He unhooks his saddlebags and throws them over his good shoulder. He loads his gun. And starts walking. Bear sees him, turns, and heads off, also walking, slowly. Sheriff Wister thinks that running would be absurd. He imagines the scene as viewed from above, two men running in a void, and thinks: we are two condemned men. Then for an instant he sees Pitt running, and running, and trying to flee, along the river, running, fleeing. God damn it, he thinks. I'll kill you, kid. He reaches Bear's horse. It's still breathing. Wister empties the gun into its head. I'll kill you, kid. Then he starts walking again. When evening comes, he sees Bear disappear in the darkness. He stops. He's crazy with the pain in his shoulder. He lies down on the ground. He grasps the gun in his hand. He tries not to fall asleep. I haven't slept for two days, he thinks.

On the fifth day Sheriff Wister feels the fever clouding his sight and making his heart race. Doesn't that bastard ever sleep? He sees him up ahead, seemingly as far away as the day before, but Wister's eyes are burning, and there are no shadows in the morning light. He starts off. He tries to remember where the trail leads, and how many miles they've covered since the pueblo. Bear, in front of him, walks without stopping. Every so often he turns. Then he keeps going. It's the way to Salina. He can't let him get that far. He can't get to Salina. He stops. He bends down. He picks up a clot of dust. Blood and dust. He looks at Bear. So I got you, kid. You didn't want to tell me, eh? He straightens. He takes a few steps. Another bloodstain. *Muy bien,* you bastard. He no longer feels the fever. He starts walking. Three hours later Bear abandons the trail and turns east. Sheriff Wister stops. He's mad, he thinks. He's going into the desert. He's mad. He takes his gun and shoots into the air. Bear stops, turns. Wister lets his saddlebags fall to the ground. Then he throws down his rifle. He opens his arms wide. Bear doesn't move. Wister walks towards him, slowly. Bear doesn't move. Wister keeps walking, lowers his arms and moves his hands to his guns. He is fifty yards from the Indian. He stops. End it, kid, he shouts. Bear doesn't move. That's the desert over there, you want to die like a fool? he cries. Bear takes a few steps towards him. Then stops. They stand there, facing each other, two black squiggles in the desert. The sun beats down. It's a world without shadows. The silence is so terrible that Sheriff Wister hears Pitt screaming inside him. He tries to remember the boy's face but he can't, he only hears that cry, so loud. He tries to focus on Bear. But the cry will not leave him in peace. You have to do your job, he says to himself. Forget the rest. Do your job. He realizes that he is staring at the ground. He lifts his head suddenly. He gazes at Bear. He sees two absent eyes. Invincible, he thinks. Then, like a lightning bolt, fear strikes him, and his legs crumple. He has held it off for days. It arrives now, like a silent explosion. He drops to his knees. He falls forwards, with his hands on the ground. They are trembling. He can't breathe, the blood is beating in his temples. With a huge effort he looks up. Bear is still standing there. Bastard. Bastard. Bastard. There are no birds in the sky, nor snakes in the dust, nor wind to riffle the grasses, no horizon, nothing. The world has disappeared. Sheriff Wister murmurs softly: go to hell, kid. He gets to his feet, casts a last glance at Bear, then turns—turns—and stumbling reaches his rifle. He grabs it. He takes a few more steps. He picks up his saddlebag and throws it over his good shoulder. Without a glance back he walks on, watching his steps. He doesn't stop until dark. He falls to the ground. He sleeps. In the middle of the night he wakes up. He starts walking again, following the faint traces of the trail. He falls to the ground again. He closes his eyes. He dreams.

On the sixth day Sheriff Wister wakes at dawn. He gets up. He sees, minuscule on the horizon, the white houses of the pueblo. He turns around. Bear is a hundred yards away. Standing. Still. Wister picks up his bags and the rifle. He starts off again. He walks for hours. Every so often he falls to the ground, pulls his hat down over his eyes, and waits. When he feels his strength returning, he stands up and sets off again. He never turns. He manages to reach the pueblo before sunset. They give him food and drink. He says: I am Sheriff Wister. They give him a bed to sleep in. They tell him in Spanish that there is a *chico*, outside the pueblo. He is camped a hundred yards or so from the first houses. They ask if it is a friend of his. No, says Sheriff Wister. He's crazy with the pain in his shoulder. He sleeps with his gun loaded, within reach of his hand.

On the seventh day Sheriff Wister gets them to give him a horse, and he heads for the mountains. He finds the wind again, and clouds of dust that blot out the trail. He stops only once, to let the horse rest. Then he sets off again. He arrives at the mountains. He goes up to Pinter Pass, crosses the mountains without turning around. Before reaching the plain, he makes a detour to an abandoned mine. He dismounts, makes a fire. He spends the night there, without sleeping. He thinks.

On the eighth day Sheriff Wister waits till the sun is high in the sky. Then he gets on his horse. He takes a few things from the saddlebags and ties them to the saddle. He leaves the rifle leaning against a wall of the mine. He descends slowly to the valley. Far away he sees the houses of Closingtown, and the trees bent by the wind. He proceeds slowly, in no hurry. He speaks out loud. Always the same sentence. When he comes to the river, he stops the horse. He gives him his head. He half-closes his eyes, and looks. Bear is a few hundred yards away. He is sitting on a horse. He is moving slowly, at a walk. Kid, says Wister. Kid. Then he turns his horse and without looking back again reaches Closingtown.

When he gets to the first houses, someone starts shouting that the sheriff is back. People rush out to the street. He continues slowly, without looking at anyone. In one hand he holds the reins, in the other a gun. No one dares approach, he's like a dead man on horseback, or a madman. Sheriff Wister crosses the town, like a phantom, then he skirts the jail and takes the trail for the Clark ranch. People follow, on foot. They hardly dare speak. Wister arrives at the ranch. He gets off his horse. He twirls the reins around a fencepost. He heads for the house, walking like a drunk. Someone goes over to help him. He points the gun at him. He says nothing, keeps walking, and comes to the house. Standing in front of it is Pitt's father. Eugene Clark. Face aged by the wind, hair gray. Sheriff Wister stops three paces from him. He's still holding the gun in his right hand. He looks at Eugene Clark. Then he says: I'm sorry, he kept crying, he wouldn't stop. He was always a good boy with me. He had never done that, before. He was a good boy. Eugene Clark takes a step towards him. Wister aims the gun at him. Eugene Clark stops. Sheriff Wister raises the barrel of his Colt .45. He says: I didn't bury him alive, I swear. He wasn't breathing anymore, his eyes were rolled up in his head, and he wasn't breathing any more. Then he sticks the gun under his chin, and shoots. Bloodstains on the face and clothes of Eugene Clark. People are running, shouting, the children want to see, the old people shake their heads, the wind ceaselessly whips up the dust, all around. It takes a while for them to become aware of Bear. He is on his horse, motionless, beside the fence. He has no eyes any more, they have disappeared into the Indian cheekbones. He breathes with his mouth open, between lips dry with dust and earth. The people are silent. He presses his heels lightly into the horse's flanks. He pulls the reins to the left and goes away. A boy runs after him. Bear, he calls, Bear. The sheriff shot himself, Bear. He doesn't turn around, he goes on, slowly, towards the river. Bear, hey, Bear, where are you going?

Bear doesn't turn around.

To sleep, he says softly.

Music.

19

"Hello, Gould?"

"Hi, Dad."

"It's your father."

"Hi."

"Everything OK?"

"Yes."

"What's this business about Couverney?"

"They've invited me to Couverney."

"What do you mean?"

"They do research there. They want me to come and work with them."

"It sounds like a big deal."

"I think it is."

"And then?"

"Then that's all, they invited me for three years, they'll give me a place to live at the university, and pay for two trips a year to come home, if I want."

"Christmas and Easter."

"Something like that."

"It sounds like a big deal."

"Yes."

"Couverney's on the other side of the world."

"It's far, yes."

"They eat like dogs there, you know? I was there once, not at the university, but in that area, you couldn't find anything to eat that didn't taste of fish."

"They say it's horrendously cold."

"Probably."

"Colder than here."

"They'll give you some money, right?"

"What?"

"I'm saying, will they pay you well?"

"I think so."

"That's important. What does Rector Bolder say?"

"He says it's a lot of money for a fifteen-year-old boy."

"No, I mean in general, what does Rector Bolder say about the whole thing, in general?"

"He says it's a great opportunity. However, he would like me to stay here."

"Old Bolder. He's a good man, you know?, you can trust him."

"He says it's a great opportunity."

"It must be like being invited to Wimbledon. If you're a tennis player, I mean."

"More or less."

"As if you were a tennis player, and one day they write to you and say, We'll pay you if you'll do us the honor to come and play here. Crazy, isn't it?"

"Yes."

"I'm proud of you, son."

"Thanks, Dad."

"It's crazy, really."

"Kind of."

"Your mother will be pleased."

"What?"

"Your mother will be pleased, Gould."

"You'll tell her?"

"Yes, I'll tell her."

"Really?"

"Yes."

"Really?"

"She'll be pleased."

"But don't tell her that I'm going, I don't know yet if I'm going to go, I mean, they just asked me."

"I'll tell her that they asked you, that's all I'll say."

"Yes."

"And that it's a big deal."

"Yes, explain to her that it's a big deal."

"She'll be pleased."

"Yes, it's a good idea, tell her."

"I will tell her, Gould."

"Thanks."

". . ."

". . ."

"When do you think you'll decide?"

"I don't know."

"Would you have to leave right away?"

"In September."

"You have a little time."

"Yes."

"It's a great opportunity, maybe you shouldn't let it get away."

"That's what they all say here."

"But you decide yourself, understand?"

"Yes."

"Listen to what everybody has to say and then you decide yourself."

"Yes."

"It's your life that's at stake, not theirs."

"Right."

"You're the one who's going into the line of fire, not them."

"What line of fire?"

"It's an expression."

"Oh."

"The way people talk."

"Oh."

"I had a colonel, once, who had a delightful way of expressing himself. When something got complicated, he would always say the same thing. When the sun's in your eyes you get a tan, you don't shoot. He said that even if it was raining, it didn't have to do with the weather, it was a symbol, the sun, you see, was an expression, and it was valid even if it was snowing that day or foggy, when the sun's in your eyes you get a tan, you don't shoot. He said it just like that. Now he's in a wheelchair. He had a stroke while he was swimming. It would have been better not to fish him out of the pool, all in all."

"Dad . . ."

"I'm here, Gould."

"I have to go now."

"Take care, son, and let me know."

"OK."

"Let me know if you decide anything."

"You'll remember to tell Mother?"

"Of course I'll remember."

"OK."

"I'll certainly remember."

"OK."

"Bye then."

"Bye, Dad."

"Gould . . ."

"Yes?"

"What about Shatzy, what does Shatzy say about it?"

"She's fine."

"No, I mean what does she think of Couverney?"

"Of that?"

"Yes, that."

"She says it's a great opportunity."

"That's all?"

"She says that if you're a deodorizer it's a great opportunity to be invited to spend three years in the men's room of a highway rest stop."

"A highway rest stop?"

"Yes."

"What the hell does she mean?"

"I don't know. I must be the deodorizer."

"Ah."

"I think it's a joke."

"It's a joke?"

"I think so."

"That girl is tough."

"Yes."

"Say hello to her for me."

"All right."

"Bye, son."

"Bye."

Click.

20

(*Gould visits Prof. Taltomar. He goes into the hospital. He walks up to the sixth floor. He enters Room No. 8. Taltomar is in the bed. He's breathing through a mask hooked up to a machine. He is very thin. His hair has been cut. Gould moves a chair over to the bed and sits down. He looks at Taltomar. He waits.*) . . . mell of soup. And of peas. Maybe peas are good for sick people, for any sort of illness, Gould thought. Maybe the smell in itself is effective, studies have been done and show that . . . Yellow walls. Yellow trailer. But more washed out. Washed out, not washed. I wonder what the toilet is like.

Gould got up, and with one finger touched Prof. Taltomar's gray hand. Like touching the skin of a prehistoric animal. Old and smooth. The machine breathed with Taltomar, giving his breath a constant, peaceful rhythm. It didn't seem to be a struggle. It seemed to be *after* a struggle. Gould sat down again. He began breathing with the rhythm of the machine. The machine breathes with Taltomar, Gould breathes with the machine, Gould breathes with Taltomar. It's as though we're walking together, Professor.

Then he got up. He went into the corridor. There were people in bathrobes wandering aimlessly and nurses speaking in high voices. The floor was of black and white linoleum tiles. Gould started walking. He kept his eyes on the floor and tried to step only in the black squares, without touching the lines. He remembered a movie he had seen in which a fighter trained by running along the railroad tracks. It was winter, and he was running with his coat on. Also, his hands were tightly bandaged, as if he were about to put on his boxing gloves, and every so often he punched the air. A winter sun overhead, city in the background, all gray, very cold, the overcoat flying, the trains not moving, rather Butch who wants to run he could come he says that he was going to run maybe not on the train tracks on the street the route up to the park and back here on the train tracks with Butch it would be less boring   but I like running alone it's always hard to know what you really like or what you want to like if I try to ask myself truly if I like running by myself or if maybe I'd rather run with Butch   with Butch we could talk he always talks about women it's fun I could tell him about Jody I wouldn't like talking to him about Jody there would be no point Jody small tits oh fuck I think dickhead come on I mustn't think about it because you always have to run away Jody we'd be good together why is it that you always have to run away she is as if she had to run away every time she has to remind you that she's not there forever or completely fuck damn think about something else bastard behind the gas tank there's the shadow freezing cold that time when there was a train right there running between the train tracks Mondini is a genius he strengthens your ankles connects feet and eyes you run without looking at your feet but place your feet on the ties look for them out of the corner of your eye the corner of your eye is what reads the feet of your opponent OK Maestro punches come from the feet the feet are punches not yet born   abort punches abort yourself bam bam right right left right Mondini great man beautiful shadow I make with my coat flying swaddled hands striking the air they're mad at me for running with my hands swaddled you shouldn't be fighting at all what bullshit it's always a fight you're always fighting that's what I like about boxing it's endlessly fighting when you run when you eat when you jump rope when you get dressed how I tie my shoes when I sing before the match I'd like to run with my gloves on my shadow is beautiful you are so beautiful Larry Larry Lawyer Larry Lawyer against Stanley Poreda bullshit bam bam uppercut   bam Poreda shit name bam   I'll cut off my hair, shave it to nothing, just a tiny bit longer on the top of my head touch me here Jody she laughs runs her hand over my head I want the robe to say "Lawyer" on it get it take away "Gorman" and write "Larry Lawyer" get it so that you get it bam Mondini will say it's all bullshit Mondini bam bam doesn't want to understand those things Mondini fuck you Larry fuck goddam cold how much is still in shadow it's almost an hour still an hour and a half bam look at that he had it in for my gold watch you don't go running with a watch on especially if you have a gold one but look at that but mind your own business mind   I even like the breath coming out of my mouth in this fucking cold you're strong Larry Lawyer ask me why I box you with that microphone what kind is it Dan De Palma my mother listens to him in secret on the radio in secret from my father who doesn't want to know about it my mother listens to him and it's not true that she cries bam it's not true bam Dan De Palma ask me once and for all why I box I do it because everything about boxing is great you're great you can become great Larry Lawyer my cashmere coat flying along the railroad tracks in this winter bam bam right left right and fast get your feet on the ties again I could close my eyes and I'd find them under my feet you've never seen another like this Mondini you've never seen it you and your Poreda shit name bam bam bitch   listen here Dan De Palma you want to know why I box you want to know I want you to say it's because I'm in a hurry that's why bam I didn't want to wait boxing is a whole life in a few minutes engrave this in your mind I could have waited you don't know my father if you knew him you'd understand what it means a lifetime to arrive at the right moment you're hanging in the balance between success and disaster that is the right moment you and your talent and that's all no need to wait you know how it's going to end and it ends in an evening it's all over if you've tried something like that you'll keep on wanting it like living a hundred lifetimes nothing will make me stop nothing imagine someone like Poreda fifty-seven bouts fourteen defeats all sold all for KOs who made you return you thief they put it in your head to rob Lawyer you're a poor bastard who do you think will pay for a ticket to see you and your broken arms he hurt you I'll hurt you worse I will Poreda bam   that time in Saratoga maybe and once against Walcot but only at the beginning I always came out always and anyway it wasn't really fear they're always telling you that you shouldn't think about it who thinks about it I don't think about it make me see fear I haven't seen it Poreda's taking care of that says Mondini we'll see I want fear Maestro bam bam bam I'm not afraid to be afraid bam left right left two steps back then again low bam keep it short don't dance yes I'm dancing I like to dance they can't figure out a thing if I dance read it in their eyes they can't figure out a fucking thing any more my shoes are beautiful with the red fringe and that guy over there who couldn't stop shitting before a fight he was so afraid I want to be afraid old Tom always in the gym played like a bag too many punches in the head he's a good old man Tom you can die or get like Tom I'd rather die I don't care about dying but not like Tom I want to die in a hurry if they can give me a beating I won't let the job stop halfway I'll keep getting up until I die did you hear me Dan De Palma I like all this it's fast you don't have to wait years I'm in a hurry do you understand me I'm in a hurry don't ask me why it's strange but if I think of dying up there I'm happy I must be mad like thinking of throwing your-self off a height strange but fuck I think bam it was better if Butch came we talked if Butch came running stop it dickhead think of

Poreda shit name bam bam if he wants to play dirty so what we'll play dirty if that's what you want or slip him one in front brilliant back and forth back and forth I never hit him but I'm smashing his brain with fakes think how would it be to win a bout with a single punch all the rest ideas that take the breath out of that poor bastard until he's stunned and you come on give the knockout punch bam but not with Poreda with Poreda it will all be dirty not the beginning maybe but afterwards it will be a mess a shit match fight and forget it I wish it were tomorrow I wish it were now calm down Lawyer calm down run Lawyer now run.

Gould stopped. In Room No. 3, a woman was crying, she was crying loudly and every so often she cried out that she wanted to leave, she was angry with everyone because they wouldn't let her leave. Her husband was outside the door. He was talking to another man, who was rather fat, and old. He was saying that he no longer knew what to do, she had thrown herself down the stairs on Christmas night, it had happened very suddenly, since her return from the clinic she had seemed well, quite normal, then on Christmas night she went and threw herself down the stairs, I don't know what to do anymore, I can't take her back to the psychiatric clinic, her leg is broken in two places and three ribs are cracked, but I can't go on, I've been here for eighteen days, I can't go on. He was leaning against the wall, and he spoke without tears and without moving his hands, very calmly. From the room came the voice of the woman crying. When she cried you seemed to hear a child crying. A very small woman. Gould began walking again. When he reached Room No. 8 he went in and sat down again on the chair next to Prof. Taltomar's bed. The machine continued to breathe. Taltomar was in the same position as before, his head, slightly turned, on the pillow, his arms outside the covers, his hands shriveled. Gould stayed for quite a while, watching the stationary film of an old man who was departing. Then, without getting up from the chair, he leaned over the bed and said

"Fifteenth minute of the second half. Nothing-nothing. The referee whistles and calls the two captains. He tells them that he is very tired, that he doesn't know what's come over him, but he's so tired, and wants to go home. I'd like to go home, he says. He shakes their hands, then turns and, walking slowly, crosses the field, toward the locker rooms. The crowd watches in silence. The players stand still. The ball is sitting in the middle of the penalty area, but no one is looking at it. The referee sticks the whistle in his pocket, murmurs something that no one can hear, and disappears into the tunnel."

Taltomar's hands didn't move. His eyelids trembled slightly, the machine breathed. Gould sat motionless, waiting. He looked at Taltomar's lips. Without the cigarette butt they looked uninhabited. You could hear from the corridor the woman who was crying with the voice of a child. Time was passing, time, passed.

When Gould got up, he put the chair back in its place. He picked up his jacket and held it over his arm because it was stiflingly hot there. He glanced at the breathing machine. Then he stopped at the foot of the bed, just for a moment.

"Thanks, Professor," he said.

Thanks, he thought.

Then he left. He went down the six flights of stairs, crossed the big entrance hall where a man was selling newspapers and sick people in pajamas were calling home. The door was glass and opened by itself when you got close to it. Outside the sun was shining. Poomerang and Diesel were waiting for him, leaning against a garbage can. They went off together, along the tree-lined avenue that led downtown. They all three danced Diesel's crooked steps, but skillfully, and gracefully, like professionals.

After a while, when they had reached the intersection with Seventh, Poomerang rubbed one hand over his shaved head and didn't say:

"The two captains consult, then the teams start playing again. And they don't stop until the end of eternity."

Gould had an old piece of chewing gum stuck to the bottom of his jacket pocket. He found it, unstuck it from the material, and then put it in his mouth. It was cold and quite hard, like a friend from elementary school whom you haven't seen for years and run into on the street one day.

21

It was five in the morning when Shatzy got home. She hated to spend the night after she went to bed with someone. It was silly, but she always found some excuse and left.

She sat outside on the steps. It was still dark. There were strange noises, noises that you didn't hear during the day. Like bits of things that had been left behind and now were busy trying to reach the world, to arrive punctually at dawn in the belly of the planetary noise.

You always lose something along the way, she thought.

I ought to stop it, she thought.

Ending up in the bed of someone you've never seen before is like traveling. At the moment it's a lot of trouble, even a little silly. It's nice later, when you think back on it. It's nice to have done it, to go around the day after, clean and impeccable, and think about how the night before you were doing those things and saying those things, above all *saying* those things, and to someone you'll never see again.

Usually she never saw them again.

I ought to stop it, she thought.

You end up nowhere, that way.

It would all be simpler if they hadn't hammered into you this business of ending up somewhere, if they had taught you, rather, to be happy standing still. All that nonsense about your road. Finding your road. Taking your own road. Maybe we were made to live in a plaza, or a park, instead, to stay there, as our life passes, or maybe we are a crossroads, and the world needs us to stand still, it would be a disaster if, at some point, we were to go off on our road, what road?, others are roads, I am a plaza, I lead nowhere, I *am* a place. Maybe I'll join a gym, she thought. There was one nearby, which was open at night. Why do I like to do everything at night? She looked at her shoes, and her bare feet in the shoes, and her bare legs above the shoes, up to the edge of her skirt, which was short. Her stockings, which were nylon, were rolled up in her purse. She never managed to put them back on when she got out of the bed to get dressed and leave. It was like reloading your gun after a shoot-out. Stupid. What would you say about it, old Bird? Did you put your guns back in the holster unloaded after firing them? Did you roll them up and stick them in your purse? Old Bird. I'll arrange a lovely death for you.

She thought about going in and going to sleep. But in the glow of the street lamps she saw the trailer, sitting motionless in the yard, slightly less yellow than usual. Once a week she washed it thoroughly, even the windows and the tires, the whole thing. Because she had been seeing it there, every day, for months, it had become a part of the landscape, like a tree, or a bridge over a river. All of a sudden, in the dark at the end of the night, with her whore's stockings rolled up in her purse, Shatzy understood: motionless, sparkling, yellow: *it was no longer something that was waiting to leave.* It had become one of those things whose task is to remain, to anchor the roots of some piece of the world. The things that, when you wake up or come home, have been watching over you. It's strange. You go in search of some amazing contraption to have yourself transported *far* away, and then you cling to it with such love that *far,* sooner or later, comes to mean far from it.

Bullshit, it's only a matter of finding a car, she thought.

It couldn't be done without a car. Trailers don't move by themselves.

They'd find a car, that was it.

And they'd go far away.

It's like a tree, she thought. She felt something rising inside her that she didn't like, she knew it and she didn't like it, a kind of distant rumble of defeat. The secret, in this situation, was not to give it time to get out. It was to shout so loud that you couldn't hear it anymore. It was to put on a pair of black nylon stockings, leave the house, and end up in the bed of someone you've never seen before.

Already done, she thought. So she went for a version of "New York, New York" at the top of her lungs.

"Did you hear that drunk last night?" Gould said the next morning while they were making breakfast.

"No, I was sleeping."

The telephone rang. Shatzy went to get it, and it was a while before she came back. She said it was Rector Bolder. He wanted to know if Gould was all right. Gould asked if he was still on the phone.

"No. He said he didn't want to disturb you, he just wanted to know if you were all right. Then he said something about a seminar, or something like that. A seminar on particulates?"

"On particles."

"He says they had to put it off."

Gould said something that was hard to understand. Shatzy got up and put a cup of milk in the microwave.

"Is Rector Bolder fat? I mean, is he fat, or what?" Shatzy asked.

"Why?"

"He has a fat voice."

Gould closed the cereal box, then looked at Shatzy.

"What did he say exactly?"

"He says it's been twenty-two days since they've seen you at the university, and so he wanted to know if you were all right. And then he said that thing about the seminar."

"You want some more cereal?"

"No, thanks."

"If you get to two hundred boxes you win a trip to Miami."

"Splendid."

"And it took all that time just to tell you those two things?"

"Well, then I suggested some stratagems for losing weight, people usually don't know that with just a couple of tricks you can spare yourself a lot of pounds, you just have to eat with a little intelligence. I told him that."

"And what did he say?"

"I don't know, he seemed uncomfortable. He said something that didn't make sense."

"He's very thin. He must be seventy years old, and he's very thin."

"Oh."

Shatzy began to clear the table. Gould went upstairs, and came down with his jacket on. He looked for his shoes.

"Gould . . ."

"Yes?"

"I wonder . . . imagine a boy who is a genius, OK?, and who ever since he was born has been going to the university every blessed day that God puts on earth, OK?, well, at a certain point it happens that for twenty-two days in a row he leaves the house but he doesn't go to his damn university, not even once, ever, so I ask myself, do you have any idea where a boy like that might go, every blessed day?"

"Around."

"Around?"

"Around."

"It's possible. Yes, it's possible. Likely, that he goes around."

"Bye, Shatzy."

"Bye."

That morning he ended up near the Renemport school, the one that had a rusting fence all around it, high enough so that you couldn't get over it. Through the windows you could see children in class, but on the playground there was a boy who wasn't in class because he was on the playground and, to be precise, was playing with a basketball, precisely in the corner of the playground where there was a basketball net. The backboard was peeling, but the net must have been replaced recently, it was almost new. The boy was maybe twelve. Thirteen, something like that. He was black. He was dribbling the ball, confidently, as if looking for something within himself, and when he found it he stopped and took a shot at the basket. He always hit it. You could hear the sound of the net, a kind of breath, or a tiny gust of wind. The boy went over to the basket, retrieved the ball, which was coming to a stop, as if worn out from exhaling that microscopic breath, picked it up, and began dribbling again. He didn't seem sad, or happy, either, he dribbled the ball and shot at the basket, simply, as if it had been written thus, for centuries.

I *know* all that, Gould thought.

First, he recognized the rhythm. He closed his eyes so that he could hear it better. It was that rhythm.

I am seeing a thought, Gould thought.

Thoughts when they take the form of a question. They bounce, strolling around to pick up all the fragments of the question, following a course that seems random, an end in itself. When they have reconstructed the question they stop. Eyes on the basket. Silence. Lifted off the ground, intuition gives it all the strength necessary to sew up the distance to a possible response. Shoot. Fantasy and reason. In the air unrolls the logically deduced parabola of a thought sent spinning by a flick of the wrist initiated by the imagination. Basket. The statement of the response: a sort of breath. To state it is to lose it. It slips away and already it is the bouncing pieces of the next question. From the beginning.

Shatzy, the trailer, a psychiatric hospital, Prof. Taltomar's hands, the trailer, Couverney would be an honor for us to be associated with the chair of, either you watch or you play, Prof. Kilroy's tears, when Shatzy smiles, the soccer field, Couverney, Diesel and Poomerang, the railroad tracks, bam, right left, mother. Eyes on the basket. Lift. Shoot.

The black child played, and he was solitary, inevitable, and secret, like thoughts when they are true and take the form of a question.

Behind him was the appointed home of knowledge, the school, armored and separate, with its production of questions and answers in accordance with an established method, within the comfortable framework of a community intent on rounding the sharp corners of the questions, and astutely transforming into a public ritual that which, isolated, would be hyperbole, and abandoned.

Expelled from knowledge, thoughts struggle, Gould thought.

(Fellow-child, you in the emptiness of an empty playground, you and your questions, teach me that confidence, the sure movement that finds the net, the breath, at the other end of every fear.)

He walked home, his steps closely following the imaginary bounces of a hypothetical ball pushed into the emptiness by his hand; he heard it hitting the pavement, warm and regular, like heartbeats rebounding away from a quiet life. What people could see, and saw, was a boy who as he walked played with a yo-yo that wasn't there. So they stared, struck by that rhythmic glimpse of the absurd, incorporated into adolescence, as if to announce, far in advance, madness. People are afraid of madness. Gould, then, went along like a threat, although he didn't know it—without knowing it, like an attack.

He arrived home.

In the yard was a trailer. Yellow.

22

An English scholar arrived at Gould's university. He was very famous. Rector Bolder introduced him in the Great Hall. The Rector rose to his feet and, standing at the microphone, reviewed the scholar's professional life and accomplishments. It took a long time, because the English scholar had written numerous books and in addition had translated and founded and promoted, and in addition to that had been the chairman of a lot of things, or an adviser to them. Finally, he collaborated. He did that to a truly massive degree. He collaborated like a madman. So Rector Bolder had to speak for quite a while. He spoke standing, holding up the pages of the speech in his hand as he read.

Next to him, seated, was the English scholar.

It was a curious situation, because Rector Bolder was speaking of him as if he were dead, not out of rudeness but because such situations require the speaker to say things that inevitably seem to be from a eulogy, that have something funereal about them, and the odd thing is that usually the dead person is very much alive, and is sitting right there, and, contrary to every expectation, is sitting there contentedly, without protesting, although he is being subjected to this torture, and is sometimes, in fact, unaccountably enjoying it.

It was one of those times. Instead of sinking into embarrassment, the English scholar let Rector Bolder's funeral eulogy pour down on him in an utterly knowing and natural way. Although the loudspeakers of the Great Hall emitted phrases like "with driving passion and incomparable intellectual rigor" and *"last but not least,* he accepted the honorary chairmanship of the Latin Alliance, a post already endowed with," he seemed to be shielded from any embarrassment, armored, so to speak, in his own, already tested hyperbaric chamber. He stared out into space with a fixed expression, but he did so with a firm and noble determination; a slightly lifted chin supported this, along with a few wrinkles that furrowed his brow, demonstrating a serene state of concentration. At regular intervals, he clenched his jaws slightly, sharpening his profile and allowing an observer to imagine an inner vitality that had never been tamed. Every so often, the English scholar swallowed, but the way someone else might turn over an hourglass: with a graceful gesture he introduced an immobility into another immobility, sealing the impression of a patience that had been dueling with time forever, and forever winning. Altogether he presented a figure that displayed to near-perfection concentrated power and absent-minded detachment simultaneously: the first confirming the praises of Rector Bolder and the second relieving them of the weight of vulgar flattery. Wonderful. At one point, just as Rector Bolder was speaking of his pedagogical activities ("always in the midst of his students, but as *primus inter pares*"), the English scholar surpassed himself: he suddenly abandoned his hyperbaric chamber, took off his eyeglasses, inclined his head, as if overcome by an unexpected trace of weariness, brought the thumb and index finger of his right hand to his eyes and, dropping his eyelids, allowed himself a light circular pressure on the eyeballs, a most human gesture in which the entire audience could see, summed up, all the moments of pain, disillusion and difficulty that a life of successes had not eliminated, and the memory of which the English scholar now, before all, wished to share. It was lovely. Then suddenly, as if reawakening from a dream, he raised his head again, put on his glasses with a rapid but precise gesture, and returned to his perfect immobility, staring into space, with the strength of one who has known pain but has not been defeated by it.

It was precisely at this point that Prof. Mondrian Kilroy started vomiting. He was sitting in the third row, and he started vomiting.

Apart from weeping—something that he did often now and with a certain pleasure—Prof. Mondrian Kilroy had begun to vomit from time to time, and this, too, had to do with his research and in particular with an essay he had written which, oddly, he termed "the definitive and redeeming refutation of whatever I have written, write, or will write." In fact it was a very special essay. Mondrian Kilroy had worked on it for fourteen years, without ever taking a note. Then one day, when he was shut in a porn-video booth where, by pressing numbered keys, you could choose among 212 different programs, he understood that he had understood, and he left the booth, grabbed a brochure that listed the prices of the "contact room," and on the back wrote the essay. He wrote it right there, standing at the cashier's counter. It didn't take more than two minutes: the essay consisted of a series of six brief theses. The longest was no more than five lines. Then he returned to the booth, because he still had three minutes of paid-for viewing left, and he didn't want to waste them. He pushed the buttons at random. When he ended up with a gay video, he was irritated.

It may seem surprising, but the essay in question did not have to do with Prof. Mondrian Kilroy's favorite subject, that is, curved objects. No. To stick to the facts: the essay was entitled:

ESSAY ON INTELLECTUAL HONESTY

Poomerang, who was a great admirer of it and knew it practically by heart, had once summed up the contents like this:

If a bank robber goes to jail, why do intellectuals roam free?

It should be said that, with banks, Poomerang had a "suspense account" (the phrase was Shatzy's, she found it ingenious). He hated banks, even though it wasn't clear why. At one time, he had undertaken an educational campaign against the excessive use of ATM machines. Along with Diesel and Gould he was constantly chewing gum, and he would stick the gum, still warm, on the keypad of an automatic teller machine. Usually he put it on the 5. People would go up to the machine, and right as they were entering their secret code they would notice the gum. If they didn't need the number 5 they would keep going, paying careful attention to where they put their finger. If their code had a 5 they panicked. The anguished need for money had to do battle with the revulsion at the chewed gum. Some tried to remove the sticky substance; they used all types of objects. Usually they ended up plastering the whole screen. A minority gave up and left. Sad to say, most people swallowed hard and then hit the number, their finger on the gum. Once Diesel saw an unfortunate woman who had three 5s in a row in her secret code. She hit the first with great dignity, and on the second her mouth was weirdly contorted. On the third she started vomiting.

In this connection: the first thesis of the *Essay on Intellectual Honesty* went like this:

1. Men have ideas.

"Clever," remarked Shatzy.

"It's only the beginning, Miss Shell. And then, careful, it's not at all obvious. Someone like Kant, for instance, wouldn't let it pass so easily."

"Kant?"

"He's a German."

"Oh."

"Do I wash here, too?"

"Let me see."

Every so often, when they washed the trailer, Prof. Mondrian Kilroy joined them. After the business of the Vancouver purée, he and Gould had become friends. And the professor liked the others a lot, too, Shatzy, the giant and the mute. They talked while they washed. One of their favorite topics was the *Essay on Intellectual Honesty*. It engaged them.

1. Men have ideas.

Prof. Mondrian Kilroy said that ideas are like galaxies of little intuitions, a confused thing, he declared, which is continually changing and is essentially useless for practical purposes. They are beautiful, that's all, they are beautiful. But they are a mess. Ideas, in their pure state, are a marvelous mess. They are *provisional apparitions of infinity*, he said. "Clear and distinct" ideas, he added, are an invention of Descartes, are a fraud, clear ideas do not exist, ideas are obscure by definition, if you have a clear idea, it's not an idea.

"Then what is it?"

"Thesis No. 2, kids."

Thesis No. 2 went like this:

2. Men express ideas.

Here's the trouble, said Prof. Mondrian Kilroy. When you express an idea you give it a coherence that it did not originally possess. Somehow you have to give it a form that is organized, and concise, and comprehensible to others. As long as you limit yourself to thinking it, the idea can remain the marvelous mess that it is. But when you decide to express it you begin to discard one thing, to summarize something else, to simplify this and cut that, to put it in order, by imposing a certain logic: you work on it a bit, and in the end you have something that people can understand. A "clear and distinct" idea. At first you try to do this in a responsible way: you try not to throw away too much, you'd like to preserve the whole infinity of the idea you had in your head. You try. But they don't give you time, they are on you, they want to know, they attack you.

"They who?"

"The others, all the others."

"For example?"

"People. People. You express an idea and people listen. And want to understand. Or, even worse, they want to know if it's right or wrong. It's a perversion."

"What are they supposed to do? Swallow it and that's the end?"

"I don't know what they're supposed to do, but I know what they do, and for you, who had an idea, and are now trying to express it, it's like being attacked. With impressive velocity you think only of how to make it as compact and strong as possible, to withstand the attack, so that it comes out alive, and, using all your intelligence, you strive to make it an unassailable system, and the better you succeed the less you realize that what you're doing, what you're really doing at that moment, is losing touch, little by little but with impressive velocity, with the origin of your idea, with the marvelous instinctive infinite mess that was your idea, and you're doing this for the sole, sad purpose of expressing it, that is, of establishing it in such a way that it is strong and coherent and refined enough to withstand the shock wave of the surrounding world, the objections, the obtuse faces of those who don't understand, the telephone call from the head of your department who . . ."

"It's getting cold, Professor."

Often they talked about it while they ate, because Prof. Mondrian Kilroy liked pizza the way Shatzy made it, and so, especially on Saturdays, they ate pizza. Which, cold, was inedible.

2. Men express ideas.

But they are no longer ideas, Prof. Mondrian Kilroy burst out. They are the detritus of ideas, arranged in masterly fashion to become solid objects, perfect mechanisms, instruments of war.

They are artificial ideas. They have only a distant relationship with that marvelous and infinite mess in which they began, an almost imperceptible relationship, like a faint perfume. In reality they are now plastic, artificial stuff, with no relation to the truth, mere gadgets to make a good show in public. Which, according to him, led logically to Thesis No. 3. Which went like this:

3. Men express ideas that are not theirs.

"Are you joking?"

"I'm totally serious."

"How do they express ideas that are not theirs?"

"Let's say that they are *no longer* theirs. They were. But they very quickly slip out of control and become artificial creatures that develop almost autonomously, and they have a single objective: to survive. Man lends them his intelligence and they use it to become ever more solid and precise. In a certain sense, human intelligence is constantly working to dissipate the marvelous infinite chaos of original ideas and replace it with the stainless perfection of artificial ideas. They were apparitions: they are now objects: and man takes hold of them, and knows them perfectly, but would be unable to say where they came from and, finally, what possible relationship they now have to the truth. In a certain sense it doesn't even matter to him any more. They function, they withstand attack, they succeed in dissecting the weaknesses of others, they almost never break: why should he rock the boat? Man looks at them, discovers the pleasure of holding them, using them, seeing them in action. Sooner or later, inevitably, he learns that one can fight with them. He had never thought of that before. They were apparitions: he had thought only of making others see them. But in time: nothing of the original desire survives. They were apparitions: man has made them into weapons."

This was the part that Shatzy liked best. They were apparitions: man has made them into weapons.

"You know what I often think, Professor?"

"Tell me, Miss Shell."

"Gunfighters, you know, the gunfighters of the West?"

"Yes."

"Well, they were fantastic shots, and they knew everything about their guns, but if you think about it, well: none of them would have known how to make a gun. You see?"

"Go on."

"I mean: it's one thing to use a weapon, another to invent it, or produce it."

"Exactly."

"I don't know what it means, but I often think about it."

"You're doing very well, Miss Shell."

"You think so?"

"I'm absolutely certain."

On the other hand, Gould, if you think about it, look what happens in a man's head when he expresses an idea and someone standing before him raises an objection. Do you think that that man has the time, or the *honesty*, to return to the apparition that was the long-ago origin of that idea and check back, to see if the objection is reasonable? He will never do it. It is much easier to refine the artificial idea now in his possession in such a way that it can withstand the objection and maybe move to the offensive, and attack, in turn, the objection. What does respect for the truth have to do with all this? Nothing. This is a duel. They are establishing who is the stronger. They don't want to use other weapons, because they don't know how to: they use ideas. It may seem that the point of all this is to elucidate the truth, but in reality what both of them want is to establish who is the stronger. It's a duel. They may seem like brilliant intellectuals, but they are animals who are defending their territory, they are fighting over a female, they are hunting for food. Listen to me, Gould: you will never find anything more savage and more primitive than two intellectuals dueling. Anything more dishonest.

Years later, after everything was over and there was nothing to be done about it, Shatzy and Prof. Mondrian Kilroy met by chance in a train station. It was a long time since they had seen each other. They went to have a drink and talked about the university, and about what Shatzy was doing, and about the fact that the professor had stopped teaching. It was clear that he would have liked to be able to talk about Gould, and what had happened to him, but it was too difficult. At a certain point they were silent, and only then did Prof. Mondrian Kilroy say

"It's funny, but what I think about that boy is that he is the only honest person I've met, in all my life. He was an *honest* boy. Do you believe me?"

Shatzy nodded her head yes, and thought that maybe that was the heart of the matter, and that everything fell into place if only one made the effort to remember that Gould, above all else, was an *honest* genius.

Then, at the end, the professor stood up and, before he left, embraced Shatzy, a little awkwardly, but hard.

"Don't pay any attention if I cry, I'm not sad, I'm not sad for Gould."

"I know."

"It's that I often cry. That's all."

"Don't worry, Professor, I like people who cry."

"That's good."

"Seriously. I've always liked them."

They never saw each other again, after that.

Anyway, Thesis No. 3 (Men express ideas that are not theirs) was followed, with a certain logic, by Thesis No. 4. Which went like this:

4. Ideas, once they have been expressed and therefore subjected to public pressure, become artificial objects lacking a true relationship with their origin. Men refine them so ingeniously that they become lethal. In time men discover that they can be used as weapons. They don't think about it for a moment. And they fire.

"Grand," said Shatzy.

"Rather long, but it came to me long, I still have to work on it," Prof. Mondrian Kilroy declared.

"I think it could even go just like this: *Ideas: they were apparitions, now they are weapons.*"

"Perhaps a little compressed, don't you think?"

"You mean?"

"You see, it's a tragedy, a real tragedy. One must beware of summarizing it in a few words."

"A tragedy?"

The professor chewed his pizza and nodded. He really was convinced that it was a tragedy. He had even thought of giving the *Essay* a subtitle, and the subtitle would have been: *Analysis of a necessary tragedy.* Then he decided that subtitles are repulsive, like white socks or gray loafers. Only the Japanese wear gray loafers. It was possible, however, that they had eye trouble, and were absolutely convinced that their loafers were brown. In that case it would be imperative to warn them of their mistake.

You know, Gould, it's taken years to resign myself to the evidence. I didn't want to believe it. On paper the relationship with the truth is so beautiful—unique, inimitable—and the magic of ideas, magnificent apparitions of the confused infinite in your mind . . . How is it possible that men choose to renounce all that, to deny it, and agree to mess around with insignificant, artificial little ideas—little marvels of intellectual engineering, for goodness' sake—but in the end trinkets, pathetic trinkets, masterpieces of rhetoric and logical acrobatics, but trinkets, in the end, gadgets, and all this just because of an uncontrollable taste for *fighting*? I couldn't believe it, I thought there must be something behind it, something that had escaped me, and yet, in the end, I had to admit that it was all very simple, and inevitable, and even comprehensible, if only you could overcome your repugnance and look at the matter from close up, very close up, even if it disgusts you, try to see it from close up. Take a person who lives on ideas, a professional, say, a scholar, a scholar of something, OK? He must have begun out of passion, surely he began because he had talent, he was one of those who have apparitions of the infinite, let's imagine that he had had such apparitions as a young man, and was awestruck by them. He must have tried to write them down, first maybe he talked with someone, then one day he must have thought he would be able to write them, and he started out, with the best intentions, and he wrote, though he knew that he would succeed in conveying only the tiniest portion of the infinity in his head, but believing that he would have time later to deepen the discussion, to explain himself better, to set it all down properly. He writes, and people read. People he doesn't even know search him out to learn more, others invite him to conferences where they can attack him, he defends himself, expounds, corrects, attacks in turn, begins to recognize a small band that is on his side and an alliance of enemies that wants to destroy him: he begins to *exist*, Gould. He doesn't have time to realize this but he is inspired, he likes the struggle, he discovers what it means to enter a classroom under the adoring gaze of the students, he sees respect in the eyes of ordinary people, he is surprised at his desire to attract the hatred of some famous person, and in the end seeks it out, gains it, maybe three lines in a footnote in a book on something else, but they are three lines that drip with rancor, he is smart enough to quote them in an interview with some journal in the field, and a few weeks later, in a newspaper, he finds himself labeled as the adversary of the famous professor, there is even a photograph, in the paper, a picture of him, *he sees a picture of himself in a newspaper,* and many others see it, too, it's a gradual thing but with every passing day he and his artificial idea become a single entity that makes its way in the world, the idea is like the carburetor, and he is the engine, they make their way together, and it's something, Gould, that he never imagined, you must understand this clearly, he didn't expect all this to happen, he didn't even want it, in truth, but now it has happened, and he *exists* in his artificial idea, an idea that gets farther and farther away from the original apparition of the infinite, having been serviced a thousand times to stand up to attacks, an artificial idea, solid and permanent, already tested, without which the scholar would immediately cease to exist and would be swallowed up again in the swamp of ordinary existence. Put like that, it doesn't even seem too serious—to be swallowed up again in the swamp of ordinary existence—and for years I couldn't grasp the gravity of it, but the secret is to get even closer, an even closer look, I know it's revolting, but you've got to follow me there, Gould, hold your nose and come look, this scholar, this scholar had a father, look at him even closer, a harsh father, stupidly harsh, who for years was intent on crushing his son, making him feel the weight of his constant and blatant inadequacy, and he does this up until the day he sees his son's name in a newspaper, printed in a newspaper, it doesn't matter why, the fact is that his friends start saying Congratulations, I saw your son in the paper, it's revolting, right?, but he is impressed, and the son finds what he never had the power to find, that is, a belated revenge, and this is tremendous, to be able to look your father in the eye, there is no price for revenge like this, what does it mean to fool around with your ideas a little, forgetful of any connection with their origin, when you are finally able to be the son of your father, the properly authorized and approved son? No price is too high to pay for the respect of your father, believe me, nor, if you think about it, for the freedom that our scholar finds in money, his first real money, which a professorship at a second-rate university begins to put in his pockets, removing him from the daily grind of poverty and guiding him along the inclined plane of small luxuries that at last—finally, in the end—leads to the longed-for house on the hill, with study and library: a mere nothing, in theory, but tremendous, actually, when, in an article by yet another journalist, it shows up as the scholar's private refuge, where he finds a haven from the scintillating life that besieges him, a life more imaginary than not, but, as displayed against the reality of his shelter, it is true, and therefore impressed in the mind of the public, which from that moment will have a regard for the scholar that he can no longer do without, because it is a regard that, by abstaining from any sort of verification, gives, a priori, respect and eminence and impunity. You can do without it when you don't know it. But afterwards? When you have seen it in the eyes of your neighbor on the beach, and of the man who sells you a car, and of the publisher you would never even have dreamed of knowing, and of the television actress and—once, in the mountains—of the Cabinet secretary, in person? Nauseating, right? Rather, it means we're close to the heart of things. No pity, Gould. It's not the moment to give in. You can get even closer. The wife. The wife of the scholar, the girl next door since the age of twelve, he's always loved her, married her almost automatically, as a legitimate defense against the neglect of destiny, a faded, sympathetic wife without passion, a good wife, the wife now of a successful professor and his deadly artificial idea, a wife happy to the core, look at her carefully. When she wakes up. When she gets out of the bath. Look at her. The bathrobe, everything. Look at her. And then look at him, the scholar, a man on the short side, with a sad smile, flaking dandruff, not that there's anything wrong, but flaking dandruff, beautiful hands, yes, pale slender hands that unfailingly cup his chin in the photographs, beautiful hands, the rest pitiful, you must make an effort, Gould, and try to see him *naked,* a man like that, it's important to see him naked, believe me, white and soft, with flabby muscles and, in the middle of his groin, nothing to be proud of, what *chances,* in the daily struggle, can a male animal like that have for mating?, very few and very modest, no way around it, and that would be the case, in fact, if not for the artificial idea, which has transformed an animal headed for the slaughter into a fighter, and even, in the long run, the pack leader, who carries a leather briefcase and adds an artistic fake limp, and who now, if you look carefully, walks down the steps of the university and is accosted by a student, a girl, who shyly introduces herself and, talking, bumps along with him to the street and then down the slippery slope of a friendship that gets more and more intimate, it's disgusting just to think about, but so useful to contemplate, thoroughly, however revolting it may be, so useful to study, to grasp in all its details, down to the final triumph in her apartment, a rented room with a big bed and a Peruvian bedspread, he gets there, with his briefcase and his dandruff, on the excuse of correcting a bibliography, and through hours of laborious disguised courtship strips away the girl's resistance with the forceps and scalpel of his artificial idea, and, thanks to a little column that for some weeks he's had in a weekly, he finds the courage, and in a certain sense the right, to lay a hand, one of his beautiful hands, on this girl's skin, skin that no destiny would ever have allotted him but which his artificial idea now offers up, together with the unbuttoned blouse, the tongue illogically parting his thin gray lips, the feminine breath panting in his ear, and the dazzling glimpse of a tanned, beautiful young hand tight around his sex. Incredible. You think there's a price, for all this? There isn't, Gould. You think that that man would ever be able to give all this up on the mere formality of being honest, of respecting the infinity of his ideas, of going back to ask what is true and what isn't? Do you think it will ever occur to that man to wonder, even in secret, even in absolute, impenetrable solitude, if his artificial idea still has anything to do with the truth, with its origins? No. (Thesis No. 5: "Men use ideas as weapons, and in doing so they detach themselves from the ideas forever.") He is by now too far away from the point where he started, and it has been too long since he inhabited his ideas, in honesty, simplicity and peace. You can't reconstruct that sort of honesty once your betrayal of it has given you an existence, an entire existence, you who would not have been able to exist, would have gone on for years until you dropped dead. You don't give back an entire life, after stealing it from destiny, just because one day you look at yourself in the mirror and are disgusted. Our professor will die dishonest, but at least he will die having lived.

As he spoke, he became, obviously, emotional. Not that he actually cried. But glistening eyes and a catch in his throat, that sort of thing. He was made that way.

Once Poomerang asked Prof. Mondrian Kilroy why he didn't publish the *Essay on Intellectual Honesty*. He didn't say you could make a nice thick book, with a lot of blank pages, and here and there, inserted at random, the six theses. Prof. Mondrian Kilroy said it was a good idea, but he didn't think he would publish the essay, because deep down he had a suspicion that it was too naive. He found it infantile. He also said, however, that in a certain sense he liked it precisely because it was a hair's breadth away from being naive and infantile but was never that way completely; it hung, so to speak, in the balance, and this made him suspect that it was, in reality, an idea, in the full sense of the term. In the *honest* sense of the term. Then he said that, in truth, he no longer understood a damn thing. And he asked if there was any more pizza.

One thing was certain, that he was now vomiting more and more often, not because of the pizza, but whenever he got too close to various professors and intellectuals. Sometimes all it took was reading an article in the newspaper, or a book blurb. The day of the English scholar, for example, the one who stared fixedly into space, he would have liked to stay and listen, he was interested in hearing him speak and all, but it was completely impossible, in the end he had vomited, and it had been a big mess, so that afterwards he had to go and apologize to the rector and the only thing he could think of saying was to obsessively repeat the phrase "You see what a fine person he is, I'm sure he is a fine person." He was referring to the English scholar. Rector Bolder looked at him speechless. "You can see that he's a fine person, I'm sure he's a fine person." And the next day, while they were washing the trailer, he kept on with that nonsense about how the man was a fine person. To Gould it seemed ridiculous.

"If he were a fine person he wouldn't make you throw up."

"It's not that simple, Gould."

"It isn't?"

"Absolutely not."

Gould was washing the tires. More than anything else, he liked washing the tires. Black shiny soapy rubber. A pleasure.

I've thought about it, I've thought about it a lot, Gould, and with all the rigor I'm capable of, but I've come to understand that no matter how obscenely men abandon the truth, devoting themselves to the maniacal pursuit of artificial ideas with which to destroy one another, no matter how much anything that stinks of ideas nauseates me, no matter that I cannot, objectively, help throwing up at the daily display of this primitive struggle disguised as an honest search for truth—no matter how immense my disgust is, I must say: this is right, it is revoltingly right, it is simply *human,* it is what must be, it is the shit that belongs to us, the only shit that we are equal to. I came to understand this by watching the best of them. Close up, Gould, you have to have the courage to look at them from close up. I've seen them: they were revolting and right, you see what I mean? revolting but inexorably innocent, they wanted only to *exist,* can you take that away from them?, they wanted to *exist.* Consider men with high ideals, with noble ideas, men who have made their ideas a calling, who are above every suspicion. The priest. Take the priest. Not an ordinary one. The other kind, the one who is on the side of the poor, or the weak, or the excluded, the one in the old sweater and the Reeboks, he must have started out with some dazzling chaotic apparition of the infinite, something that in the dim light of youth dictated to him the imperative of taking a stand, even a suggestion of which side to stand on, and it all must have begun in honesty, but then, holy God, when you come upon him again, grown-up now and famous, Christ, famous, just to say it is disgusting, *famous,* with his name in the papers and his picture, with the telephone ringing constantly because journalists have to get his opinion, on this or that, and he answers, fucking shit, he *answers,* and joins in, and marches at the head of processions, a priest's telephone doesn't ring, Gould, let me tell you with all the necessary cruelty, you may not know it but a priest's telephone doesn't ring, because a priest's life is a desert, it is by definition a desert, a kind of protected national park, where people can look, but from a distance, he is an animal in a national park, and you're not allowed to touch him, can you imagine it, Gould?, for a priest it's a problem just to be touched, have you ever seen a priest who kisses a kid or a woman, in greeting, for no other reason, a meaningless gesture, normal, but he can't do it, because people would immediately feel a sense of unease and of imminent violence, and this is the harsh daily condition of the priest in this world, he who is a man like other men, and instead has chosen that dizzying solitude, from which there would be no exit, none, if not for an idea, maybe even a good idea, that comes from the outside and changes that landscape, restoring to him some human warmth, an idea that, used properly, refined, revised, sheltered from risky encounters with the truth, leads the priest out of his solitude, and little by little makes him the man he is now, surrounded by admiration, and by people's wish to get close to him, and even by desire in its pure state, a man in a sweater and Reeboks, who is never alone, who goes around enveloped in children and brothers, who is never lost because he is always tied to some media terminal, every so often in the crowd he fleetingly catches a woman's eye charged with desire, think what this means for him, that dizzying solitude and this explosive life, is it surprising if he is ready to *die* for his idea?, he *exists* in it, what does it mean *to die for that idea*?, he would be dead anyway if it were taken away from him, he is *saved* in that idea, and the fact that he may save hundreds and even thousands of his fellows doesn't change the point by one iota, which is that he saves himself above all, with the optional alibi of saving others, stealing from his destiny that dose of recognition and admiration and desire essential to make him alive, alive, Gould, understand this word clearly, alive, all they want is to be alive, even the best, those who establish justice, progress, freedom, the future, even for them it's all just a matter of survival, get as close as you can, if you don't believe it, see how they act, whom they have around them, look at them and try to imagine what would become of them if one day they happened to wake up and simply change their mind, what would be left of them, try to get an answer out of them, one that is not an instinctive self-justification, see if one single time you can hear them explain their idea with the wonder and hesitation of someone who is right at that moment making a discovery, and not with the assurance of someone who is proudly showing off the devastating efficacy of the weapon he is holding, don't be taken in by the apparent mildness of their tone, by the words they choose, purposefully mild, they are fighting, Gould, fighting with their teeth for survival, for food, the female, the den, they are animals, and they are the best, you see?, can you expect anything different from the others, from the petty mercenaries of intelligence, from the bit players of the great collective struggle, from the nasty little warriors who scavenge the debris of life on the edges of the battlefield, pitifully sweeping up laughable salvations, each with his artificial little idea, the top doctor in search of funds for his son's college education, the critic who alleviates neglect in his old age with forty lines a week brought out where they can make a little stir, the scientist and his Vancouver purée, with which he feeds the pride of wife, children, lovers, the pathetic appearances on television of the writer who is afraid of disappearing between one book and the next, the journalist who takes a stab at anything to make the front page, to be sure of existing for another twenty-four hours—they are only struggling, you see?, they fight with ideas because they don't know how to use anything else, but the substance doesn't change, it is a fight, and their ideas are weapons, and, sickening as it is to admit, it is their right, their dishonesty is the logical deduction from a primal need, their disgusting daily betrayal of the truth is the natural consequence of a natural state of acknowledged deprivation, you don't ask a blind man to go to the movies, you don't ask an intellectual to be honest, at least I don't think you can, although it's depressing to admit it, but the very concept of intellectual honesty is an oxymoron

6. Intellectual honesty is an oxymoron.

or, rather, a highly prohibitive and perhaps inhuman task, since no one, in practice, would even dream of undertaking it, being content, in the more admirable cases, to do things with a certain style, a certain dignity, let's say with good taste, that's it, the exact term would be with good taste, in the end you feel like saving the ones who at least manage to do things with good taste, with modesty, who don't seem proud of the shit that they are, not so proud, not so damn proud, not so shamelessly, arrogantly proud. God, how sickening.

"Something wrong, Professor?"

"I was wondering . . ."

"What, Professor."

"What, exactly, am I washing?"

"A trailer."

"I mean: what, precisely, is the role of this yellow object in your ecosystem?"

"For now, the function of this yellow object in our ecosystem is to wait for a car."

"A car?"

"A trailer can't go anywhere without a car."

"This is true."

"Do you have a car, Professor?"

"I had one."

"Too bad."

"To be precise, my brother had one."

"It happens."

"Having a brother?"

"That, too."

"In fact it happened to me three times. And you?"

"No, it never happened to me."

"I'm sorry."

"Why?"

"Hand me the sponge, please."

They talked. They enjoyed it.

Once Gould, Diesel and Poomerang stopped because they had a game to watch, down on the field.

Professor Mondrian Kilroy and Shatzy stayed. They washed everything thoroughly and then they sat on the front steps, looking at the yellow trailer.

They talked.

At one point Professor Mondrian Kilroy said it was strange but he would sadly miss that boy. He meant that he would sadly miss Gould. Then Shatzy said that if he wanted he could come, too, the trailer was small but they would figure something out. Prof. Mondrian Kilroy turned to look at her and then asked if they really intended to go all the way to Couverney in the trailer, and if all of them were going. To which Shatzy said

"Couverney?"

"Couverney."

"What does Couverney have to do with it?"

"What do you mean, what does it have to do with it?"

"What are we talking about, Professor?"

"About Gould."

"So then what does Couverney have to do with it?"

"It's Gould's university, isn't it? Gould's new university. A place where your blood freezes, by the way."

"They *asked* Gould to go to Couverney, they only *asked* him."

"They asked him and he's going."

"As far as I know, he doesn't know that."

"As far as I know, he knows it perfectly well."

"Since when?"

"He told me. He decided to go. He starts in September."

"*When* did he tell you?"

Prof. Mondrian Kilroy thought for a while.

"I don't know. A few weeks ago, I think. I'm never very clear on when things happen. Isn't it ever like that for you?"

"..."

"Miss Shell ..."

"..."

"Do you always know when something happened?"

"..."

"Yes, I'm only asking out of curiosity."

"Did Gould *really* tell you he's going to Couverney, Professor?"

"Yes, I'm certain of it, and he also told Rector Bolder; you know, he would like to have a goodbye party, or something like that, and Gould would prefer to avoid it, he says it would be ..."

"What the hell does he mean by a *goodbye party*?"

"It's only an idea, an idea of Rector Bolder's, he is a man who appears to be hard and inflexible but a sensitive soul is hidden inside, I would almost say ..."

"Have you all lost your minds?"

"... I would almost say ..."

"Jesus, that boy is fifteen years old, Professor, Couverney is a place for grown-ups, a person isn't grown-up when he's fifteen, he is when he's twenty, if a person is twenty he's grown-up and then maybe, if he really wants to throw his life in the toilet, he can consider the curious possibility of going to bury himself in a den of ..."

"Miss Shell, may I remind you that that boy is a genius, not a ..."

"But who the hell said so?, I'd like to know who said so? I would like to know how it is that you all decided point-blank that a boy like that is a genius, a boy who has seen nothing but your goddam classrooms and the road that leads to them, a genius who wets his bed at night and is afraid if someone on the street asks him what time it is, and hasn't seen his mother for years and listens to his father Friday night on the telephone, and will never go up to a girl even to pray to her in Arabic—what score does all this add up to? I imagine that it adds up to a fantastic score in the special category of geniuses, too bad he doesn't stutter, that would make him nearly unbeatable ..."

"Miss Shell, you shouldn't . . ."

"Of course I should, if all the professors like you insist on keeping their brains pickled in the brine of . . ."

". . . you shouldn't at all . . ."

". . . of their self-love, convinced that they have found the goose with the golden eggs and have become so completely . . ."

". . . Miss Shell, I invite you to . . ."

". . . completely besotted by this business of the Nobel, because—let's speak plainly—that's what you're aiming at, you and . . ."

"WILL YOU PLEASE CLOSE THAT SHIT-FILLED MOUTH OF YOURS?"

"I'm sorry?"

"I asked you if you would please close that shit-filled mouth of yours."

"Yes."

"Thank you."

"You're welcome."

". . ."

". . ."

". . ."

". . ."

"Miss Shell, it is an unfortunate situation, I agree, but that boy is a genius. Believe me."

". . ."

"I would like to add one more thing. Birds fly. Geniuses go to universities. Although it may seem banal, that's the way it is. I've finished."

Months later, the day before she left, Shatzy went to say good-bye to Professor Mondrian Kilroy. Gould had already been gone for a while. The professor went around in slippers and continued to vomit. It was clear that he was sorry to see them all leave, but he wasn't the type to be weighed down by things. He had a formidable capacity to accept the necessity of events, as they happened. He spoke a lot of nonsense to Shatzy, and some of it even made her laugh. At the end, he took something from a drawer and gave it to Shatzy. It was the brochure with the prices of the "contact room." On the back was the *Essay on Intellectual Honesty.*

"I would very much like you to keep this, Miss Shell."

There were the six theses, one written under the other, in block letters, on a slight slant, but in orderly fashion. Under the last there was a note, written with a different pen, and in script. It didn't have a number in front of it, nothing. It went like this:

In another life, we will be honest. We will be able to be silent.

It was the passage that made Poomerang literally freak out. It was the thing that made him crazy. He never stopped repeating it. He didn't say it to everyone, as if it were his name.

Shatzy took the brochure. She folded it in two and put it in her pocket. Then she embraced the professor and the two of them performed some of those actions that put together are called goodbye. A goodbye.

For years afterward, Shatzy carried with her that yellow brochure, folded in four; she always carried it with her, in her bag, the one that said *Save the Planet Earth from Painted Toenails.* Every so often she reread the six theses, and also the postscript, and heard the voice of Prof. Mondrian Kilroy, who was explaining and becoming emotional, and asking for more pizza. Every so often she had the desire to get someone to read it, but the truth was that she never met anyone who was still innocent enough to understand any of it. Sometimes people were intelligent, and all, smart. But it was clear that it was too late to bring them back, to ask them, even for a moment, to come home.

She ended up losing the yellow brochure and the entire *Essay on Intellectual Dishonesty,* when, early one morning, at the house of a doctor, while she was trying to sneak away and couldn't find her black stockings, she turned the bag upside down. It made a big mess and while she was putting everything back in he woke up, so she had to say something silly, and was distracted, and went away as usual, and the yellow brochure stayed there.

It was too bad. Really.

On the other side, where the prices for the "contact room" were printed, there was a whole list of services, and the last, the most expensive, was called "Crossing contact."

It remained one of the things that Shatzy never understood: what in the world was a "Crossing contact"?

23

"At the microphone is Stanley Poreda, we're here with him in the gym where he is training for his upcoming bout with Larry 'Lawyer' Gorman, scheduled for eight rounds, on Saturday the 12th. So, Poreda . . . confident?"

"Very."

"A lot of rumors are circulating on the subject of your return to the ring . . ."

"People like to talk."

"They're wondering why a fighter whose career was over has decided after two years . . ."

"Two years and three months."

". . . two years and three months, an eternity, if you like, people wonder why a fighter who was finished with professional boxing . . ."

"People wonder about fucking stupid things."

"Surely Poreda means to say that . . ."

"Poreda means to say that they are fucking stupid questions,

I'm coming back for the money, why else? Boxing has hurt me, you can see my arms, they're a mess, I made so many punches my arms are mangled, that's what boxing did for me, but it's the only thing I know how to do and if someone's giving me money, a lot of it, I come back, and . . . what was the fucking question?"

"People are saying the fight is fixed."

"Who says that?"

"It's been in the papers. And the bookmakers say they won't take bets until the night before the match. Not even they get the picture."

"And when do they ever get the picture, I've enjoyed screwing them for years, they never get it, they've lost more money on my fights than my ex-wife's bills . . ."

"You mean to say it's a clean fight?"

". . . you know my ex-wife, right?, she was a money pit, it was impressive, she was always saying she didn't have enough money for clothes, I didn't believe her, I left her saying it, but she insisted, she didn't have enough money for clothes, well, I had to believe it when I saw the pictures of her in *Playboy* . . ."

"Will it be a clean fight, Poreda?"

". . . in *Playboy*, get it? . . ."

"You don't want to answer?"

"Listen, fag: boxing *isn't* clean. And this fucking fight won't be. Expect it to be dirty. Blood and shit. Listen, you little faggot: I bring the shit. Lawyer has the blood. OK?"

Gould got up, flushed, pulled up his pajama pants, glanced in the mirror over the sink, then opened the door and went out. Shatzy was sitting at the top of the stairs. She had her back to him and didn't turn around even when she started talking. She didn't turn around once, all the way to the end.

"OK, Gould, let's make it short so no one gets mad, you're going to Couverney, I didn't know, now I know, and it doesn't matter how I found out, anyway Professor Kilroy told me, he—although in a certain sense he's a fine person—he talks just a little too much, he likes to gossip, but you shouldn't be mad at him, since sooner or later I would have found out just the same, maybe you would have sent me a telegram, or something like that, I'm sure it would have crossed your mind, at Christmas, let's say, or after a reasonable number of weeks, I know you would have told me, you'd just need time to get settled, of course, it must not be easy to show up like a parachutist in a war zone dominated by neurotic and potentially impotent brains, surrounded by colleagues who pay to study whereas you are paid to study, however hard you try to be pleasant it's predictable that you'll find a certain aversion to big smiles and pats on the back, among other things you have to explain all this stuff like how you don't play on the soccer team, you're not in the chorus, you don't go to the dance at the end of the year, you don't go to church, you're petrified by anything that is or appears to be an association or a club or anything that requires meetings, and, on top of that, smoking doesn't appeal to you, you don't collect anything, you couldn't care less about kissing girls, you don't like cars, and they will end up asking you what the fuck you do in your free time, and it won't be easy to explain to them that you go around with a giant and a mute sticking chewing gum in ATM machines, I mean it won't be easy for them to absorb, you can always try telling them that you watch soccer games because the mute missed a move he saw years ago and has to find it again, this is slightly more reasonable, they might even let it pass, I'd be for keeping to generalities, though, a good answer might be I don't have any free time, play the hateful genius, but since it's what they'll want to think about you, that you're a hateful genius, you could be Oliver Hardy and they would still think you're hateful—they *need* to think it, it soothes them—and above all presumptuous, to them you will always be presumptuous, even if you go around saying Excuse me all the time, excuse me excuse me excuse me, to them you will always be presumptuous, it's their way of turning the tables, mediocrities don't know they're mediocre, that's a fact, since by definition mediocrities lack the imagination to see that someone might be better than they are, and so anyone who is better must have something wrong with him, or he cheated somewhere, or must be a lunatic who imagines that he's better, and that is presumptuous, as they will certainly let you know very quickly and in ways that are none too pleasant, and even cruel, at times, this is typical of mediocrities, to be cruel, cruelty is the virtue par excellence of mediocrities, they need to practice cruelty, it's an activity that doesn't require the least intelligence, which is helpful, obviously, and makes it easy for them, makes them excel, so to speak, in that activity which consists of being cruel, whenever they can, and therefore often, more often than you might expect, since they'll surprise you, this is inevitable, their cruelty will stab you in the back, probably it will happen like that, it will stab you in the back, and then it won't be easy at all, it's better for you to know it now, if you still don't see, they'll stab you in the back, I have never really survived anything that stabbed me in the back, and I know there's no way, finally, to defend yourself from what comes at you from behind, there's nothing to do about it, just continue on your way, trying not to fall, or stop, since no one is so stupid as to think that he can get anywhere except by staggering, picking up wounds from every direction, and in particular from behind, it will be like that for you, too, especially for you, if you like, since you won't get this curious idea out of your head, this fucking stupid idea, of walking in front of everyone else, on a road that I don't want to say but, school and all that, the Nobel, that business, you can't claim that I really understand it, if it were up to me I'd tie you to the toilet bowl until it passes you by, but on the other hand I'm not the most suitable person to understand, I've never had this thing of walking in front of everyone else, I don't know, and then school was always a failure, without exception, so naturally I don't understand anything, even if I make an effort, all that comes to mind is the stuff about rivers, if I want to find some way to digest all this stuff, I end up thinking about rivers, and about the fact that people began to study them because it didn't make sense this business about how a river takes so long to reach the sea—that is, it chooses, deliberately, to make a lot of curves, instead of aiming directly at its goal, and you have to admit there's something absurd, and this is precisely what people thought, there's something absurd in all those curves, and so they started studying the matter, and what they discovered, incredibly, is that any river, it doesn't matter where it is or how long, any river, just any river, to get to the sea takes a route exactly three times as long as the one it would take if it went straight, which is astonishing, if you think about it, that it takes three times as long as necessary, and all on account of curves, on account of the stratagem of curves, and not this river or that river but all rivers, as if it were required, a kind of rule that's the same for all, which is unbelievable, really, nuts, but it was discovered with scientific certainty through studies of rivers, all rivers, it was discovered that they are not crazy, it is their nature as rivers which constrains them to that continuous, and even precise, winding, since all, and I mean all, navigate a route three times as long as necessary—three point one four times, to be exact, I swear, the famous Greek pi, I didn't want to believe it, but it seems that it really is true, you take the distance from the sea, multiply it by pi, and you have the length of the route, which, I thought, is really great, because, I thought, there's a rule for them, can it be that there isn't for us—I mean, the least you can expect is that it's more or less the same for us, and that all this sliding to one side and then the other, as if we were crazy or, worse, lost, is actually our way of going straight, scientifically exact and, so to speak, predetermined, although it undoubtedly resembles a random series of errors, or rethinkings, but only in appearance, because really it's just our way of going where we have to go, the way that is specifically ours, our nature, so to speak—what was I saying?, oh yes, that business of the rivers, if you think about it, it's reassuring, I find it very reassuring, that there is an objective principle behind all the stupid things we do, it's been reassuring, ever since I decided to believe in it, and then, lo and behold—what I meant is that it hurts me to see you navigate revolting curves like Couverney, but even if every time I had to go and look at a river, every time, to remind myself, I will always think it's right, and that you are right to go, although just saying so makes my head feel like it's splitting, but I want you to go, and I'm happy that you're going, you're a strong river, you won't get lost, it doesn't matter if I wouldn't go there, not even dead, it's just that we're different rivers, I guess, I must be another model of river, in fact if I think about it I feel like more than a river, I mean, it may be that I'm a lake, I don't know if you understand, maybe some of us are rivers and others are lakes, I'm a lake, I don't know, something like a lake, once I went swimming in a lake, it was very strange because you see that you're moving forwards, I mean, it's all so flat that when you swim you realize you're moving forwards, it's a strange sensation, and then there were a lot of insects, and if you put your feet down, near the shore, where you could touch, if you put your feet down it was really disgusting, like greasy sand, you would never have known from the surface, a kind of greasy, oily sand, disgusting, really, anyway I only meant to say two things, the first is that if they try to hurt you I'll come there and put up a high-tension wire and hang them by the balls, yes, by the balls, and the second is that I'll miss you, that is, I'll miss your strength, it doesn't matter if you don't understand it now, maybe you'll understand later, I'll miss your strength, Gould, you strange little boy, your strength, goddam fucking shit.

Pause.

"Do you know what on earth time it is?"

"No, I don't. It's dark."

"Go to sleep, Gould. It's late, go to sleep."

24

It was all so sudden and, in a certain sense, *natural*.

That morning Gould had gone back down to Renemport, the school—it had occurred to him that he might see that black kid again, with his basketball, and all the rest—to be precise, he *felt* that he was there, he had awakened with the *certainty* that he was there.

It took a while, then he got to Renemport. Maybe it was recess, or some holiday or the last day of something. The fact is that the playground was overflowing with boys and girls and they were all playing, making a noise that sounded like an aviary, but an aviary where someone was shooting invisible silent bullets, fiercely and with very bad aim.

There were a lot of balls, of all sizes, which bounced around and set off geometries against feet, hands, book bags and walls.

The school, behind the great aviary, seemed empty.

There was no sign of the black kid. Every so often someone shot at the basket. But almost no one made it.

Gould sat down on a bench near the street, a dozen yards from the school fence. The street ran behind him—grazed by speeding cars and trucks. In front of him there was some grass and then the rusty iron mesh, extending upwards, and finally the playground full of children. There was no rhythm in all that, no order, or center, so that it was difficult *to think* there, in a sense impossible—to have thoughts. So Gould took off his jacket, laid it over the back of the bench, and sat there, not thinking.

The sun was high in the sky.

The ball went over the fence, not by much, a few inches, no more. It landed on the grass, bounced a few yards from Gould and rolled towards the street. It was black and white, a soccer ball.

Gould was not thinking. Instinctively his eyes followed the parabola of the ball, watched it bounce on the grass and disappear behind him, in the direction of the street. He went back to not thinking.

A voice pierced the confusion, shouting

"Ball!"

It was a girl. She was leaning against the fence with her fingers hooked around the rusty iron links.

"Hey, throw me the ball?"

Years of study with Prof. Taltomar had taught Gould not to feel the slightest embarrassment. He sat staring straight ahead, back to not thinking.

"Hey there, will you throw me that ball, hey, I'm talking to you, are you deaf?"

It went on for a while, with the girl shouting and Gould staring straight ahead.

Minutes.

Then the girl got fed up, abandoned the fence, and went back to her game.

Gould watched her run over to another girl, taller than she was, and then disappear somewhere in the great animal pen of children and balls and shouts and happiness. He focused on the fence where moments earlier her hands had been, and imagined the rust, on his palms and in the creases of his fingers.

Then he got up. He turned around and looked until he saw the black-and-white ball on the other side of the street, stopped at the edge of the sidewalk, spinning with the dust swirled up by the speeding cars.

It was all so sudden and, in a certain sense, *natural*.

The bus driver saw the boy from a distance, but didn't think he would actually cross the street. He thought he would at least turn his head, would see the bus and stop. Instead the boy walked into the street without looking, as if he were in the driveway of his own house. Instinctively the bus driver pressed the brake pedal, gripping the steering wheel in his hands and leaning back into the seat. The bus began to skid, its rear heading toward the center of the street. The boy kept walking, looking at something in front of him. The driver let up a little on the brake so that he could regain control of the bus, saw the few feet he had to go, and thought that he was killing a boy. He swerved violently to the right. He heard the shouts of passengers thrown forward from the seat behind him. He saw the side of the bus pass a few feet, no more than a few feet, from the boy, and felt under his hands the friction of the tires scraping the curb.

Gould reached the other side of the street, bent over, and picked up the ball. He turned, looked to see if any cars were coming, then crossed the street again. A bus had come to a halt there, slightly angled against the sidewalk: it was honking its horn madly. Gould thought it was saying hello to someone. He stepped up onto the grass and got to the bench. He looked at the fence, at how high it was. Then he looked at the ball. On it was written *Maracaná*. He had never seen a ball so close up. In fact he had never even touched a ball.

He glanced at the fence again. He knew the move, he had seen it a thousand times. He went through it mentally, wondering if he would ever manage to transmit it to all the parts of the body that were needed. It seemed unlikely. But it was so clearly necessary, that he make the attempt. He went through it all carefully, in order. The sequence of moves wasn't complicated. You had to get up speed, that would be difficult, synchronize the timing, and put all the pieces together into a single movement, without interruption. You couldn't stop halfway through, it was clear. It had to be a thing that began and ended, without your getting lost on the way. Like the refrain of a song, he thought. The children, on the other side of the fence, were still shouting. Sing, Gould. Anyway, go on to the end, it's the moment to sing.

The bus driver's legs were trembling, but he climbed out and, leaving the door open, headed towards that idiotic boy, who was standing there motionless, staring at the ball he was holding in his hand. He must be a real imbecile. The driver was about to shout to him, when finally he saw him move: he saw him raise the ball in the air, with his left hand, and then send it into flight with his right foot, nailing it over the fence into the school playground. Just look at this imbecile, he thought.

The curve of black-and-white leather meets in the air the catapult of foot leg calf, inner right instep, perfect soft impact that goes back along the flesh to the brain—pure pleasure—while the body rotates around the matador's flag of the left leg intent on keeping its balance during the rotation in order to restore it to the right leg as soon as it touches earth again, returning from the great flight with a thud, keeping the body from rolling forwards while the eyes instinctively look up to see the ball that is scaling fences and doubts, rolling out in the sky a trajectory like a rainbow in black and white.

"Yes," Gould said softly. It was the answer to a whole lot of questions.

The bus driver came up a few feet away from the boy. His legs were still shaky. He was angry.

"Are you completely out of your mind or what?, hey you, what is it, are you nuts?"

The boy turned to look at him.

"Not anymore, sir."

He said.

25

"Hello?"

"Hello."

"Who is it?"

"It's Shatzy Shell."

"Oh, it's you."

"Yes, it's me, General."

"Everything all right down there?"

"Not exactly."

"Good."

"I said: not exactly."

"I beg your pardon?"

"I called to tell you that there's a problem."

"The fact is, you did telephone me. Why?"

"To tell you there's a problem."

"Problem?"

"Yes."

"Nothing serious, I hope."

"It depends."

"It's not the moment, you know?, to have serious problems."

"I'm sorry."

"It's just not the moment."

"Will you listen to me?"

"Of course, Miss Shell."

"Gould has disappeared."

"Miss Shell . . ."

"Yes?"

"Gould left for Couverney."

"That's true."

"That's not the same as *disappeared*."

"True."

"He only left for Couverney."

"Yes, but he never got there."

"Are you sure?"

"Very sure."

"And where on earth did he go?"

"I don't know. I think he decided to disappear."

"Pardon?"

"He's gone, General, Gould is gone."

"Something must have happened to him, did you call the university, the police, did you telephone everywhere?"

"No."

"You must do so immediately, Miss Shell, call me back in five minutes, I'll take care of everything, in fact I'll call you back, in five minutes . . ."

"General . . ."

"Don't lose your head."

"I'm not losing my head, I'd just like you to listen to me."

"I am listening to you."

"Don't do anything, please."

"What on earth are you saying?"

"Listen to me, don't do anything, don't say anything to anyone, and, please, come here."

"Me, come there?"

"Yes, I'd like you to come here."

"Don't talk nonsense, Gould must be found, there's no point in my coming there, will you please do me the favor of . . ."

"General . . ."

"Yes."

"Trust me. Take one of your airplanes, or whatever, and come here."

" . . . "

" . . . "

" . . . "

"Believe me, it's the only useful thing you can do. Come here."

" . . . "

"Then I'll expect you."

" . . . "

"General?"

"Yes?"

"Thank you."

26

Somebody lights a cigarette—maximum volume, noise of feverish tobacco, loud as the crumpling of a mile-long sheet of paper—his cheeks hollowing as they suck in the smoke, cheeks beneath eyes like oysters floating in a ruddy face that turns to the woman beside him, a blonde who laughs with a hoarse strong laugh like a promise of bed which bathes the minds of the men packed in, each in his place, within a ten-yard radius, and little by little fades over men and women sitting in close rows, bodies touching, minds speeding, rows and rows that descend gradually from the top, penetrating the air pierced by waves of rock music expelled from giant speakers, by shouts that rising up call out names from one side of the arena to the other, traveling through the mottled light and FLASH bulbs, among the odors of tobacco, expensive perfume, aftershave, armpits, leather jackets, popcorn, advancing in the big collective roar, lap belly of millions of words, excited foolish dirty drunk of love that swarm like worms over that earth of bodies and minds, that plowed field of lined-up heads, sloping down concentrically, inevitably, towards the dazzling well that at the center of it all concentrates eyes fears blood pressures, focusing on the blue of the carpet where a red legend shouts out PONTIAC HOTEL and will do so throughout the excitement of this night, God bless it, now that it has finally arrived, coming from afar and riding up to

... here in the ring at the Pontiac Hotel, where at the Radio KKJ microphone Dan De Palma welcomes you to this marvelous night of boxing. Everything ready here FLASH for the challenge which has inspired rivers of ink and thousands of bets, a challenge that Mondini wanted desperately, and achieved, perhaps even against the wishes of his favorite FLASH of course between the general surprise FLASH and the skepticism of the media, skepticism that, we must say, has been transformed into an agonizing wait, to judge from the size of the crowd and the tension that you can breathe FLASH here beside the ring, where it's only a few seconds now to the start of the match FLASH the referee will be Ramón Gonzales of Mexico, we have 8,243 paying spectators, twelve radio feeds, in the red corner FLASH in white shorts with gold trim, thirty-three years old, fifty-seven fights, forty-one wins FLASH fourteen losses, two ties, twelve years in the ring, twice challenger for the world championship, retired two years and three months ago in the ring at Atlantic City, a controversial fighter, loved and hated FLASH bookmakers' nightmare, a lefty, a formidable boxer, a fighter of rare power, Stanleeeeeey "Hooooooooooooker" Poreeeeeeeeeda FLASH in the blue corner, black shorts, twenty-two years old, twenty-one fights, twenty-one wins, twenty-one inside the distance FLASH and knocked to the canvas only once, one of the hopes of championship boxing, boxes both orthodox and southpaw FLASH he can move FLASH in dizzying rhythms, he's got spectacular agility, young, unpredictable, arrogant FLASH hateful, the kid who maybe in a few years we'll call the greatest, Larrryyyyyyy "Laaaaaaaaawyer" Gooooooooorman

(feel Mondini's fingers moving up and down my neck loosening the knots of fear, I'm not scared Maestro, but do it anyway, it feels good)

"Don't be in a hurry, just forget the bullshit, Larry."

"Right."

"Back up, watch out for his head."

"Right."

"Do the easy things and you won't have any problems."

"You promised, Maestro."

"Yes, I promised."

"I win and you take me to the world championship."

"Think about the fight, stupid."

"You'll like it, you'll see, the world championship."

"Fuck you, Larry."

"Fuck."

BOX cries referee Gonzales, and it's on, Poreda takes the center of the ring, Lawyer uses the right defense, moves around Poreda . . . Poreda goes with a very close defense, with his gloves together in front of his face, he prefers to leave his body exposed, blank gaze and . . . fierce behind the red gloves, he is apparently the FLASH Poreda of old, not pretty but like a rock . . . solid, Lawyer flies around him, keeps changing direction FLASH very loose, for now he's using his legs, doesn't even throw a jab . . . the two seem to be studying each other, feint by Lawyer FLASH another feint . . . Poreda doesn't work much with his legs but seems agile enough with his body, another feint, and again from Lawyer FLASH Poreda doesn't back up, he keeps to small upper-body movements . . . there still hasn't been a single punch, a very cautious start on the part of the (you're so ugly, Poreda, hasn't anyone ever told you?, he doesn't have legs, either he's pretending not to or he doesn't have the legs anymore, with those he can't get away, and hit him on the arms, I ought to hit there, are the arms broken or not?, yes they are son of a bitch and so) *USE THE JAB, LARRY, THE JAB, IN THE AIR, LIKE THIS* very graceful around the center of the ring, but Lawyer doesn't draw punches, he seems to mock his opponent FLASH typical of Lawyer, though, he likes to put on a show . . . even too much some of his detractors say (is this what you want, huh, Poreda?, want me to get tired out running around you, beautifully, while you wait there for the right moment to screw me, you think I fell for it, huh, fine, end of the show, it was just for) FLASH FLASH RIGHT FROM POREDA an unexpected right hook FLASH not even prepared, but he took Lawyer by surprise, got him in the face, the tension rises here at the Pontiac Hotel (fucking bastard) LARRY, WHERE THE FUCK ARE YOU? (I'm here, I'm here, Maestro, OK, end of the dance, you bastard) feint from Lawyer, another feint, changes defense, jab ANOTHER JAB, AND LEFT HOOK FLASH POREDA SWEPT AWAY FROM THE FLASH CENTER OF THE RING, Poreda on the ropes, LAWYER, FLASH TWO-HAND COMBINATION, IMPRESSIVE SERIES FLASH TO THE BODY FLASH Poreda doesn't lower his hands, he protects his face FLASH Lawyer hits then regains his distance, now he goes down, keeps hitting his body GET THE FUCK OUT OF THERE, Lawyer back and then forward again, Poreda still on the ropes, Lawyer with two hands, Poreda's body sways, he doesn't come out of his defense, OUT OF THERE, Lawyer perseveres, UPPERCUT FROM POREDA, AND HOOK, RIGHT HOOK TO THE FACE, LAWYER STAGGERS, POREDA GOES TO THE CLINCH, MOUTHPIECE FLIES, LAWYER'S MOUTHPIECE HAS FALLEN OUT, REFEREE INTERVENES, that powerful hook from Poreda shook Lawyer's head, tore out his mouthpiece, the referee picks it up, now hands it to Lawyer's cornermen, Lawyer can breathe, he seems to have really felt Poreda's one-two, Poreda seemed trapped on the defensive, then with an uppercut he surprised Lawyer, hitting him again right away, great timing, Lawyer puts back the mouthpiece, BOX, they start again, there's blood on Lawyer's face, maybe a little cut above the eyebrow, the two fighters are studying each other again, rather, it seems to be a cut on his mouth, a lot of blood right now, dripping down Lawyer's neck, maybe the referee should THIRTY SECONDS, LARRY (OK, thirty seconds, stay cool and) THIRTY SECONDS, GET

AWAY, LET THEM GO, THIRTY SECONDS it's Lawyer now who's looking for the ropes, Poreda presses him but cautiously, he moves in close, in his characteristic position, head forward between his shoulders, Lawyer tries to push him back with the jab, the referee stops, warning to Poreda for low head, fight resumes, GONG, end of the first round, a round that passed practically in a single flash, action that

"He's a son of a bitch."

"Let me see."

"He did it with his elbow . . . the elbow right in the mouth as soon as he saw the mouthpiece gone, fucking . . ."

"Shut up and let me see."

". . ."

"OK, WATER, GET THAT WATER OVER HERE . . ."

"It hurts, Maestro."

"Don't talk crap."

"My mouth is . . ."

"SHUT IT and listen to me. LARRY!"

"Yes."

"Start again from the beginning. Forget everything, start again, as if it were the first round . . . no hurry and a clear head, OK? It's all like before, you're stronger, you're confident, get up there and do your job, that's it."

"How many did he screw me out of?"

"Two or three, nothing serious."

"TWO OR THREE?"

"I have the number of a good dentist, no problem. Get up, come on, breathe, are you thirsty?"

"I'll kill that great big son of a bitch, I swear I'll . . ."

"LARRY, GOD DAMN IT, NOTHING HAPPENED, START AGAIN FROM THE BEGINNING, DO YOU UNDERSTAND OR NOT, FROM THE BEGINNING, everything from the beginning, nothing happened, clear head, Larry . . ."

"OK, OK."

"First round, right?"

"First round."

"Nothing's happened."

"OK."

"You know something, you're missing three teeth, there in the front."

"Baseball bat, years ago."

"OK, fuck you, Larry."

"Fuck."

Second round here in the ring at the Pontiac Hotel, we're live for the listeners of Radio KKJ, Larry "Lawyer" Gorman took an ugly blow to the mouth, he now holds the center of the ring . . . Poreda not too quick on his legs, but keeps his arms up and ready to strike, straight right from Lawyer, again a straight, Poreda doesn't lower his arms, Lawyer moves around him, seems to be looking for the HARD JAB, FOLLOWED BY ANOTHER JAB AND HOOK TO THE BODY, POREDA ON THE ROPES, Poreda in the corner, moves out on the left, Lawyer doesn't stop him (pay attention to the head, and the uppercut, he'll certainly try that again) Poreda again in the corner, tries an uppercut, misses, Lawyer works him on the body, quick punches to the ribs, Poreda still protecting his face, bends his body, tries to go out on the right, DOWN, POREDA DOWN HAS SET ONE KNEE DOWN (what are you doing you bastard?) THE REFEREE PUSHES LAWYER AWAY, IT WAS PROBABLY A PUNCH TO THE LIVER, A PUNCH AT CLOSE RANGE, POREDA'S RIGHT LEG BUCKLES, AS IF BROKEN IN TWO, NOW POREDA GETS UP, breathing hard while referee Gonzales counts, he seems lucid, nods his head that everything is all right LARRY! (eyes the same as before, nothing happened, it's a trap) LARRY LEAVE HIM ALONE! (I understand, Maestro, I know, I'm not going in there, I'm not going there, I'm dancing now, hey?, a little dancing will do him good) while Lawyer moves around him, changing direction, he seems to have no intention of attacking, or maybe he's waiting for the moment . . . Poreda moves in, Lawyer isn't there, he backs up, he slips away gracefully to the right, moves around Poreda, now he changes direction, Poreda tries again to shorten up, Lawyer leans on the ropes, hook from BUT IT'S A STRAIGHT COUNTER FROM LAWYER AND POREDA STAGGERS, STILL UP, LAWYER WITH TWO HANDS, POREDA IN TROUBLE, POREDA, POREDA LANDS A HOOK, ANOTHER, NOW HE'S THE ONE PUNCHING, A VIOLENT EXCHANGE, LAWYER TAKES ONE, LEANS ON THE ROPES (where the fuck) AGAIN POREDA ON THE ATTACK, *OUT OF THERE LARRY,* POREDA AIMS LOW AND THEN WITH A HOOK MISSES *WILL YOU GET OUT OF THERE LARRY?* (when he breathes) POREDA KEEPS GOING, GAP CLOSING, LAWYER TRAPPED AT THE ROPES, POREDA, POREDA LARRY! (when he breathes) POREDA LANDS THE RIGHT, AGAIN WITH THE RIGHT, MISSES THIS TIME, POREDA LETS GO, two steps back (go on) LAWYER LIKE A CATAPULT, STRAIGHT RIGHT, STRAIGHT AGAIN, POREDA IN THE CENTER OF THE RING, CURLED OVER, SAVAGE HOOK FROM LAWYER, POREDA STAGGERS, LOOKS FOR THE ROPES (the hook, he doesn't see the hook), POREDA ON THE ROPES, LAWYER KEEPS HIS DISTANCE, SEARCHING FOR AN OPENING, POREDA'S BODY SWAYS (there you are, boy), Lawyer with the jab, again with the jab, Poreda doesn't respond, he's still looking for HARD JAB AND RIGHT HOOK, POREDA DOWN, LIGHTNING ONE-TWO, POREDA DOWN (get up, you clown) POREDA TAKING THE COUNT, HE STANDS UP (get up, I haven't finished), JUMPS UP AND DOWN, SIX . . . SEVEN . . . EIGHT . . . makes a sign that he wants to keep going, the fight starts again, and Lawyer immediately takes off, shortens up, gets Poreda jab, another jab, COUNTER-PUNCH, POREDA ANTICIPATED HIM, STRAIGHT COUNTER-PUNCH, LAWYER SWAYS, LEGS BUCKLE, STRAIGHT COUNTER, LAWYER HURT BUT STANDING (what the fuck . . .), looks for the clinch, now (fuck your head, you bastard), this is an extraordinarily intense moment here, audience on their feet, referee orders the break, Lawyer is breathing with his mouth open, it was the counter-punch that got him (that piece of crap, Larry) still in the clinch, Poreda works the sides, hook from Lawyer on the mark, uppercut misses, Poreda still on the sides, head to head (what's he doing, talking?) Poreda seems to move better in the clinch (shut up, you bastard, shut up), the referee separates the two fighters AND WHAT IS THAT, REF? On the way out Poreda punches him in the body, Lawyer protests REF, WHAT WAS THAT? OPEN GLOVE!!! Hard to judge from here (thumb in the diaphragm, I know it, you bastard), it looked like a clean hit, Lawyer now catches his breath, Poreda doesn't persist, he takes the center of the ring, gets his legs going, it's the Lawyer GONG we know, end of the round, a round that in my personal opinion sees the two fighters essentially

"Everything all right, Larry?"

"Shit fight."

"Let me see your mouth."

"It's a fucking shit fight."

"OK, you win and we go home."

"He fakes going down."

"It's his way of resting."

"What the hell do you mean, he can't go down like that without . . ."

"He doesn't give a shit, he goes down, gets his breath, and meanwhile you lose your mind, he's always done that."

"I didn't even touch his liver."

"He goes down beautifully, it's his specialty."

"Fucking . . ."

"Breathe."

"He tries it every time, with the head . . ."

"Be quiet, breathe."

"And he talks, that guy talks, you know?"

"Let him talk."

"I don't like him talking."

"Breathe."

"He says you paid him to beat me."

"WILL YOU SHUT UP AND BREATHE?"

". . ."

"Listen, don't you ever let up, Larry, even if you see him looking dead, don't let up . . ."

"Is that story true?"

"What story?"

"Did you pay him?"

"FUCK, LARRY, THIS IS A BOXING MATCH, NOT A DEBATE, KEEP YOUR HEAD IN THIS RING OR THAT GUY WILL PEEL OFF YOUR GODDAM MOMMA'S BOY FUCKING FACE . . ."

GONG

"You're stronger, Larry. Don't throw it all away."

"OK."

"You're stronger."

"Whose side are you on, Maestro?"

"Fuck you, Larry."

"Fuck."

Third round here in the ring at the Pontiac Hotel, Larry "Lawyer" Gorman against Stanley "Hooker" Poreda, tension is high, it's a match that lives on sudden, lightning punches . . . Lawyer's class against Poreda's experience and power . . . those who predicted a farce whose only purpose was to fill the pockets of the bookmakers will have to think again DON'T LET HIM GET CLOSE, LARRY with two tough opponents (get the fuck out of my way) Poreda tries to get closer, forces Lawyer to the clinch (fuck you), head to head, unloads punches to the sides in the direction of NO BRAWLING LARRY, GET AWAY FROM THERE the referee orders a break, Poreda locks again immediately, he doesn't let Lawyer breathe, he has evidently decided not to give him any more breathing room when SPEED, LARRY, QUICK AND OUT again a jumbled exchange in the clinch (quick, quick, OK, quick), the referee calls another break, but Poreda gets low, head between his shoulders, the classy Lawyer slips away, goes around his opponent, changes his step, changes direction, Poreda tries again to shorten up, FLASH FROM LAWYER, a straight that opened up Poreda's defense, ANOTHER JAB, AND STILL ANOTHER, rapid punches,

Lawyer punches and then goes back to dancing (now, all in a moment, now) he's at his best, agility and velocity, ANOTHER JAB, FAKES THE HOOK, POREDA SLIDES HIS BODY OUT, BUT LAWYER HITS WITH THE STRAIGHT, POREDA TAKES IT IN THE FACE, SLOW DOWN, *LARRY, SLOW FUCKING DOWN,* he's like a rubber band Lawyer, forward and back, quick bursts, Poreda doesn't seem to get it, he waits on the ropes and submits, Lawyer's show, he's at his best *LARRY, FUCKING CHRIST, STOP,* SINK IT DECISIVELY THIS TIME LAWYER, POREDA'S BOUNCING ON THE ROPES, TWO-HAND COMBINATION FROM LAWYER, UPPERCUT FROM POREDA, HIT, LAWYER HIT HARD BUT STILL CLOSING, TO THE BODY NOW, LANDS A HOOK, POREDA STAGGERS, TRIES TO GET OUT, LAWYER BLOCKS HIM, CLOSE HOOK, LAWYER AGAIN ON THE MARK (breathe and close) LAWYER BACKS UP TWO STEPS, Poreda breathes, the entire audience is on its feet, *AND NOW GET OUT LARRY GET OUT,* LAWYER'S nerves on edge, A FLASH, STRAIGHT RIGHT AND HOOK, A SHOT (go down, you bastard) POREDA BOUNCES OFF THE ROPES (the fuck down) HE BUCKLES, LAWYER WITH TWO HANDS (fuck you, fuck you, fuck you) POREDA SLIDES TO THE SIDE, ROUND-HOUSE HOOK, LAWYER TAKES IT (enough, Christ) AND RESPONDS WITH A STRAIGHT, MISSES (breathe, how long is it since I breathed?) POREDA DROPS HIS SHOULDER, COMES OUT WITH THE UPPERCUT, ON TARGET AND RIGHT HOOK, LAWYER BACK *LARRY!!!* POREDA CHASES HIM *LARRY UP WITH THOSE ARMS!!!* (arms up) POREDA TWICE IN THE FACE (breathe, I have to manage to breathe) *DON'T LOWER YOUR ARMS GODDA* (how much time left?) POREDA WITH THE HOOK, MISSES, AGAIN WITH THE HOOK (upper-cut) UPPERCUT FROM LAWYER MISSES (arms up) KEEP YOUR HANDS UP LARRY!!! FEROCIOUS RIGHT FROM POREDA LAWYER HIT, LAWYER DOWN (   ) LAWYER DOWN, LAWYER DOWN (where is he?) A FEROCIOUS RIGHT FROM POREDA HAS SENT LARRY LAWYER GORMAN TO THE CANVAS, HE'S LYING ON HIS BACK (lights, buzzing, lights, cold) HE RAISES HIS HEAD, REFEREE GONZALES IS BENDING OVER HIM FOR THE COUNTDOWN (nausea, blood on those shoes, the referee's shoes, where the fuck did that punch come from?) THREE (I've got to sit up, sit up, lights, cold, faces watching, enormous faces, nausea, Jesus I'm tired, how could I not see it coming, you dickhead) FOUR (he caught me in the gut, fucking Christ, look at the ropes and count, three, I see them, three, OK, all those faces, a woman shouting, I can't hear her shout, shit) FIVE (the legs, the legs, there are my legs, it's all OK, now get up, the buzzing, where is Mondini?, breathe, oxygen to the brain, breathe) SIX (I can't feel my mouth, shit, Mondini, what's missing?, my legs are there, I have to make my head stop, look at a fixed point, my eyes stop, why is that shit referee coming so close, a gold tooth in his mouth) SEVEN (OK, I have to wait for my head to come back, buzzing and vision dancing, the legs will have to get me away, they'll do it, no problem, I can't feel my mouth, Mondini, up and down with the body and dance with the legs, no problem) EIGHT (of course I can go on, I'm going on, you shit referee, what's missing Mondini?, I'll keep going, everything's OK, where's Poreda?, let me see Poreda's face, the bastard, I what kind of face do I have?) BOX, still twenty-three seconds to go in this dramatic third round, Poreda tries to force Lawyer to the ropes, Lawyer backs up, works with his legs, uses the jab to keep Poreda away, eighteen seconds, POREDA ADVANCES Lawyer slips away on the left, BUT HE STAGGERS, POREDA IS ON HIM, HITS WITH THE RIGHT, LANDS IT, AGAIN WITH A RIGHT TO THE FACE, LAWYER GOES TO THE CLINCH, HE SEEMS EXHAUSTED, POREDA KEEPS GOING, LOOKS FOR THE RIGHT OPENING, LAWYER TRIES TO REACT, RIGHT LEFT, MISSES THE TARGET, AGAIN THE RIGHT, HIT BELOW THE BELT, POREDA PROTESTS, REFEREE STOPS THE ACTION, WARNING TO LAWYER, FIVE SECONDS, POREDA LIKE A WILD ANIMAL ON LAWYER, IT'S A FURIOUS CLINCH,

GONG

AND IT'S THE BELL THAT TAKES LAWYER OUT OF A SITUATION that is certainly not too comfortable, after the knockdown that

"Breathe."

". . ."

"Sit down and breathe, go on."

". . ."

"Let me see, OK, look at me, all right, and give me the salts, breathe."

". . ."

"I liked the idea of the low blow . . . Poreda isn't what he used to be, he should have pretended to faint and you would really have been screwed . . . he isn't what he used to be."

". . ."

"Arms and hands, all OK?"

"Yes."

"Breathe."

"I didn't see it."

"A straight right hand, you didn't see it from the start."

". . ."

"Water, come on."

"Maestro . . ."

"Swish, don't drink, DON'T DRINK, spit, like that."

"What should I do, Maestro?"

"OK, like that, and now breathe, BREATHE."

"What should I do?"

"How's your mouth?"

"I can't feel it."

"Better that way."

"I don't know what to do out there, Maestro."

"THAT'S ENOUGH OF THE SALTS, can you breathe?"

"Maestro . . ."

GONG

"Fuck you, Larry."

"What's happening, Maestro?"

"Fuck you, Larry."

"Maestro . . ."

Fourth round here in the ring at the Pontiac Hotel, a cry goes up from the eight thousand spectators, Poreda and Lawyer square off in the center of the ring, their faces both show marks of the struggle, Lawyer's mouth is bleeding, one of Poreda's eyes is half closed, they're moving slowly now, still studying each other in the center of the ring (everything so far away   everything goes more slowly, Poreda is slower   my red gloves like someone else's   flash pins and needles in my hands bam bam it's the pain that keeps me awake, wonderful pain   it's an orgy bam Poreda you whore, fuck you I didn't even feel it I can't feel any hit any more if you want I can't feel I'll make you come inside if you want come on you old bastard   right right left the left scares you you don't see the hook you don't have an eye there any more to look you look with the blood it throbs in your head come forward I'm not coming to get you   fuck yourself I didn't feel it   I won't feel anything any more there's no one any more it's hell come to hell bam   the corner's nice the ropes on your back smell of bam you whore bam bam dance great legs bam you bastard head like a rock my fingers   you can't see it shithead you can't see it any more come to hell now) LEFT HOOK FROM LAWYER, A STUNNER, INCREDIBLE, POREDA STAGGERS BACK HE'S IN THE CENTER OF THE RING, HE CAN'T KEEP HIS ARMS UP, HE STAGGERS, LAWYER SLOWLY COMES CLOSER, POREDA TAKES A STEP BACK, LAWYER IS SHOUTING SOMETHING AT HIM, HE GETS CLOSER, LAWYER, POREDA NOT MOVING, LAWYER, LAWYER, THE CROWD ON ITS FEET

Gould saw the latch on the door turn and the door open. A man in uniform appeared.

"Hey kid, why didn't you answer?"

"What?"

"I knocked, for the tickets, and you didn't answer, what are you doing, sleeping in the toilet?"

"No."

"You have a ticket?"

"Yes."

"Everything all right?"

"Yes."

Still sitting on the toilet, Gould held out his ticket.

"I knocked, but you didn't answer."

"It doesn't matter."

"You need anything?"

"No, no, everything's all right."

"You know, sometimes someone's in trouble, feeling sick, we have to open up, according to regulations."

"Of course."

"What about you, you coming out?"

"Yes, I'm coming out now."

"I'll close the door for you, OK?"

"Yes."

"Next time, answer."

"Yes."

"OK, have a good trip."

"Thanks."

The conductor closed the door. Gould stood and pulled up his pants. He looked in the mirror for a moment. He opened the door, went out, and closed the door behind him. There was a woman, standing there, who looked at him. He went back to his seat. The countryside slid by past the windows without surprises. The train moved along.

27

Gould's father arrived late in the evening, when it was already dark. He looked around.

"It's all changed here."

He wasn't in uniform. There was something boyish about his face. Like his smile. And he was wearing rather elegant brown shoes, laced shoes. It was hard to imagine that he could fight a war, with shoes like that. They seemed more suitable to making peace, a dull, reassuring peace.

Shatzy looked out the window because she expected soldiers or bodyguards, or something like that. But there was no one. She thought it was odd. She had never imagined that man *alone*. And now he was there. Alone. Hard to figure.

Gould's father said his name was Halley. He said he would like it if Shatzy simply called him Halley. And not: General.

He also said, in the desire to be precise, that he wasn't really a general.

"Oh, no?"

"Well, it's a boring story. Call me Halley, all right?"

Shatzy said that was all right. She had made pizza, so they began to eat, at the kitchen table, with the radio on, and all. Gould's father said it was a good pizza. Then he asked about Gould.

"He's gone, General."

"Will you explain to me exactly what that means?"

Shatzy explained. She said that Gould had left, but he hadn't gone to Couverney, he had taken a train somewhere, she didn't know where, and had telephoned her from there.

"He telephoned you?"

"Yes. He wanted to tell me that he wouldn't be back, and . . ."

"Will you tell me what his exact words were?"

"I don't know, he said only that he wouldn't be back, and please we were not to look for him, we were to let him go, he said exactly that, let me go, everything is fine, and then he said now I'll explain what to do about money. And he explained it to me."

"What money?"

"Money, just money, he asked if I could send him some money, for the first weeks, then he would get settled."

"Money."

"Yes."

"And you said nothing to him?"

"I?"

"You."

"I don't know, I don't think so, I didn't say much. I was listening. I was trying to figure out from his voice if he was . . . I don't know, I was trying to figure out if he was afraid, something like that, if he was afraid or . . . or if he was content. Do you see?"

". . ."

"I think he was content. I remember thinking that his voice was peaceful, and that he seemed almost happy, yes, now it may seem strange to you, but it was the voice of a happy boy."

"He didn't tell you where he was?"

"No."

"And you didn't ask him, right?"

"No, I don't think so."

"There must be a way to identify the call by checking the telephone company computer. It shouldn't be difficult."

"Don't try to do that, General."

"What do you mean?"

"If you love Gould, don't do it."

"Miss Shell, he's a child, he can't go around in the world like that, without anyone, *it's dangerous* to go around in the world, I certainly won't let him . . ."

"I know it's dangerous, but . . ."

"He's only a child . . ."

"Yes, but *he's not afraid,* that's the point, he's not afraid, I'm sure of it. And so we mustn't be. I think it's a question of courage, you see?"

"No."

"I think that we should have the courage to let him go."

"Are you serious?"

"Yes."

She was serious. She was convinced that Gould was doing exactly what he had decided to do, and when things are like that you don't have much choice, all you can do is not interfere, that's all, interfere as little as possible.

Gould's father said she was crazy.

So Shatzy said

"That has nothing to do with it"

and then she told him the story of the rivers, that business about how if a river has to get to the sea it does so by turning to the right and the left, when undoubtedly it would be quicker, more *practical,* to go straight to the goal instead of complicating life with all those curves, which serve only to make the route three times as long—three point one four times, to be precise—as the scientists have ascertained with marvelous scientific precision.

"It's as if they were *obligated* to wander, you see?, it seems absurd—if you think about it you can't avoid seeing it as absurd—but the fact is that they *have* to advance like that, one curve following another, and it's not absurd or logical, neither right nor wrong, it's simply their way, that's all."

Gould's father was quiet for a moment, thinking. Then he said:

"Where did he say to send the money?"

"I won't tell you even if you tie me to a nuclear warhead and drop me on a Japanese island."

Then they stopped talking for quite a while. Shatzy cleared the table, while Gould's father paced, back and forth, stopping every so often at the windows, and glancing outside. At one point he went upstairs. Shatzy could hear his footsteps overhead. She imagined that he was looking at Gould's room, and touching the objects, opening closets, holding up the pictures, things like that. She heard him go into the bathroom. She also heard the toilet flush, and Larry "Lawyer" Gorman came to mind, and she realized that she missed him, goodness how she missed him. Gould's father came back down. He sat down on the sofa. One of his brown shoes was untied, but either he didn't realize it or didn't give a damn.

Shatzy turned out the light in the kitchen. She left the radio on, but turned out the light, and came and sat on the floor, leaning against the sofa. The other sofa, the green one. Gould's father was sitting on the blue one. There was traffic information on the radio. An accident on the interstate. No one dead as far as anyone knew. But who can ever say.

"My wife was a very beautiful woman, Miss Shell. When I married her she was truly beautiful. And she was *fun*. She didn't sit still for a moment, and she enjoyed everything, she was one of those people who give meaning to the silliest, most insignificant things, who expect something even from those, she had faith in life, she was just made that way. When I married her I didn't know her very well, we had met three months earlier, no more, it wasn't like me, but she asked me to marry her, and I did, and what I think is that it's the best thing I've done, in my whole life. Seriously. We were very happy, please believe me. And when she discovered she was expecting a baby, it didn't occur to me to be frightened, it was a joyful moment, we both simply thought that it would be wonderful, that it was a good thing. Every year we were in a new place, the Army is like that, it moves you around, and she was with me, and wherever we went it was as if she had been born there, her home town. She made friends everywhere. When Gould arrived we were at the Almenderas base. Radar and reconnaissance, things like that. And Gould arrived. I worked a lot, what I can remember is that she seemed happy, I remember we laughed, and it was as before, a wonderful life. I don't know when things began to get complicated. You see, Gould was never an easy child, I mean, he wasn't a normal child, assuming that there are normal children, he was a child who wasn't like a child, so to speak. He was like a grown-up. As far as I remember, we didn't do anything special with him, we treated him as he was, we didn't think we had to do anything special for him. Maybe we were mistaken. When he went to school, then all that about him being a genius came out. They tested him, did scientific examinations, and then they told us that everything led them to believe that that child was a genius. They used just that word. Genius. It turned out that his brain was in the highest rankings of the delta band. Do you have any idea what that means?"

"No."

"That's the Stocken parameters."

"Oh."

"A genius. I wasn't glad or sorry, and my wife didn't know what to think, either, to us it didn't matter, you know? Ruth is my wife's name. Ruth. She started feeling unwell when we were in Topeka. There were these moments of emptiness, so to speak, when she didn't remember who she was; afterwards she returned to normal, but it was as if she had done something enormously laborious, and was exhausted. It's strange what can happen in a brain. In hers everything was sort of upside down. You could see that she was trying to regain her strength, and also her interest in life, but every time she had to start again from the beginning, it wasn't easy, it was as if she had to put back together all the pieces of something that had been broken. They said it was fatigue, merely a question of fatigue, then they started giving her a lot of tests. Then, I remember, we were no longer happy. We still loved each other, we loved each other very much, but it was hard, with her suffering in between us, it was all a little different. During that period she and Gould were together a lot. I'm not sure that it was ideal for Gould, and now, thinking back on it, I see that for her, too, being with that child couldn't have been very healthy. He was a child who complicated things for you, in your head. She didn't need things to get complicated. But it seemed that they got along well together. You know, people are usually afraid of someone like Ruth, they don't like being with someone who has, let's say, psychological problems, real problems, I mean. Gould wasn't afraid. They understood each other, they laughed, they had all sorts of non-sense of their own. It seemed like a game, but I don't know, I don't think it could have been very good, for Ruth or for him. I'd say it wasn't, given how it ended. At a certain point Ruth began to get worse very quickly and then they told me that she should be cut off from everything, and, however painful, she should be per-suaded to go into a clinic, with constant care, she was no longer able to live in a normal place. It was a harsh blow. You know, I've always worked for the Army, I was never trained to understand, in the Army you learn to perform a task, not to understand. I did what I was told. I took her to a clinic. I worked hard, and as soon as I had time I went to her. I was there, I wanted her to be with me, and I with her. At night I'd come home, often it was so late Gould was asleep. I remember that I wrote him notes. But I never really knew what to write. Every so often I made an effort to get home a little earlier, and then we played a game, Gould and I, or we listened to boxing matches on the radio, because we never had a television, Ruth detested television, and I was mad about boxing, I even fought a little, as a young man, I've always enjoyed it. Anyway, there we were, listening. We didn't talk much. You know, talking to your son is not something you can improvise. Either you have to start very early or it's a disaster, believe me. In my case it was undeniably a disaster. And then everything fell apart, when the Army transferred me to Port Larenque. Thousands of miles from here. I thought about it for quite a while, and finally I made a decision. I know it will seem ludicrous to you, and even mean, but I decided that I wanted to be with Ruth, I wanted my life with her back, the way it was in the beginning, and I would have done anything to make that happen. I found a clinic not far from the military base and I brought Ruth with me. But I left Gould here. I was sure that it would be better for him to stay here. I know that you will judge me harshly, but I don't feel any need to justify or explain myself. I would say only that Gould was one world, that child is a world, and Ruth and I were another. And I thought that I had the right to live in *my* world. That's how it went. I always made sure that Gould had everything he needed, and that he could grow up studying, because that was the road he was meant to take. I tried to do my duty. What remained of my duty. And it always seemed to me that, whether good or bad, the situation worked. It seems that I was mistaken. But Ruth is better, they let her go out for long periods now, she comes home and every so often truly seems what she used to be. We laugh, and people can spend time with us, they aren't afraid anymore. Every so often, she looks very beautiful. Once, when she seemed really well, calm, I asked her if she might like to see Gould, we could have him come, someday. She said no. We never spoke of it again."

It was as if someone had suddenly turned off his voice. Someone had turned it on, and now had decided to turn it off. He said

"Excuse me"

but in truth nothing could be heard. Shatzy understood that he had said

"Excuse me"

but who knows: you can never be sure.

What with one thing and another, it had grown late, and Shatzy wondered what was still to come. She tried to remember if she had something to say. Or to do. It was all rather complicated by that man who was sitting there, motionless on the sofa, staring at his hands, and swallowing, every so often, with an effort. It occurred to her to ask him what was that story that he was a general but wasn't really, completely—that whole business. Then she decided it wasn't a good idea. She also reminded herself that it would be better to face the subject of the money. Somehow, money had to be sent, to Gould. She was wondering what approach to take when she heard Gould's father say

"What is Gould like now?"

He had said it with a voice that seemed new, as if it had been returned to him at that moment, washed and ironed. As if he had sent it to the dry cleaner's.

"What is Gould like now?"

"Grown up."

"Aside from that, I mean."

"Grown up nicely, I think."

"Does he laugh, sometimes?"

"Of course he laughs, why?"

"I don't know. There was a time when he didn't laugh much."

"We've had some great laughs, if that's what worries you."

"Good."

"Side-splitting, really."

"Good."

"He has hands like yours."

"Yes?"

"Yes, he has the same fingers."

"Funny."

"Why?, he's your son, right?"

"Yes, naturally, I meant it's funny that there's a boy, somewhere in the world, who goes around with your hands, hands like yours. It's a strange thing. Would you like that?"

"Yes."

"It will happen. When you have children."

"Yes."

"You should make children, instead of Westerns."

"What?"

"Or children along with the Westerns."

"Maybe it's an idea."

"Think about it."

"Yes."

"Have friends?"

"Me?"

"No, I meant . . . Gould."

"Gould? Well . . ."

"He must need friends."

"Well . . . he has Diesel and Poomerang."

"I mean real friends."

"They love him very much, truly."

"Yes, but they're not real."

"Does it matter?"

"Of course it matters."

"I find them very sympathetic."

"Ruth said that, too."

"You see?"

"Yes, but they don't *exist*, Miss Shell. He invented them."

"Yes, but . . ."

"It's not normal, is it?"

"It is a bit odd, but there's no harm in it, they're good for him."

"You don't find them frightening?"

"Me? No."

"You don't find it frightening that a child spends all his time with two friends who don't exist?"

"No, why?"

"It frightened me, I remember it was one of the things about Gould that frightened me. Diesel and Poomerang. I was afraid of them."

"Are you kidding? They wouldn't hurt a fly, and they could make you die laughing. I swear I miss them, aside from Gould, I mean, but I liked it better when those two were around."

"You mean the giant and the mute have also vanished?"

"Yes, they went with him."

Gould's father began to laugh softly, shaking his head.

He said

"It's crazy."

and then he said again

"It's crazy."

"Don't worry, General, Gould will manage."

"I hope so."

"You must just have faith in him."

"Of course."

"But he will manage. That kid is strong. He may not seem like it, but he's strong."

"You really think so?"

"Yes."

"He has so much potential, so much talent, there's the risk that he's throwing it all away."

"He's simply doing what he wants to do. And he's not a fool."

"He has always liked studying. At Couverney they were going to pay him to do it, there was no reason to run away. Doesn't it seem to you strange for him to disappear just now?"

"I don't know."

"Is it possible that he didn't explain anything to you, on the telephone?"

"He didn't explain much."

"He must have said something."

"About the money."

"And nothing else?"

"I don't know, he wasn't feeling well."

"It was a phone booth, on the street?"

"At one point he said something about the fact that he had kicked a ball."

"Fantastic."

"I didn't understand him very well, though."

"You didn't understand him?"

"No."

Gould's father began to smile again, shaking his head. But without saying

"Nuts."

This time he said

"You really won't help me find him?"

"You won't look for him, General."

"No?"

"No."

"And how do you know?"

"I wasn't sure before, but I am now."

"Really?"

"Yes, now that I've seen you I'm sure of it."

". . ."

"You won't look for him."

Gould's father got up, and began to wander around the room. He went over to the television. It looked like wood, but then, who knows, it might very well have been plastic that looked like wood.

"Did you buy it?"

"No, Poomerang stole it from a Japanese guy."

"Oh."

Gould's father took the remote and turned it on. Nothing happened. He tried to push the buttons, but still nothing happened.

"Tell me something, Miss Shell. Truthfully."

"What?"

"Weren't you afraid living with a child like Gould?"

"Only once."

"Once when?"

"Once when he began to talk about his mother. He said that his mother had gone insane, and he began to tell the whole story. It wasn't so much what he said; it was his *voice* that was frightening. It was like the voice of an old man. Of someone who had known everything forever, and who also knew how things would end up. An old man."

"..."

"He needed someone who would help him be a little child."

"..."

"He didn't believe that you could be a child in real life without someone taking advantage of you and killing you, or something like that."

"..."

"He thought he was lucky to be a genius because it was a way of saving his life."

"..."

"A way of not seeming a child."

"..."

"I don't know. I think it was his dream, to be a child."

"..."

"I mean: I think it *is* his dream. I think now that he is grown-up, he will finally be able to be a child, for his whole life."

It turned out that they stayed up late, talking about wars and Westerns, or sitting quietly, with the radio on, playing ordinary music. Finally Gould's father said that he would like to sleep there, if she didn't mind. Shatzy said that he could do what he wanted, it was his house, and then she didn't mind, in fact she would be glad if he stayed. She said she could make the bed in Gould's room, but he gestured vaguely in the air and said he preferred not to, he would sleep on the sofa, it wasn't a problem, the sofa would do very well.

"It's not too comfortable."

"It will do very well, believe me."

So he slept on the sofa. The blue one. Shatzy slept in her room. First she sat on the bed, with the light on, for quite a while. Then she went to sleep.

The next morning they made an arrangement about the money. Then Gould's father asked Shatzy what she was thinking of doing. He meant to say did she want to stay there, or what.

"I don't know, I think I should stay here for a while."

"I would feel better if you would."

"Yes."

"If for some reason Gould should think of coming back, it would be better if he found someone here."

"Yes."

"You can telephone me whenever you like."

"All right."

"I'll call you."

"Yes."

"And if you have any good ideas, tell me right away, OK?"

"Of course."

Then Gould's father said she was a smart girl. And he thanked her, because she was a smart girl. He also said something else. And finally he asked if there was anything he could do for her.

Shatzy didn't answer immediately. But later, when he was just about to leave, she said that there was one thing he could do for her. She asked him if some day he would take her to meet Ruth. She didn't explain why, she just said that.

"Take you to meet Ruth?"

Gould's father was silent for a moment. Then he said yes.

28

On the prairie the wind bends landscapes and souls to the west, curving Closingtown like a weary old judge returning home after yet another death sentence. Music.

The music was always the same, Shatzy did it with her voice.

Night outside. In the Dolphin sisters' living room, the two of them and the stranger, the one they shot when he came into town.

Logically it was a little odd, but if you tried to tell Shatzy she shrugged her shoulders and kept going.

The stranger's name was Phil Wittacher. Stress on the i. Wittacher.

Phil Wittacher was not a man who relocated willingly. Let's say that he moved only if he was paid more, and in advance. He had received an extremely polite letter from Closingtown: and a thousand dollars for the trouble of reading it. It was a good starting point. The letter said that if he wanted another nine thousand dollars he was to show up at the only red house in town.

The only red house in Closingtown belonged to the Dolphin sisters.

Which was why they were sitting there, in the living room, chatting. All three.

"Why me?" asks the stranger.

"If we consider our problem, you seem, in every respect, the person most suitable to resolve it, Mister Wittacher," says Julie Dolphin.

"We need the best, and that's you, boy," says Melissa Dolphin.

They were the same but not the same, said Shatzy. It happens, with twins: physically two drops of water, but then it's like a single soul divided in two, with all the white in one part and the black in the other. Julie was the white. Melissa the black. Hard to imagine one without the other.

They probably wouldn't even exist, the one without the other, said Shatzy.

On the outside of the cup that Julie Dolphin brings to her lips is a curious landscape drawn in blue. A verbena tisane.

"It will not have escaped you that this town simulates a normality that is completely illusory: every day something happens here that one might euphemistically call *irritating*."

"The towns of the West are all the same, Miss Dolphin."

"Bullshit," says Melissa Dolphin.

The stranger smiles.

"I don't think I understand."

"You will. But I'm afraid we must beg you to have the kindness to listen to some stories. Can we ask you to return tomorrow, at sunset? It will be our pleasure to tell them to you."

Phil Wittacher was not a man who liked to take a long time about something. If a job was to be done, he preferred to get going.

Julie Dolphin placed on the table a bundle of banknotes that looked as if they had been ironed.

"We are sure that these will help you to consider the inconvenient possibility of staying in town long enough to under-stand the problem, Mister Wittacher."

Two thousand dollars.

The stranger makes a little bow, takes the money, and sticks it in his pocket.

He gets up. A stiff leather suitcase, like a kind of violin case, is leaning against the chair. Phil Wittacher is never separated from it.

"With what we're paying, maybe we could take a look?" says Melissa Dolphin.

"My sister means to say that it would be reassuring for us to see your, how to put it, the tools of your trade. Just out of curiosity, of course; you know, we, too, are, in a way, connoisseurs, if we may be allowed such a presumption."

The stranger smiles.

He places the case on a chair and opens it.

Sparkling metal, oiled and smooth. Mother of pearl inlay.

The two sisters lean over to look.

"Good heavens."

"Real jewels, if I may say so."

"Are they wound?"

The stranger nods.

"Naturally."

Melissa Dolphin looks at the stranger.

"Then why are they stopped?"

Phil Wittacher arches his eyebrows slightly.

"I beg your pardon?"

"My sister wonders why these splendid clocks of yours are stopped, since you assure us that you have wound them."

The stranger approaches the case, leans over to look. He observes the three dials carefully, one by one. Then he straightens up again.

"They've stopped," he says.

"Yes."

"Miss Dolphin, I assure you that it is impossible."

"Not here, in this town," says Julie Dolphin. She closes the case and hands it to the stranger.

"As I was saying, it would be extremely useful if you would have the kindness to listen to what we have to tell you."

Phil Wittacher takes the case, puts on his duster, recovers his hat, and heads for the door. Before he opens it he turns, takes out his pocket watch, glances at it, puts it back in its place, and looks up at the Dolphin sisters, his face slightly pale.

"Excuse me, can you tell me what time it is?"

His tone is that of a man who has been shipwrecked and asks how much drinking water is left.

"Can you tell me what time it is?"

Julie Dolphin smiles.

"Naturally no. It's been thirty-four years, two months, and eleven days since anyone in Closingtown has known what time it is, Mister Wittacher."

At that point she burst out laughing. Shatzy. She started laughing. You could see that she really liked this story, she enjoyed telling it, she could have gone on doing it for a lifetime. It made her happy, that was it.

"Until tomorrow, Mister Wittacher."

29

No gun—over his heart, in the pocket, business cards that say

Wittacher & Son.
Construction and repair of clocks and watches.
Medal of the Senate, Chicago Universal Exposition.

Suitcase in hand, he walks in the wind to the very edge of town, a red house, the Dolphins' house—three steps, the door, Julie Dolphin, the living room, odor of wood and vegetables, two guns hanging over the stove, Melissa Dolphin, dust that creaks under your shoes, everywhere, a strange town, dust everywhere, no rain, a strange town, good evening, Mister Wittacher.

Good evening.

For five days—every day at sunset—Phil Wittacher went to the Dolphin sisters', to listen. They told him the story of Pat Cobhan, who killed himself in a gunfight, at Stonewall, for love of a whore, and the story of Sheriff Wister, who left Closingtown innocent and returned to Closingtown guilty. They asked if he had met an old man, half blind, the two guns in his gunbelt polished to a shine. No. You will meet him. His name is Bird. This is his story. And they told him about old Wallace, and his wealth. They told him about the Christiansons, a love story, from beginning to end. On the fifth day they told him again about Bill and Mary. Then they said

"Maybe that's enough."

Phil Wittacher puts out his cigar in a blue glass dish.

"Good stories," he says.

"It depends," says Melissa Dolphin.

"We are rather inclined to consider them horrendous stories," says Julie Dolphin.

Phil Wittacher gets up, goes to the window, looks out into the darkness. He says

"All right, what's the problem?"

"It's not so easy to explain. But if there's anyone who can understand it's you."

They ask if he has noticed that all the stories have one thing in common.

Wittacher thinks.

Death, he says.

Something else, they say.

Wittacher thinks.

The wind, he says.

Exactly.

The wind.

Wittacher is silent.

Again he sees Pat Cobhan, after days of travel, get off his horse, pick up a handful of dust, let it slide slowly through his fingers, and think: no wind, here. And at last is allowed to die.

There was no wind where Sheriff Wister surrendered to Bear. Desert, sun. No wind.

Wittacher thinks.

He's been in this town for six days, and the wind hasn't stopped blowing for an instant, in a frenzy. Dust everywhere.

"Why?" asks Phil Wittacher.

"The wind is the curse," says Melissa Dolphin.

"The wind is a wound of time," says Julie Dolphin. "That's what the Indians think, did you know that? They say that when the wind rises it means that the great mantle of time has been torn. Then all men lose their way, and as long as the wind blows they will never find it. They are left without destiny, lost in a tempest of dust. The Indians say that only a few men know the art of tearing time. They fear such men, and call them 'assassins of time.' One of them tore the time in Closingtown: it happened thirty-four years, two months, and sixteen days ago. On that day, Mister Wittacher, each of us lost our destiny in a wind that rose suddenly in the sky over town, and hasn't ceased."

You had to listen to Shatzy when she explained all this. She said that you had to imagine Closingtown as a man hanging out the window of a stagecoach with the wind in his face. The stagecoach was the World, which was making its nice journey through Time: it went along, grinding out days and miles, and if you stayed inside, sheltered, you didn't feel the air or the speed. But if for some reason you leaned out the window, *zac,* you ended up in another Time, and then the dust and the wind could make you lose your mind. She really did say "lose your mind": and around here that's not just an expression. She said that Closingtown was a place that was leaning out the window of the World, with Time blowing in its face, blowing dust right in its eyes and confusing everything within. The image wasn't all that easy to understand, but everyone liked it a lot, it had gotten around the hospital, and I think that in some way everyone found in it a story he vaguely recognized, or something like that. Prof. Parmentier himself, once, told me that, if it was helpful, I could think of what was happening in my head as something not very different from Closingtown. Something tears Time, he said to me, and you are no longer punctual about anything. You are always a little bit somewhere else. A little before or a little after. You have a lot of appointments, with emotions, or with things, and you are always chasing them or stupidly arriving ahead of time. He said that that was my illness, if you like. Julie Dolphin called it: losing your own destiny. But that was the West: certain things could still be said. She said them.

"Thirty-four years, two months, and sixteen days ago, Mister Wittacher, each of us lost our destiny in a wind that rose suddenly in the sky over Closingtown, and hasn't ceased. Pat Cobhan was young and the young can't live without destiny. He got on his horse and rode until he reached the land where his was waiting for him. Bear was an Indian: he knew. He led Sheriff Wister far away, to the edge of the wind, and there delivered him to the destiny he deserved. Bird is an old man who doesn't want to die. He curses but he is crouching in this wind where his destiny as a gunfighter will never find him. This is a town from which someone has stolen time, and destiny. You wanted an explanation: is that sufficient?"

Phil Wittacher thinks.

It's completely mad, he says.

Less than you think.

They're legends, he says.

Don't talk nonsense, boy.

It's only wind, he says.

You think so?

Shatzy said that then they made him open his suitcase. Inside were all his tools and his three clocks, perfect and beautiful: inexorably stopped.

"And how do you explain this, Mister Wittacher?"

"Perhaps it's the humidity."

"Humidity?"

"I mean, it's very dry here, in this town, it's terribly dry, I suppose it's the wind or . . ."

"The wind?"

"It's possible."

"It's only wind, Mister Wittacher, since when does the wind stop a clock?"

Phil Wittacher smiles.

"Don't corner me: it's one thing to stop a clock, another to stop time."

Julie Dolphin rises—without hesitation rises—and goes over to the stranger, goes very close, and looks him in the eye, straight in the eye.

"I beg you to believe me: here in Closingtown, they are the same thing."

"In what sense, Ma'am?"

In what sense, Shatzy? we asked her. Every so often there were five or six of us listening to her stories. She was actually telling them to me, but I didn't mind if the others listened, too. They came to my room, we filled it up, someone would bring cookies. And we listened.

In what sense, Shatzy?

Tomorrow, she said. Tomorrow.

Why?

She said tomorrow, she means tomorrow.

Tomorrow?

Tomorrow.

The first time I saw Shatzy I was downstairs, in the reading room. She came and sat down near me and said

"Everything all right?"

I don't know why, but I mistook her for Jessica, one of those college girls who would come here as interns. I remembered that she had a problem with a grandmother, something like a sick grandmother. So I asked her about her grandmother. She answered and we went on talking. Only after a while, when I looked at her closely, did it occur to me that she wasn't Jessica. Not at all.

"Who are you?"

"My name is Shatzy. Shatzy Shell."

"Have we ever seen each other before?"

"No."

"Well, hello, my name is Ruth."

"Hello."

"Are you an intern here?"

"No."

"Are you a nurse?"

"No."

"Then what do you do in life?"

She stopped to think for a while. Then she said

"Westerns."

"Westerns?"

I wasn't sure I remembered what they were.

"Yes, Westerns."

They must be something that had to do with guns.

"And how many have you made?"

"One."

"Is it good?"

"I like it."

"Can I see it?"

That's exactly how the stories began. By chance.

Phil Wittacher smiles.

"Don't corner me: it's one thing to stop a clock, another to stop time."

Julie Dolphin rises—without hesitation rises—and goes over to the stranger, goes very close, and looks him in the eye, straight in the eye.

"I beg you to believe me: here in Closingtown, they are the same thing."

"In what sense, Ma'am?"

Then Julie Dolphin told him.

"You can believe it or not, but thirty-four years, two months, and sixteen days ago someone tore the time in Closingtown. A great wind arose and suddenly all the clocks stopped. There was no way to get them started again. Our brother had mounted an enormous clock on a wooden tower, right in the middle of Main Street, under the water cistern. He was very proud of it, and he went to wind it, personally, every day. There was no other clock so big, in all the West. It was called the Old Man, because it moved slowly and looked wise. It stopped that day, and never started again. Its hands were stuck on the 12 and the 37, and, in that condition, it was like a blind eye that never stopped staring at you. Finally they decided to board it up. At least then it stopped spying on everyone. Now it looks like a smaller water tank, under the big one. But inside it's still there. Stopped. If you think that these are merely legends, listen to this. Eleven years ago people from the railroad come to town. They say that they want to route the tracks through here, to link the Southern line with the great plains. They bought land and drove in stakes. Then they notice something odd: their watches have stopped. They ask around and someone tells them the whole story. So they have an expert come from the capital. A little man who was always in black, and never spoke. He stayed here for nine days. He had some strange tools, he never stopped taking clocks apart and putting them back together. And he measured everything, the light, the humidity, he even studied the sky, at night. And naturally the wind. In the end he said: 'The clocks do what they can: the fact is that there is no longer Time here.' The little man had almost got it right. He understood something. In reality, time has never stopped existing here. But the truth is that it's not the same time as in the rest of the world. Here it runs a little ahead or a little behind, who can say. What is certain is that it runs in a place where the clocks can't see it. The people from the railroad thought about this for a while. They said it was not ideal to route a railroad through a land where time no longer existed. Probably they imagined trains disappearing into a void and getting lost forever. No one made a big deal of it. People who are used to living without destiny can live perfectly well without a railroad. Nothing has happened since then. In the sense that the wind hasn't stopped blowing for an instant, and no clock has been seen that wasn't stopped. We could go on this way forever, whatever *forever* means in a place where time has been

torn. But it's hard. One can live without clocks: it's more complicated to do without destiny, to live a life that has no appointments.
We are a city of exiles, of people absent from themselves. It seems
that only two possibilities remain to us: to somehow sew up the
tear in time, or to go away. We two would like to die here, on a
day with no wind: that's why we've called on you."

Phil Wittacher is silent.

"Let us die at the right time, without dust in our eyes, boy."

Phil Wittacher smiles.

The world, he thinks, is full of lunatics.

He thinks of the little man in black and can't imagine him anything but drunk, leaning against the bar in the saloon, bewildered
by nonsense.

He thinks of the Old Man, and wonders if it really is the biggest
clock in the West.

He thinks of his three splendid clocks, with the time in
London, San Francisco and Boston. Stopped.

He looks at the two old women, their house in perfect order,
certain that they are adrift in a time that is not theirs.

Then he clears his throat.

"All right."

He says

"What do I do?"

Julie Dolphin smiles.

"Make the clock go again."

"What clock?"

"The Old Man."

"Why that one?"

"If it goes, the others will follow."

"It's only a clock. It won't restore anything to you."

"You see about making it go. Then what must happen will
happen."

Phil Wittacher thinks.

Phil Wittacher shakes his head.

"It's crazy."

"What's the matter, boy, you shitting in your pants?"

"My sister wonders if you do not by chance nourish an exaggerated distrust in the possibilities of your . . ."

"I'm not shitting in my pants. I'm only saying that it's crazy."

"Did you really think that for all that money you'd find yourself doing a *reasonable* job?"

"My sister says that we're not paying you to tell us what's crazy and what isn't. Make the clock go, that's all you have to do."

Phil Wittacher gets up.

"I imagine it's absolutely idiotic, but I'll do it."

He says.

Julie Dolphin smiles.

"I'm sure of it, Mister Wittacher. And I am truly grateful to you."

Melissa Dolphin smiles.

"Whip his ass, that bastard. No pity."

Phil Wittacher looks at her.

"It's not a gunfight."

"Of course it is."

Music.

30

The Old Man was so big that when you went inside it was like going into a house. You opened a door, climbed some steps and ended up in the clock case. It was as if you were a flea entering a pocket watch. Phil Wittacher was dazed with wonder. The works were all of wood, rope and wax. The winder mechanism was water-operated, using the cistern above the clock. Only the hands were of iron. The numbers, on a white-lacquered wooden face, were painted in different colors, but they were not normal numbers. They were playing cards. All diamonds. From the ace to the queen, who was in the place of the 12. The king was in the middle of the face, where the signature of the clockmaker would ordinarily go.

Town full of crazies, thinks Phil Wittacher.

He climbs up and then descends into that incomprehensible network of toothed wheels, tracks, hooks, ropes, weights, balances.

Everything is stopped.

If only you couldn't hear the wind whistling between the boards, thinks Phil Wittacher.

He spends three days in there, hanging lamps everywhere and making a thousand drawings. Then he shuts himself in his room to study them. One evening he goes out to the Dolphin sisters'.

"What did your brother do?" he asks.

"You're not being paid to ask questions, boy," says Melissa Dolphin.

"You mean before coming to the West?" asks Julie Dolphin.

"Before building the Old Man."

"He cheated thieves," says Melissa Dolphin.

"He invented safes," says Julie Dolphin.

"Oh, that's it," says Phil Wittacher.

Then he returns to his room over the saloon. And studies the drawings some more.

One night there's a knock on the door. He opens it and sees an old man dressed like a gunfighter. Including the guns. Two, in their holsters, backwards, with the handles jutting forward.

"Are you the clock man?" says Bird.

"Yes."

"May I?"

"If you like."

Bird comes in. Drawings everywhere.

"Sit down," says Phil Wittacher.

"I have only one thing to say to you and I can say it standing up."

"I'm listening."

"I piss blood, pain keeps me from sleeping, even whores find me disgusting, and I can't see worth a damn. Hurry up and fix that clock. I need to die."

Phil Wittacher raises his eyes to heaven.

"Don't tell me you believe that story . . ."

"There's not much else to believe in, around here."

"Then take the first stage, get out when you come to where

there's no more wind, and wait: if you really believe it, a short wait should be enough, and you'll find someone to kill you."

How is it that Bird is now pointing two guns at him? Only a second ago they were in their holsters.

"Pay attention, kid. At this distance I don't need eyes."

Phil Wittacher puts his arms up.

How is it that those two guns are again in the holster? A moment ago they were pointed at him.

"Lower your arms, you idiot. I can't kill you if I want to die."

Phil Wittacher lets himself fall on a chair. Bird takes a wad of dollars out of a pocket.

"This is all the money I have. I was saving it for a mariachi player, but I've been waiting for years and one hasn't arrived yet. There's no more poetry in this world. Fix the clock and it's yours."

Bird puts the money back in his pocket.

Phil Wittacher shakes his head.

"I don't want money, money is no use to me, I've made the mistake of taking this job and all right, I'll finish it, but leave me alone, all I want is to get away from this town of crazies as fast as possible, in fact, you know, I'll tell you something. I wonder why I haven't left already, that's the truth, do you happen to have any idea why on earth I'm still here?"

"Simple: you can't leave in the middle of a gunfight."

"It's not a gunfight."

"Of course it is."

Says Bird. Then he touches two fingers to the brim of his hat, turns, and heads for the door. Before opening it, he pauses. He turns towards Phil Wittacher again.

"Kid, you know where a gunfighter looks, during a gunfight?"

"I'm not a gunfighter."

"I am. He looks in the eyes of his adversary. His eyes, kid."

Bird nods his head at the drawings that crowd the table and the room.

"Staring at the guns is useless. By the time you see something, it's already too late."

Phil Wittacher looks at his drawings. The last words he hears from Bird are:

"Look him in the eye if you want to win, kid."

Shatzy said that the next day Phil Wittacher had them take down all the boards that had been nailed over the Old Man's face. The hands were stuck on 12 and 37. The Dolphin sisters were right: it was like a blind eye that never stopped staring at you. The Old Man and its thirteen diamonds. From his room Wittacher studied it for hours. He had moved the table in front of the window: he would work on his drawings, then lift his head and gaze at the Old Man. Every so often he went down to the street, crossed it, and went up into the heart of the clock. He checked, he measured. When he got back to his room, he sat down at the table and began to study again. Through the wind, he stared at the Old Man's blind eye. On the morning of the fourth day he woke at dawn. He opened his eyes and said to himself:

"What an idiot."

He dressed, went downstairs, and asked Carver who was the oldest person in Closingtown. Carver pointed out a half-breed Indian who was sitting on the ground, sleeping, with a half-empty whiskey bottle in one hand.

"Isn't there someone who isn't drunk out of his mind?"

"The Dolphin sisters."

"No, not them."

"Then the judge."

"Where do I find him?"

"In his bed. The house beyond Patterson's store."

"Why in bed?"

"He says that the world makes him sick."

"So?"

"He said it ten years ago. Since then, he only gets out of bed to pee and to shit. He says it's not worth the trouble."

"Thanks."

Phil Wittacher leaves the saloon, arrives at the judge's house, knocks on the door, opens it, goes into the semi-darkness, sees a big bed, and on it, half dressed, an enormous man.

"My name is Phil Wittacher," he says.

"Fuck off."

"I'm the one who's fixing the Old Man."

"Good luck."

He takes a chair, pulls it up to the bed, sits down.

"What was the man who built it like?"

"What do you want to know?"

"Everything."

"Why?"

"I have to look him in the eye."

31

The first few times Shatzy came, she stayed for a while, then left. Whole days could pass and we wouldn't see her. During that time I was in the hospital. It was one of those times. So days could pass and I wouldn't see her. Then, I don't know how it happened, but she began to stay longer, and then she told me that they had given her a job there. I don't know. I don't think she had a job. She needed one. She wasn't exactly a nurse, she wasn't trained, but she did something like that. She stayed with the sick people. Not that she liked them all, no, there were some she didn't like in the least. I remember that once they found her in a corner crying, and she didn't want to say why. Crazy people can be very *nasty,* now and then. We can be very nasty.

Stink of shit and cigars, blinds half lowered over the windows, the whole room overflowing with newspapers, old newspapers, clippings from newspapers—right in the middle is the big iron bed, and lying on it is the judge, who is enormous: his pants unbuttoned, strange-looking shoes on his feet, greasy hair combed carefully back, yellowish beard. Every so often he leans over to grab a basin that's resting on the floor, spits some brown catarrh into it, and puts it down again. Otherwise he talks. Phil Wittacher listens.

"Arne Dolphin. Say what you like, but he was a man who knew how to talk. If you gave him a little time he could convince you that you were a horse. You laughed, but meanwhile the first chance you had you took a look at yourself in the mirror: like that, just to make sure. I imagine, there, in the city, he bugged everyone with all his nonsense about the West. He had maps, and on the maps there was a valley, beyond the Sohones Mountains: a paradise, he said. He convinced sixteen families. Seventeen, including his: two sisters and a brother, Mathias. Even the newspapers mentioned it: Arne Dolphin's expedition. They traveled for six months, going farther than anyone had gone before. They had been lost for weeks when they arrived in this territory. There was nothing. Only Indians, in the surrounding canyons, hidden in their invisible villages. Arne Dolphin stopped his wagon train for the night. I don't know where he was thinking of going, the next day. Anyway, he didn't go. In the morning someone came back from the river and said that the water was shining down there. Gold. They had been looking for woods, fertile land, meadows. They found gold. Arne Dolphin decided that it should remain a secret. He proposed a pact to the heads of the sixteen other families. For five years they would work in isolation from the world, then each would be able to go his own way, with his gold. They accepted. Closingtown was born: the city that was on no map in the world.

"They worked hard. Arne Dolphin even managed to get the Indians involved. I don't know how he did it, but little by little he persuaded them to work for him. He was fascinated by them. He had learned their language, he studied their mysteries. It became his passion. He spent hours questioning them, listening to their stories, learning their ceremonies. The Indians respected him, they even gave him a name, he had become their brother. Indians, poker and clocks: these were the three things he was passionate about. To listen to him, in fact, they were a single thing, three faces of a single thing. Who knows what he meant. Indians, poker and clocks. Women he hardly looked at, liquor he didn't drink, and as for money he seemed not to care about it, relatively speaking. He felt that he was the father, the inventor of all that was happening: this was enough. It must have been rather like feeling you were a god. Not bad as an emotion.

"Every so often, out of the desert, some desperadoes arrived, or a wagonful of lost settlers. Arne Dolphin welcomed them, told them about the gold, explained the rules, and if they failed to obey he murdered them. There was not even a mention of a trial. Arne Dolphin didn't administer justice: he *was* justice. Every so often some of the new arrivals did make an attempt to get away, to bring the news to the world: he and his brother Mathias went off in pursuit. They would return a few days later with the heads of those poor wretches tied to their saddles. They burned the eyes, so that the message was clearer. He was a man who was gentle, lively and fierce.

"I don't know if the others were afraid of him. But they had no need to be. He was the man who had invented the world they lived in. Rather than fearing him, they loved him. They owed everything to him, and he very much resembled what each of them would have dreamed of being. No, they had only blind faith in him, absolute faith, if you like. For example: all the gold they found they gave to him. I'm serious. And he hid it in a safe place. A place that only he and his brother knew. It was a good system for preventing anyone from feeling a desire to leave before the proper time and cheating all the others. It was a good system for not being robbed by the first bandits who happened by. Arne Dolphin caused the gold to literally disappear: there was more in Closingtown than in all the banks of Boston, but if you arrived in the town, and didn't know it, you wouldn't find an ounce, a nugget, nothing. They had agreed that they would divide it among themselves at the end of five years. No one wanted to know where it was before then. Arne Dolphin and his brother Mathias knew. That was sufficient. Closingtown wasn't a city: it was a safe.

"After three years, three and a half years, the river stopped bringing gold. They waited, but nothing happened. So Arne Dolphin sent his brother with some Indians to follow the course of the river upstream. They thought that in the mountains they might find a seam or something like that. They returned a month later. They had found nothing. That night, at the Dolphins' house, came the disaster. A discussion between the two brothers, perhaps more. The next morning Arne had disappeared. Mathias went to where they kept the gold, and found the storehouse empty. No one wanted to believe it. Mathias took five men and without saying a word set off at a gallop towards the desert. A few days later their horses returned, walking. Tied to the saddles were their heads, with the eyes burned. The last horse was that of Mathias. The last head was his. End of the story, kid. If you ask around you'll hear different versions, everyone has his own theory on how Arne Dolphin managed to carry off all that gold. But the truth is that no one knows. The man was a genius, in his way. No one has seen him since. And nothing has happened, from the day he left. This is a ghost town. It died that day. Amen."

Phil Wittacher lets a few moments pass.

Silence.

"When was this?" he asks.

"Thirty-four years, two months, and twenty days ago."

Phil Wittacher is silent. He's thinking.

"Why didn't they go and look for him?"

"They did. They paid the best bounty hunter they could find, and sent him after him."

"And the result?"

"I followed him for twenty years, I was on his track a thousand times, and I never managed to look him in the face."

"You?"

"Me."

"But you're a judge."

"Judges are tired policemen."

"You'll never catch him lying here."

"Wrong, kid. If you lose a horse you can do two things: run after him or stay where the water is and wait till he's thirsty. At my age a man runs badly but he waits beautifully."

"Wait *here*? Why on earth should he come back?"

"Thirst, kid."

"Thirst?"

"I know that man better than my own cock. He'll be back."

"Maybe he's dead, maybe he's been in the ground for years."

The judge shakes his head and smiles. He nods his head in the direction of the newspapers, tons of paper, saturating the room with words.

"Indians, poker and clocks. He changes his name, changes his town, changes his face, but it's not hard to recognize him. Even his style is always the same. A megalomaniac. Gentle, lively and fierce. He's not a man who likes to hide. To flee, yes, of that he is a master, but as for hiding . . . it wouldn't be like him. If you know how to read the newspapers properly, it's like being stuck to his horse's balls."

Phil Wittacher looks at the judge. His hands are bursting with fat, the nails long and dirty. Fingers black with ink. He has lovely eyes, of a boyish blue. They wander aimlessly, gazing at spirits dancing in the air. Phil Wittacher gazes at them until they notice, turn, and stare at him, waiting. Then he says

"Thank you."

He gets up. He puts the chair back where he found it. He goes to the door. On the wall he sees a framed photograph of a girl pretending to read a book. Her hair is gathered at the nape, and she has a slender, shapely neck. There is something written on it, by hand, blue ink. He tries to read it, but it's in a language he doesn't know. He thinks of Bird, and the story of how he spent years memorizing the French dictionary, from A to Z. Not stupid, he thinks, looking at that slender and shapely neck. His hand is on the doorknob when he stops, and turns to the judge.

"And the clock?"

"What clock?"

"The Old Man."

The judge shrugs his shoulders.

"Typical of Arne Dolphin. He wanted to build the biggest clock in the West. And he did. He put the Indians to work, and he did it."

The judge leans over to spit. Then he lies back again. "If you want to know the truth, I've never seen it working."

"I see."

"Do you know what's broken inside?"

"It's not broken. It's stopped."

"Is there a difference?"

Phil Wittacher turns the doorknob, hears the click of the lock.

"Yes," he says.

He opens the door and goes out into the light that, clinging to the dust, whips the festive midday air, leading thoughts to fly about over the earth burned by the merciless sun, like trapeze artists in love, said Shatzy, rather, she almost sang, as if it were a ballad—smiling, I remember this very well—she smiled. Even when I began going home a couple of days a week, I'd still see her, and listen to her, when she felt like telling a story. She always had a tape recorder, so that when she thought of something she could say it to the tape recorder, and not lose it. I thought that might be a good idea. That it might be a good way of putting *order* into one's things. For a time I wanted to have a tape recorder, too, like that. That way, if by chance I should see everything clearly, everything that had happened and everything that had *not* happened, I would be able to say it into the tape recorder. And I would have explained to myself how things were. Strange ideas come into your mind, from time to time.

Once Shatzy told me she had known my child.

There were a lot of rumors about her, at the hospital. They said that she went with the doctors. That she went to bed with them. I don't know. There wouldn't have been any harm in it. Some were married but some were not, and then, in the end, what does it mean? My husband, Halley, said she was a good girl. I don't know if he was faithful to me when I wasn't all there, when I barely recognized him. It would be nice if he had been. It would be something for us to laugh about over the years.

"Not to hurry you, Mister Wittacher, but do you think you're on the right track to understanding what's not working in the Old Man?" says Julie Dolphin.

"Everything works."

"Are you making fun of us?"

"It's not broken. It's stopped."

"Is there any difference?"

Phil Wittacher takes his hat in his hand.

"Yes," he says to himself.

The name of my child was Gould.

32

All that hot and windy day Phil Wittacher is shut up inside the Old Man. A hydraulic clock, he says to himself as he opens the conduits of the cistern and lets the water flow, following every twist and turn down through the rewinding mechanism. He repeats the operation dozens of times. He can't figure it out. He sits down. Weary. He thinks. He gets up. He follows a stream that he alone knows and that takes him around inside the Old Man from one gear to the next, up to the painted clockface, with its thirteen beautiful playing cards, diamonds. He looks at them. For a long time.

Hours.

Then he understands.

At last he understands.

"Son of a bitch."

He says.

"Ingenious son of a bitch."

He climbs down from the Old Man with his head emptied out by fatigue. In the void a buzz of questions. They all begin with: Why?

He doesn't go back to his room, he goes straight to the house of the Dolphin sisters. Odor of wood and vegetables. Two guns hanging over the stove.

"What happened that night between Arne and Mathias?"

The sisters sit in silence.

"I asked what happened."

Julie Dolphin looks at her hands, resting in her lap.

"They had a discussion."

"What sort of discussion?"

"You repair clocks, there are some things there's no point in your knowing."

"That is a peculiar clock."

Julie Dolphin again looks at her hands, resting in her lap.

"What sort of discussion?" asks Phil Wittacher.

Melissa Dolphin raises her head.

"The river no longer yielded gold. In the mountains they had found nothing. Mathias had an idea. He made an agreement with the heads of five other families. The idea was to take all the gold and leave, at night."

"Run away with the gold?"

"Yes."

"And then?"

"Mathias asked Arne if he was with them."

"And he?"

"Arne said he didn't want any part of it. He told Mathias that he was a shit, and so were the other five, and everyone else in the world. He seemed to be sincere, he could put on a good act when he wanted to. He said that if that was to be the end of Closingtown he didn't want to see it. He said that for him it was all over right then and there. I remember that he took his watch, a silver pocket watch, and gave it to Mathias, and he said to him: The town is yours. Then he picked up his things and left. He said he would never return. He never returned."

Phil Wittacher thinks.

"And Mathias?"

"He was drunk. He started breaking things up, then he went out, and he stayed out for hours. He came back in the morning. He went to where they kept the gold. He found nothing, and realized that Arne had taken it all. He got the five others and they left at a gallop, on Arne's trail."

"The same five family heads?"

"They were his friends."

"And then?"

"Four days later their horses came back. And on the saddles were their heads, with the eyes burned."

Phil Wittacher thinks.

"What time was it when they arrived?"

"Stupid question, around here."

Phil Wittacher shakes his head.

"OK, what was it, day, night, what?"

"Evening."

"Evening?"

"Yes."

Phil Wittacher gets up. He goes to the window. He looks at the street and at the dust flying in front of the windows.

It takes some effort, but finally he says:

"Was it Arne who murdered time?"

The Dolphin sisters are silent.

"Was it?"

The Dolphin sisters sit there, heads bent, hands in their laps. It's not clear which it is, of the two, who says

"Yes. He took it with him, when he left."

Phil Wittacher picks up his duster. And his hat. The Dolphin sisters stay seated. It's as if they're waiting to be photographed.

"That watch . . . the silver watch, did you ever find it?"

"No."

"It wasn't attached to the saddle, or among Mathias's things?"

"No."

Phil Wittacher says softly: yes.

Then, louder,

"Good night."

He goes out. He crosses the town, enters the saloon, is about to go up to his room when he sees the old drunk Indian, sitting as usual on the floor with his back against the wall. He stops. He goes over and crouches in front of him.

He looks at him and says:

"Arne Dolphin, does that name mean anything to you?"

The Indian's eyes are wet rocks set in a mask of wrinkles.

"Can you hear me? . . . Arne Dolphin, your friend Arne, the great Arne Dolphin."

The Indian's eyes are motionless.

"I'm talking to you . . . Arne Dolphin, that big creep bastard Arne Dolphin, great big son of a bitch."

And then, in a much lower voice:

"The assassin of time."

The Indian's eyes don't move.

Phil Wittacher smiles.

"You'll remember when it's useful."

The Indian lowers and raises his eyelids.

Will he start the clock again? I asked Shatzy, and some of the others asked, too. She smiled. Maybe even she didn't know. I don't know how a Western is made. I mean, if you already know from the start how it's going to end or if you find out later, little by little. I've never made a Western. Once I made a child. But it's a strange story. And with that, too, you didn't know, at first, how it was going to end. The doctor says that when I'm better I'll have to start there, and, patiently, *tell myself the story*. But I don't know when that will be. I remember that his name was Gould, and also many other things, some of them nice, yet they are painful, all of them. It was the only thing I hated about Shatzy. She talked about that child, my child, as if it were nothing, and I couldn't bear it, I didn't want her to talk about him, I don't know how she could have been his girlfriend, she must have been fifteen years older, I didn't want to know what there was between them, I don't want to know, take that girl away, I don't want to see her anymore,

Doctor, leave me alone, what's that girl doing here? take that girl away, I hate her, take her away or I'll kill her.

She said that Gould no longer needed anything or anyone.

She stayed here for six years. At some point she left for Las Cruces, she said she'd found a job in a supermarket there. But then, after a few months, we saw her come back. She didn't like it that in the place where she worked everything was a special offer. She said that she spent her time getting people to buy more than they needed, and this was stupid. She started working in the hospital again. Here in fact it's unlikely that for every two hysterical crises they give you a third, which entitles you to a lottery ticket for a free electroshock treatment. In this sense you couldn't blame her. She lived by herself, in a room nearby. I always told her that she should get married. She told me: she already had. But I don't remember the rest of the story anymore. Certainly she had no one. It's odd, but she was a girl who had no one. It's the thing I never understood about her: what she had done that she remained, in the end, so alone. Here at the hospital everything went to pieces on account of that business about the theft. They said she had stolen money, from the safe in the pharmacy. That is, they said she'd been doing it for months, that they had warned her, but to no avail, she kept doing it. I didn't think it was true, there were people who hated her here, who were perfectly capable of sabotaging her. So I told them I didn't believe it, that I thought it was all a setup. She didn't say a thing. She took her things and left. Halley, my husband, found her a job as a secretary at an association for war widows. It doesn't sound like much, but it was quite entertaining. War widows do a bunch of things you would never imagine. Every so often I went to see her. She had her own desk, the work wasn't onerous. She had plenty of time to do her Western.

Phil Wittacher stands up, glances at the old Indian and heads for the stairs.

"It's like squeezing blood from a stone. It's years since I've heard him say a word," says Carver, drying yet another glass.

"Right."

"Whiskey?"

"There's an idea."

"Whiskey."

Phil Wittacher leans on the bar.

Carver pours him a glass.

Phil Wittacher tries not to think. But he thinks.

"Carver."

"Yes."

"Was there anyone in this damn town who hated Arne Dolphin?"

"Before he left?"

"Now they all do."

"Yes."

"But before?"

Carver shrugs his shoulders.

"Who in the world doesn't have an enemy?"

Phil Wittacher drinks. He puts down the glass.

"Carver."

"Yes?"

"Mathias, his brother Mathias, did he hate him?"

Carver stops. He looks at Phil Wittacher.

"Have you ever had a brother who was a god?"

"No."

"Well, you would have hated him, every day of your life, in secret and with every ounce of your strength."

On the desk she had two framed photographs. Shatzy. One was of Eva Braun, the other of Walt Disney.

33

Phil Wittacher in the noonday sun, leaning against the wall of the saloon, his hat pulled down over his eyes and his bandanna pulled up over his mouth for protection from the dust. He gazes at the face of the Old Man, its hands and numbers, like a poker player. He starts walking. He likes to walk with the wind behind him. It makes no noise, and he is in the lead.

He thinks how it's an old story and he has nothing to do with it. Joyfully he repeats that he is only a clock repairman. He says aloud I'm out of here, time to go, sorry, but it's not the job for me, adios amigos. He doesn't have a single reason to stay, he thinks, and make that clock run. Then he stops. He looks up ahead. He sees Melissa Dolphin: she's sweeping the street in front of her house, whipped by the river of whirling dust, with irrational care, and futile, she sweeps. Her white hair flies away, out of the neat arrangement that her old hands must have tried to impart, as she stood before the mirror, that morning, as every morning. She looks like a slender ghost, patient, invincible and vanquished.

Shatzy said that at precisely that point Phil Wittacher turned and spat, and, since the wind was against him, he spat practically on his pants. Then he sent them all to hell.

34

Phil Wittacher goes into the judge's house. Semi-darkness, stink of shit and cigars. Newspapers everywhere.

He takes a chair and pulls it up to the bed. He sits down.

"Still on the idea that sooner or later the horse will come to water?"

"You can bet on it, kid."

"He doesn't seem to be very thirsty."

"He'll come. I'm not in a hurry."

"I am."

"And so?"

"If he's not thirsty we'll have to make him come."

As Phil Wittacher says this, he holds out a typewritten page. It says that on Sunday 8 June, at 12:37, with great pomp, Phil Wittacher, of Wittacher & Son, will make the historic clock of Closingtown, the biggest in the West, run again. Food, drink, and a surprise finale.

Phil Wittacher nods at the piles of newspapers.

"I've put out this announcement in such a way that he can read it. After all, he's been sending messages for thirty-four years: it's time to answer."

The judge raises himself off his pillows, puts his legs down over the side of the bed, rereads the paper carefully.

"You don't think that bastard's so crazy he'll come."

"He'll come."

"Bullshit."

"Will you believe me if I tell you he'll come?"

The judge looks at him as if he were an algebra problem.

"And how do you know that, asshole? Are you by some chance in Arne Dolphin's head?"

"I know where he is, what he's doing, and what he'll be doing tomorrow. I know everything about him."

The judge starts laughing and lets out a gigantic fart. He laughs like a madman for several minutes. A monstrosity of bronchial tubes and catarrh. But with silver in the middle. All of a sudden he becomes serious again.

"All right, clockmaker, I'm damned if I understand it, but OK."

He leans forward and brings his big face close to Phil Wittacher's.

"You're not going to tell me that you can really make that clock run?"

"That's my affair, let's talk about your part."

"Simple. As soon as the bastard sets foot in town I plant a bullet between his eyes."

"Anyone could do that. Don't waste yourself. For you I've thought of something more refined."

"Which is?"

"*Not* to plant a bullet between his eyes."

"Are you nuts?"

"In this town, that man is dead. I need him alive. You solve the problem."

"Alive in what sense?"

"Judge: I bring him here to you. You find a way to make him sit at the table with me. Long enough to tell us a couple of stories. Then do what you want with him. But I want him at that table, without witnesses, and without a bullet between the eyes."

"It won't be easy: that man is a wild beast. If you give him time, you're a dead man."

"I told you it was a job worthy of you."

"It won't be a walk."

"No, so maybe you'd better find yourself another pair of shoes."

"Go fuck yourself, snotface."

"I don't have time. I have to see Bird."

So he goes to see Bird.

"Bird, do you know how Arne Dolphin used to shoot?"

"Never met him."

"I know, but you know what people say about him?"

"A little slow to draw. Dead aim. A family trait, it seems. The sisters used to make a little show out of it, at one time."

"That story about the jack of hearts?"

"Right."

"How the hell did they do it?"

"I don't know. But where cards are involved there's always a trick. Only guns never lie."

Phil Wittacher doesn't think that's true.

"Bird: one man against six, in an open field: does he have any chance of coming out alive?"

"There are six shots in a Colt. So yes."

"Forget the poetry, Bird. Does he come out alive or not?"

Bird thinks.

"Yes, if the six are blind."

Phil Wittacher smiles.

"We're the ones who are blind, Bird. We see only what we expect to see."

"Forget the philosophy, kid. What the fuck did you come to ask me?"

"Still have that idea about dying?"

"Yes, so hurry up and get that clock going."

"Do you have any engagements for June the 8th?"

"Apart from pissing blood and throwing stones at dogs?"

"Apart from that."

"Let me think."

He thinks.

"I'd say no."

"Good. I'll need you, that day."

"Me or my guns?"

"Do you still work together?"

"Only on special occasions."

"It *is* a special occasion."

"In the sense of?"

"We're going to start that fucking clock."

Bird narrows his eyes to look Phil Wittacher carefully in the face.

"Are you shitting me?"

"I'm utterly serious."

How is it that the gun was in the holster and now it's pointed at Phil Wittacher's head?

"Are you kidding?"

"I'm utterly serious."

How is it that that gun is once again in its holster?

"Count on me, kid."

"I need your eyes, Bird."

"Bad news."

"How are they?"

"Depends on the light."

"What card is this?"

Bird narrows his eyes on the card that Phil Wittacher slides out of his sleeve.

"Clubs?"

Phil Wittacher pinches it between two fingers and throws it in the air.

Bird draws and shoots. Six shots. The card ricochets off the six bullets as if on an invisible glass table. Then it falls like a dead leaf.

"Could you hit it at twenty paces?"

"No."

"And if it weren't moving?"

"At twenty paces?"

"Yes."

"With a bit of luck I could manage."

"I need you to do it, Bird."

"It'll take a bit of luck."

"Wouldn't glasses be better?"

"Go fuck yourself, clockmaker."

"I don't have time. I have to go see the Dolphin sisters."

So he went to the Dolphin sisters'.

"Two Sundays from now, at 12:37, I'm going to restart the Old Man."

The Dolphin sisters stare at him without moving. It's incredible, but it seems to Phil Wittacher that he sees Melissa Dolphin's eyes shining with something like: tears.

"It will be a big mess, but it's what you wanted."

The Dolphin sisters nod their heads yes.

"I'd like to tell you to stay home until it's all over, but I know you won't, so I'd prefer that you come, and play your part. But let's be clear: no improvisations, and obey orders."

The Dolphin sisters again nod their heads yes.

"OK. When it's time, I'll let you know. Good night, ladies."

Duster, hat.

"Mister Wittacher . . ."

"Yes."

"We'd like you to know that . . ."

"Yes?"

"It's not easy to find the right words, but we have an obligation to let you know . . ."

"Yes?"

Melissa Dolphin has no more tears in her eyes when she says:

"Nothing personal, but in a moment your cock's going to come out, kid."

"Pardon?"

"What we mean is that it might be more prudent if you were to button the relevant opening of your pants, right under the belt, Mister Wittacher."

Phil Wittacher looks down. He buttons his pants. He looks up again at the Dolphin sisters.

What did I do wrong? he thinks.

That was more or less the last part of the Western that I heard in Shatzy's voice. I don't know if there was more, but if so she took it with her. The way she went was terrible, and I say that this was an injustice, because each of us should be able to choose the music we dance out on. It should be a *right,* or at least a privilege, of great dancers. I hated Shatzy, for a lot of reasons. But she knew how to dance, if you know what I mean. She was in a car with a doctor one night, they'd had a little to drink, or smoke, I don't remember. They hit a pylon on the viaduct, straight on, down in San Fernandez. The man was driving, and was killed instantly. When they pulled Shatzy out, though, she was still breathing. They brought her to the hospital and then it was a long, painful affair. She had a lot of injuries, including something in her spinal cord. Finally she had to be confined to a hospital bed, immobilized except for her head. Her brain still worked, she could look, hear, speak. But the rest was as if dead. It was heartbreaking. Shatzy had always been one who didn't give up easily. She had talent, if it was a matter of squeezing something out of life. But this time there wasn't much to squeeze. For a few days, motionless there in her bed, she said nothing. Then one day my husband, Halley, went to see her. And she said to him: General, for pity's sake, let's end this. She said it just like that. For pity's sake. The fact is, my husband, I don't know, was fond of that girl, she represented something for him, he would never let her get lost, or anything like that, he would never do it. So he found a way. He had her brought to a military hospital. Certain things are easier to do there. The military is accustomed to it, if one can put it like that. It was also kind of ridiculous because it was a hospital for soldiers, and she was the only woman. She even joked about it. The day before she left, when I went to say goodbye, so to speak, she wanted me to come close and then she asked me if I would go around through the hospital and find a boy who would like to come and see her for a moment. She wanted him to be cute. I tried to understand what she meant by cute, but she just said could I find one with nice lips. So I went and in the end I came back with a guy who had a lovely face, dark hair and a lovely face, an amazing guy, really. His name was Samuel. When he got there, Shatzy said to him: Would you kiss me? And he kissed her, a real kiss, a movie kiss, endless. The next day a doctor did what had to be done. I think it was some kind of an injection. But I don't know exactly. She went in a moment.

At home I have hundreds of her tapes, full of Westerns. And in my mind I have two things that she told me about Gould, which I will never tell anyone.

We buried her here in Topeka. The words on her tombstone she had chosen herself. No dates. Only: *Shatzy Shell, nothing to do with the oil company.*

May the earth lie light upon you, little one.

35

The wind blows under a jaguar sun, the main street of Closingtown smokes dust, like a chimney rising from a hearth where all of Earth is burning.

Desert everywhere.

Arriving from the outside and penetrating the town's every pore.

Not a sound, not a voice, not a face.

An abandoned city.

Scraps of nothing fly about, and silent dogs wander in search of shade in which to park their limbs and regrets.

Sunday June 8, sun at the zenith.

From the east, in a cloud of dust, out of the past, twelve horsemen appear, one beside the other, hats pulled down over their eyes, bandannas pulled up over their mouths. Revolvers at their belts, and rifles under their arms.

Slowly they advance, against the wind, keeping their horses at a walk.

By the time they reach the first houses of Closingtown, their outlines are distinct.

Eleven are wearing yellow dusters. One: black.

They advance slowly, one hand on the reins, the other on the rifle. They examine every inch of the town, around them. They see nothing.

They do not speak, they move forward in a line, one beside the other, taking up the entire width of the street. A comb. A plow.

Minutes.

Then the one dressed in black stops.

They all stop.

On the right is the saloon. On the left the Old Man.

Hands stopped at 12:37.

Silence.

The saloon door opens.

An old woman comes out, her cloud of white hair flies every which way as soon as it meets the wind.

Eleven rifles are raised and aimed at her.

She protects her eyes from the sun with one hand, crosses the porch, goes down three steps, approaches the twelve and stops in front of the one in black. The gun barrels have not lost sight of her for an instant.

"Hello, Arne," says Melissa Dolphin.

The man doesn't answer.

"If I were one of your men I would grip with my chaps very tight and not move a muscle. They have more guns fixed on them than I have years on me. We have counted them: a hundred and thirty-eight. Not the years: the guns."

The man raises his eyes. Gun barrels, sticking out of all possible hiding places, are looking at him.

"You know, you didn't exactly leave pleasant memories around here."

The eleven look about nervously, guns lowered.

Melissa Dolphin turns and goes slowly back to the saloon,

climbs the porch steps, tries to fix her hair, opens the door, and disappears inside.

The hundred and thirty-eight guns remain fixed on the twelve. They do not shoot. They do not go away.

Silence.

The man in black nods to the others. He dismounts from his horse and, leading it by the reins, walks to the saloon's hitching post. He throws the reins over the wooden rail. He hangs the rifle on his saddle. He pulls the bandanna off his face. Thick white beard. He turns to look at the hundred and thirty-eight rifles. All dedicated to his friends. He crosses the porch, puts one hand on the door and the other on the butt of his revolver. He opens. He enters.

The first thing he sees is an old Indian, sitting on the floor. A statue.

The second thing he sees is the saloon is empty.

The third is a man sitting at a table, in the farthest corner.

He crosses the room and comes up to the man. He takes off his hat. He places it on the table. He sits down.

"You must be the clockmaker?"

"I am," says Phil Wittacher.

"With that baby face?"

"Right."

The man in black spits on the floor.

"What do you care about that clock?" he says.

"It's not a clock. It's a safe."

The man in black smiles.

"Full," adds Phil Wittacher.

The man in black clicks his tongue.

"Bingo," he says.

"Ingenious. You open the cistern, the water flows down, starts the mechanism, and the mechanism makes the hands go. Only, if you try that, nothing happens. And you know why?"

"You tell me."

"Because it works backwards. You start the hands, they start the mechanism, the mechanism starts the water flowing, the water rises, sets off three pistons that open an underground cell and pump more water from underground: full of gold and stopped there for thirty-four years, three months, and eleven days. It looks like a clock. But it's a safe. Ingenious."

"Congratulations. You know a lot."

"More than you think, Mathias."

Like an electric shock. For an instant the man in black is a man who is about to get up, draw two guns and shoot. The next he is a man who hears a voice cry:

"Stop!"

He takes the third instant to stop. The fourth to sit down again. The fifth to slowly turn around, keeping his hands on the table.

The judge is wearing polished boots with colored rowels, studs, and all. He has scented his hair, and is freshly shaved. He stands at the other end of the saloon, with a gun pointed at the man in black.

"The conversation isn't over yet," he says.

The man in black stares at Phil Wittacher.

"What do you want from me?"

"I want to tell you a story, Mathias."

"Hurry up, then."

"Do you have an appointment?"

"To kill that fat man over there and get out of this stupid town."

"He's a patient type. He'll wait."

"Hurry up, I said."

"OK. Thirty-four years, three months, and eleven days ago. Night. You propose to your brother Arne to skip out with the other five and all the gold. He refuses. He sees that it's all over, and that the rest will be just a nasty battle for that gold. He does something that you alone can understand: he gives you his silver watch. Then he takes his things and goes off, in the middle of the night. It must be intolerable to have a brother who is so just, right, Mathias? Never a mistake. A god. What was it like to live in his shadow for years, dozens of years? It's one of those things that make a man go mad, right? But you didn't go mad. No. You waited. And that night your moment arrived. I seem to see you, Mathias. You go to the clock, open the safe, find it full, take as much gold as you can hide in your horse's saddle. In the morning you rush out of the house, crying that Arne has run away with all the gold, you take your five friends and follow him. He's still in the desert when you find him. Arne is one against six: he can't win. How many did he kill before dying, Mathias? Two? Three?"

". . ."

"It doesn't matter. You take care of the ones who are left. They wouldn't have expected it, they were your friends. You shoot them from behind, while they are decapitating your brother, right? You cut off their heads, too, burn the eyes. You tie the heads to the saddles. And you tie the head of your brother Arne to the saddle of your horse. Clever. The horses arrive in Closingtown that evening. It's almost dark, the heads are mutilated, the horse is yours. And above all: people see what they expect to see. A brother who has been the loser his whole life, why should he have won that time? They expected you to be dead and they saw you dead. If it should happen a hundred more times, a hundred times they would see your head, attached to that saddle. But it was Arne's."

The man in black doesn't move a muscle.

Phil Wittacher looks out the window. There are eleven horsemen in yellow dusters with a hundred and thirty-eight guns pointed at them.

"The rest is thirty-four years, three months, and eleven days of revenge. Half a lifetime pretending to be Arne Dolphin and every day enjoying the thought of an entire city hating the god who betrayed it, the thief, the murderer of his good brother Mathias, the man who had always had a plan to screw them all, the bastard who went around playing poker and collecting clocks, while they were here, dying slowly in the wind. Clever, Mathias. You had to give up all that gold, but you had the revenge you sought. End of the story."

Mathias Dolphin speaks softly, in a low voice.

"Who knows this besides you?"

"No one. But if you want to try to kill me don't do it now. The fat man, over there, knows what to do. And a hundred pounds ago he was a bounty hunter: he has no problem with shooting in the back."

Mathias Dolphin clenches his fists.

"OK, what do you want for your silence?"

"Your silver watch, Mathias."

Mathias Dolphin instinctively looks down at his leather vest, black. Then he looks again into the eyes of Phil Wittacher.

"If you're so smart, clockmaker, why do you need the combination to open the safe?"

"I'm not interested in opening the safe. It's the Old Man I'm interested in. And to start it without breaking it I need that combination."

"You're mad."

"No. I'm a clockmaker."

Mathias Dolphin shakes his head. He even manages a smile. Slowly he opens the front of his duster, takes the watch from a pocket, and with a clean gesture tears the chain that connects it to his vest. He puts the watch on the table.

Phil Wittacher takes it. He lifts the cover.

"It's stopped, Mathias."

"I'm not a clockmaker."

"Right."

Phil Wittacher holds the watch up to his eyes. He reads something on the inside of the cover. He lays the watch, open, on the table.

"Four queens and the king of diamonds," he says.

"Now you can make the Old Man run, if you really want to."

"Now yes."

"I think it will be a great big surprise for everyone, when you do it, and I don't feel like being there. So tell that fat man to put down the gun, I have to go now."

Phil Wittacher nods to the judge. The judge lowers his gun. Slowly, Mathias Dolphin gets up.

"Goodbye, clockmaker."

He says. He turns. He looks the judge in the eyes.

"Am I wrong or have we seen each other before?"

"Maybe."

"You were young and you always arrived a moment too late. Was that you?"

"Maybe."

"It's curious: people make the same mistake their whole life."

"Which is?"

"You always arrive a moment too late."

He draws and fires. The judge barely has time to raise his gun. A bullet hits him in the chest and he falls against the wall and slides onto the floor. At the sound of the shot all hell breaks loose outside. Mathias throws himself on Phil Wittacher and lying on top of him, on the floor, points the gun at his head.

"OK, clockmaker, this is my hand."

Outside a fierce gun battle rages. Picking up Phil Wittacher like a rag, Mathias stands. He crosses the room, holding him tight and staying away from the windows, to keep from being seen. They pass the judge: collapsed on the floor, his chest bleeding and the gun still clutched in his hand. He has trouble speaking, but he does.

"I told you, kid. You didn't have to leave him time."

Mathias kicks him in the face, the judge crumples.

"You shit," says Phil Wittacher.

"Shut up. All you have to do is be quiet. And walk. Slowly."

They approach the door. They pass the old Indian, sitting on the floor. Mathias doesn't even look at him. He stays out of the way, behind the doorpost.

He hears the shooting die down, almost suddenly, as if swallowed up into the void.

Still a few isolated shots.

Then silence.

Silence.

Mathias pushes Phil Wittacher forward, keeping the barrel of his gun pointed at his back.

"Open the door, clockmaker."

Phil Wittacher opens it.

The main street of Closingtown is a cemetery of horses and yellow dusters.

Only wind, dust, and corpses. And dozens of men, weapons in hand, positioned on the roofs, everywhere. Silent.

Watching.

"OK, clockmaker, let's see if they like you in this town."

He pushes him out and comes after him.

Light, wind, dust.

Everyone watches them.

Mathias pushes Phil Wittacher across the porch and into the street. He sees his horse tied to the post. It's the only horse still standing. He looks around. They're all watching him. All with their guns lowered.

"What the fuck's got them, clockmaker? Have they lost the will to kill?"

"They think you're Arne."

"What the fuck are you saying?"

"They would never kill Arne."

"What the fuck are you saying?"

"They'd like to, but they can't. They'd prefer that he do it for them."

Phil Wittacher nods toward the middle of the street. Mathias looks. Shiny black hat, pale, full-length duster, polished boots, two silver-handled guns in their holsters. He advances with his arms crossed and his hands just touching the guns. He looks like a prisoner or a madman. A bird with its wings folded.

"Who the fuck is he?"

"Someone who shoots faster than you."

"Tell him if he doesn't stop I'll blow your brains out."

"You'll do it anyway, Mathias."

"Tell him!"

Phil Wittacher thinks: you're magnificent, Bird. Then he shouts:

"BIRD!"

Bird keeps walking, slowly. Behind him the Old Man looks at the scene with his poker-hand eyes.

"BIRD, STOP. BIRD!"

Bird doesn't stop.

Mathias presses the barrel of the gun against Phil Wittacher's neck.

"Three more steps and I shoot, kid."

"BIRD!"

Bird takes three steps and then stops. He's twenty paces away. He stands still.

Phil Wittacher thinks: what nonsense. Then he says, into the wind:

"Bird, let it go. The game's lost. He has the winning hand."

Pause.

"Four queens and a king."

Then Bird spreads his wings. But whirling around, as the duster opens in the wind.

Four rapid shots, fired at the face of the Old Man.

Queen.

Queen.

Queen.

Queen.

Mathias aims at Bird and fires.

Two shots in the middle of the back.

Bird falls, but falling he fires again.

Fifth shot.

King.

The Old Man goes: CLACK.

From a window in the saloon, Julie Dolphin lines up eye, sight, man, says Farewell, brother, and pulls the trigger.

Mathias's head explodes in blood and brains.

The Indian, in the saloon, sings softly and opening one fist lets gold earth slide between his fingers.

The silver watch, on the table, begins to tick.

The hand of the Old Man trembles and then moves.

12:38.

Phil Wittacher is on his feet, spattered with blood. So tired, he thinks.

In the silence, the Old Man shakes and murmurs something with a voice that sounds like thunder shot from the center of the earth.

All Closingtown looks at him.

Go, Old Man, says Phil Wittacher.

Silence.

Then an explosion.

The Old Man is opening up.

A drop of water hits the sky.

It shines in the light of midday and keeps on going, a sparkling stream shot in the air.

Water and gold.

All Closingtown looks up.

Phil Wittacher has his eyes on the ground. He bends over, grabs a handful of dust. He stands up. Opens his fingers.

There's no wind here, he thinks.

Bird closes his eyes.

The last thing he says is:

"Merci."

Bird was buried with his arms crossed on his chest: his hands were just touching the guns; they were there in the coffin, too, polished till they sparkled. Many people carried the coffin up to the top of the hill, because they thought it would be an honor, in later years, to say: I went with Bird, that day, to the other world. They had dug a big hole, deep and wide, and put up a dark stone, with his name on it. They lowered the coffin into the hole and then took off their hats and turned towards the minister. The minister said he had never buried a gunfighter, and wasn't sure he knew what to say. He asked if the man had ever done anything good, in his life. He asked if anyone knew anything about him. Then the judge, who had a bullet somewhere in his dorsal spine but couldn't care less about it, said that Bird had shot four queens and a king, at thirty paces, without wasting a bullet. He asked if that might be enough. The minister said he was afraid not. That started a debate, and they dug around in their memories trying to remember a good thing, just one, that Bird had done in his life. It was funny, but all they could think of was a lot of nasty stuff. What they finally came up with was how he had studied French. At least it seemed to be something *nice*. They asked the minister if that would be enough. The minister said it was like fishing for trout in a glass of whiskey. Then the judge pointed a gun at him and said: "Fish."

So the minister said a lot of interesting things on the possibilities of redeeming a life of sin by taking up the study of languages. He didn't do too badly. Amen, they all said at the end, quite convincingly. They filled the hole with earth, and went home.

With the money that was found on Bird they had a mariachi come to town. They led him up the hill and asked how many songs he could play for that sum. He made two calculations, then he said: one thousand three hundred and fifty. They gave him the money and told him to begin, and added that he could go at his own pace, since Bird wasn't in a hurry. He picked up the guitar and began. He sang songs in which everything went very badly, but the people, inexplicably, were quite happy. He went on for seven hours. Then came the first gunshots from the town. He got the message, climbed on his mule, and took off. But he was an honest mariachi, and didn't stop singing until he disappeared on the horizon, and he kept going for days and months and years.

That's why, around here, when people hear a mariachi singing, they raise a glass and say: Here's to you, Bird.

Not a breath of wind. Bright bursts of red sunset along the horizon of Closingtown. Phil Wittacher puts on his hat and mounts his horse. He looks ahead into the distance. Then he turns to the Dolphin sisters: standing motionless, white hair carefully combed, not a strand out of place.

Silence.

The horse lowers its head a couple of times, then raises its nose to sniff the air.

Julie Dolphin's eyes are shining with tears. She presses her lips together. She waves her hand, just lightly, but to Phil Wittacher it seems beautiful.

"Tight ass and loaded guns, kid," says Melissa Dolphin. "The rest is useless poetry."

Phil Wittacher smiles.

"Life isn't a gunfight," he says.

Melissa Dolphin opens her eyes wide.

"Of course it is, you fool."

Music.

THE END

Epilogue

"No, it's something completely different."

"Do you think it's a question of experience, or . . . of wisdom, if we can use that word?"

"Wisdom? . . . I don't know, I think, rather, it's . . . let's say the way in which you experience pain is different . . ."

"In what sense?"

"I mean . . . when you're young the pain hits you and it's like you've been shot . . . it's the end, it seems like the end . . . the pain is like a gunshot, it makes you jump, like an explosion . . . it's like there's no relief, no remedy, it's absolute . . . the point is *you don't expect it,* that's the heart of the matter, when you're young you don't expect pain, and it surprises you, and it's the shock that gets you, *the shock.* Shock, you know?"

"Yes."

"As an old person . . . that is, when you get older . . . the shock isn't there anymore, it can't take you by surprise . . . you *feel* it, of course, but it's like tiredness added to tiredness, there're no more explosions, you see?, a huge weight has been placed on your shoulders . . . or it's like you're walking and your shoes are getting soaked, more and more saturated, caked with mud, heavier and heavier. At some point you stop, and that's the end. But you don't jump in the air, the way you did when you were young, it's not that anymore. That's the reason you can box as long as you live, if you want. It doesn't hurt anymore, after a while, in my view, it doesn't hurt anymore. One day, you're just too tired and you leave, that's all."

"You left because you were tired?"

"I thought I was tired. That's all."

"Tired of fighting?"

"No . . . I still liked fighting, throwing punches, and taking them, I liked boxing . . . I didn't like losing, of course, but I could have gone on for a while and kept winning . . . I don't know . . . at some point I realized that *I just didn't feel like being up there anymore* . . . up where everyone's watching you, and there's no escape, all those eyes on you, if you shit in your pants they see you, whatever you do they're watching you, and I was tired, of that . . . I think that all of a sudden I had a tremendous desire to be in a place where no one could see me. So I left. That's all."

"You went out in a spectacular way, though, right in the middle of a challenge for the world championship . . ."

"Fourth round, with Butler, yes . . ."

"Well, it made quite an impression, the images have become famous, you suddenly stop fighting, you turn . . ."

"I hate those pictures, I look stupid, or scared, whereas it was something completely different . . . you can't choose the moment when you're going to have an important realization, mine came there, right in the middle of the fight, suddenly everything seemed marvelously clear to me, and it was perfectly obvious that I had to get out of there, and find a place where people weren't watching me, it didn't matter that I was right in the middle of the fight, it was irrelevant . . ."

"... it was a challenge that had been talked about for months and months ..."

"... yes ..."

"... it was a world championship ..."

"Yes, well, but ... OK, it was a world championship, what can I tell you, I knew what a world championship was, I wasn't stupid ... I had the world championship stuck in my mind from the first day I went into the gym ... It sounds ridiculous, but what was important to me wasn't boxing, what was important was to get to the top, to the peak, to be the champion of the world. Then things changed, but at the beginning ... Christ, what ambition, when you're a kid you can dream about things ... you really believe in it, maybe people hate you because you're arrogant, or you seem crazy, egotistical, and it's all true, but inside ... Christ, what strength you have inside, a beautiful strength, life in its pure state, not like those people who are always calculating, hiding their hopes under the mattress, just in case someone notices later, the ones who camouflage themselves and then cheat you in the last round, maybe with a dirty hit ... oh, I was unbearable, but ... Mondini hated me for that, he always hated me ... but ... that was when I learned to be alive. Then it's a sickness that never goes away."

"What about Mondini, what did he mean to you?"

"It's not a nice story."

"Do you feel like talking about it, Larry?"

"I don't know. It turned out badly, and maybe there was no way to make it turn out right."

"You and Mondini separated after the fight with Poreda."

"You remember that fight, Dan?"

"Of course."

"OK, let me tell you something. Before the fourth round, remember?"

"The last ..."

"Yes, before the last round, in the corner, during the interval, well, Mondini wasn't there anymore, he had already gone ..."

"He didn't go to the corner?"

"No, it's not that, he was there, in the corner, he did everything he was supposed to do, the water, the salts, all that crap . . . but he was no longer there, he was no longer Mondini, he was no longer my Maestro, he had abandoned me, am I clear?"

"Poreda often said that Mondini had paid him to win that fight."

"Forget what Poreda says."

"But he . . ."

"What Poreda says doesn't count for shit."

"There was an investigation . . ."

"Bullshit. I got up from the stool and I was alone, that's all that counts."

"It was one of the most violent rounds I've ever seen."

"I don't know, I don't remember much about it, only it wasn't boxing anymore, at that point, it was hatred and violence, I wasn't myself, up there, it was something that was fighting in my place . . ."

"Mondini threw in the towel at twenty-two seconds from the end of the round."

"He didn't have to."

"Afterwards he said he didn't like seeing his students smashed to pieces."

"Bullshit. Listen to me carefully, I could have gone on, I could have kept going like that for the whole week, I was young and Poreda was old, and listen to me carefully, maybe I don't remember everything about that round, but one thing I do remember, and that's Poreda's face, he was a man who was hurting up to his asshole, a guy at the end of his tether, he would have been dead before me, that's the truth, by God, and when I saw the referee interrupt and that towel fly onto the canvas, I thought they'd taken it from Poreda's corner, I swear, I thought they'd finally understood, and I think that I raised my arms, because I thought I had won. But the towel was mine. Absurd."

"Poreda's punches were powerful, Mondini knew it."

"Mondini shouldn't have thrown the towel."

"Why did he do it?"

"Ask him, Dan."

"He has always said it was to save you."

"From what?"

"He said that . . ."

"Let's change the subject, all right?"

" . . ."

"Christ, so many years have passed and it still makes me jumpy, that business . . . I'm sorry, Dan, maybe we should cut this bit? Is that possible?"

"Don't worry, it's no problem . . . we can edit the interview however we like . . ."

". . . it's just that it's . . . I don't know, I've never understood it, that is, I understood it but then . . . well, it's all bullshit."

"Afterwards you went to the Battista brothers."

"I had to go somewhere, they had the resources to take me to the world championship . . ."

"There was a lot of talk about that family, some said that . . ."

"You know something about Mondini?, I want to tell you something about Mondini, I've never told anyone, but I want to tell you, here on the air . . . well, four years after that match . . . we hadn't seen or heard from each other or anything . . . I was with the Battistas, no, it was when I was getting ready to fight Miller, whoever won would challenge Butler for the world championship, it was during that period, well . . . one day they had me read a newspaper and in it there was an interview with Mondini. It wasn't the first time, every so often I happened to read something about him, and he almost always managed to get in something against me, a comment, even just a word or two, but it was like he intended every time to say something vicious. Well, so I started reading, and the interviewer asked Mondini if I had any chance, against Miller. And he said: now that he is with the Battistas, of course he has a chance. Then the interviewer made him repeat it, because he wanted to get it right. And in the interview he said: Lawyer is a fraud, he was good when he was young, but the money has ruined him, now he's a puppet in the hands of the Battistas, and they will take him where they want, maybe even the world championship. Then he also said some crap about my car and the women I went around with . . . fuck, he had been my Maestro, he *knew* I was great, he knew how I was made, he couldn't forget everything because of a picture in the paper, or some crap he'd read somewhere, he had seen my fights, he knew I could do without all the Battistas in the world, he understood boxing, he truly understood, it was only spite, and rancor. So I did something ridiculous, I went straight to his gym, and before anyone could stop me I got to him and I said Fuck you, Mondini, and I started hitting him, I know it's terrible, but after all he had been a fighter, he could defend himself, and he did, and I hit him, without gloves, I hit him until I saw him on the ground, and then I said Fuck you, again, and that's the last image I have of him, lying on the ground running a hand over his face and then looking at it, filthy, bloody, it's the last time I saw him. I never read an interview with him, I never wanted to know anything else about him. Pretty terrible, isn't it?"

"*You never heard from him?*"

"He was my Maestro, fuck. Have you ever had a Maestro, Dan?"

"*I?*"

"Yes, you."

"*Maybe . . . yes, maybe, someone . . .*"

"It must be difficult to be a Maestro, no one really manages to do it well, you know?"

"*Maybe.*"

"It must be difficult."

"*. . .*"

"*. . .*"

"*Have you had others? . . . I mean another Maestro.*"

"No. After Mondini, no. In the corner, with the Battistas, it was like having a plumber, or an insurance agent, it wouldn't have made any difference. I fought alone, all those years. Alone."

"They didn't teach you anything?"

"Not to overcook the spaghetti. The only thing."

"And the fight with Miller?"

"Miller?"

"Yes."

"Miller was hungry. Mondini would have liked him. He came from the ghetto, I don't know where, but he was always bragging about how he was from the streets, and so nothing could frighten him. Bullshit. Everyone is scared."

"Everyone?"

"Of course, everyone . . ."

"You were scared?"

"I . . . it's strange . . . at the beginning no, I wasn't scared, truly, then later it changed . . . you know something, something that might help you understand . . . before every fight . . . you go up there, right?, and in those few instants before you start you have your opponent in the other corner, you jump up and down, you throw a few punches in the air . . . right before the match, right? . . . well, a lot of trainers, if you notice, will stand in front of their fighter, they plant themselves right between him and his opponent, so he can't see the enemy, you understand?, they get in the middle, staring their boy straight in the eyes and shouting things in his face, and all this is so he doesn't see his opponent, so he doesn't look at him, doesn't have time to think, and to be afraid, you see? . . . Well, Mondini did the opposite. He'd stand beside you and look at the other guy as if he were looking at the view of the countryside from his balcony. Cool. He'd make observations, comments. Take Sobilo, for example . . . Sobilo had a shaved head, and a skull tattooed right on the top of his shaved head . . . I remember Mondini kept saying Tell me, Larry, did they shit on his head? And I said It's a tattoo, Maestro, and he no, really, you think? and he looked for his glasses so he could see, but he couldn't find them and . . . so like that it wasn't exactly easy to get scared. Later, things changed. The fighters were different, too . . . they really were frightening . . . Miller had already killed two people, for example, when I met him, of course it was bad luck, but still they had died . . . that was rough boxing, Mondini had always told me, the punches were different, there was this odd feature, that you could die . . . odd . . . die . . . you know what Pearson once told me? Pearson, you remember him, champion middle . . ."

"Bill Pearson?"

"That's him. He said something intelligent. He told me that you *had* to be afraid of your opponent: that way you didn't have time to be afraid of death. He said it just like that."

"That's great."

"Yes, great. And he was right. Somewhere I learned to be afraid of my opponents. It kept my mind occupied. It brought out the best in you. It was a good system."

"Was Miller so terrifying?"

"Well, of course he . . . he was impressive . . . then he wasn't as bad as he seemed, but . . . I remember the strange sensation the two or three times I found myself trapped in the corner, he had surprised me, with him you shouldn't, ever, but I had fallen for it, and there I was, it must have happened two or three times, but I remember it very clearly, for a second you felt like . . . finished, done for, in some part of your brain you thought that if you didn't hurry up and find a way out you'd be dead, it wasn't just a question of losing or winning, you'd be dead . . . God, what a lot of ideas came to you on how to get out of there, I guarantee you, you became an eel, I swear . . ."

"In the end, though, he was the one who went down."

"He was powerful but slow. In boxing you can't let yourself get slow. He was fine till the fourth, fifth round . . . then his legs got heavy, he slowed down completely . . . the thing with him was to get through those first rounds, then came the easy part . . . if you can call it easy . . ."

"He went to the canvas four times, before the referee stopped the fight."

"Yes, he had courage, and he was proud . . . maybe that stuff about hunger entered into it, he came from hunger . . . he was a good guy . . . that is . . . he was just what you'd imagine a fighter to be, everything, hungry, fierce, mean, and . . . a child, rather childlike . . . once, a few years ago, I go into a bar and there he is, sitting at the bar, wearing these expensive clothes, a silver jacket and a blue tie, something like that you could die laughing but he thought he was very classy . . . he bought me a drink and started talking as if he'd never stop, said he was thinking of a comeback, he'd had a good offer from a casino in Reno, he was still in shape, and even if he spoke a little slowly . . . you know, dragging out his words slightly?, well . . . he seemed in shape enough, he said that the only problem was his left hand, he had a left hand that would break if it so much as turned a doorknob, and then I told him that he didn't have to give a fuck, the right was enough for him, I still remembered that right, I remembered it every time I got out of bed . . . and he was pleased, he smiled, and drank, and smiled . . . at some point he told me something that stayed with me, he told me that, before a fight, he had to touch a child on the head, like so, a caress, something like that, a child, it brought him luck, and he told me that that day, against me, he goes out of the dressing room and then, as usual, heads for the ring, walking through the crowd, and the whole time he's looking around, and there's not a kid to be seen, and when he gets to the ring, and everyone's clapping and shouting, all he can think about is that he hasn't found a child to touch on the head, and even then, standing in the ring, in the last seconds before the gong, he's still looking for a kid in the first rows. And he said that all he saw was adults. Old people. And he said it's really terrible when you look for a kid and you don't see one. Just that. It's really terrible when you look for a kid and you don't see one."

"*Then in fact he did make a comeback, he went ten rounds with Bradford, quite a sad show.*"

"You people out there call it sad . . . you . . . but it's not sad . . . what does sad have to do with it . . . it's not like that, Dan, you know? . . . it's not sad, it's beautiful . . . maybe they fight and it's painful, and you remember when they were quicker and not so fat, and you say How sad, but . . . if you think about it . . . they're only trying to steal a little more luck out of life . . . they've got the right, it's like two people who love each other and after years and years of living together, say after thirty years they've been living and sleeping together, there comes a night when they're in bed and . . . maybe they turn out the light, maybe they're not even completely naked, but there comes this night when they make love again . . . and is that sad?, just because they're old and . . . to me it seems beautiful, if you've been a fighter fighting seems beautiful to you, and I saw that fight . . . Miller, my God, he was fat like . . . but I thought OK, it's all right like that, the punches were real, they had nothing to be ashamed of, if they wanted to do it why shouldn't they, I hope they were paid properly, they deserved it . . ."

"But you yourself never went back to the ring."

"No."

"Have you ever been tempted?"

"Oh God, ever . . . hard to say . . . but . . . no, I never really considered going back."

"After the victory over Miller . . . after five years of professional boxing, with a record of thirty-five wins and only one loss, you became Butler's official challenger, for the world championship. What do you remember of that period?"

"Those were the days: we ate well and the time flew by. You know who said that? Drink, Mondini's assistant . . . he fought for two years, two years only, when he was young, but for him it had been paradise, still was . . . I think he had been beaten in every fight, but he was young and . . . I don't know what else, anyway it seemed that they were the only two notable years of his life, and so everyone was always asking him Hey Drink, what was it like? And he'd say: Those were the days: we ate well and the time flew by. Quite a guy."

"You have always said that you had great admiration for Butler. Were you afraid of him, before meeting him, the first time, in Cincinnati?"

"Butler was intelligent. He was a particular type of fighter. You would have said he was cut out for . . . pool or something like that . . . something that required nerve, precision, calm . . . something without violence . . . you know what Mondini said about him, when we watched his fights? He said: Learn: he writes the letters with his head: the fists merely deliver the mail, that's all. I watched and I learned. At the time, I recall, many people said he was a dull fighter, there was all this talk about how he made boxing dull, it was dull, like watching someone read a book, they said. But the truth is that he was giving a lecture, every time he fought he was giving a lecture. He was the only one stronger than me."

"In Cincinnati, that time, you took the world championship crown away from him, sending him to the canvas thirty-two seconds from the end of the match."

"The best round of my life, all in one suspended breath, amazing."

"Butler said that at a certain point he would have liked to go into the audience so he could enjoy the sight."

"Butler was a gentleman, a true gentleman. You know, the other year, in Madison, before Kostner-Avoriaz, we saw each other, he and I, and some other old champions, the usual parade of former champions before the match, up in the ring, with everyone clapping, well, anyway, it was a long event, endless, yet another former champion kept appearing, and at one point Butler, who was next to me, turns to me and says Do you know what a boxer's worst nightmare is? And I say No, I don't . . . I thought it was a joke, so I said No, I don't . . . and yet he was serious. He said to me: To die without money for the funeral. He wasn't joking. He was serious. To die without money for the funeral. Then he turned away and didn't say another word. Well, now it may seem silly, but I thought about that, and you know, it's true? If I think of all the fighters I've talked to, sooner or later that business about where they're going to be buried comes up, and the funeral—it seems ridiculous but it's true, as Butler says, and . . . it's something that made me think, because . . . Me, for example, it never occurred to me, I don't think I've ever once thought about my funeral, I don't know, it's not the sort of thing that occurs to me . . . you know? no, even that, it didn't seem to have much to do with me, with . . . it's like it's not my world, the ring and all . . . I think that was the idea Mondini had, that I had nothing to do with that world, with boxing, and that it didn't matter if I had talent or anything, I had nothing to do with it and that was all, I think that was the reason he never believed in me, truly believed, that, ultimately, was the reason, he thought it wasn't my place, he always refused to change his mind, about that, and . . . never . . . so."

"Eight months after the match in Cincinnati, you conceded the rematch to Butler. And you went to the second loss of your career."

"Yes."

"Many people said that you weren't prepared for that match, some even spoke of a fix, they said that the Battistas were already planning the third fight, and a huge amount of money . . . it was said that they had forced you to lose . . ."

"I don't know . . . things were very weird around that time. . . they never asked me to do anything, I promise you . . . but then the Battistas never told me anything . . . I don't know, it was sort of like we all had it in mind that the right thing was to have a final bout, to determine who was the stronger. I think that even I in some way would have liked that, not so much for the money, that wasn't so important, it was that . . . it seemed more fair, I don't know, it was like things just ought to go that way. So I went into the ring without knowing very well what I wanted . . . I think I wanted to box . . . to put on a show . . . and, look, if he had been afraid, or even if he'd thought only for an instant that he could lose . . . well, he would have lost, it would have been over for good, for him . . . I certainly wouldn't have dragged myself back . . . only that . . . the fact is that he went up there with a single idea, pounded into his head, a single, precise idea, and that idea was to knock me out of there. And he did it. He saw everything a moment before I did, he knew what I would do, and where I would go, it was like he was figuring out my moves before I did. And meanwhile he hammered. At some point I realized that it was over, and then I vowed that I would at least stay on my feet till the end, I vowed to myself, while I was sitting in the corner, and Battista was giving me I don't know what bullshit that I wasn't even listening to, I said to myself Fuck you, Larry, you will come out of this fight on your feet, if it's the last thing you do. Then the bell rang, there were four rounds till the end, I decided to throw all the strength I had into my legs and put on the best dance Butler had ever seen. I didn't even think about throwing punches, only about flying around him, yes. I could manage it, for four rounds I could manage it. So I started dancing and I began to take Butler for a walk. He fell for it for a minute, a little more than a minute. Then I saw him smile and shake his head. He planted himself in the center of the ring and left me to do my number. Every so often he feinted, but in reality he was waiting, that was all. When he went in with the jab I almost didn't see it coming, I only felt that my legs were gone, and without legs you're not much of a dancer . . ."

"*You know that many people said it was a phantom punch, that you threw yourself down?*"

"People see what they want to see. At that point they were convinced that the fight was fixed, and so . . . that was a real punch, I'm telling you . . ."

"*Have you ever sold a fight, Larry?*"

"What sort of question is that, Dan? . . . we're on the radio . . . you don't ask questions like that . . ."

"*I only wondered if you'd ever sold a fight . . . it's been years now . . .*"

"Come on . . . what sort of question is that . . . why should I have sold a fight . . . what difference does it make now anyway . . ."

"*OK, as if not said.*"

"You know how things go, right? . . . you yourself . . . come on . . ."

"OK, listen, now that you've left and . . . have another life . . . I'd like to know if you miss the ring, and the public, and the headlines in the newspapers, and the gym, that world, those people."

"If I miss them? . . . oh God, it's . . . it's hard to say, things are different, that's over, that . . . it's not that I think about it every day . . . I miss it, yes, I miss something, of course I miss it . . . there were some wonderful things, you know boxing makes you experience some truly unique things, there's nothing like . . . anyway it's something special, truly, I often was . . . I found that I was happy, it gave me a lot of happiness, maybe in odd ways, it's not easy to explain, but . . . how to say . . . it was . . . it made me a happy man, that's it, for example, I remember once, in San Sebastiano, I can't even recall now who I was supposed to fight, well, I had some weight problems, every so often it happened, and so to get me back to my weight Mondini woke me, at five in the morning, when it was still dark . . . I put on the heavy track suit, and on top of that my robe, with the hood over my head, and the idea was to jump rope for a solid hour and sweat like a pig, and that's what I'd do, it was the only sure method for losing weight in a short time . . . but . . . the problem was that we were in a hotel, and Mondini said he didn't want me to jump rope in my room, I'd wake everyone up, and so we went downstairs to look for a place, and there was no one around, at that hour, so we opened doors at random and ended up in a big ballroom, you know, the sort of place that's used for weddings, parties, and so on, there was a long table and a little stage for the orchestra, and big windows looking out onto the city. I remember that the chairs were stacked upside down on the table and there was also a drum set, on the stage, you know?, but covered with a sheet, a pink sheet, just imagine. Mondini turned out the light and said to me Jump, and don't stop until you see the color of the cars in the street. Then he left. So I stayed there, alone, all wrapped up, the hood pulled over my head, and I began to jump rope, alone, in the dark, with the whole sleeping city around me, and there I was, with the rhythm of the rope, and the sound of my feet on the wood, and the hood over my head, and my eyes staring straight ahead, and . . . the heat, and then the dawn, little by little, through the big windows, but slowly, *delicately*, Christ, it was like being . . . I don't know, it was wonderful, I remember I was jumping, and my thoughts moved to the rhythm of my feet, and what I was thinking was I am unbeatable, I am safe, just that, I am safe, I am safe, while I was jumping, and I was thinking, I am safe . . . like that."

" . . ."

"I imagine that's what it is, to feel happy."

"Yes."

"Yes."

" . . ."

" . . ."

"How is life now, Larry?"

"Life?"

"Yes, I mean, how are things going for you?"

"That's a personal question, Dan, not a question to ask on the radio."

"No, sincerely, it was my own curiosity, I'd like to know, how things are going . . ."

"OK, but turn off that tape recorder, what's the public got . . ."

"Maybe they'd also like to know . . ."

"Come on, don't give me that bullshit, turn the thing off . . ."

"OK, OK."

"Then you can turn it on again, all right?"

"OK, if you pref—"

Click.

Gould turned off the light in the men's room. He looked up at the clock. Three minutes before seven. He opened the locker, and took off his white shirt and hung it on the plastic hook. He picked up from the table the card that said "Thank you" and put it away, on the shelf above. Then he looked at the glass jar with the tips in it. He had worked out a system for predicting the total before he counted the money: it was a system that involved many variables, such as the atmospheric temperature, the day of the week, and the percentage of children who had used the toilets. So he began to calculate as usual and at the end he fixed the figure in his mind. Then he emptied the jar onto the table and started counting. Generally he had a margin of error no higher than 18 percent. That day he was very close to hitting the exact figure. Seven percent over. He was improving. He picked up the money and put it in a nylon bag. He tied the bag and stuck it in his briefcase. He gave a look around, to see that everything was in place. Then he took his jacket from the locker, and put it on. In the locker there was a pair of rubber boots, an atlas, and a few other things. There were also three photographs, attached to the door. There was one of Walt Disney, and one of Eva Braun. Then there was a third.

Gould closed the locker. He put the chair away, pushing it under the table, picked up the briefcase, went to the door, turned back to give another glance around, then switched off the light. He went out, shutting the door behind him, and went up the stairs. The supermarket, above, was also closing. Half-empty checkout counters and workers pushing trains of carts. He went over to give the keys to Bart, in the little office.

"Everything all right, Gould?"

"Perfect."

"Take care, OK?"

"See you tomorrow."

He left the supermarket. It was dark and a cold wind was blowing. But the air was clean, of clean glass. He pulled up the collar of his coat and crossed the street. Diesel and Poomerang were waiting for him, leaning on a garbage can.

"How was the shit?"

"Abundant."

"It's the season, shitting is a pleasure in winter," Poomerang didn't say.

All three had their hands in their pockets. They hated gloves. If you think about it, of all the nice things you can do with your hands there's not one you can do if you're wearing gloves.

"Shall we go?"

"Let's go."

ALSO BY ALESSANDRO BARICCO

*"Alessandro Baricco is a novelist who weaves words into a
fabric as delicate as Venetian lace."* —Chicago Tribune

OCEAN SEA

At a remote shoreline hotel, an artist dips his brush in ocean water
to paint a portrait of the sea. A scientist pens love letters to a woman
he has yet to meet. An adulteress searches for relief from her pro-
clivity to fall in love. And a sixteen-year-old girl seeks a cure from a
mysterious condition which science has failed to remedy. When they
meet, their fates begin to interact as if by design. Enter a mighty tempest and a ghostly mariner with a thirst for vengeance, and the Inn
becomes a place where destiny and desire battle for the upper hand.
In *Ocean Sea*, Baricco presents a hypnotizing postmodern fable of
human malady—psychological, existential, erotic—and the sea as a
means of deliverance. Playful, provocative, and ultimately profound,
it is a novel of striking originality and wisdom.

Fiction/Literature/0-375-70395-0

SILK

This startling, sensual, and compelling novel tells a story of adventure, sexual enthrallment, and a love so powerful that it unhinges a
man's life. The year is 1861. Hervé Joncour is a French silkworm
merchant who combs the world for their gemlike eggs. Circum-
stances compel him to travel to a country that is legendary for the
quality of its silk and its hostility to foreigners: Japan. There, in the
court of a nobleman, he meets a woman. They do not touch; they do
not even speak. And he cannot read the note she sends him until he
has returned to France. But in the moment he does, Joncour is possessed. The same spell will envelop anyone who reads *Silk*, a work
that has the compression of a fable, the evocative detail of the greatest historical fiction, and the devastating erotic force of a dream.

Fiction/Literature/0-375-70382-9

VINTAGE INTERNATIONAL
Available at your local bookstore, or call toll-free to order:
1-800-793-2665 (credit cards only).